What Happens on Sunday

Laurie Koozer

Week 1: Steelers vs. Tennessee Titans (W 34-7)

Jen

Jen wasn't upset that she was twenty-one, unmarried, and unexpectedly pregnant. She wasn't upset that it was September 11 or that her brother Bobby was in Iraq. She was upset because all of it—the broken condom, her brother's departure, and the positive pregnancy test—had happened so suddenly this summer, threatening to ruin her favorite day of the year—the Steelers home opener.

All season long, the Steelers tickets were exchanged amongst her dad's family, but thanks to a poker game about three years after she was born, her dad Larry always had dibs on opening day tickets and extended the favor by hosting one hell of a tailgate for the entire brood.

This morning, they arrived early to set up long folding tables, a network of grills, and a stereo and TV system where guests without tickets could watch the game. Before most people were out of bed, Jen and her mom were securing tablecloths, mixing drinks, and arranging trays of pierogies, hot sausage, and stuffed pepper soup.

With the game only about an hour from its one o'clock kick-off, Jen watched as her dad and his friend Glenn grilled burgers and her mom stood in a circle talking and laughing with a handful of aunts and cousins, each of them holding red plastic cups and dressed in black and gold from their earrings to their socks. Beyond them, a handful of male relatives crowded around the keg, talking about their hopes for this year's team. On the other side of that, Audrey and Shannon, the bartenders from her dad's favorite watering hole, Morgan's, played a friendly game of cornhole with two older gentlemen from a neighboring tailgate. Against this backdrop of festivities, Jen stood beside her boyfriend Dave, holding a cup of orange juice.

"I can't believe I'm drinking plain orange juice at a tailgate."

Dave raised an eyebrow. "I thought that you weren't going to call attention to it."

"Yeah? And I thought you would have the decency not to knock me up before football season the year I turned twenty-one. But I guess we thought wrong."

Dave's brown eyes flashed as bright as the diamond stud in his right ear. He wore a black Polamalu jersey, baggy jeans, and a backwards baseball cap. At twenty-two, he didn't look a day over seventeen. After the pregnancy test, they'd made a deal not to tell her parents until after this day. Or until he gave her an engagement ring.

Jen poked him in the ribs. "I'm not calling attention to it in front of them, but to you I can do it all I want. And how about that ring, hon? Maybe you can get that ring so we can finally tell them?"

"Finally? We've only known for a couple of weeks." Dave rolled his eyes. "The ring is coming. Don't worry." Jen smiled, pretending she was having fun. Across the way, her mom finished her drink and started pouring another. She looked glassy-eyed and nervous. Something about the way her lips curled together made Jen think of Bobby just like she had earlier that morning when she saw his favorite BBQ chips, and then when Dave tapped the kegs, and then again when a cousin set up the stereo system. Bobby was always in charge of sound.

Thinking about Bobby and that missing engagement ring were all she did lately, and she had promised herself that today would be different. She wasn't going to spend it worrying. Over at the cornhole game, Jen noticed Shannon leaning over to pick up a sack with long, slender fingers and then flick it effortlessly into the hole. Her family had taken in Shannon as their unofficial fifth member for family picnics, dinners, and the occasional wedding. Shannon was nice, pretty, could talk sports better than any man, and had a perfect hourglass figure, to boot. Jen sneaked a peek at Dave to see if he, too, had noticed Shannon's skills, but he looked more interested in the grill.

Just then, Jen's mom grabbed her waist and shook her back and forth.

"C'mon Jen, let's get you a drink!"

Jen shook her head. "No."

"You're twenty-one now, kiddo. You can drink legal."

"I know. I just don't feel like it. I'm full."

"Don't be silly. Whaddya want? Rum slushie? Whiskey and coke? Beer?"

Jen winced. Of course she wanted beer. But drinking in the first trimester could affect the baby's brain. That was nothing to mess with.

"Nah, I think I'll pass."

Raising an eyebrow, her mom slapped her on the butt, then turned toward Dave with a delirious grin. "What can I do you for, David?"

He tilted his head, shrugging his narrow shoulders. "If you're askin', then I guess I'll take another beer." Jen's mom smiled, walking over to the keg.

Jen looked at him, wrinkling her nose.

"Ya know, you could at least, like, not drink with me so I don't feel like such an outcast."

"But wouldn't that make it obvious? I don't know what the big deal is, anyways. My cousin Theresa drank and smoked the whole way through her pregnancy, and her kid turned out just fine."

Jen narrowed her eyes. "There's a whole lot of stuff your cousin Theresa does that I wouldn't do."

"Like what?"

"Like be twenty-four years old with three kids to two different guys and be shacked up with a third in an Armstrong County trailer park."

Dave looked away from her. They'd been dating for nearly four years now, and she'd never felt weird about his family until she found out she was pregnant. Dave was fine, but her baby would be getting DNA from the whole damn family, not just him. She'd grown up in a split entry house in Shaler Township, and Dave had grown up in ramshackle apartments in Millvale with his single mom. Like most Pittsburgh families, they had bonded over their shared love of the Steelers, Pens, Pirates, and even the occasional NASCAR race. But there was something unmistakable about Dave's family that just screamed Wal-Mart. Her family shopped there, too, but at least they didn't look the part.

Not that her mom was too far off at this particular moment, nearly spilling Dave's drink all over him as she passed it over. Ever since Bobby left, nothing surprised her when it came to her parents. They were stressed and acting out in ways she'd never seen. Her mom drank more and her dad shopped more—for big toys like riding lawnmowers and a hot tub. She couldn't imagine how they'd react to her news about the baby. There'd probably be a brand new Ford F-150 in the driveway and three pitchers of margarita in the fridge in three hours flat.

Her mom looked at her with eyes as gray and pointed as a cat's. "You're acting strange, Jen."

"I'm fine."

"You look like you have a secret."

Jen laughed, nervous. "No secret here. Just excited for the game."

A few spaces away, another group of tailgaters turned on the "Steelers Polka," a fight song to the tune of the "Pennsylvania Polka."

Jen's mom bobbed up and down, swaying with the music. Watching her move, Jen couldn't help but imagine what she must have looked like twenty-some years ago, a young mother herself, smiling and carefree, without the weight of a son on duty halfway across the world. As her mom sang along to the song, Jen grabbed her hand, pulling her into a clumsy polka. Immediately, her mom responded, almost like she'd been waiting for her to ask. Around the parking lot they danced, laughing loud and wild. Jen knew people were watching, that nearby tailgaters had stopped to stare, but something about the way her mom's face flushed pink and her long hair danced in loops made Jen feel okay. Almost proud. She knew it was something that Bobby would do.

Desiree

Coming back from the bathroom at halftime, riding on the wave of a strong Steelers lead and several Yuenglings, Desiree was irritated to find that a young mother holding a little boy had invaded her seat. In straight-leg jeans tucked into black stiletto boots and a v-neck Steelers shirt, she waited on the concrete step, perplexed. Making eye contact with her husband Tom, she raised an eyebrow. *Can you even believe this?* Tom shook his head, shrugging as the young mother leaned forward, talking to an older couple in the next row.

"Do something," mouthed Desiree, pointing at her heels. Her feet were killing her.

"She'll just be another minute," he said. Another minute? Desiree didn't wait another minute for anybody, and she did not like the idea that this woman, whoever she was, probably thought she had the right to take somebody's seat just because she was holding a little kid. People with little kids were so self-centered—completely insufferable people whose life's work was to make everybody else miserable by talking about their child's every bowel movements.

She leaned into the row, pushing past Tom to tap the mother's shoulder. Tom's brown eyes widened, turning into that *What the hell are you doing?* expression he usually reserved for condemning her erratic driving or extravagant purchases.

"Excuse me," Desiree said. "That's my seat."

The young mother looked up. Something about her face looked squished, as if she'd been squeezed through a vice. Pity the poor man who had impregnated this ugly chick.

"Yes, I know, we'll just be another minute." With a smug expression on her tight little mouth, the mom turned back to her conversation. "Yes, well, he's two now and we are working on potty-training, but there have definitely been some accidents." Both women laughed. Oblivious, the blond-haired boy reached a tiny hand into his mother's hair and tugged. Desiree smirked. Even the kid's smart enough not to like her.

Desiree leaned in again. "No really, that's my seat. And I want it back." She crossed her arms over her chest, ready to slug it out like she was in the parking lot of Shaler High School about twenty years ago. "Now."

The woman looked to Tom, huffy, like she expected an apology. He offered none. She grabbed her son and pushed past Desiree, clicking her tongue and shaking her head.

Desiree rolled her eyes, pushing into her seat and pulling out her Coach hobo handbag. Time for lipstick and powder.

"I wish my face wasn't so oily, I mean I know it keeps me from getting all wrinkly but—"

Tom cut her off. "Desiree, do you know how much you just embarrassed me? How could you treat that lady like that? She had a child."

"A child? Please. First of all, who the hell brings a baby to a Steelers game? And second, just because somebody has a kid, are we just automatically supposed to make exceptions for them? It's not my fault they didn't use birth control."

Tom shook his head, his teeth clenched. "I'm a father. So what are you trying to say about me?"

Desiree waved him off. "Parents of teenagers, I'll excuse. Now those are people who need exceptions. I've seen how dramatic Kristen and Robbie are, and I'll give you that one. But little kids are just about showing off." She put on a falsetto voice, "Oh look at me, I had a baby, aren't I sooooo special?"

Tom shook his head, but she could see behind his sunglasses that he was trying hard not to laugh. "You're unbelievable, Des."

Desiree shrugged, going back to her mirror and powdering her nose. Tom leaned into her ear and whispered, "Can you honestly tell me you don't want one?"

She bit her lip. "Yes. Do you know how hard I work to stay in shape?" She slapped her solid abs and laughed. Just then, she noticed the young mother and little boy standing at the bottom of their section. As the quarter started, they headed back up the steps to their seats. From behind her sunglasses, Desiree watched as the little boy struggled to climb the steep concrete steps. As they slowly passed, he locked eyes with her. His eyes were a light shade of blue, watery in the midday sun. His chubby cheeks were streaked with a stripe of sunburn. Desiree shifted, uncomfortable. His gaze felt accusatory. As he walked past her row, she stuck out her tongue, real fast so Tom wouldn't see. The little boy smiled, looking away and laughing merrily into the distance.

Megan

By the middle of the fourth quarter, the Steelers led 34 to 7. The outcome was clear. And in a corner table at Lot 17, it was also clear that Megan's roommate Emily had drank way too much and was becoming overly friendly with Mike, a clean-cut kid with dark hair, blue eyes, and a cleft chin who was just some rando about three quarters ago, when Emily had first pointed toward the group under a flat-screen television.

"Mm, those ones are cute," she had said. Megan leaned past her, trying to get a look. There were four boys, but she could only see the faces of two. They were okay, but their short, styled hair and freshly shaved faces were pretty mundane. Some days it felt like every guy in this town looked exactly the same—especially on game days, when they were all wearing black and gold.

Megan shrugged. "You can have'em. They look kinda lame."

Emily laughed. "You're so hard on everybody. What's boring about them?"

"For starters, one of them is wearing a Steelers polo shirt. Unless he's over the age of forty-five, that is completely unacceptable. This isn't corporate black-and-gold day at the office."

Emily flashed a quick smile in the directions of the randos, her bright white teeth as blinding as the midday sun on the PPG building, those green eyes of hers as cool as mint and condescending as a Philosophy major. At twenty-five, Emily was only three years younger than her, but sometimes she acted super boring, like a totally old lady. They met about two years ago when Megan answered Emily's ad for a two-bedroom house in Friendship. Their place was great and, so far, cohabitation had been good. But Emily was pretty uptight, not even down for a casual hook-up.

Megan cleared her throat. "So I suppose you want me to go over there and talk to him?"

Emily blushed, shaking her head. "You don't have to. I'm fine without looking for boys. But they are cute."

Emily was always fine without boys. But what she really needed was a good lay. One good lay might be the final step to dislodging that stick from her ass.

But this doofus Mike attempting to explain the finer points of football? He did not seem like a candidate for a good lay, no matter how dreamy Emily looked. But at least Emily was distracted, making it a lot easier for her to find her own rando for the afternoon. None of these boys made the cut and one of them, a Kevin, who it turned out recognized her from the restaurant, kept trying to talk to her, even when the ball was in play. She was so glad her dad had taught her the right way to watch football. Not like this Kevin asshole. Of course his name was Kevin. He couldn't be more boring if he tried. She noticed him eyeing up Emily and Mike and tried to look away before he could make another attempt at conversation.

"Looks like they're hitting it off," he said.

Megan bit into an ice cube, not taking her eyes off the TV. Too late. This dude didn't quit. "Yep," she mumbled, wondering if it was possible to be any more disinterested.

"So, you're a waitress, huh?"

"Yep." She spit the ice back into her glass.

"So, where do you go to school?"

"I don't."

"Oh."

"What's that supposed to mean?"

Kevin smiled, his hazel eyes lighting up. Megan zeroed in on his dimples, immediately reminded of a little boy she used to babysit in high school, a little shit who used to take a dump in the bathtub and then laugh the whole time she cleaned it up. Dimples couldn't be trusted for a minute. Still, in spite of his standard-issue dude haircut, there was something strikingly handsome about him. Had all the whiskey gone to her head or were his eyelashes quite possibly the nicest ones she'd ever seen?

"It wasn't supposed to mean anything. You look young. I thought maybe you were in school."

Megan had a feeling she was older than him. She didn't like to tell people her age, and, besides, she knew if she told him, she'd get that same blank stare her mother gave her when they talked about her job.

She lifted up her glass, biting another ice cube with her front teeth. This was exactly the kind of thing she'd feared in coming over to this table—an in-depth discussion on something boring like the state of her career, or lack thereof. Kevin here might be cute, but she had more important fish to fry than explaining to him why she was perfectly content being a waitress. She stood up, nodding toward the table. "Anybody need anything?"

They shook their heads. She walked to the bar with perfect posture, pushing out her chest, which was already popping out of her faded shirt. She liked to go to thrift stores and find old Steelers gear and create her own masterpieces. This particular one advertised the ill-fated 1996 Super Bowl when the Steelers lost against the Dallas Cowboys. She had sliced it along the sides and sewn it together with gold shoelaces, then cut it off just above her navel. At the bar, she slid her glass toward the bartender, Todd. He was new at Lot 17 and had been flirting with her for weeks.

He winked. "What can I do ya for?"

She leaned toward him. "First, you can get me another whiskey. And second—" She lowered her voice, looking at the length of the bar. "You can have sex with me tonight."

Todd's brown eyes widened. He wore a starched white button-down shirt stretched tight over his muscular torso. Orange and black tattoos peeked over his collar: the tips of flames, like a fire raging on his back.

"Maybe," he said. He held his hand to his neck, swallowing. And that's when Megan noticed it, the gold ring on his left hand. She blinked. She wasn't drunk, but she definitely felt tipsy. She hadn't noticed the ring before. She really hadn't. And he was the one throwing her free drinks and winks. He had given her that sign, that devious sparkle in his eyes indicating interest. And she wasn't one to let an opportunity pass her by, no matter how ill-conceived it might be.

"I don't believe in maybe," she said. She wrote her phone number down on a napkin and slipped it across the bar with a quick kiss in the air.

Angela

Monday morning, Angela swung her red Chevy Cavalier into her best friend Robbie's driveway and honked the horn. It was seven and already shaping up to be a beautiful day. Robbie lived in a cul-de-sac in Whitehall, a small suburban street filled with brown and red brick houses with small, tree-lined yards. On a crisp morning like this, with barely a cloud in the sky, the whole scene looked picturesque, like something straight out of a movie except with way smaller houses. While everybody else she knew liked, hell, loved these kind of days, Angela was already looking forward to three months from now—the whole city barren and snow-covered, potholes marring the roads and thick gray clouds blocking out the sun. She liked gray days, the rainier the better. The sunshine made her feel like she needed to be accomplishing something. Gray days lent themselves to long afternoons spent by the record player, surfing the internet, drinking coffee, and drawing with charcoal. There were a lot of those days in Pittsburgh, but it still wasn't enough. For college, she had decided to start looking at schools in Seattle. From what she could gather from the internet, movies and music, Seattle epitomized everything good in the world—coffee, music, and rain. It didn't hurt that it was on the opposite side of the country. This time of the year especially, she could use some distance between her and the proverbial state of Steelers Nation that this town entered at the end of July and didn't leave until some time in January. Football. The only good thing about football season was that the roads, malls, and movie theaters were mostly empty during game time.

When Robbie & Kristen still hadn't come out, she lay on the horn again. Just then, the front door opened. Kristen loped down the sidewalk, her dishwater blonde hair just grazing her shoulder. Her round moon face and permanent grin wasn't so much happy as it was oblivious, like a puppy dog wagging its tail as its owner berates it in a very soothing tone of voice. Angela didn't care for Kristen, but Robbie's mom Patty was a stickler for fairness: "If Robbie gets a ride, so does Kristen." Approaching the car, Kristen scrunched her face, and Angela felt pleased, thinking that Kristen was most likely reacting to the chop job she'd done on her hair over the weekend—a fake black bob longer on the left side than the right. Angela liked making people feel uncomfortable, especially generic people like Kristen. Just like every other girl at Baldwin High School, she wore a cut-off denim miniskirt and a spaghetti strap tanktop under a hoodie. No creativity or imagination. Angela didn't exactly feel like her ripped black Nirvana t-shirt and skinny gray jeans were particularly cutting edge either, but compared to her classmates, she was downright counterculture.

"Angela," Kristen said, climbing into the backseat. "Mom said to tell you not to honk the horn this early in the morning. It'll make the neighbors mad."

Angela backed out of the driveway, biting her lip ring. "Mm, does she really think I care about the neighbors?"

Robbie buckled his seatbelt. Tall and thin, Robbie wore his shoulder-length brown hair in a ponytail at the nape of his neck. Today he wore black Dickies and a faded KISS t-shirt they found this summer at the Red, White and Blue thrift store. Angela smiled, remembering how excited they were to find that shirt. It was uncommon to find an authentic band shirt that wasn't some hackneyed country or classic rock act. This KISS t-shirt was the real deal. It looked way cooler than all those faux-vintage shirts any moron with a credit card could pick up at Hot Topic or Urban Outfitters. This was authentic, worn by a real fan. Angela had a feeling that the former owner was a local, the kind of guy they'd call a yinzer. The kind of dude who had a thick Pittsburgh accent, either currently did or at one time had sported a mullet, couldn't eat a salad without adding some french fries, wore socks and sneakers with shorts, thought dressing up was wearing a gold chain with a Steelers, Pirates, or Pens polo shirt, and drank cheap beer like Coors Light or the local favorite, Iron City. Basically, anybody who was like her dad or his buddies down at the Clairton Steel Mill. Every last one of them was a yinzer and completely proud of it.

Robbie leaned forward, fiddling with the radio, turning it through every station on the dial. None were playing any music, just shrill laughter and grating voices.

"Put it on KISS-FM," demanded Kristen. Angela shook her head and pushed in the latest Postal Service CD.

Kristen groaned. "You guys listen to the most depressing music ever."

"No, Kristen, we listen to real music. You just don't know because none of the stations around here play anything that was recorded since, like, 1998 because they all suck. If I have to listen to one more Alice in Chains song, I swear I'm gonna kill somebody."

"Whatever. I like Alice in Chains."

Angela turned onto Route 51, and they began their slow crawl to the school, red light after red light of suburban staples—drug stores, doctors' offices, beer distributors, and chain restaurants. She drummed her hands against the steering wheel. "Why was your mom home anyways? Did she have to take the day off for your first day of school?"

"Shut up," said Robbie. "She always takes the day off after the first Steelers game."

"Why? It's not like she's getting drunk like Dom and Nancy."

"I don't know. Geez, Angela, it's just something that she does. But I really hope she does some baking today."

Angela nodded. Patty baked cookies all the time and they were delicious—probably the best chocolate chip cookies she'd ever tasted, and a pumpkin roll to die for. Patty was a sweet lady and a great mom, but Angela had known the woman since she was five years old and couldn't think of one interest she had other than eating and the Steelers. And considering those two interests described about three quarters of the population in Western Pennsylvania, they didn't exactly make her unique. At the next traffic light, Angela made the dreaded left into the high school's parking lot. This location always made her stomach hurt, even when she drove past on the weekends or during the summer. Just the sight of the purple-and-white marquee and the knowledge that the building was a few hundred yards away made her nauseous. Except for Robbie, the people at her school were pretty awful. Not awful in the sense that they picked on her or made her life miserable, but awful in the sense that they all seemed so much the same, like a million little clones who dressed alike and spoke with bad Pittsburgh accents and didn't care about things like reading, or philosophy, or good music, or life outside of Pittsburgh. She pulled into the student lot, driving through a flurry of shiny, smiling kids dressed head to toe in American Eagle. When she parked the car, Kristen jumped out. Angela watched her in the rearview mirror, catching up with a group of girls with similar hair and skirts. She looked at Robbie and let out a long exaggerated sigh.

"It's going to be a long week," he said, head pressed against the window. Angela nodded. It was going to be a long year.

Patty

Patty stood at her bedroom window, peeking through the curtains. She watched Angela's car pull out of the driveway, then begin its slow descent down the street. In the backseat, Kristen's ponytail bobbed up and down. Patty smiled to herself, sure that Kristen was chattering nonstop, much to Robbie and Angela's chagrin. That girl talked so much she changed her own conversations. When they finally disappeared, Patty turned around, flooded with relief.

They were gone. They were finally gone. At least one of them, and sometimes one of their friends, had been at home all weekend. Patty loved her kids, but she loved her privacy too. And with kids, you seldom got any of that. There was always some crisis to fix or fight to resolve.

She crossed the room, not wanting to think about that at all.

Football season was here, her favorite time of the year. She approached her dresser, kneeling to open the bottom drawer. Underneath a pile of sweaters, she pulled out a metal box. Opening it, two pairs of panties popped out. She picked them off her comforter and dangled them in front of her. A sheer pink thong and powder blue lace boyshorts. Looking at them, she blushed. She held onto the shorts, pushing the other pair into the box, and fished out a stack of red, heart-shaped cards.

She already knew who was going to get the panties this week. There was no doubt about it. Number 36, Jerome Bettis. He was a big old running back nicknamed "The Bus" for his ability to barrel through defensive lines. He hadn't even played in yesterday's game due to an injury, but it didn't matter. He was her favorite player. And this was probably going to be his last season. After last year's loss to the New England Patriots in the AFC Championship game, Patty was afraid he might retire. She hated thinking of him going out that way, with such a terrible loss. She wanted to see him go out on the top. He deserved that much. And his teammates felt the same way. In a melancholy post-game interview last year, wide receiver Hines Ward had openly cried as he explained to reporters how badly they had wanted to win for The Bus. Eight months later, that image of a crying Hines Ward still haunted her.

Picking up a purple gel-tip pen she printed: *Dear Jerome, I believe in you and the team. The Super Bowl trophy is coming back to the 'Burgh. Love Always, Ginger Mae.* Patty shut the envelope, sealed it with a lipstick kiss and filled in the log sheet where she recorded the game final score, date sent, recipient, and type of panty.

She started shutting the box fast like she usually did, then remembered the kids weren't home and she didn't have to be at work. She smiled, running her fingers through the panties. They were tiny, every last one of them an XS. Patty was a size 16, and she didn't know anybody who could fit into something so small, save for her ex-husband's new wife, Desiree. Desiree was about the skinniest person she knew. And perhaps the prettiest, something that Patty really didn't want to think about on a day like today.

She pushed the panties back into the box, pressing them deep into the drawer and then shoving it shut, eager to head to the post office.

Shannon

In the parking lot at Chili's, Shannon looked at her watch and groaned. It was already noon. Darla was fifteen minutes late. Habitually. And sometimes, she didn't show up at all. "It totally slipped my mind," she would say later when confronted with her absence.

Shannon slammed the door of her Ford Explorer and pulled out her cell phone. She'd told Darla that she had to be back in the office by one for her weekly staff meeting, but Darla had insisted.

"I feel like I never see you," she'd said on Saturday when she called to ask her to lunch. "I miss my sister."

A familiar powder blue Hyundai raced into the lot and pulled crooked into a parking space. Darla jumped out of the car, wearing a navy t-shirt and a jean skirt. She ran toward Shannon, the wind blowing her chin-length hair and bangs around her heart-shaped face.

"I'm sorry, babe," she said, breathless. "It totally slipped my mind I was supposed to meet you."

Shannon pushed open the door to Chili's. In the tiled lobby, there was a small huddle of dayjobbers in suits and shoppers from the nearby Waterworks Shopping Plaza. Shannon pushed through them to put her name in. "Smeltzer. 2. First Available."

Darla wrinkled her nose. "Ew, I hate smoking."

"Well, you're stuck with it now, I have to be back at the office at one, so we don't have much time."

The hostess sighed. "You could sit at the bar if you're in a real hurry."

Shannon nodded. "Yes. We'll do it."

Sitting at the closest stools, Shannon flipped through the menu even though she knew she'd order the black bean burger, just like always.

"So how are you, sis?"

"I'm kind of pissed right now."

"Why?"

"Because you were the one who insisted on meeting for lunch and then it almost slips your mind just like always. You need to start using a calendar or something. We don't all operate on Darla Standard Time."

Darla laughed, thumbing through the menu. Shannon watched her, thinking that they couldn't look any more different. Shannon was tall and lean—with olive skin and black hair. Darla was short and petite. She had fairer skin and dark blonde hair. Dark brown eyes were the only trait they shared.

"Oh, you. You sound like Jack." Darla pointed at a picture in the menu. "Yum, the burger looks good. I think I'll have a burger."

Shannon shrugged. Jack was Darla's latest boyfriend. They had been dating since last March. By age twenty-eight, Darla had two broken engagements and one live-in boyfriend under her belt. In the same timespan as those, Shannon had one failed three-year relationship.

"So what'd you do yesterday?"

"Mm, Audrey and I went down to Larry's opening-day tailgate. It was fun. Do you know that Jen is twenty-one now? Isn't that wild?"

Darla shut the menu and turned toward Shannon. "I guess, yeah. I always think of her as such a little kid. But don't you ever get sick of hanging out with the Morgans' crew?"

Shannon groaned. "No, I don't get sick of them. Don't you get sick of always riding my back about every goddamn thing?"

Darla frowned, her pink lips pouty. "I'm sorry. I just, you're my big sis and I want to see you happy, and I just wonder why you want to spend all your time with a bunch of old people. But anyways, I wanted to hang out with you, so I'll try not to pick. You know I like to pick. I have a big mouth. Just ask Jack. He's totally mad at me because of this stuff with the house."

"What stuff with the house?" Darla had recently bought her own place, a fixer-upper in the city's Morningside neighborhood. It was a two-story brick house with two bedrooms and a spacious porch and deck. She'd got it for below sixty thousand dollars, a steal within city limits, but the house had been in disrepair since the early 1990s. It needed to be refurbished and brought up to date. Fortunately for Darla, Jack flipped houses for a living and could do all the remodeling she wanted. Shannon had been renting the same one-bedroom apartment in Blawnox for the past five years. She hated the idea of throwing her money away on rent, but she didn't make enough to save for the down payment or repairs of buying.

"He's just busy all the time. I mean, I bought this house thinking he was going to help me, and it's been two months and nothing has gotten done."

"Maybe he's working on his own house."

"That's exactly what he says!"

"Maybe that's because it's true!"

"I guess," said Darla. "But I want him to work on my house." She emphasized the word "my" and for a second she sounded just like she had as a child, always begging for her own way.

"He'll get to it eventually."

The waiter stopped by, taking their order and their menus. Shannon sat back on her hands.

"I know he'll get to it eventually. I want him to get to it *now*."

Shannon turned away, scanning the room. She happened to think Jack was a really great guy. Of Darla's many boyfriends, he was one of the few that she actually liked. And she hated hearing Darla complain about him or something he had done.

"I don't know what to tell you, Darla. Just be lucky you have him, okay, and I'm sure he'll get around to it in time."

Darla smiled, a mischievous sparkle in her eye.

"Wow, you sound exactly like him, Shannon. I mean, seriously, it's like scaring me that he gave you this script to you to tell me. You guys aren't dating behind my back, are you now?" She laughed. It was a tinkling laugh that made other people along the bar look at her and smile. That was Darla. She had a way about her that drew people in. Shannon looked away, uncomfortable. She glanced up at the television above the bar. Channel 4 was recapping yesterday's game, meaning that it must have been almost twelve-thirty. The food couldn't come fast enough.

Week 2: Steelers at Houston Texans
(W 27-7)

Jen

Right after the Steelers won 27 to 7 against the Houston Texans, Dave rushed Jen into her pink and white childhood bedroom. Smiling, he handed her a velvet box. "Here it is."

She snapped it open, already knowing exactly what it was—her engagement ring.

Dave looked nervous. "What do you think?"

She slipped it on her ring finger, a .25 carat princess cut on a solid white gold band. It fit just fine. But she had never imagined this moment quite like this. Five, even two, years ago, she would have imagined Dave getting down on one knee and begging for her hand. But ever since Bobby had left, she lived with a sense of urgency. Life felt too short, like she had to act now instead of waiting for something else.

"It fits."

"It fits? That's all that you can think to say?"

"What am I supposed to say? I mean, you didn't exactly woo me with any romantic gestures just now." She stuck her tongue out, mimicking him.

He laughed. "Aw, come on, you know I'm not like that. I already know you're gonna marry me, so why go through the hoops of asking." She laughed, looking into the mirror. Last week, Amy from work had cut her hair into a geometric bob that was shorter and sculpted in the back. In the front, it fell just long enough that she could tuck it behind her ears. The new style made her brown eyes look bigger and highlighted the peachy glow of her skin, something she attributed to pregnancy considering her usual sallow complexion. She dangled her hand in front of the mirror, trying to see the ring how others would.

"Come on, quit being so silly," Dave said, interrupting her brief fantasy. "Now comes the hard part."

Her smile disappeared. She knew exactly what he meant. Her parents. They had to tell her parents. It wasn't going to be easy, but at least the Steelers had won. She couldn't have planned that any better if she'd tried. "I know. But they're in good moods now, so maybe it won't be that bad."

Dave rubbed his chin. "Yeah, if we woulda lost that game today, you know we wouldn't be telling them tonight."

"Right. No bad news on top of a Steelers loss." As soon as she finished the sentence, she bit her tongue.

Dave put his head down. "Bad news, huh?"

She stood up. "No, no, I didn't mean it like that. Not bad news for us."

With her hand on his shoulder, his gray-blue eyes looked particularly vulnerable. She hated seeing him like this, but it seemed like her big mouth was always getting them to this point.

"We don't have to do this if you're not—"

"No!" The firmness in her voice surprised her. "It's not that. I'm ready. I'm just saying that to my parents, this will be a shock. Bobby gone to Iraq and me being married and pregnant in the span of a month will be hard for them to adjust to. But even if they do think it's bad news, I think it's good news and that's what matters." She leaned her face into his shoulder, avoiding those eyes. After a moment, he slapped her butt. She giggled, comfortable that all was well.

From downstairs, she heard her mom screaming that dinner was ready.

They looked at each other, then headed down.

About twenty minutes later, she and Dave sat directly across from her parents, eating their dinner in a comfortable silence. The table was filled with barbeque chicken, garlic mashed potatoes, and grilled squash and zucchini.

She picked at her plate with one hand, barely able to swallow.

"We're doing well so far," Larry said. "But we haven't really been outmatched yet. Next week, we'll see what we're made of."

Of course. Any silence too long or awkward could be squashed by some football talk. Jen smiled, relieved. Next week they were scheduled to play the New England Patriots, the team who had ruined their Super Bowl chances in last year's AFC Championship game.

Dave grinned. "Did you see all those sacks today? I'd like to see our defense take Brady down like that."

Larry laughed. "Me too."

Troy Polamalu was Jen's favorite player and earlier that day he had trounced all over the Texans' quarterback, David Carr. She loved the way his curly mane of black hair billowed beneath his helmet as he ran and the way he snuck up on his opponents, streaking across the field like white lightning to bring them down without warning. But tonight she thought of the other team. How it felt to know that Troy was on the field, that at any second, they could be completely blindsided.

She watched her parents eating slowly, with soft smiles.

Her mom looked at her dad, beaming. "You really outdid yourself with these grilled vegetables."

Her dad laughed, and Jen braced herself. It was time. She slid her left hand across the table. When they didn't look up right away, she drummed her fingers against the table.

Her mom's eyes widened. She picked up Jen's hand and looked at it, her mouth closed and her expression blank.

Larry appeared a lot more animated. Excited, even. "What's that I'm seeing? Is somebody going to make an honest woman out of my little girl?" He started to get out of his chair, but Dave cleared his throat.

"There's something else," he said. Jen pulled her arm back and turned sideways, pushing her hair over the side of her face. Did he really have to say it like that? *There's something else.* Like he was about to say that one of them had six months to live or he was enlisting in the army.

Her dad looked at them expectantly. Her mom leaned back, limp, as if she was melting into the back of her chair. "You're pregnant, aren't you?"

Jen felt like her throat was swelling shut. In her mind, this had been completely different. There was supposed to be a jubilant moment of celebration about the engagement. Then, after the excitement wore off, they would announce the pregnancy. Now it seemed like the engagement wasn't intentional, but some kind of an obligation. She glared at Dave.

Nobody said anything. She thought of the email Bobby had sent after she'd told him, a rather curt reply: "Good luck telling Mom and Dad." If he was here, though, she knew that he would say something to alleviate the tension. That was his special gift.

Her dad cleared his throat. "Is that true?"

"Yes, but that's not why we're getting married. We love each other. I mean, we were planning on getting married. This is just speeding things up." Her voice sounded shaky and overly cautious.

Dave covered her hand with his. "Yeah, we're just speeding things up."

"You're sure? You're really sure you want to do this?" said her mom.

Her dad looked at her mom. "What's that supposed to mean?"

Her mom picked up her plate and walked into the kitchen. "I'm just saying that they don't have to make this decision right now. They should think about it." Jen cringed as the garbage disposal roared to life with a loud crashing noise, like it was about to suck all the air out of the room.

She felt frozen, just watching her parents.

"If they say they want to get married, then we should support their decision," said her dad, furrowing his brow.

Her mom walked back into the room, her voice rising. "They are still kids and they obviously don't even know how to be responsible if they can't even use birth control."

"Stop talking about us like we aren't even here!" Jen stood up. "We are adults and this is what we are doing. We're getting married and we'll be out of your hair if we're such a problem, then. We will have our own lives and you don't even have to see your grandbaby if you don't want to...."

Dave cleared his throat. "Hey, calm down. I mean, I'm sorry that this is upsetting news, but this is what we want to do, so we don't ask that you agree with it. We just ask that you support us."

Her dad stood up. "Of course we support you." He walked into the kitchen, where Jen heard him cracking open a can of beer. "Right, Beth?"

Jen looked at her mom, hopeful. Her mom continued to glare, a hard edge to her voice. "I wish Bobby was here."

It was something they said all of the time, but tonight it didn't carry the same hope or nostalgia. It felt like an accusation: *I wish Bobby was here, because he would never do something like this to us.*

Shannon

Earlier that day while getting ready to watch the game, Shannon couldn't find her favorite jersey. She looked everywhere, but it was nowhere to be found. She knew it was no big thing, but she had worn it every game last season during their winning streak, and she wanted to keep with tradition. It wasn't until her bed was full of clothes and her closet was nearly empty that she remembered. Darla. At some point after the season, Darla had borrowed it. Giving something to Darla was like giving something to the Bermuda Triangle: you just shouldn't expect to get it back. At least not in one piece. Ever since they were little kids, Darla had always been fascinated with whatever toys and clothes Shannon had, a fascination that she usually pursued until Shannon got tired of haggling over it and just finally let Darla have whatever it was that she wanted. Things were just easier that way. But since her form-fitting Joey Porter jersey was her absolute favorite and she had worn it through all of last season when they'd played so well, she called Darla. Darla was at work but knew right where it was and said that Jack would be around if Shannon could stop by later.

Later that night, just as twilight spilled its dim orange glow across the cityscape, Shannon parked on tree-lined Jancey Street and bounded up the steps.

Jack opened the door before she knocked. He nodded her in, then settled back into a recliner, drinking a Yuengling and looking completely nonplussed about her arrival. Standing on the red tile entryway, she hesitated.

"Um, Darla told me to come pick up my shirt."

Jack nodded, getting up. "Yeah, yeah, she said you'd be over. I'll get your shirt." He disappeared around the corner into the dining room and Shannon stood frozen in the green and white living room. Save for a couple of mirrors, the couch, recliner and TV, the room was mostly bare.

Jack returned with her jersey. She looked it over, checking for any stains or other signs of Darla's carelessness, but it looked completely fine.

On the TV, announcers called plays for that evening's game.

"Thanks," she said, trying to be casual. Except around Jack, she never felt casual. Nervous? Yes. Quivering in the knees? Certainly. Embarrassed and awkward? Definitely. But never ever casual. She felt him watching her and looked away. A good five or so inches taller than her, Jack had a rugged face that looked sculpted out of a dark tan clay. His brown hair, clipped short with long skinny sideburns, highlighted his prominent cheekbones. But it was his eyes that really killed her—a light but piercing shade of green. They were at once disarming and reassuring. Jack pointed to the couch. "You want to stay for a minute?"

A minute? She'd like to stay for five, maybe twenty, as long as it would take to memorize every line on that face. That didn't seem right, but neither did going home. That afternoon, Audrey's house had been packed with rowdy friends and family and the excitement had charged her up. Returning to the stone-cold quiet of her apartment felt like torture. And Sunday evenings were always the worst; the thought of the upcoming week filling her with dread: the endless days at work and the long nights at Morgan's tending bar. It was an endless cycle without change or variation, except the Pittsburgh sports seasons—football, hockey, and baseball.

She sat down.

Jack smiled. "Wanna beer?" Shannon nodded. While Jack disappeared, she looked around the room, imagining how easy Sunday afternoons were for Darla when she wasn't working: lounging around in sweats, watching the Steelers game with a beer in one hand and Jack's hand on her leg.

Jack handed her a cold can and sat down.

"Thanks," she said, cracking it open.

"So did you get to see that game today?"

She nodded. "Yeah, pretty good—"

"I wish I could have seen more. I was upstairs painting all day. She needs to get a TV up there."

Shannon noticed that his dark arms were speckled with splatters of white paint. "Painting?"

He looked at his arms and laughed. "Yeah, well you know, now that she's doing Thanksgiving here, she wants to get things finished before then. Or should I say she wants me to get things finished."

"She's doing Thanksgiving here?"

Jack nodded. "Yeah, she said she wanted to host everybody, you know, take the burden off your mom this year."

Shannon raised her eyebrow. Take the burden off her mother? It was more likely that Darla just wanted an excuse to get Jack to start doing the work. With Jack studying her face, she tried to hide her gut feeling.

"Something wrong?" he asked.

"No, I'm just, just wondering who's going to cook."

Jack looked surprised. "She said you were."

"She what?" Shannon felt her entire face turning red. That was exactly the sort of thing that Darla would do, just like the time she'd hosted a BBQ at another apartment, then had the place fumigated and moved everything to Shannon's place at the last minute.

Jack laughed, waving his hand toward her. "Joking! Joking! Geez, Shannon, you looked about ready to blow a gasket there."

"Sorry. It's just that I wouldn't exactly put it past her."

He looked at her for a moment, his eyes full of something akin to sympathy. Then he turned away. They sat there for a few minutes, turning their attention to the Raiders and the Chiefs game. She finished her beer, then leaned forward, putting it down. He turned toward her, his arm poised as if he was about to stand. "Another?"

She'd barely eaten anything at Audrey's house and she was feeling a little something from that one beer. She felt like it was probably a good idea to leave but didn't want to. But she definitely shouldn't take another drink.

"So what's she having you do?"

Jack smiled, launching into a long speech on cabinets and countertops.

As he talked, Shannon leaned into the couch, nodding. His voice was so smooth and soothing that she felt herself opening up like a flower, each word peeling back a petal from its bud. She imagined her own one-bedroom apartment—four square rooms above a bakery in Blawnox. It was cold, beige, and undecorated. When she'd first moved there, she'd planned to paint and decorate but never really got around to it. She spent most of her time at Morgan's anyways.

She leaned forward, interrupting. "I'm sorry, is it just me or is this whole remodeling thing kind of weird?"

Jack stopped. "Weird? You do know I remodel homes for a living, right?"

"No, not like that. I guess it's just weird for me to think of my younger sister building herself a home. I mean, before I do."

"There's nothing to stop you from building a home, Shannon."

"But there is. I'll get these ideas, ya know, about things to do and things to buy, but then it always seems so pointless, like it'll never really be a home. But like seriously, I'm thirty-three. What am I waiting for?"

Jack leaned back in his chair, rubbing his elbow. He looked stumped, like he wasn't sure what to say. Shannon felt embarrassed. She'd said too much. She'd said way too much. What was she thinking saying all those personal things to her sister's boyfriend? He wasn't going to understand and he didn't need to understand. It wasn't his place to understand. She picked up her beer can, ready to throw it out. Ready to leave.

"I'm sorry, I have to—"

"No." Jack leaned forward. "I understand what you mean. Really, I do. I mean, I'm your age and I don't feel like it's home, either. I always live in my places while I do the work there, so it literally isn't my home. What I'm doing is my job. I'm just building a house for somebody, and then they're going to come in to make it a home." He looked at her, his smile soft and inviting. "It is kind of strange. And here's Darla, twenty-eight and knows exactly what she wants."

Shannon shifted on her feet. "Yeah, I wonder how that works."

He shrugged. "I don't know. She's just Darla, I guess. That's just how it is."

Yeah, thought Shannon. Darla always knew exactly what she wanted and exactly how to get it.

"I should probably be going."

She waited for a moment, looking at Jack, waiting for him to say something more. The heat between them was palpable, an electric kind of sensation that made her wish he was running finger down the side of her neck.

Jack blinked, then looked at the TV. "Yeah," he said. "You probably should."

Angela

On Monday morning, Angela walked to her locker between first and second period and traded in her books for her gym bag. Gym was the absolute worst.

Beside her, Brad Wellesley pulled out his physics textbook.

"Yo, Bad Luck," he said, slapping her on the back with a heavy fist. He was a quarterback with blond hair and blue eyes, that All-American look that made all the other girls swoon and Angela want to puke. Alphabetically, they were always stuck together, but it helped that he had a sharp wit and latent nerd tendencies—like his locker being wallpapered with old Marvel comics. Because he wasn't a total cliché, she didn't hold him in complete contempt, but he never helped himself by calling her Bad Luck.

"Yo, Brad," she said, returning the punch to his arm. "Don't call me Bad Luck."

He laughed. "But it's a good name. And this season, it doesn't make me hate you because we're awesome."

A few years ago at a tailgate, WTAE, the local ABC affiliate, had interviewed her dad about game day superstitions. There, on live TV, he drunkenly announced that she wasn't allowed to watch any games because she was "bad luck." Brad, of course, was watching and hadn't dropped it since.

"Keep up the punching me in the arm and I might start watching the games and wrecking up the season."

Brad narrowed his eyes, tilting his head. "Now, Bad Luck, if you keep talking like that, I might have to subject you to a gun show." He flexed his arm, slapping at his muscle and preening.

"I'm going to barf."

He pushed her into her locker.

She rubbed her arm. "Dude, seriously. Stop with the roughhousing."

"C'mon, you know I'm jokin'. Where you headed with that bag?"

Angela groaned. "Gym class. Wanna trade places? I'll gladly go to physics."

Brad winked. "Does that mean I get to change in the girls' locker room?"

"Oh, stop it. I freakin' hate this class. All the stupid bitches in my class are so competitive. It's second period gym, not the Summer Olympics."

Brad shrugged. "Skip it. That's what I do during Trig. Go out, get in my car, and head home during seventh period."

Angela's eyes widened. "But how do you not get caught?"

"Seriously, you think anybody's gonna notice? They won't." Brad shook his head, tugging at the pink streak in Angela's hair. She'd done it over the weekend while the rest of the town was watching the Steelers game. "Man, Bad Luck, for somebody who looks so crazy, you sure are a wuss."

Angela held the bag to her chest. "I'm not a wuss, I'm trying to keep my records clean for college applications."

Brad smiled, his blue eyes sparkling. His eyelashes were so long it almost looked like he was wearing mascara. "Wuss!" He pushed at her one more time.

"I'm not a wuss," she said, only to find that she was alone. Surrounded by a group of other football players and cheerleader girls, Brad was halfway down the hall.

Megan

The grand lobby at the Renaissance Hotel was an elegant space—creamy marble pillars and a red-carpet staircase in the shadows of an ornate golden rotunda. Late Monday morning, Megan marched through the spacious lobby and the brown doors of the hotel restaurant. Like most days after a Steelers win, she was in an unusually good mood. The night before, she had finally sealed the deal with Todd the tattooed bartender. Turns out those flame tattoos only circled his neck, not his entire back like she had expected. Megan had three tattoos—a faded daisy on her ankle that she'd gotten when she turned 18, a Steelers logo just above her hip bone, and the most recent, a huge bouquet of purple orchids, pink hibiscus, and orange lilies on the back of her left shoulder that dangled all the way down to her elbow. It had taken her three sessions to get the color and details just right and she lost a little respect for a guy as big as Todd who couldn't endure the same. Plus, their nearly six minutes together was entirely too fast and totally unforgettable. At its anti-climactic end, he had the nerve to growl for more, making faces and cussing when she toppled over him in a race to dress and go home.

He'd patted the bed. "C'mon, I've got the night off. Let's do this some more."

"Gotta go," she'd said, shaking her head and getting out of there as fast she could. She'd left him wanting for more, of course. That was the only way she did it.

In the kitchen, she tossed her purse and hoodie into the break room and tied on an apron. Five days a week, she served there during lunch and dinner, plus the occasional wedding or other event during the weekend. It wasn't exactly a dream come true, but she'd been there since she dropped out of Pitt about seven years ago, and if nothing else, it was comfortable.

As she made her way through the kitchen, the head chef, Marlon, spotted her and whistled. "My, my, Megan. Looking beautiful as always, even on a Monday morning."

He was a tall man with faded cocoa skin and a bald head. This morning, he wore his white chef's outfit and a diamond stud in his left ear. Strikingly handsome, he was ten years older than Megan and thrice-divorced. He'd tried many times in the past five years to start something with her, but she'd always discouraged his advances. It wasn't that she didn't think he was sexy. It was mostly because it seemed so easy with him. He was always suggesting things and making flirtatious innuendos. With guys like Marlon, it was more fun to play it coy.

As she pulled her hair into a bun, he stood by watching her as the other staff slowly filtered their way in. "So," he said. "You know I gotta get your post-game analysis. What's the word?"

Megan smiled, adjusting the collar of her black shirt. "Defense. Did you see all those sacks we had?"

Marlon smiled coyly and crossed his arms over his chest. "Mm, mm, I love it when you talk dirty, I mean, football, to me."

She was about to give him a friendly push when the manager of catering, Larissa, walked up behind him in her brown business suit and nodded to Megan. "Megan? I was wondering if you'd have a word with me in my office?"

Marlon let out a low whistle. "Ahhh, see, I told you you'd eventually get fired if you didn't sleep with me."

Larissa shot Marlon a dirty look and turned back to Megan. "Megan? Do you have a minute?"

This time, as Megan passed Marlon, she poked him in the gut. He crumpled over like a sacked quarterback, then winked at her before heading toward the stove.

Aside from some light chit-chat about the gray weather, Larissa and Megan walked silently toward the elevators and then to the sales and catering offices on the third floor. Megan knew what was coming. Last week during a wedding, she'd ended up drinking a little too much while she was helping out with the open bar. She'd gotten so tipsy that she'd slow danced with a cute wedding guest. That sort of stuff wasn't really tolerated, and if Larissa had found out, then she was probably getting a lecture.

Larissa sat down at her desk and folded her hands over a black leather organizer.

"You've been here for what 6, 7 years now? You've done hosting, serving, catering. Pretty much everything."

Megan shifted in her seat.

"I don't know if you're aware of this or not, but Tonya has decided to stay home after she has the baby, so we are looking for somebody to take over as a Banquet Event Manager. And before we look outside the hotel, a couple of us were talking, and we were wondering if you were interested in the position. Obviously, there would be a pay increase. Now, I think you already know the job pretty well, but I'm still not expecting you to make a decision today."

Megan sunk back into her chair, surveying Larissa's eager expression.

"Megan, you look so worried, like I'm about to fire you. I'm offering you a promotion."

A promotion. Why did she need a promotion? Everything was just fine the way it was. Why didn't anybody in her life ever get that? Things didn't need to change. They needed to stay the same. But a raise? Now that she could use.

"It's steady work, Megan. No more checking the weekly schedule. A regular eight-thirty-to-five day. And full benefits."

Larissa emphasized eight-thirty to five like it was a good thing, yet, the idea of arriving here at eight-thirty every day seemed like a nightmare. But at least it would be something to tell her mom and maybe Emily. Maybe it would make them take her a little more seriously.

Megan shrugged. "I'll do it."

Larissa raised her eyebrows, then smiled. "Okay, that's good to hear. Well, you should probably get down for the lunch shift right now, but I'll talk to you over the next week or so to finalize things and start the transition, Tonya plans to leave sometime in mid-October so yeah, that's great. I'll let you know when we'll be getting you started." Megan jumped up, anxious to leave.

"Oh and Megan? One more thing."

She turned around. Larissa sat up straight, her shiny brown hair gleaming in the fluorescent lights.

"Event Managers should only slow dance with the wedding guests if they're actually, you know, guests at the wedding."

Megan's eyes widened. "Oh, so you knew about that?"

Larissa laughed. "The whole hotel knows about that one, Megan. But it's okay; we kind of expect that sort of thing from you."

"Oh." Megan tried to muster a fake smile, not sure whether Larissa was paying her a compliment or an insult.

Desiree

On Thursday night, Desiree came home to an empty house. It wasn't an uncommon event. It was much more uncommon for Tom to actually be home in the evenings. Most nights, she filled her evenings with workouts at the gym or yoga classes so that by the time she got home, there wasn't a lot of time to dwell on being alone. Yesterday in a Pilates class, she'd pulled a muscle in her neck and had been having spasms ever since. All day at work, she'd been up and down from her desk, unable to concentrate on anything longer than about twenty minutes at a time. The whole office must have thought she was insane, especially when she announced she was leaving at five. She always stayed until six. That way, on the rare nights when Tom was actually in the office, they could ride home together.

She was the head of Conference Planning, and he was a Vice President of Brokerage Services at PNC Bank. This week, he was in Florida working with some new brokers. He'd accepted this position shortly after they were married three years ago, and ever since, he'd been gone almost every week. This week, he'd come home on Saturday afternoon, long enough for them to watch the Steelers game together before he headed to the airport for another two-week stint in Florida.

Desiree threw the keys to her BMW on a hook in the foyer and grabbed the mail. All of it was junk. Since pretty much everybody she knew was either in Pittsburgh or in regular e-mail contact with her, she knew that there was no reason for her to get personalized mail. Still, sometimes she found herself looking through it with hope, imagining that somewhere, Tom was dropping off a postcard. That was how their relationship had started a million years ago: after multiple encounters at corporate functions, they had embarked on a series of flirty correspondence through the company's inter-office mail that abruptly ended when Tom's wife, Patty, stopped by his office and found a perfume-drenched thong from Conference Planning, 12th Floor.

At that point, she and Tom didn't have a relationship other than this office flirtation, but the aftereffects of that discovery killed his marriage and pushed them closer together. It wasn't something she was proud of, but it also wasn't something she spent too much time feeling guilty about. Life was too short for that.

Desiree set the junk mail in a basket on a black lacquer table. The place was quiet. She walked into the kitchen and opened the chrome-colored refrigerator. Aside from a gallon of soy milk, greek yogurt, and a bag of mixed greens, it was empty. Not that she was even hungry. Somebody had brought back a pizza from Monte Cello's at lunch, and two slices was more than enough to tide her over for the rest of the day. She put her hand to the back of her neck and stretched, letting out a long sigh.

Slipping off her black suit jacket, she looked around. The kitchen, like the rest of the house, was clean and modern, beautiful and precise. She'd grown up amidst a lot of clutter and liked to keep things neat. Tom complained that the place felt antiseptic. But that was fine with her. Things were supposed to be in their appointed places. When his kids came over on the weekend, it drove her crazy how they left their shoes and clothes laying about. Kristen would just drop her purse and her cell phone any which way it fell, and Robbie had once decided to dye his hair in the bathroom and gotten black dye all over her white terrycloth shower curtain.

Teenagers now, the kids were often moody and seldom easy to handle, but she did love them. They were funny and surprisingly witty and the way they looked at Tom sometimes made her jealous. Her own father had left when she was too young to remember and her mother's subsequent husbands were mostly losers, just extra bodies in the house, not the kind of men who commanded any sort of presence or respect.

She stood in the kitchen as if waiting. Sitting down seemed like a choice to stay in for the rest of night, and she wasn't quite ready to resign herself to that. Maybe she could go shopping. But even then, she'd be alone. Unless Kristen wanted to go with her. Sure, it would be a bit of hike to go pick her up, but they could head out to the Galleria Mall. And Kristen always wanted to go shopping.

Picking up the phone, she dialed their number and waited. Kristen picked up on the first ring, sounding breathless and excited like she always did. She always sounded like she was late for a party.

"Hello?"

"Kristen? It's me, Des."

"Oh, hey."

"I was just gonna see if you wanna go shopping tonight. I got off work a little early, thought maybe I'd run out to the Galleria, could pick you up on the way."

"Really? Isn't that kind of far?"

Desiree lived in the North Hills, two bridges and a tunnel away. "Yeah, you know, I just need to get out, just thought maybe you'd like to join."

"I would, ya know, but Mom is making us do this, like, family dinner thing tonight, so yeah, I can't really get out of it."

"Family dinner? We could go after that."

"No. Sorry, Des. She's like all about us bonding or whatever, so I'll, like, have to clean up, too, and by then it will be too late."

"Oh." Desiree's voice fell, and she slumped against the counter. Leave it to Patty to plan family dinner on the one night she needed Kristen.

Kristen cleared her throat. "Maybe I can ask Mom if you can come over?"

"No. No, don't worry about it. I'm good, just thought I'd offer. We can just do something next weekend."

"Mm, actually I was going to tell you guys that next weekend is bad because it's fall formal on Saturday night, but maybe on that Sunday, I can do something."

Fall formal? Kristen had never mentioned fall formal. Desiree wondered where she had gotten a dress. She was an expert on formal dresses. Why hadn't Kristen asked for help?

"Okay. It sounds like you're busy, so I'll let ya go. Have fun at your dance—"

Desiree was still saying goodbye as Kristen hung up the phone.

Patty

Patty peeled the foil from the lasagna, breathing in the savory aroma of oregano and basil.

"Kristen, did you set the table yet? Seriously, I told you—"

Kristen popped her head in from the dining room. "I already did it. Geez, Mom. Chill out."

"When I came down here you were on the phone. Who were talking to?"

"Des. She wanted me to go shopping with her."

Patty wrinkled her nose, picking up the pan with an oven mitt and carrying it into the dining room. As she set it on the deep mahogany tablecloth, she yelled for Robbie. "Robbie!!!! Get down here, dinner is ready!"

She motioned for Kristen to sit down and started serving up generous portions onto square white plates. "So what'd you tell her?"

"Tell who?" Kristen picked at the lasagna with the tip of her fork. "Did you use the lowfat cheese and lean meat? This looks packed with calories."

"You're fourteen, you can use some extra calories. What did you tell Des about shopping?"

Kristen made a face. "I told her that we were having dinner. And that we won't be coming out there next weekend because of fall formal."

Patty nodded, folding her napkin into her lap. "Where is your —"

"I'm here," said Robbie. As usual, he looked mildly annoyed. He wore a pair of skinny jeans and a faded t-shirt that said Joy Division. Patty wasn't sure what Joy Division was, but the faded gray shirt and Robbie's expression led her to believe that it had little to do with joy.

Patty looked at her kids. They seldom ate together, but she'd decided that at least one night a week, they needed a proper dinner together. Usually she cooked something for dinner and the kids ate it in their rooms: Robbie watching *The Simpsons* reruns and Kristen on her phone. Most nights, Patty ate alone, standing at the kitchen counter.

But this summer she'd finally finished redecorating the dining room, and its dark mustard color walls and the copper and amber chandelier made it feel so cozy this time of year that she wanted them to start using it for something more than a resting place for coats and schoolbooks.

Kristen took a small bite of lasagna and cleared her throat. "Can I stay over at Vanessa's house after the formal?"

"Why can't Vanessa stay here?"

Kristen groaned. "I knew you were going to say that. Seriously, Mom, why does everybody always have to stay here?"

"So I know where you are. Vanessa's parents are never home."

Robbie looked up from his plate and laughed, sticking his tongue out at Kristen. Patty knew it was about to start. It was always like this with the two of them: a moment of relative calm giving way to a fight. "Ha, you're just mad because Mom's onto you. I bet you were planning on staying over night with Jeff not Vanessa."

"Mom! Tell him to shut up. That is a lie, Robbie. A lie. I would not do that!"

Patty took a drink of iced tea. "Calm down, Kristen. And I'm not telling anybody to shut up."

Kristen crumpled up her napkin and threw it onto the table, bouncing out of her chair like she was about to run away screaming. "Mom! You always take up for him. I should have went shopping with Des. I hate it here."

Robbie glared at her. "Stop being overdramatic, Kristen. Why do you always have to be such a freakin' drama queen?"

"I am not a drama queen!"

Patty hit her fist onto the table. "Both of you. Stop it. And Kristen, I see you trying to get out of your seat. Sit down! We're going to sit here and eat like a family."

Kristen and Robbie groaned but went back to their food. From the living room, Patty heard the opening credits to *Wheel of Fortune* playing on the abandoned TV. Was it really that difficult for Kristen to turn off the TV when she came into the dining room? She turned to Robbie. "So are you going to the fall formal?"

He looked at her like she had just asked if he was going to sign up for the football team. "No. Angela doesn't work that night, so we are going to the movies."

"Why don't the two of you go to the dance?"

"Because we don't go to dances. We don't like anybody at school."

"The two of you isolate yourselves so much, I don't think it's healthy. You should have more friends than Angela."

Kristen laughed. "Yeah, right. Robbie should be glad that Angela's friends with him. Otherwise he'd probably get beat up all the time, but Angela's such a weirdo that nobody wants to mess with her."

"Shut up, Kristen. You don't know anything."

"I know that everybody makes fun of you."

Patty put her hand to her forehead. "Both of you, stop. Really. Just stop."

For a second, they were quiet. Patty watched Robbie as he ate. She knew that he got picked on at school. He was extremely intelligent and didn't tolerate stupidity in others. If he treated his classmates like that, they might think he was a know-it-all. He carried himself with a quiet sense of rage that she sometimes felt when he snapped at Kristen or her. She tried to give him a pass most times because she knew the divorce had been hard on him and she imagined it would be hard to grow up as a boy in an all-female house. It didn't help that his only friend in the world was yet another female. Angela had always been a sassy little girl, but now she verged on being cruelly sarcastic. She was tough enough to deal with the consequences of any drama she created, but Patty had a feeling that Robbie wasn't as good at dealing with such backlash. She also worried that Angela might be involved with drugs. No particular reason, just something about her appearance that brought drugs to mind.

"Robbie, maybe it would be a good idea if you hung out with somebody other than Angela all the time. Like, what about Gary Marsh? You and him used to get along so well."

Robbie put down his fork and stared at her. "Look, Mom, I don't like Gary Marsh anymore, okay? And I don't think that you of all people should be telling me about making friends. At least I have one friend. That's one more than you have."

Patty frowned. He didn't know anything about her friends. She had friends. There were plenty of women at work who she talked to. But then she thought of Monday morning, the day after a win over the Texans, wrapping up a pink lace bikini brief for Troy Polamalu. Was she close enough to anybody to tell them about that? No, but that was different. That was something she kept to herself because she wanted it to be a secret. She didn't need to explain that to anybody.

She looked at Robbie, uncomfortable. His skin was a dead white, like the inside of an igloo. "Go to your room."

He shrugged, walking away with hunched shoulders.

Once he was gone, Patty looked at Kristen. "You said the kids pick on Robbie. What do they say?"

Kristen paused, her usually wide eyes uncertain and heavy. She looked at Patty, very serious. "They call him a fag."

Patty took a deep breath, feeling the slightest ache in her head. Standing up, she began to clear the table. "I'll clean up, Kristen." She'd had enough family time for one evening.

Week 3: Steelers vs. New England Patriots
(L 23-20)

Megan

Last season when the Steelers snapped a New England Patriots winning streak, Megan celebrated the big win with a good-looking doorman from the hotel named Daniel. This year, she watched the Pats snap a Steelers regular season winning streak in her apartment, alone and hungover. Sunday hangovers could be long and tedious. Even the wildest of her friends usually gave it a rest on Sundays and people like Emily and her grad student friends filled their Sundays with vegan brunches or repurposing furniture, so she was always grateful for football season, when the parties usually extended for one more day.

Megan stood up from the couch, switching the channel to another game and heading into the kitchen for a glass of water. Her head pounded louder than stadium music. Last night, she had worked dinner for a wedding, then Emily picked her up and they went to Oktoberfest at the Penn Brewery.

It was one of her favorite Pittsburgh traditions—beer by the jugful in a brick courtyard complete with wiener schnitzel and a polka band. She vaguely remembered the band and her genuine annoyance when she'd realized that Emily was meeting up with that Mike guy and that his crony Kevin was also there. At one point, she remembered being a part of a big group of clean-cut guys with popped collars and girls with crewneck sweaters and tweed jackets. And then it had become rather apparent that Emily and Mike, who she caught cuddling in line for the Porta-Pottys, were more than just friends. Miffed that she found out from a Porta-Potty canoodle and not directly from Emily, she ditched that group and caught up with some high school friends who were also there. She went home with a friend of a friend, Will, who wasn't nearly as cute this morning.

Filling up her cup of coffee, she was surprised when the doorbell rang. Pulling down her tank top to cover the slight pouch of her belly, she headed to the door. Her parents Nick and Shelley stood on the front porch. Her mom, with perfectly-coiffed short brown hair, looked disappointed, and her dad, with gelled hair and an ample belly spilling over his belt, just looked plain irritated.

"What are you guys doing here?"

"Lovely hello. Nice to see you too, Megan," said her mom, pushing into the house. Her dad patted her shoulder. "You look a little sick, kiddo, everything okay?"

"Well, that game —"

He shook his head. "Tell me about it, I'm sick too."

Before Megan could even process what was happening, her mom was taking off her shoes and making herself comfortable. "We were in the neighborhood, watching the game with some friends and thought we'd stop by. Can I use your bathroom?"

She nodded, watching her mom mount the wooden staircase. "Watching the game in the neighborhood? What's with that?"

Her dad shrugged. "One of your mom's co-workers was having a birthday party during the game. It was over at Lot 17." He grinned. "I'll tell you one good thing: they make their drinks stiff there." He rubbed his elbow, hanging his fleece on the stair railing. "God, Megan, you really don't look good. You sure you're all right?"

Megan shifted on her feet, imagining the quiet horror of her dad and Todd making small talk about the game during drink orders.

"I went to Oktoberfest last night."

He held up his hand. "Say no more. Understood. But for god's sake, Megan, can you put some clothes on?"

She knew her breasts were practically popping out of her tank top but this was her house, not a convent. "And could you give me a warning call next time you decide to drop by?"

"We weren't going to stop, but your mom said that you hadn't returned her calls all week."

She hadn't returned her mom's calls? Try the other way around.

Returning from the bathroom, her mom piped in, "Yes, Megan, I'm sorry I couldn't reach you all week. We're getting ready for a grant deadline. We need to get this renewal for one of our projects, or about 20 people will lose their jobs." She sighed, rubbing her hand on her cheek and smiling weakly. Her mom always made whatever she was doing sound like it was of the utmost importance. It was great that she was trying to save peoples' jobs, but was it really that time-consuming that she couldn't take five minutes to call her only daughter? The thought of arguing made Megan feel even more exhausted.

"Whatever. I just wanted to tell you something."

"And what's that?"

Megan swallowed. This was good news, right? This was the kind of thing that would get her mom off her back, right? But she was pretty darn sure that her mom would find something condescending to say even if Megan blurted out that she'd found the cure for breast cancer. "I got a promotion at work."

Her dad clapped his hands together. "That's great! What will you be doing? Managing the hotel? Head chef? CEO?"

Her mom didn't crack a smile. In spite of thousands dollars worth of beauty creams, her skin was beginning to show signs of its age, especially in the corners of her mouth and on her neck.

"Conference Services Manager. This girl, Tonya, she's having a baby so they're moving me up. I'll be doing some office work and then at the events, instead of serving, I'll be in charge of making sure the catering staff is doing their job."

Her mom tilted her head. "So did you really get a promotion, or are you doing a temporary favor?"

A favor? Really? Did anything that ended with a paycheck really ever count as a favor?

"No, it's not a favor. This will be full-time job with a raise and benefits. You know, Mom, like you've been begging me to do for, like, my entire life."

Her dad squeezed her. He smelled like beer and Drakkar Noir. "That's great."

Her mom crossed her arms over her chest. She wore a black turtleneck with a camel-colored blazer. In her ears were diamond studs, and on her neck hung a thick gold herringbone necklace. "That is great. But do you really want to settle for this? I thought you wanted to finish your degree."

Megan groaned. "Oh my god, Mom. Did you really have to go there? If I said I was going to school, you would tell me that I should get a full-time job. You make my head explode."

"Megan, don't be such a victim. Is it wrong to want to see my daughter doing better for herself than being event staff?"

Her dad groaned. "She's just fine." He rolled his eyes. "You know, Shell, I was almost in a good mood there for a minute, and then you had to go and make me mad."

"Don't start with me, Nick. I didn't make you mad. You're just mad because the Steelers lost and now you've lost your buzz. A grown man and you can't even watch how much you drink. I was embarrassed there, Nick. You were drunk in front of my co-workers."

He threw up his hands. "Oh, really? I embarrassed you? I wasn't even drunk. And you were the one who was embarrassing—you were talking so loudly during the whole game, nobody could hear the goddamn announcers."

"You don't even like the announcers!"

"I'd rather hear them than your incessant chatter about work. Can you talk about anything else? Those people were trying to have a nice afternoon, and all you could do was remind them about things they needed to do at work tomorrow."

"You have no idea, Nick. I know these people, and they need to be reminded. And I was only doing that because we were obviously losing the game and I wanted to create a distraction."

Megan stepped in between them. "Shut up! Seriously, if you came here to fight, then just leave." She pointed at the door. Her parents momentarily glared at one another, then turned toward her, almost as if they had choreographed the whole bickering couple routine.

"I'm sorry," her mom said. "It's been a long day. If you put some clothes on, do you want us to take you out to eat or anything? Do you have any food here? We could go to Giant Eagle and get you some groceries."

Her dad nodded, putting a hand around her arm. "You're gettin' too skinny. Let's get you some groceries."

Megan laughed. Her dad knew exactly how much she ate and that there was no mistaking her for skinny, but he liked to tease. And for free groceries, she'd gladly play along.

"If you want." She shrugged, thinking how nice it would be if she was gone when Emily came home, especially if she returned with Mike. Megan skipped up the stairs, pulling the door to her room shut. It looked like a boutique had exploded, clothes and shoes piled ankle deep on the floor. She waded through them, looking for a clean pair of jeans. From below, her parents spoke in a low rumble. They'd been married for almost 30 years but were always at odds about something. And people wondered why she didn't want a boyfriend. The real question was why everybody else did.

Angela

As soon as she heard the garage door opening, Angela decided it was a good idea to head up to her room. That afternoon during work, her co-workers at the theater had listened to the game on the radio. She was well aware that they had lost. And based on about an hour's worth of listening to their collective bitching and moaning, she also knew that this was a loss that particularly hurt; something about the end to a winning streak and the New England Patriots, a team considered evil incarnate by most Steelers fans. Angela jumped up from the couch and turned off the latest episode of E! True Hollywood Story. She was halfway up the stairs when her dad's gruff voice growled behind her.

She spun around. He stood in the half-opened front door, his hair tousled and sticking up on the sides. Angela smiled at him, then stomped toward her bedroom.

"Get back here, Angela!" She heard him calling out as she shut her door. She collapsed on the edge of her bed. This summer, she'd painted her whole room black, including the ceiling. The effect was a lot more claustrophobic than she'd anticipated. She stood up, opening a window. The wind was chilly. Goosebumps rose on her arm. She flicked on the radio. She needed The Smiths in her life right about now.

There was a knock at the door. What the hell did they want now? Furious, she opened it. Dom stood there, his lips puckered. "Did they let you watch the game today?"

"Seriously? I have homework to do." She started to close the door, but he held his hand up, stopping it.

"Homework is for nerds. I asked you a question."

She shrugged. "They had it on the radio. I might have been out there at some point."

"Was that some point around the end of 3rd, beginning of 4th quarter?"

"Possibly. You wanna make something of it?"

Dom laughed, a hearty chuckle. "Do I wanna make something of it? What are you, a joker? When the Patriots scored three in a row, I told your mom you had to be somewhere watching or listening. Sounds like I was right." His finger still pointed in her face, he glanced down the hall toward her mom, who stood a few feet away with a disapproving expression.

"C'mon Dom," said her mom, pushing him away and somehow sidestepping right into Angela's room. Her mom surveyed the room. It was hard to tell which was worse, her dad blaming her for the stupid game or her mom standing there in her room looking so curious.

"Don't mind him, Ang. He had too much to drink today. You know how he gets."

Angela rolled her eyes. "Did Sally Wiggin or anybody interview him for the news or anything else you should tell me? Radio? Newspaper? Online web show?"

She could see that her mom was suppressing a laugh. "No. He did not get on the TV news. And Ang, that was so long ago. You know he felt bad about that. But don't worry."

"Worry about what?"

"You did listen to it on the radio, but you know it wasn't your fault that they lost today."

"Um, yeah. I'm aware of that. It's never been my fault."

Her mom bit her lip. "Right. I know. You're good."

"Whatever." Angela turned around, shutting the door behind her and booting up her laptop. She needed to start working on her application to the University of Washington. Seattle looked better and better every day.

Jen

Kneeling over the toilet, she felt completely overcome. She coughed then gagged, finally heaving an evening's worth of orange juice, ice cream, and microwave popcorn into the bowl. Finishing, she flushed, slumping against the wall. She glanced at the clock: 9:15. Damn. She was going to be late for work. But compared to this nausea, nothing else really seemed very important. She rubbed her stomach, concentrating on the blue monogrammed hand towels hanging from a chrome rack. BM and LM. Beth and Larry Michalski. She covered her eyes with her hands.

Since last Sunday, she had stayed with Dave. Right now, she didn't even want to look at her parents. They'd left several apologetic messages during the week, none of which she'd returned. Last night, Bobby sent her an e-mail encouraging her to make things right. Even on the other side of the world, he was the family peacemaker, the tie that bound them all. That e-mail and her need for clean clothes were enough to bring her home. Besides, after the Steelers lost yesterday, Dave went to the bedroom and wouldn't come out or talk to her. She needed a break. This morning, she briefly saw her dad before he left for work, and he hugged her so tight, she thought he might squeeze out the baby. He smelled like soap and eggs, and she thought of how rare it was to find him before he became saturated with the harder smells of his garage—motor oil and cigarettes. The way he kissed her forehead good-bye reassured her that things with them were going to be fine.

She heard her mom knocking at the door. "Jen? Is that you? Are you okay?" Squeezing her eyes shut, she grimaced. Okay? She felt so sick she didn't know if she'd ever feel okay again. But she wasn't about to tell her mom that. "Yeah, I'm fine. Everything's fine."

"Are you sure? Do you need anything? Can I come in?"

There was a long, exaggerated silence. Jen felt her mom's anxious hovering outside the door like she was standing right beside her. "Can I come in?"

"Whatever." Jen eased herself upright and leaned on the blue counter. Her mom looked at her in the wall-length mirror and for a moment they were framed perfectly: each of them looking just beyond the other.

Jen wiped her mouth. "I'm okay. Just you know, a little queasy."

Just out of bed, her mom hadn't yet softened her face with layers of foundation and powder and Jen found the sight of her naked wrinkles unsettling. Her mom looked at her, serious. "Maybe some crackers?"

"No. I'm not hungry. The doctor said it's normal."

She nodded. "So you've already been to the doctor? Who took you?"

"Dave. I have another appointment in a couple of weeks."

Shutting the toilet lid, her mom sat down on it. Jen turned on the sink, scrubbing her hands before rinsing her mouth.

"I can go with you. If you need moral support or anything."

Jen spit water into the sink and watched it swirl down the drain. "Dave's gonna take off work that day, but thanks." She reached into her make-up bag for her burgundy lipstick, not that lipstick was really going to be much help on a day like this. Her entire face looked waxy and green—so much for that pregnancy glow.

"Your father and I talked, and I know you said that you want to elope, but we'd really like to plan you a wedding."

Lipstick poised to her mouth, Jen stopped. "A wedding?"

Her mom stood up, shuffling on her feet. "Yes. Something small, just close family and friends, but something official. We just, once this baby comes, it's going to change your life and we'd like to do something for you. And Dave, of course." She tilted her head, putting her hand on Jen's shoulder.

Her mom's hand felt like it weighed as much as the Allegheny Mountains. She knew the request came from a good place, but right now, imagining feeling well enough to be in a wedding seemed nearly impossible.

"You're so busy, Mom."

Her mom put her hand on her waist, pulling her close. "I'll make the time."

"Do you think Bobby could come home?"

She could feel her mom hesitating. "I don't know about all that. But if we start planning now, there's always a chance. So is that a yes?"

Jen nodded and as her mom smiled she realized she couldn't remember the last time her mom had looked so pleased without the help of her favorite beverages.

Shannon

If there was anything more frustrating than a Steelers loss followed by a long, tedious Monday spent working, it was the Pittsburgh traffic patterns. Although using the word patterns to describe them was dubious at best. The city's geographical position in a valley at the tip of three rivers made the usual grid-like streets and by-ways of most major cities a near impossibility. Unlike other places, where six and eight lane expressways were the norm, the roads around Pittsburgh were four lanes that narrowed down to two and sometimes one to enter and exit the city via bridges and tunnels. The whole place was a bottleneck.

Sitting on Route 28 North at four-thirty in the afternoon, she cursed a long laundry list of items: the Ford Expedition blocking her view, the road construction, accident, or rockslide that had caused the traffic jam, and herself for going this way at all. If she'd have gotten off at the 40th Street Bridge and drove through Lawrenceville, she'd be there by now. But at half past four, she had expected to miss rush hour traffic and get back to the office early enough that she'd have a couple of hours to kill before she worked at Morgan's. Now, it was ten to five. She'd have to rush through her end-of-day stuff at the office and grab something quick to eat on the way to Morgan's.

Earlier in the day, she'd been stuck outside the Fort Pitt tunnel for forty-five minutes while an accident was cleared inside the tunnel. And here she was stuck again. She clicked through the radio, trying to find an explanation for this particular traffic backup. Instead, every deejay in town was still commiserating about Sunday's Steelers loss and bemoaning the upcoming bye week. She hated the bye week, too, but she hated this traffic more. Finally, she clicked onto Kelly Clarkson's new song and found herself singing along. Shannon sang, tapping her fingers, then noticed that her cell phone was ringing.

The screen read, "Darla." She held it for a minute. Her ringtone was set to the old school *Monday Night Football* theme song and, listening to it, she couldn't help but remember chilly Monday nights when she was younger, curling up in a fleece Steelers blanket watching *MacGyver* and then football with her parents.

"Whaddya want?"

Darla laughed. "Now promise you're not going to be mad at me."

"That doesn't sound good."

"Well, it is. It's just fine. But I know how you are, so promise you won't get mad."

Shannon swallowed. "Okay. I promise. Maybe."

"That's good enough. Yesterday a friend of Jack's came over to watch the game with us, and he mentioned that he was single and looking for somebody and I mentioned that I had a sister and I may have, you know, showed him your picture and said that maybe we can arrange something, like a dinner date or a night at the movies."

Shannon turned down the music.

"You didn't."

"I did! But Shannon, it's not bad. He is a nice guy."

"That means he is ugly."

"He is not ugly, Shannon. But he dresses, well, he's kind of stuck in the nineties when it comes to clothes, but you can fix that. I mean, seriously, Shannon, he is a good guy and your age and very, very interested. He said he thought you were super hot."

"What picture did you show him?"

"The one of us at Dad's birthday this summer. You were wearing the white sundress."

"That is a nice picture. But Darla, I have told you a million times I do not want to be fixed up. I am not interested in dating."

"But Shannon, I just don't believe that. I know you think that you don't want it, but if a nice man comes along, you should really take advantage of it. I mean, it's been a couple of years since you really dated anybody, and I just want to see you happy."

"And why do you think that I'm not happy? I'm just fine, Darla, freakin' fine, and you should just butt out of it."

"You're just freakin' fine? Because you sound a little angry."

"I am angry, Darla. Because I've been stuck in traffic for almost an hour now on 28 and I was stuck in traffic for an hour earlier today and I'm just so freakin' tired of driving around this damn town and getting stuck everywhere I freakin' turn."

There was a long silence. Shannon felt embarrassed. Her hands shook. She didn't mean to sound so angry. As usual, Darla was unaffected. "Okay. He's coming over next week for the game, and I told him I'd try to get you to come over, but you know that it's up to you, so just do whatever you want."

The Ford Expedition moved forward.

"We're moving! We're finally moving!"

"Okay, good. Just think about what I said and get back to me."

"What does Jack think about the friend and me? I assume you told him your devious little plan."

"It's not devious, it's helpful." Darla paused. "But Jack said I need to butt out of your life."

Shannon smiled, thinking about Jack defending her like that and then of last Sunday night, the way he'd looked at her with such concern as she'd talked. He'd really been listening. At work and with her family, it always felt like she did all the listening. Talking was a nice change of pace.

"So me and him are on the same page again? I'll come over. I'm not promising anything, Darla, I'm seriously not, but I'll at least meet him if it's such a big deal to you."

"Good. Great! I knew you'd come around."

Shannon frowned. Darla knew she'd come around because she always did. That was the way it worked with them—Darla bugged her until she caved. It was kind of like when a team was on the field too long: no matter how good your game, if you've been playing defense for the majority of a quarter, somebody's eventually going to sneak right into the end zone.

She hung up the phone and drove, slow but steady. The afternoon traffic stretched far ahead with no end in sight, a dull metallic march toward the horizon.

Week 4: Bye

Megan

Friday afternoon at a quarter till twelve, Megan walked through the kitchen in a daze, hoping that nobody would be there to bitch about her being late, trying to ignore Marlon's attempts at flirting as she buttoned up her white shirt, leaving the top two open to reveal a tie-dye Steelers tank top. Marlon inched closer, the scent of waffles baked deep into his skin. "Rough night, huh?"

"Huh?"

He nodded. "Your eyes. They're a little bloodshot. What's on tap for the weekend?"

Even though they worked with plenty of single people, as the self-proclaimed queen of party, most of her co-workers spent Fridays and Mondays following her around like a pack of annoying six-year olds, trying to get the scoop on what to do next. Most times she was happy to offer up some ideas for where to go and maybe the occasional wild story about a party gone awry, but sometimes it was just plain irritating. Would it kill any of them to pick up the City Paper and find their own weekend activities for a change?

"No plans. I think I'm getting a cold or something. I might pick up a shift tomorrow night if I feel like it."

Marlon smiled. "Oh, sure, a cold. Whatever you say, baby."

Wrinkling her nose, she marched away with some righteous indignation. Last night, she didn't sleep because she was coughing, and now her throat burned. Sniffling, she stepped into the main dining room. The dim lights cast a warm glow on the dark red room. Ellie, the hostess, told her that she'd already sat people in her section: "A two-top in the corner. One of them's cute."

Megan groaned, rolling up her sleeves. She didn't care if one of them was a male model, she wanted to go home. Everything hurt. And it hurt even more when she saw Kevin sitting in the corner booth with an older gentleman wearing a navy suit.

At Oktoberfest last week, Kevin had showed up in the early part of the night along with a tiny brunette with pursed lips who wore a navy blazer and a pair of khaki pants that looked more like she was ready for nine holes at the Mt. Lebanon Golf Course than an evening at a brewery. Megan hated those kind of girls and felt relieved when they left after one beer.

"Megan," said Kevin, smiling.

"Hey." She really didn't feel like making small talk. He introduced her to the other gentleman, Don.

"Did Ellie tell you about the specials?"

Kevin nodded. "Yes, but she didn't tell us we'd be working with the best waitress in the house."

Megan wanted to punch him in the face.

He continued, "Megan here lives with my best friend's girlfriend. We're in good hands today."

We're in good hands? It was obvious that Kevin was some kind of salesman or he was with some kind of a salesman, but even this was over the top for all the little yuppie boys. She hated the yuppie boys. Those fresh-faced college graduates with their apartments in Shadyside or the South Side who worked in the banks and financial companies Downtown and thought they ruled the world. But Megan had been around long enough to know that most of those boys would turn into yuppie men, married to nagging wives and moving to upscale neighborhoods like Mt. Lebanon or Upper St. Clair so that they could brag about how good their school district was while they spent every waking moment in the office or traveling for work to avoid their families.

Megan cleared her throat. "What do you mean 'girlfriend'?"

"Emily. She's Mike's girlfriend."

"No. They're just dating. There's a big difference."

"No, there's not really a difference."

"Yes, there is." Kevin pulled at his tie, looking truly uncomfortable. He rolled his eyes toward the other gentleman as if begging for help, but Megan didn't really care. Emily and Mike were not boyfriend and girlfriend yet.

Don laughed. "You kids these days. There were never so many vagaries when I was young. It must be hard to date today."

What did he know? He looked like the kind of guy who acted chivalrous as he fed you drinks all night, then tried to stick his thumb in your asshole once you passed out.

She started to say something else, but a quick glance at Kevin stopped her. He looked truly embarrassed. Maybe this was his boss or something. Or even worse the bitchy brunette's dad. Of course, that could be kind of funny.

"So I guess that brunette you brought to Oktoberfest is your girlfriend?"

"Kevin, you didn't tell me about any brunette!" Don gave Megan a playful wink, shaking his head as he turned toward Kevin.

"She's not my girlfriend. But why are you so interested, Megan? Trying to fix me up with a friend or are you asking for yourself?"

Don let out a loud, obsequious laugh. "Kevin! You're a real live-wire. If you're this quick with our waitress, I'd love to see what you can do in the courtroom."

The two started laughing and Megan felt herself shrinking. Lawyers. He was trying to impress somebody in his firm. What a cliché. And what a little bitch for asking if she was interested. Lawyers and their egos. Disgusting.

"What would you like to drink?" she said, breaking up their chatter long enough to take their orders.

As she stomped into the kitchen, blinded with fury, she nearly ran into Marlon.

"Whoa, Megan! You look like somebody stole your flask. What's going on?"

"Nothing. I'm waiting on a couple of douchebags."

"Let me know if you want me to spit in their food."

"Normally I would say no, but this guy—God, I really don't like him."

Marlon smiled, his brown eyes flashing. "I've never seen you this angry, but damn it's sexy. I'm gonna run out there and tell this guy to come in more often."

"Shut the hell up," said Megan. She walked out of the kitchen, looking for her next table and forcing a smile.

Patty

There was nothing more dreadful than a fall Sunday without a Steelers game, especially so early in the season. Football was a game of momentum. After last week's loss, she was anxious to see them prove themselves again, but they wouldn't get another chance until next Monday night against the San Diego Chargers. That meant two Sundays in a row without a game. At three in the afternoon, she turned off the TV and looked at the Terrible Towel hanging from her mantle.

Last night, Kristen went to her fall formal dance. She wore a one-shoulder, brown knee-length dress that showed way too much skin for Patty's taste but looked positively Puritanical next to the short, tight, strapless dresses all of her friends were wearing. What were these other parents thinking? That was an easy one. Most of them weren't thinking. Most of the other parents she knew were more interested in partying than parenting. A couple of beers or a glass of wine was fine every once in a while, but forty-somethings who lived for ladies' night seemed sort of sad and desperate. Not that she was any less sad or desperate, of course, but at least she wasn't prowling the South Side in clothes twenty years too young for her After the dance, Patty picked up Kristen and Jeff at Eat'n Park, dropped Jeff off at his house and brought home a sullen Kristen, still pouting because she wasn't allowed to stay over at Vanessa's.

This morning, Patty took it easy on Kristen and let her sleep through Mass. When she got home, both kids were gone. Two separate notes were posted to the fridge, one saying that Robbie was at Angela's house, the other that Kristen was shopping with Desiree. That had been about four hours ago and just as she wondered how much longer they could shop, she heard Desiree's unmistakable laugh on the porch.

Throwing off her afghan, she sat up straight, grabbing her most recent copy of *O* magazine and flipping toward Oprah's favorite things as if she actually cared or could even afford any of the overpriced merchandise.

"Hi, Patty. Kristen wanted me to come in while she tried on some of her new clothes," said Desiree. Both her and Kristen carried large bags from Kaufmann's and American Eagle Outfitters. And what was that pink one that Kristen had half-hidden under her purse? It looked like Victoria's Secret, and if it was anything other than a modest bra or pair of underwear, Patty and Desiree were going to have a nice, long chat.

"What did you do—buy the entire mall?"

Kristen grinned ear to ear. "I wish." She pulled a faded denim mini-skirt out of an American Eagle bag. It looked exactly like every other skirt she had. "Look, Mom, isn't this so cute?"

"Don't you already have one just like that?"

"Don't be silly, Mom. That one is dark denim. This is stonewash."

Desiree nodded, her eyes sparkling as if she'd been lecturing Kristen on denim washes the whole way home and admired her pupil for learning.

Kristen skipped up the stairs, dragging the bags. "I'm gonna try this on and show you, Mom. Wait, Des, I want you to see it too."

Overhead, Patty heard her clunky shoes stomping into her room and slamming the door shut. Patty imagined her dropping the bags on her cluttered floor and throwing clothes on top of clothes. Next week, Kristen was going to wake up for Mass and clean her room.

Turning to Desiree, Patty tried to act grateful, even though she wanted to tell Desiree to go take her stonewash mini-skirts and take them right back to the store. Kristen had enough clothes. Patty knew that she should be happy that Desiree took such an interest in the kids, but she wished that Desiree had a less materialistic hobby. But any time she tried to bring that up with Tom or Desiree, they became so defensive. And if there was anything Patty hated, it was starting a fight. "Thanks, Desiree. You really didn't have to do that."

Desiree waved her hand as if all those purchases were merely nothing, which, to her and Tom, they probably were. "Don't worry about it. It's just some belated school shopping."

Standing in the entryway, a brown leather Coach tote on her shoulder, Desiree looked like she wasn't sure if she should sit down or run out the door.

Patty nodded toward the couch. "Would you like to sit down?" Desiree shook her head, looking out the screen door like she had somewhere to be. With her long, straight blonde hair and flawless skin, she looked much younger than thirty-eight. Today, she wore a pair of black pants and a silky burgundy blouse. Her waist looked tiny enough for Patty to wrap her hands around. As strange as it was, Patty didn't entirely despise her. Desiree might have looked elegant and classy, but Patty knew her well enough to know that she was just a brash Western Pennsylvania girl at heart, equally comfortable shopping at Saks Fifth Avenue or shooting pool in a beer and whiskey joint. Patty was comfortable with neither.

"Would you like a drink of water?"

"Sure."

"Come in to the kitchen," said Patty, motioning for Desiree to follow her.

As Patty poured her a glass of water, Desiree settled at the counter. "Can I ask you something, Desiree?"

Desiree looked alarmed. "What?"

"Is Tom going to take Robbie to a game this year?"

"Oh." Desiree put her hand on her heart. "You scared me there for a minute. You looked so serious I thought maybe you were going to tell me you had cancer or something. Sure, tell Robbie to tell us what game he wants to go to and we'll set it up."

Patty watched Desiree drinking her water. As she moved her arms, the muscles rose in her bicep. Once upon a time, it had been her and not Desiree who had shared those season tickets. Once or twice since the divorce, he'd offered her the tickets to take one of the kids, but she always refused. There was something about going to the games now that felt foreboding. Like that was something from another life where she no longer belonged.

"I'll tell him. But Des, I really think Tom should take more of an interest in him."

"What's that supposed to mean?"

"He's having a hard time in school. Kristen told me that the other kids pick on him. All he does is hang out with me and Kristen or Angela. I think he needs a stronger male presence in his life. I wanted to tell him this myself, but I can never get ahold of him."

"He's not intentionally avoiding you. Tom is just never home anymore. I barely see him except on Sundays. That's why we haven't asked the kids to a game yet because that is really the only day we see each other. He's away this week too." Desiree shifted on her chair, looking around the room. Her gaze stopped on the fridge. "What's with all the cereal?"

Patty shrugged. What kind of a question was that? "We all like something different."

She ate Raisin Bran, Robbie ate Count Chocula and Kristen only liked Apple Cinnamon Cheerios. The kids were very particular about food.

Desiree nodded, but her eyes betrayed her with a hint of sadness. "When I was growing up, my mom always said, if you don't like it, that's tough, this is what you're getting." Patty knew that Desiree had grown up poor, mostly because she'd once told Patty that the only constants in her childhood were food stamps and government cheese. Desiree laughed now, coarse and determined, but it was obvious something was bothering her.

"I do what I can," said Patty. "It's rough being a kid, you know."

"That's nice."

"I just wish Tom would do the same."

"Patty, he does the best he can."

"I know he has another life with you and his job, but these kids need a father, Des."

"These kids HAVE a father. And I do my best to try to see them every week too. It seems like everybody forgets about that. I'm a damn good stepmom." Her voice rose as she finished her speech and Patty felt immediately uncomfortable. This was why talking to Desiree and Tom about anything was so difficult. Both of them were so sensitive and defensive, she couldn't imagine how they could sustain a relationship.

"I wasn't talking about you, Desiree. You are a good stepmom. I just wondered if you could try to say something to Tom about Robbie."

Desiree nodded. "I'll talk to him if you want me to. I'll try. Honestly Patty, it's not like he's intentionally ignoring Robbie, he's just never here anymore."

The chord of melancholy in Desiree's voice made it sound like this wasn't just a problem for Robbie and Kristen.

"Do you need to talk?"

Desiree looked at her with a mix of surprise and confusion. "Talk? About what?"

"I don't know. It just seems like maybe you need to talk about something."

Desiree answered definitively, that brief glimmer of sadness disappearing as fast as it had appeared. "No. Nothing to talk about here. I'm fine."

From the living room, Patty heard Kristen crashing down the stairs.

Desiree stood up, turning away from Patty and gushing about how cute Kristen looked in her new outfit. The skirt was too short and the shirt looked wrinkled, but Patty smiled and nodded that it was nice. She would tell Kristen the truth later. For now, she was grateful for the interruption. Seeing Desiree vulnerable felt wrong, the same sickening feeling she had experienced last night watching Jeff and Kristen kiss goodbye, like it wasn't meant for her to see.

Angela

On Tuesday morning, Angela pulled her gym bag out of her locker and contemplated her next move. There was nothing worse than volleyball. She looked around, trying to delay the inevitable and wondering why Brad wasn't at his locker, surrounded by his usual posse of blonde girls in mini-skirts and platform shoes and beefy dudes with tattoos and Steelers pins on their bookbags.

Steelers pins. This past Sunday, the Steelers didn't play so it had been a nice change of pace not spending her entire afternoon at work forced to listen to WDVE's game coverage on a one-speaker AM/FM stereo from 1985.

Even better, after her shift was over, Robbie came to her house and ate dinner with the family and, unlike most Sundays in fall, it didn't end in some dramatic football-related conflict. Robbie complimented her mom on her stuffed peppers and Dom even offered to help them build a car for their upcoming physics project.

Thinking about it now, she kicked her locker shut, wishing for a fire drill or some other means of escape.

"Bad Luck!" Brad's baritone voice sounded urgent. Angela spun around, concerned.

"Is something wrong?"

He shrugged. "Not with me, but your friend Robbie might be in trouble."

"What?"

Brad lowered his voice. "You didn't hear this from me, but Robbie was smartin' off to Decker and T-Dog in homeroom this morning, and they plan to make him pay for it in gym class today."

Angela groaned. Decker and T-Dog were two clueless jocks with big mouths and even bigger biceps. "What are they going to do?"

Brad looked up and down the hallway. "Not sure but if I were you, I'd find Robbie and get the H out of here. Like I told you last week, go out the side door and if you run into one of the security guards, mention my name. They think we're friends and they'll let you do anything."

"We need to leave? It's really that bad?"

Brad nodded, serious. "I swear."

"I need to find him." Angela pulled her bag close to her body.

"Do it now," he said, flicking The Clash pin on her bookbag. "Time to Rock the Casbah, if ya know what I mean."

Angela pursed her lips. "Did you really just say that?"

Brad punched her shoulder. "Quit pickin' and go, dude. And don't tell anybody."

She looked at him. He pushed about 6'5 and 250 and wore a big gray shirt and mesh shorts. One of his hands could wrap easily around her neck.

"Hey," she said, hovering. "Thanks."

He blew a raspberry, shaking his head. "No prob. But seriously, Bad Luck, get the hell out."

She ran down the hallway, breathless until she found Robbie trudging toward the locker room. She grabbed him by the neck. "Come on, dude, I'm not playing volleyball today."

He removed his earphones. "What do you mean?"

"It's a beautiful day in the neighborhood and we're gonna go and enjoy it."

She shook her car keys.

Robbie's eyes widened. "Seriously?"

She intertwined their arms. "Seriously," she said, dragging him along.

Jen

On Wednesday night, Jen was finishing up Desiree Salvatore's hair. Desiree was Audrey's daughter and a regular customer ever since she got her beauty license two years ago. Growing up, she had always admired Desiree, mostly because she was at once rude and outspoken but when it came right down to it, she was one of the sweetest people around. It was still unbelievable to think that Desiree would trust her with her hair considering that she could easily afford the priciest salons in Shadyside or Downtown. It surely helped that Jen worked around her insanely busy schedule, even making the occasional house call or keeping the salon open late, like tonight.

Jen pulled up strands on either side of Desiree's hair to make sure that they were even. One was a little longer than the other. She clipped that side and let it fall slack.

"So," said Desiree. "How long are you going to take off of work to have the kid? What if I need my roots done?"

Jen grinned, combing Desiree's hair. "I don't know how long I'll take off, but if you want, I could always do your hair anyways. At your place or my parents'."

"What about your place? Your little lovers' nest."

Little lovers' nest. That was the last description she'd used to describe Dave's four-room apartment. They only moved half of her stuff in over the weekend and space was already tight. Especially the bedroom—Dave's clothes were now stuffed into two dresser drawers and the closet crammed full of hers. And that was just the summer stuff. She still had to bring over her winter wardrobe, and then there would be all the maternity clothes. "It's not so much a nest as a pigsty. It's small."

"You mean like your ring?"

Jen laughed. Desiree wore a two-carat marquis-cut diamond. Earlier in her appointment, they compared their rings side by side and Jen readily admitted that hers looked like a speck.

"Yes. Like that. Except I think it might be smaller."

They both laughed.

"But don't say anything, ya know, about what I said about the ring. Dave can't really afford anything right now."

Desiree waved her hand. "Jen, I would never say anything. And seriously, the size of the ring is not what counts. It's the size of his —"

Jen blushed. "That's just fine."

"Then you're fine." They both laughed.

"What about the wedding?"

Jen groaned.

A week had passed since she let her mom take over the wedding plans and already she regretted the decision. Once she'd found out about the pregnancy, she'd abandoned her dreams of a horse-drawn carriage and a butterfly release in the garden at Phipps Conservatory. But her extended family's idea of a wedding usually involved a fried chicken-haluski-and-pierogie buffet, a firehall or VFW, an open bar that ran out of whiskey by nine, and a drunken rendition or two of the chicken dance and the Steelers polka. Those weddings were always fun, but she had always envisioned something different for her own wedding. And if all of Dave's family came out from their farms and trailer parks, the open bar would run dry before dinner and there was a ninety-five percent chance of fisticuffs.

Jen rose on her tiptoes to cut the front of Desiree's hair. Once her manager had left, she had slipped off her chunky black platform heels in favor of bare feet. Standing all day made her calves ache and her feet swell. She looked in the mirror, regretting the noticeably distressed look on her face in between the taped pictures of Troy Polamalu, her brother Bobby in his army fatigues, and a shot of her and Dave at last year's opening day tailgate.

"That bad?"

"Not bad. Just typical. Her and my aunts are working on it and it's going to be just like most of my cousin's weddings—the Polish Club, the buffet, you know the drill."

Desiree held up her hand. "Say no more. What do you want?"

Jen shifted, uncomfortable. With all the people in her family buzzing about the wedding, it was hard to believe that this was the first time somebody had actually asked her what she wanted. "I was hoping for something a little more elegant, maybe at a hotel, you know, or at least with a plated meal. But I can't really say too much right now. Beggars can't be choosers."

"Phooey on that. It's your wedding. Do you know if your mom's signed anything yet?"

"I don't think so."

"Look, I've got personal relationships with just about every hotel and catering place in town. Give me a week or so and I'll check around and see if I can get a deal for you."

"We were hoping for something in November before I really start showing. That's so close. Everything is probably full."

"Not necessarily. What about a Sunday?"

"A Sunday? Why?"

"During the football season, most hotels have banquet space on Sundays. Nobody wants to get married on game day. If you were willing to do it, we could probably make it work. Probably something pretty special, too." Desiree pointed at her bangs. "Can you trim that side a little more?"

Jen clipped it. "I don't want to get married during a game either. I mean, half my family probably wouldn't show. Dave might not even be willing to go."

"I'll look at the schedule. If it's a one o'clock game, we could plan something for the evening. Do you want me to look?"

Jen nodded. Desiree had grown up just down Freeport Road in Sharpsburg, the very same ash-covered town where she now called home. But now Desiree drove a black BMW, lived in a gated community near Sewickley, carried a Louis Vuitton tote bag, and wore tailored pantsuits. If there were anybody whose tastes Jen trusted, it was hers.

Shannon

On Friday night, Morgan's was unusually slow. Shannon didn't mind, but Audrey got anxious when the place wasn't filled by eight.

Audrey looked between the clock and door. "It's all the damn road construction keeping people home. Nobody wants to be out here driving on these roads when they could just drink at home."

Shannon tilted her head. "It has the opposite effect on me. I spend all week driving those stupid roads, so by the time Friday rolls around, I need to get drunk to survive."

Audrey laughed. "You? Drunk? I can't imagine. Maybe that's what we should do if it's still like this at ten, just go to town."

Shannon smiled, pulling at the bottom edge of her white tank. "If it's still like this at ten, I'm going home and going to bed."

Audrey moaned. "Oh please. We could call it a night here by midnight and go on over to the VFW until three or four. Now, that would be a night to remember. Or better yet, not to remember."

"That sounds like a nightmare."

"You are the most boring young person I know."

"I'm not that young, Audrey. I'll be thirty-four in a few months. I'm tired."

"34? Gimme a break. When I was thirty-four, I was still out partying every night."

Shannon laughed. "Right, because when you were my age, you were on your third marriage and had teenage children."

"So? I never let that keep me from a damn party." Audrey kept her fried blonde hair cut short. A tarnished gold necklace hung around her neck and six silver studs decorated each ear. Leaning against the counter in a tight black shirt, she looked young enough to be Shannon's older sister, but was actually old enough to be her mom.

The brown door opened, a flash of streetlights filling the dark, smoky room. Darla closed the door and waved. She wore a pair of purple scrubs with a Steelers lanyard around her neck. "Hey, ladies!"

"What are you doing here?"

"Jack's working on the house tonight. Thought I'd get him a six pack."

Audrey walked toward the cooler. "What'll it be?"

Darla tilted her head, studying the case. "Miller Lite." She dug through her tote, pulling out cash. "Kinda slow in here, isn't it?"

"It's only nine. It'll pick up."

"If you leave early, you can always come over and help out."

"Right," Shannon said. "Because that's how I want to spend my night, painting with my sister and her boyfriend."

Laughing, Audrey handed Darla her change then set her hands on her hips, shaking her head. "I don't see how that would be any worse than going home early on a Friday night and being in bed alone by eleven."

Darla nodded, a mischievous gleam in her eyes. "Right. Oh, Shannon, forgive me for suggesting human contact."

"Guys, lay off for a second, can ya? I can't help it I'm tired and want to go to bed early on Fridays."

Darla turned to Audrey, conspiring. "Did she tell you I have a guy for her?"

Audrey raised an eyebrow. "No, she didn't. Tell me everything."

Shannon groaned. "There's nothing to tell. Darla wants me to meet some friend of Jack's, so she's forcing me to watch the game with them on Monday night."

"Can you believe how disgusted she sounds? You'd think I'm asking her over for a colonoscopy, not a football game."

"Don't take it personally, Darla. This girl's a tough cookie to crack. But maybe this guy will melt her heart."

"Hey, guys," Shannon said, waving at them. "I'm still here, remember?"

They laughed, putting their heads together and smiling, their conversation moving from Shannon's dating life to the remodeling work at Darla's house. Even Audrey was easily taken in by Darla's wide smile and nonstop chatter. Why did everybody act like she was an ice princess just because she rarely dated? The number of boyfriends you had said nothing about your capacity to love. What Shannon couldn't understand was somebody like Darla who moved so easily between men.

The door opened again. Larry marched into the bar.

"Hey, Audrey. Shannon," he said, taking his seat at the far end of the bar. He had heavy shoulders and a protruding belly covered by a Penguins shirt. His bald head was covered with a Penn State ball cap. He took a pack of cigarettes and smacked it on the counter. Shannon poured him a Coors Light draft.

"What's goin' on?" he said, setting his wallet down by the ashtray.

She shrugged, looking around the room. Darla and Audrey chatted at the end of the bar. The jukebox sat silent. The light over the men's room flickered, its bulb ready to die.

"What am I doing? Waiting for the night to start," she said, loud enough for Darla and Audrey to hear.

Larry nodded. He scratched at the scruffy hair on his neck and looked up at the television. She waited for somebody, any one of them, to make a reply. But nobody answered, like she hadn't even spoken at all.

Desiree

At Ross Park Mall on Saturday afternoon, Desiree stood in front of the Pro-Image Sports store. Inside the shiny window just beside a Pirates display, a rack of Steelers-themed baby clothes caught her eye. Usually she didn't pay any mind to baby clothes, but ever since she'd found out that Jen was pregnant, she couldn't help but notice the infants' section. It was hard to believe that little Jen was old enough to be grown and starting a family of her own. It felt like only a few years ago that she'd been a toddler and Desiree used to babysit her. In many ways, Jen's family was like a second family. None of her little brothers had kids yet, at least as far as they knew, and she hoped that maybe Jen's baby would be the niece or nephew she always wanted.

Last week she had actually considered asking Patty about what kind of baby gift to buy, but as usual, Patty launched into a full-scale tirade on Tom's lack of fathering skills, a conversation that left her upset and a little disgusted at both Tom and Patty. Sometimes she felt like Tom and Patty were so busy worrying about each others' parenting problems that she ended up being the better parent. While Patty rambled on about how Robbie needed a father, Desiree couldn't help but think about the conversation she'd had earlier that day with Kristen about birth control and oral sex. At least the kids had one adult in their life who gave it to them straight: "If you decide to have sex, I'll get you birth control. Never do it without a condom. And for god's sake, don't go down on him unless he does the same for you."

Desiree knew that both Patty and Tom would be furious if they found out she had said that to Kristen, but she couldn't help it. The truth was the truth. And besides, Kristen's flustered reaction to her honesty made her pretty damn sure that Jeff hadn't even hit the ball hard enough to get them to first base.

A group of teenagers carrying coffee cups and Dippin' Dots distracted her as they walked between her and the store. One of them, an ugly girl with a sunken face and thin hair, gave her a dirty look as they passed. The only thing she hated worse than little kids were ugly teenagers. She walked into the store, her stilettos tapping loud against the tiled floor.

Over the loud speakers, Bon Jovi blasted. Desiree rubbed the onesie between her fingers. It was softer than she had expected, almost velvety. Up close, the details were exquisite. Earlier she had considered buying a silver rattle from Tiffany & Co., but this little outfit was too cute. Pink was her favorite color. She threw it over her forearm, then picked out a pair of black and gold pajamas just in case they had a boy. She had a feeling that Jen and Dave would appreciate this gift more than the silver rattle. The Tiffany's catalog could wait until the next time one of the girls in her office got knocked up.

At the register, a boy with curly hair and acne rang up her order.

"Is that for your kid?" he said, stuffing them into a black bag.

Desiree turned sideways, running her hand over the flat front of her khaki pants. "Do I LOOK like I have a kid?"

"I guess not, no."

Desiree grabbed the bag before he handed her the receipt. "If I were you, I'd make it a policy not to insult your customers."

He shrugged. "It wasn't an insult."

Huffy, Desiree walked out of the store and into the main mall, balancing her purchases as she zig-zagged through bored teenagers and harried young mothers with babies on their hips and shopping bags in their strollers.

She kept thinking about that clerk: "It wasn't an insult." Stranger than anything, she completely agreed.

Week 5: Steelers vs. San Diego Chargers
(W 24-22)

Megan

Monday night games threw off the rhythm of the week. Sunday games were predictable. Familiar. What happens on Sunday sets the tone for the week to come. If the Steelers lost, she knew to expect a foul week. If they won, even if her week still sucked, at least she'd be in a better mood to deal with it. Monday games meant that she spent the first day of the week in eager anticipation, her stomach jumpy and her mind racing as she waited for the game.

She had been so out of sorts and nervous earlier that day, she had agreed to watch it at Del's Restaurant and Bar with Emily, Mike, and some of Mike's friends. They sat wrapped around the corner of the bar, Megan on one edge, Mike & Emily on the other, a plate of fried appetizers and a bucket of Miller Lite bottles hovering between them. Megan watched the overhead TV with one eye then scanned the bar. Except for a guy with a bad comb-over but nice smile at the far end, there were no prospects in the crowd.

The digital Steelers clock read 9:30. Megan wiped her mouth and cracked open another bottle. It was her fourth. Or fifth. Or maybe more. She'd lost count after the first bucket.

As the game entered the second quarter, Mike's friend called. Mike clicked off his phone.

"Sorry, Megan. He's not going to make it tonight."

"Why are you sorry? I'm fine, I've got beer and football and my best friend." She squeezed Emily's arm, smiling. Emily wore a navy blue sweater and a delicate gold necklace with a moonstone pendant. She offered a weak smile and leaned in closer to Mike. He wrapped his arm around her. At his touch, Emily's pale skin flushed. Megan knew what that meant—sex. Good sex, too. The female body only responded like that if it was looking forward to something.

Mike excused himself to the bathroom and Emily looked at Megan, wistful and glassy-eyed.

"He's great, isn't he?"

"I'll take your word for it." Megan pinched Emily's wrist. "He's doing it to ya, isn't he?"

Emily blushed, closing her eyes. "Megan!"

"He is! He is! Good for you." Megan hit Emily's shoulder, waving for another beer and thinking about that encounter with Kevin last week. Emily still wasn't referring to Mike as her boyfriend. "Are you, like, going steady?"

"Don't make fun. But I guess. I mean, I don't just do it unless I'm dating. I'm not a slut." Emily broke off, her face falling. "I didn't mean it like that."

Honestly, she didn't even think that Emily was implying she was a slut until that last part. *I didn't mean it like that.* Translation: That's exactly what I meant.

"Then how did you mean it?"

"Megan, I—"

"Stop, Em. No worries." She wasn't about to sit here all night long, playing the third wheel to somebody who had just called her a slut. Looking at the commercial, she fumbled through her purse for cash. She only had a couple of ones, not nearly enough to cover her share. If she crumpled them up, it would look like enough. She shoved them toward Emily.

"I'm gonna head out now."

"Megan, don't go. I'm sorry, please—"

"Sorry about what? I'm fine. I'm tired. I have to get up for work early. I'll finish this one at home."

"What's going on?" Mike said.

Megan pushed her hair out of her eyes. "I'm tired. Going home." Before Mike could stop her, she walked out of the bar and onto Liberty Avenue. The sidewalks and street were mostly empty. She walked along, past an empty Chinese restaurant, record store, and art gallery. Across the street, loud music blared from the broken windows at Howlers bar. At Tessaro's and Lot 17, the standing crowds were visible through the dark windows, expectant eyes looking upward at the TV as if waiting to be told that they were going to make it through Judgment Day. She thought of going to Lot 17. Todd sent her texts occasionally telling her she was welcome any time, but a friend of a friend said his wife wasn't very nice, and a run-in with her didn't seem very fun.

It was early October, but the night air was chill, hinting at the impending winter. She put her hands into her pockets and pulled her hoodie tight against her body, wishing she wasn't wearing a skirt. She kept thinking about a commercial from earlier that night, some body spray ad featuring a woman wildly pressing her body into a man's to smell his deodorant. Thinking about it, their faces turned into those of Emily and Mike. That wasn't something she wanted to picture. Hands shaking, she pulled out her cell and dialed. She had to do something, anything, to get that sight out of her head.

Marlon answered on the first ring. The connection sounded distant, like cordless phones from the eighties. "My lady calls?"

"Where you at? I was watching the game at Del's but there were too many people in there."

"I'm at home." Marlon lived about five minutes away in Lawrenceville.

"Can I come over?"

He laughed, a rich baritone. "You can, but you know what's gonna happen if you do."

She laughed. "We'll see about that. I just want to watch the game."

"Oh sure. The game. Then come on over. I'll get the sex swing ready."

Megan smiled to herself. Sometimes it was too easy. "Don't be so sure of yourself. Got any booze?"

"Of course, but you won't need too much of that once I get to ya."

"Okay, behave for a minute. I'm getting close to my car. I'll be there in a few."

She pulled out her keys, fumbling with the lock on her Volkswagen Gulf. Inside, the floor was lined with empty Diet Pepsi bottles, CDs, clothes, and high heels. She turned on the radio to follow the game and headed toward Marlon's. Her hands felt heavy, and she felt uncertain driving. Good thing he lived close. Iconic local announcer Myron Cope had retired earlier this year and she missed his colorful broadcasts. If he were on the radio now, she imagined that nasally voice of his cutting through the fog in her head like the weather beacon on the Gulf Tower slicing through a dark black sky. Instead, she rubbed her temples, thinking of her mom and dad at their sprawling ranch house in the middle of a cookie-cutter suburban development in Bethel Park.

She turned up the radio. The Steelers were winning. She thought about Marlon, about what she was about to do. Her skin felt hot and her head felt light, like she was about to be sick.

Shannon

In the half-painted kitchen, Shannon folded her arms over her chest and glared at Darla.

"Balding AND fat? Really?"

"He's not fat, Shannon. He's husky." Darla perched on her tiptoes to grab a new bottle of ketchup for the tray of fries still steaming on the oven. Five inches taller, Shannon leaned forward, pulling it down easily. She tucked it under her arm.

"I'm not giving you this until you apologize."

"Apologize for what?"

"For setting me up on false pretenses."

"Shannon, looks aren't everything!"

"That only works if the guy has half a brain. But I'm sorry, Darla, this guy is weird. I don't even get why he's friends with Jack."

"They went to high school together."

"I don't care if they went to charm school together, this guy is a grade A creep. He's been staring at my chest all evening."

Darla gazed at Shannon's chest, laughing. "They're double D, Shannon. Sometimes, people stare."

"No, sometimes creeps stare, not people. I don't even want to go back out there."

Darla grabbed the bottle. "You are going back out there, and you're going to be nice. Can't you just be nice? And can you carry the fries?"

Shannon didn't want to be nice. To creepy guy Alan or to Darla. As usual, the only person she could tolerate was Jack. Carrying the plate of fries, she followed Darla through the dining room. The table was covered with tarp and the walls were outlined with painter's tape.

In the bright living room, Shannon set the fries on a coffee table and sat at the edge of the couch, as far away as she could from Alan. For the fifteen-hundredth time that night, he was totally checking out her chest. She grabbed a pillow and hugged it tight against her torso.

"So," said Alan, thrusting his arm across the empty space between them. His voice was coarse and irritating like a piece of glass in her eye. "Tell me again, what it is that you do for work?"

Shannon gritted her teeth. It was the third time he'd asked that question. "I work for the Water Authority. I'm a field tester."

"What's that?"

She kept her eyes glued to the game. "I go around the city collecting tap water samples, then bring them into the lab for testing."

"That's a weird job. So, what, are you in your car most of the time?"

A weird job? Shannon bristled. This asshole owned a couple of Subway restaurants and he was an expert on jobs? "It's not really weird. And I happen to like it. It's actually pretty interesting. I always liked chemistry—"

"I thought Darla said you were a bartender." He looked sideways at Darla. "Dar, didn't you say your sis here was a bartender? You lyin' to me?"

Darla shook her head, her blonde bangs covering her eyes. She sat on the floor in front of Jack's chair, leaning on his legs. The way she sat looked uncomfortable, and something about her face seemed uncertain.

"She has two jobs."

"Scientist by day and bartender by night. Sounds like the beginning of a porno." Alan chortled—a loud, grating laugh. Shannon found it highly offensive. She swallowed, ready to tell him off: *How dare you distract me from the game AND imply that I'm some low-level porn floozy? Have you looked in the mirror lately, Alan? Has anybody ever told you that you're gross and obnoxious?*

Jack cleared his throat, rising from his chair. "Hey, Alan, why don't you come in the kitchen and help me get some more beer?"

As he stood up, Shannon noticed that he stepped over Darla without looking at her. This evening, he was unusually quiet. At several points, he fell asleep. Shannon assumed he was tired, but now he sounded aggravated. Alan and Jack went into the dining room. She leaned toward Darla.

"Is everything okay?"

Darla moved to the couch. "He's in a mood. We had a fight earlier."

"What about?"

"About this. He didn't want to set you up with Alan. Said it was a bad idea." Darla sighed. "I guess it was."

They fought about her? Jack wanted to save her from Alan's cheesy advances? That was pretty flattering.

"I'm sorry. I was just trying to help you out," Darla continued. "I mean, you need to meet somebody. You can't go on being single forever."

Shannon leaned back, deflated. On the television, a San Diego Charger plowed right into Ben Roethlisberger.

"Oh my god," she screamed, covering her mouth.

"What? What?" Alan and Jack ran into the living room for the replay.

As they showed the hit again, Jack slapped his hand against the recliner. Shannon looked at him. They eyed each other uneasily. "Shit," said Jack. "He's hurt."

"Calm down, Jack," said Darla. "It's just a game." She talked to Jack like she was a teacher and he was an errant student.

He slouched, his arms crossed. He looked truly irritated, ready to explode.

Shannon looked him straight in the eyes, ignoring Darla and Alan, talking directly to Jack: "I know exactly how you feel."

Patty

As soon as the game ended, Patty headed up the stairs as fast as she could, not even bothering to stop and straighten the crooked family portrait that Robbie and Kristen always hit on their way out the door. The photo was an early nineties nightmare—her with permed and teased hair, Tom beaming in a navy suit and thick plastic glasses, Kristen cheesing so hard that her eyes looked like slits, and Robbie looking at something out of the frame, irritated but irresistible in an argyle sweater and dress pants. She'd seen enough episodes of *Oprah* and *Dr. Phil* to know that she should take down the picture, that letting go of the past was the only way to move forward. But she hated the idea of taking down that photo. Perhaps they weren't a family now, but once upon a time they were. Their family, hers and Tom's, had existed. Maybe it didn't now, but once it did—as real as the final score in tonight's game and the black scuffmarks on the steps.

Patty shut her bedroom door, her heart racing from her flight upstairs. She sat down on the bed with a deep exhale. God. She really needed to start exercising more. She watched enough video from Coach Cowher's training camp to know that none of her boys in black and gold got winded walking up a set of stairs, and they probably wouldn't expect their admirer Ginger Mae to wear out so easily either. A woman like that would have to be quite physically fit to wear those tiny panties.

Patty crouched down on her knees, pulling out her box with a pause. Her heart still raced. She hoped that it had more to do with Robbie and Ben Roethlisberger's injury than it did that walk upstairs.

While she'd always enjoyed Monday night games when she went to them, now they complicated her panty-sending schedule. She rushed around, packing things up late, and then had to get up extra early to stop by the post office on her way to work. Once she made the mistake of taking a package to work to mail during her lunch hour. That morning, she watched her tote with an eagle eye, nervous that a hapless co-worker would stumble onto her secret.

She ran her hand through the pile and picked out a rainbow-striped cotton bikini for Ben Roethlisberger. They were bright and cheerful. After this game, she felt like Ben needed something with a little color. She folded them into a neat square. Usually, she felt sexy folding underwear. For about twenty minutes each week, she let herself relax and become Ginger Mae. Ginger Mae who didn't have kids. Ginger Mae with her string of admirers. Ginger Mae with perky breasts and pouty red lips. Tonight, though, even Ginger Mae couldn't stop her mind from racing. Ginger Mae didn't have to worry about her teenage son and the way he was being treated at school. She didn't have to wonder if his silence during tonight's game was because he hated spending time with her or because he secretly hated football and just wanted to be upstairs watching the *Rocky Horror Picture Show* and listening to depressing music. Ginger Mae didn't have to worry that Kristen might at that moment not be at her friend Vanessa's house at all but climbing into the backseat of a car with her boyfriend.

Patty sighed, pushing the panties into the envelope and picking up a heart-shaped card: *Dear Ben, Here's hoping for a fast and safe recovery. Love Always, Ginger Mae.*

Life as Ginger Mae was uncomplicated, almost blissful. All she had to do each week was pick panties, prepare a package, and go to the post office. Her life was good. Really good. Patty dropped the envelope into a brown briefcase, trying to channel good feelings, trying to think about a new postal worker she'd noticed last week—the first man in years she'd really thought of as good-looking. But tonight, even conjuring up a crush was useless. The envelope felt heavier than normal, weighty, like an eleven-pound baby that she'd have to carry for another month. It felt like just another thing to endure, kind of like everything else in her life.

Angela

At Taco Loco for lunch, Angela watched as Robbie bit into his taco then stuck out his tongue. Shreds of lettuce and a chunk of tomato fell out of his mouth and onto his plate.

"Gross." She stabbed at her refried beans. It was the second Tuesday in a row they had skipped school. Probably not the best idea, but it sure beat going to class.

"At least I don't have a secret crush on Brad Wellesley."

"I do not have a secret crush on Brad Wellesley!"

"Yeah, right."

Angela rolled her eyes, avoiding his accusing glare. Last week, she had told Robbie that it was Brad's suggestion that they skip school, and luckily Robbie didn't ask too many questions about why Brad would do that. This week, though, she didn't need a push from Brad to skip gym class. She had heard through the grapevine that their teacher Ms. Monahan was planning to make them do aerobics, or more specifically, "Sweatin' to the Oldies with Richard

Simmons," and she had no intention of spending forty-five minutes of her life jumping around to one-hit wonders by Herman's Hermits while some dude from the '80s with a 'fro encouraged her to love her body. Some things in life just didn't need to be experienced.

"I don't like him, Robbie. Seriously."

Robbie rolled his eyes, tugging at the collar of his black t-shirt, his neck appearing slender and long. With his new haircut, Robbie's face portrayed a certain softness that had once looked hard with his long, greasy hair but now made him appear exposed. Vulnerable. It was her idea to cut his hair shorter. He protested at first, but went along with it in the end, just like he always did. Now she felt guilty, wondering if this new look had put him up for even more than the normal adolescent torment.

Watching him pick at the remnants of his taco with a fork, he reminded her of a little kid, sticking the fork in and out of the shell, smiling as it cracked apart. Here, away from the prying eyes and judgmental glares of the cafeteria crowd, the act felt innocuous. But the same thing back at school could very well get him made fun of for the rest of the day. He was nearly eighteen, but still a boy who played with his food rather than eating it. It wasn't that he didn't eat. He did eat. A lot. But spending so much time playing with his food and wearing skinny girl-cut jeans was enough to get his ass kicked in the halls of Baldwin High. And that was why it felt so relaxing to be here—away from classmates and teachers. Away from anybody who judged them or teased them for being different. How nice it would be next year to get away from that. Robbie seemed to believe that going to Pitt would be different enough, and she hoped he was right. Especially because what she really wanted was to be away from everything, including him. It wasn't that she didn't love him or want to be his best friend. There came a time when she needed to get out on her own—start dating and finding her own life. Going to Pitt next year meant more of the same, always watching out for Robbie. Still, on a day like this, with the sun shining and the tacos so tasty and the Mountain Dew flowing, things felt perfect.

"Sometimes I think I could stay here forever."

"At a Mexican restaurant?"

"What? No! In Pittsburgh."

Behind Robbie, the green curtains on the window were framed by chili-pepper lights, and above them, pink and blue lanterns swung on brown hooks. It was festive albeit cheesy, but certainly a welcome break from the suburban sameness of Whitehall.

"Forever might be a long time. I figured after we graduate from Pitt we should go to New York or maybe to Europe or Asia."

Angela swallowed. This was how it always was with him—this long-term planning like they were going to be together forever. Didn't he ever think that at some point, one of them was bound to get a boyfriend and they wouldn't be spending the rest of their lives on the same path? That kind of talk was why she needed to get away from Pittsburgh and Robbie sooner than later. The truth was that Robbie probably wanted to move somewhere else, too, but he was the good kind of local boy who would go to Pitt for no other reason than because that's where his mom and dad went. And then he would probably become one of those people who moved out of town for a few years, met a whole bunch of expatriate Steelers fans, got homesick and moved back, then wrote an essay for the *Post-Gazette* about how moving away had taught him the true meaning of Pittsburgh. It seemed like somebody wrote an essay like that every other week in the local papers. Hell, they could print an entire daily paper just about people who left Pittsburgh crying about how much they missed it. That was NOT going to be her. Never.

Now Robbie stirred his refried beans in a counterclockwise motion. He always did that when he was finished eating. She'd never had a little brother or sister but she imagined that this might be how it felt—this constant worry and fear always tugging at you like it was your job to protect them from all that might come their way: parents, teachers, and even friends. More than anything, she wanted to escape that feeling. Robbie was her best friend, not her responsibility. There was a difference.

"Come on," she said, picking up the check.

He followed her to the register. A bored-looking girl with dark skin and braids checked them out. Robbie rifled through a tin of peppermints, spilling a few of them onto the counter. Angela leaned forward, picking them up. As she did, she noticed a Steelers sticker stuck to the side of the cash register.

She bristled, suddenly irritated. So this place wasn't any different than anywhere else. You could never get away from the Steelers in this town.

Robbie popped a candy into his mouth and loped out of the door. Angela followed, watching him stride toward her car in sideways jumps around mud puddles. It was nice to see him laughing for a change. It made her feel less guilty about leaving him. Like everything would be just fine without her.

Desiree

Thursday night, Desiree stood in her guest bedroom, looking at the pink Steelers onesie. She smiled then pulled a series of packages out of a Kaufmann's bag. This was getting to be ridiculous. Goddamn ridiculous. If Tom found out how many presents she was buying for Jen's baby, he would be furious. But it wasn't like she was using his money. She made her own damn money, and she could spend it any way she pleased.

She just couldn't help herself. Shopping was so much fun and besides, she had enough clothes and jewelry to last her three lifetimes. It felt nice to buy things for somebody else, especially somebody like Jen, who always looked at her luxury purses and shoes with a mix of envy and admiration. Jen liked the finer things in life, and she wasn't going to find them shacking them up with a mechanic, so if Desiree could help her dreams come true in some small way, she would. Once upon a time, Kristen used to look at her like that, but now Kristen was so busy with her boyfriend, she could barely be bothered with Desiree's shopping trips. Last night she'd turned down a trip to Anthropologie. Anthropologie! That was just plain ungrateful. Why, when she was that age, if somebody besides her mother would have wanted to take her to Horne's Department Store and buy her things, she would have damn near started a religion in their honor. And there was Kristen, smacking her chewing gum and refusing.

"I'm talking to Jeff on the phone now. Can't we go another night?"

Desiree clenched her teeth, still mildly irritated. Just for that, she went to Anthropologie by herself and bought a silk kimono robe that was big enough for Jen to wear through her whole pregnancy. After that, she headed to Pottery Barn Kids and bought a silver-plated comb set that included a brush, mirror, and a box lined in blue velvet to save your child's first hair cut and subsequent loose teeth. Then, at Gymboree, she found a pair of crocheted booties in the exact same shade of pink as the onesie. They were a little expensive, but pink was the kind of nuanced color that could encompass a multitude of shades so if you find an exact match, you just had to get it. Looking at all of it, she smiled. The pink may have been a bad idea, since Jen had told her they weren't going to find out the sex, but Desiree felt deep down that it was going to be a girl and usually when she had feelings in the pit of her stomach, they turned out to be true. As a child, she had sniffed out the true character of her mom's boyfriends before they could even take their shoes off and sit down for a beer. And they always proved her right. Sure, sometimes it took a few years of marriage but in the end, they always showed themselves to be the louses she knew they were.

The robe was especially delightful. She picked it up, rubbing the velvety texture between her fingers. Slipping off her white tailored jacket, she pulled the robe on over her suit.

Looking into the mirror, she smiled, waving her arms in circles, watching the gentle drape of the sleeves. She stood sideways then, pulling out the robe, seeing how far it would stretch. She grabbed two pillows and stuffed them against her stomach, then retied the robe. Standing at an angle, she looked pregnant.

She blinked. It was something she couldn't have imagined herself doing ten years ago, hell not even ten weeks ago, but standing here, it actually seemed like something to consider. She wasn't getting any younger. Besides, her and Tom had been together for six years, and she needed something else. She wasn't dumb enough to think that their marriage was going to last forever. She'd seen enough of marriage to know that eventually one of them would fall out of love and be ready to move elsewhere. And lately, she was starting to think that it would be Tom. Before, she always figured that it would be her, but all these long work trips were starting to make her paranoid. She wondered if this was how Patty had felt so many years ago. The thought of feeling like Patty was bizarre. Patty always seemed fine—impenetrable really—a little nervous-acting sometimes, but mostly the kind of woman who seemed like she didn't need to depend on a man. Her mom was like that, but it had taken her four different marriages to finally decide to pawn the old wedding rings and buy a handgun. "Who needs a man if I've got a gun?" she always quipped.

Thinking of her mom, she picked up the onesie and turned around to look at herself holding it in the mirror. It was surprising to her how natural she looked holding something so tiny. She changed her position then and cradled it like a baby. It looked natural. It really did, and she wasn't just telling herself that. She meant it.

"You look like a mom," she said. "Like a really super hot mom, of course."

She laughed but then looked away, embarrassed. It was one thing to admire the clothes that she was getting for Jen. It was another thing to actually think of them as her own. She took off the robe and threw the pillows onto the bed, like the mere imprint of the moment might linger on her skin like White Shoulders, the drug store fragrance her mom always wore on dates.

Jen

Where was he? Earlier that morning, she told him about twenty-five times that her appointment was at 12:45 and he needed to pick her up by noon. But here it was twenty minutes past, and no sign of Dave.

Tapping her foot on the sidewalk, she counted to herself. He had one more minute. Only one. Any minute, one of her coworkers or customers was bound to come outside and make a snide comment about her being stood up. The last thing she ever needed was snide comments, but especially not today and especially not about Dave. The doctor said she would be far enough along to hear the baby's heartbeat at this visit, and she didn't want some rude remarks to ruin what was meant to be a special day. But glancing at her cell phone, her head hurt and just as she was about to give up on him altogether, a horn honked and Dave pulled into the lot in his blue Ford Ranger. Fuzzy Steelers dice hung from the rearview mirror. She jerked the car door open, sliding in and slamming it shut so hard the dice shook.

On the radio, Lynyrd Skynyrd blared. She hit the power button, silencing the noise as Dave pulled onto Freeport Road.

"You're late." She pulled out her doctor's card, checking the suite number and address.

He nodded. "I got caught up watching the news. They were giving updates on the injured list for Sunday, and I wanted to see if Ben was going to play."

"Half the city could tell you that. It was all over the radio this morning."

"I missed it. Hey, I said I was sorry. I lost track of time."

Jen rolled down the window. It was a cool day, but the car smelled like the bottom of an ashtray. Dave had stopped smoking in the house but had obviously moved all his smoking activities to the car. She wanted to gag, not like that was anything new. Everything made her gag these days—garbage cans, certain hair dyes at work, Chinese food, and mayonnaise. Pregnancy controlled every aspect of her life right now and she didn't like it one bit.

"I'm always early for doctor's appointments. If they tell you to be there fifteen minutes early then I'm going to be there fifteen minutes early. Once I went for an appointment and they wouldn't see me because I was late."

"They wouldn't see you? Why not?"

"Because I was late."

"No, it wasn't because you were late. It was because you weren't aggressive enough. The barking dog gets the food."

The barking dog gets the food? Wasn't it the squeaky wheel gets the oil? Dave was wrong, but for once, she was too exhausted to point it out. Last week he'd told her that they weren't allowed to paint in his apartment but after she called the landlord she discovered that they were allowed to paint under the condition that they paint it back when they move. Dave didn't pay attention to things and was on her last nerve. But the Steelers injury report? Apparently he paid so much attention to that, he was willing to sabotage her doctor's appointment. And what about her dad? He knew that Dave was taking off early for her appointment. The only

TV was in his main office and he would definitely have known if Dave was watching it. Why hadn't he said anything? She didn't even want to think about it. Her head was starting to hurt for real. They cruised down Freeport Road at a fairly good pace now, right past the faded purple bridge to Oakmont and toward the doctor's office in Harmarville.

As they approached the intersection near the doctor's, she held her purse in her lap, clenching her teeth. Her 12:45pm appointment had started ten minutes ago. And Dave didn't even care. He was blaring the music loud again like everything was business as usual. Was this how it was going to be now—she would have to take care of everything or it wouldn't get done? Back at the apartment, a stack of dishes waited in the sink, three baskets of dirty laundry in the hall, and the filthy bathroom floor hadn't been cleaned in months. The thought of it pissed her off.

"Just let me off at the door," she said, spitting the words out like skunked beer. Dave slammed on the brakes. She jumped out without a word: no thanks or goodbye or I'll be in Suite 309 or I'll see you in five minutes. Just the angry slam of the door, the peel of his tires, and the loud angry shouting inside her head: I hate you. I hate you. I hate you. Good-bye.

She knew she'd get over it, that just as mad as she'd been at him earlier this week about the painting clause in his lease, this, too, would pass. But for right now, hitting the elevator and riding to the third floor, her feet swollen, her head aching and her stomach about to heave, she just wanted to be mad. She just wanted somebody to blame.

Week 6: Steelers vs. Jacksonville Jaguars
(L 23-17 OT)

Desiree

As he parked their BMW, Desiree watched Tom from a side angle. Despite the fact that she talked the whole way home—about the conditions of the parking lot at Heinz Field, the annoying rain, the older woman in her department who commented recently on the length of her skirts, and the hard work she was putting in to trying to find a reception room for Jen, Tom hadn't said one word since the Jacksonville Jaguars had scored in overtime, winning the game by a touchdown. During the ride home he nodded, sighed, and shook his head at a couple of points during her monologue, but no words at all.

Screw you, Tommy Maddox, she wanted to scream, stomping into the house behind Tom.

Her plan, all day, was to start hinting about having a baby. The idea of it still unsettled her a little bit—did she really want to open that box? Tom had already been there, done that, and would he really want to do it again? But she couldn't stop thinking about babies. Her brain was on auto-pilot all the time now, mulling over names and tiny shoes and tuition funds and ballet classes.

The sheer volume and intensity of her thoughts made her pretty sure that this wasn't just some indulgent whim about shopping for baby clothes or the fact that she was sick and tired of not having anything at work to say when all the other women talked about pregnancy weight and bowel movements. For the first time in her life, she wanted a kid. And damn back-up quarterback Tommy Maddox had ruined Tom's good mood by throwing too many interceptions and botching the game.

In the kitchen, he opened the fridge and pulled out leftovers from their dinner last night at Morton's. He opened it now and began eating it cold. Pulling out a knife and fork, she slid it across the counter.

"Here. You can at least use utensils."

Tom picked them up with a weak grin. "Thanks."

She sat down on a barstool. Her clothes were damp and starting to smell. She wanted to change but didn't want to lose her courage. "Are you going to talk tonight or what? I'm not the one who lost the game, so you better start talking to me or I'm going to start taking this personally."

He turned toward her. His wide brown eyes imbued the hard lines of his face with a sense of fragility. On size and strength alone, he was not the sort of gentleman you wanted to encounter in the boardroom or a dark alley. But the amber flecks in his eyes and the tender way he looked at people made him vulnerable. Other people in their office credited his sensitive face with his success—he was a salesman who could be trusted. But sometimes Desiree saw it as just plain weak—he was somebody who could be taken advantage of. Manipulated.

"It's not personal, I just don't feel like talking right now. You go ahead. I'll listen."

He hung his head, returning to the cold baked potato. *I'll listen.* He told her that a lot. So on and on she talked, uncomfortable with silence. Growing up, the only silent moments she knew were right before something bad happened—one of her little brothers getting injured in a bike or a motorcycle accident or her mom packing up their belongings and telling them it was time to move again.

She always had to talk. And when Tom said he would listen, her mind always rushed back to Patty. Patty wasn't a talker. Patty would have never followed Tom around the house talking at him. And she was such a huge football fan that she probably knew exactly how to behave after a loss. They'd been together five years and sometimes Desiree felt like she was still catching on, still walking the tightrope trying to make it from girlfriend to wife while Patty stood silently underneath, waiting for her to fall.

"There was something I wanted to talk about."

Tom turned. He looked mournful, indescribably sad like he had after his father died. It didn't seem the appropriate reaction to a football game, and Desiree suddenly became concerned that something else was going on—was he having an affair? He was certainly away from home enough to carry it out. And he was always so tired when he was home. Last night, he'd turned down sex even after she came on to him in some sexy new lingerie.

Maybe kids were a bad idea. A really bad idea. What if he was planning to leave her? Her own childhood was hard enough. Maybe it was better not to put that on somebody else.

She sighed. "It can wait. I just wanted to talk about painting, you know. The living room."

Tom raised an eyebrow, then came toward her. He put his head into her shoulder. She felt his warm breath through her fleece jacket and slipped her hand into his pocket.

"Oh Des, I'm so glad we understand each other about this."

She stiffened, surprised. "About what?"

He put his chin on her shoulder. "The game. Remember when we found out that we'd both cried after the Super Bowl 30 loss? I knew I'd found my girl then. And you're just as upset tonight. It's cute."

He kissed her on the cheek. "Think you can buck up for bed?" He brushed his nose across her cheek. She felt relieved that he mistook her chatter for anger. He dropped his hand to her thigh and she suddenly felt more confident than she had in weeks. "Of course I can." Coyly, she smiled, pulling him up the stairs.

Megan

She woke up with a start, not sure where she was except that she was trapped beneath the weight of a body and the whole place smelled like kielbasa and dead fish. Straining to open her eyes, she saw a narrow screen door. An escape. For a second, she felt hopeful and scanned the contents of the room looking for some clues to her location—a pile of black-and-gold plastic leis, a half-eaten black-and-gold cupcake, a couple of cans of Iron City Light, some beer koozies, and a pair of tongs. Above it all, a banner that once boasted "You're in Steelers Country" was ripped in half, the two sides swinging just above the beer cans on the counter.

Earlier in the day, she went down to the game with Emily and Mike, got annoyed by their PDA and ran off with some guy she met that morning at the tailgate who had a boat. She remembered kissing not one, not two, but possibly three different guys at different points in the day. Or had they all been the same? She poked at the beefy arm of the guy bearing down on her right shoulder. He wore a Jack Lambert jersey that had definitely seen better days, the number 58 cracked and faded. When his head flopped toward her, revealing his bald head, ruddy complexion and bushy blonde eyebrows, she prayed fervently that he wasn't one of the 3 she'd kissed. She'd been with some doozies in her day—like that 58-year old guy with one testicle who she met at a friend's wedding or a frequent diner at work, cross-eyed Johnny Mariani who she'd found downright unattractive until he broke down in tears telling her the story of his fiancee's untimely demise. But unless this bastard told her that his entire family was murdered, there wasn't one good reason to touch him.

She pulled her arm out from underneath him in one swift move. He faltered on the couch, rousing from his position with the confusion of a wrestler knocked out cold.

"What the—" He sat up, his irritation turning into a slow satisfied smile. "Well, well, if ain't Sleeping Beauty?"

Megan pushed him aside, searching the room for her shoes and purse, which she quickly located on a counter alongside the other party debris—melted candy bars, batteries, a pack of hotdogs, empty potato chip bags, and red plastic cups.

"What the hell is that supposed to mean?"

"You came in with Ronny, totally blitzed and been passed out ever since. I got so tired of trying to wake you, I decided to join you."

Ronny. A high school jock turned obnoxious frat boy turned working stiff. She remembered running into him and kissing him too, the unexpected taste of smoke on his breath as he cupped her ass and pushed her against the side of a bathroom wall. But she couldn't remember coming to this particular boat with ol' Lambert or whoever the hell he was.

"You could have spared me the spooning."

Lambert smiled, amused. "And how do you know we didn't do anything else?" His piercing blue eyes were attractive but entirely disarming. He had a face that looked innocuous on its own, but when he smiled, with dimples and a snaggletooth, he was definitely somebody who couldn't be trusted.

Megan grabbed her cell phone. "Because I freakin' know. I always remember that."

"Your mother must be proud. Who you calling? Your boyfriend?"

"I'm calling my roommate to come get me." She stopped, furious. Her battery was dead. She shoved it back into her purse, slipping on her shoes and fully prepared to walk toward Downtown and catch a cab. But when she looked out the window, she stopped again, confused. Instead of Heinz Field, the window revealed the soft blue lights of a faraway bridge. She blinked, pressing her face closer to the glass. Just barely, she made out a row of yellow lights climbing a hill. It looked like an incline; which one, she wasn't sure.

"Where the hell are we?"

Lambert rolled his eyes, running a hand over his shiny head. "The marina. I can get your friends here if you need directions."

"My cell's dead."

"You can use mine."

"I don't know any of their numbers."

Lambert moved back to the bench, folding a blanket crosswise and stacking it up on a table. "Guess you're screwed."

For the first time, she felt anxious. She didn't just want to go home, she needed to go home. She began her new job in the morning, and this would be a less than stellar way to start. Thank God the Steelers had won so her Monday morning hangover would be worth something.

"Look, can you, like, call me a cab or take me home? I need to get out of here."

Lambert shrugged. For all she knew, he was a sicko, a real twisted pervert, the kind that her mom and Emily and even Marlon always warned her about. She'd had some bad experiences in her days—left drunk and shoeless in Schenley Park once or twice in undergrad, stranded without cash or a phone in the back room of a dive bar in Butler County when the girls at the hotel had insisted on going to a country bar and left way too soon to see it through. But she always seemed to come out of things okay—had never run into any man or woman who she couldn't outwit, out drink, or out fight. Emily always said that eventually everybody comes to the end of the rope and what if this was hers? She'd die alone on the Ohio River, a meat cleaver to the head or her strapless bra tied around her neck. For a while, she'd be in the news: "Local Steelers Fan Murdered after Tailgate." There'd be a thinly attended funeral and viewing, with her parents, Emily, and people from work, and perhaps a few players or coaches, some bigwigs from the teams' front office showing their respects to the victim of this horrific crime. For the rest of the season, there would be a stronger police presence in the parking lots and by next year, things would return to normal. She felt tiny, like she was shrinking. Lambert turned around, smiling.

"I was gonna sleep down here, but it's a little cold out. I'm heading out Fox Chapel way. Where you need a ride to?"

"Uh, I'm in Bloomfield."

"Give me a few minutes. I'm gonna clean up a little around here."

Megan tapped at her silver watch. "Time is money." She crossed her legs and stared out the window, admiring her own reflection. For just waking up from a drunk coma, at least she still looked good. She uncrossed her legs and sighed, loudly, as Lambert shoved debris into a garbage bag.

"It'd be faster if I had some help." He tied the bag and dropped it on the floor. It sounded like glass breaking and water running.

"I thought you might say that," she said, reaching for a bag and picking beer bottles off the table. "At least we won."

"Won? What game were you watching?"

Megan dropped her bag. "What's that supposed to mean?"

"It's supposed to mean we lost the game. Damn girl, how drunk were you?"

She swallowed, her mind racing. She was sure they had won. Sure of it. They were leading in the third—wait, was that the second? There had been some interceptions and the crowd had taken to booing for a time but they rallied. Or had they? Just thinking about it hurt.

"We lost. 23 to 17. I figured that's why you were so out of it. Had to numb the pain somehow."

Megan pressed her hand into the table, crushing cheddar popcorn and pretzel sticks. Getting too drunk to know what happened during the game was amateur hour bullshit. She felt embarrassed, confused, everything slowly spinning out of focus. Sticking her hand to her forehead, her skin felt clammy.

"I think I'm gonna be sick."

Lambert looked up, his tongue hanging from his mouth like a dog in August. "Huh?"

"Sick. I feel sick." Megan crashed through the screen door and onto the deck of the boat. Leaning over, she vomited into the black water. Her stomach heaved and her head throbbed as she hung onto the metal railing. Fighting back tears, she looked out into the dark night. The boat was docked at a small marina, a handful of other powerboats swaying in the water along a narrow wooden dock. The river looked wider as it glided past the expansive hills of Mt. Washington and under the soft blue lights of the West End Bridge. The night felt big and black, an open mouth ready to swallow. She rubbed the hair on her arms, looking at how different the river was in the dark. During the day, the water looked murky and green, dirty with random debris—logs, styrofoam, used condoms, and the like. Now it looked like a long black belt winding through the forested hills, flecks of silver reflecting like buckles and spikes.

It was the kind of night people disappeared into, senile elderly people walking toward a slow death, kidnapping victims vanishing without a trace. Megan looked down at the water gently lapping the boat and imagined falling into it, how quickly it would cover her entry, no sign of her at all.

A stoner she dated back in college once told her that right before a person drowns, they get the most intense hallucination of their life. Megan had laughed at him, wondering how any person could know this if the person really drowned.

"Because, dude," he always said. "Sometimes people fight it back and then they have one helluva story to tell." He told this story with an expression of awe, like it was a natural progression for people who liked to get high—the ultimate hallucination. She always found it ridiculous and hated it when he started telling that story, but standing on the edge of a boat, she found it enticing—

the idea of pushing so hard against the edge of something that if you didn't pull back, it was all over. In real life, sometimes that's what she wanted, to push so hard that everything—the working and paying bills and having awkward conversations with strangers at parties and worrying about what would happen in the future—would go away. But it was always there, pressing upon her like it did even now. You have to be at work in the morning, she told herself. You have to be at work. She turned, slipping inside the cabin where Lambert greeted her with his reassembled Steelers banner.

"You're in Steelers Country now," he said, pointing at it and grinning.

Megan swallowed. His brusque voice sounded vaguely threatening.

Patty

In spite of the fact that she seldom drank more than two glasses of wine at a time and had only slept with two men in her entire life, the day after a Steelers loss, Patty always felt a kindred connection with women from episodes of *Sex and the City* or R-rated movies—those kind of women who occasionally woke up with a vague sense that something had happened the night before, only to be confirmed by the lack of clothing and the strange man snoring next to them.

At this point in her life, the sight of a man, no matter how strange, sleeping next to her probably wouldn't be such a bad thing. But if a lot of drinking had been involved, she knew there would be a sense of embarrassment and disappointment as she tried to piece together exactly what happened. This morning, opening her dresser drawer, she recalled yesterday's game in fragments, just like how her father used to tell stories after a big night out with the guys at the mill—no coherent narrative—just a bunch of plot points that you were supposed to add together to make a story: The overtime. The interceptions. The booing.

She hated the booing. Back when she went to the games she often felt like she was the only one in Three Rives Stadium not booing, but she didn't care. A true fan stands behind their team no matter what. And as hard as it might be to accept, losses were a part of the game. And usually they were a team effort and not one person's fault. But overanalyzing the performance of one team member was easier to make sense of, thinking that if they could have just changed one thing—their coverage during a shotgun pass or a missed tackle—then things could have been entirely different.

Still, she couldn't be mad at Tommy Maddox, no matter how many interceptions he had thrown. Nobody knew this, not Robbie, not Kristen or even the nosy women at work who were forever prying into details of her home life, but once upon a time, her and Tommy Maddox had a moment. It wasn't much of moment, but it was a moment and she couldn't shake it.

It was at Ross Park Mall, two years ago around Christmas. She sat alone in the food court eating a steak burrito and waiting for Kristen. When she first saw the handsome gentleman carrying trays for his wife and patiently wrangling his kids into their seats, she thought she knew him from work.

Is that Ed? Or Joey from Marketing? She stared, trying to figure out why this guy's profile was so familiar. And then he looked up, his brown eyes meeting hers. Immediately she knew exactly who he was. She swallowed, dabbing her napkin on the stray sauce running down her chin. For a quick minute, she didn't look away and neither did he. Her insides quivered, thinking of so many panties and red lipstick kisses that had passed between them unknown. And then he smiled, not the kind of insincere smile the players saved for local news crews, but a genuine expression of happiness, as if he had seen her catching him in his moment of domestic bliss but that he didn't mind, that perhaps he even wanted her to watch. For a second, she was certain there was electricity in the air, like perhaps he somehow knew exactly who she was, an invisible force leading them to each other, to this moment. But then one of his kids spilled a drink and the whole family turned to clean up the mess.

But today, listening to those loud boos in stereo-surround, all she could think about was Robbie. What if that was Robbie on the field—being jeered and taunted in front of a national audience? The thought made her skin crawl like babies after a Cheerio on the floor. Ever since Kristen had told her what the other kids said about Robbie, she'd treated him more gently than ever, not giving him a hard time about cleaning his room or the way he dressed and asking him daily about what was going on at school and even how Angela was doing.

She couldn't be sure if it was this new approach or something else, but she noticed a difference over the past few weeks. When she came home from work, she found him in the house working on homework and smiling or watching *The Simpsons* and laughing out loud as he recited entire conversations word for word. She knew that a happy teenager was nearly as delicate as a peaceful newborn baby, if not more so. Once a baby's fragile state of happiness is interfered with and it begins to cry, it's not terribly hard to cajole it back into that original state. Or even when it is hard to return to that original state of bliss, at least the baby doesn't remember their previous agony. On the other hand, teenagers remember every slight, every misspoken word and perceived insult that ever occurred, and they are quick to flaunt it. It was better to try and appreciate Robbie's improved spirits rather than investigate. One wrong question and they'd be right back where they started.

Patty sighed, looking down at the blank card and wondering what to write. Again she thought of Robbie and wrote as though she were addressing him: *Dear Tommy, No matter what anybody says about you, hold your head up high. Be proud. I love you. Love Always, Ginger Mae.*

That sounded a little bit over the top. She usually didn't tell the players that she loved them. But this was different. Tommy, like Robbie, needed a self-esteem boost right now. And sometimes a secret admirer, like a parent, is the only one who can deliver.

Angela

No matter what she did, it was impossible to concentrate on her homework from Mrs. Gianni's English class. Normally, writing a four-page essay about the symbolism in "The Yellow Wallpaper" would be right up her alley, but tonight the whole thing seemed a little obvious and tired. Her senior year was looking to be a colossal waste of time. She could learn more from an hour on the internet than she ever learned having to listen to her asshole classmates talk about the gender roles in *Taming of the Shrew*. They were all dumb, but it wasn't their fault. So were most of the teachers. Occasionally at the beginning of the school year, new teachers would make snide comments about her piercings. She loved the looks on their faces later in the first semester as they slowly realized that she, and not one of the little All-American girls with their American Eagle threads and Ugg boots, was actually the most intelligent student in the class. Not that being the most intelligent person in her classes really meant anything. Maybe if she had a challenging class it would, but even in her supposedly advanced classes, things seemed like they were being dumbed down just to make sure that no child was left behind. Please. Some of these teenage crybabies she knew desperately needed to be left behind. Just last week, Marci Updyke threw a full-on preschool tantrum in the bathroom because her mom had just texted her that the homecoming dress she wanted was sold out.

Ugh. Marci was in her English class and thinking of that, she wanted to skip it even more than she usually did. Putting her book away, she fell backwards onto her bed, staring at the ceiling as her mom opened the door. Startled, she jumped. Didn't a closed door mean anything to these people?

"Can't you freakin' knock?"

Putting a hand on her hip, her mom looked about the room, her expression of disapproval rising as she surveyed the piles of black clothes, books, shoes and the magazine cutouts covering every inch of the walls. "How about I start to knock when you start to clean your room?"

A petite woman, Angela's mom wore her blonde hair permed and chin-length, the perfect frame for her heart-shaped face. She was the kind of woman who people described as cute, something that people had once said about her too until the summer after freshman year when she finally shed the baby fat, earned enough baby-sitting money to buy her own clothes, and met a bunch of guys at a tattoo shop down in the South Side who would pierce her no matter what her age, probably only because they wanted to sleep with her cousin Megan. Whatever. Everybody wanted to sleep with Megan. So when she told the boys to start piercing, they did, no questions asked. After enough hardware to the face and hair dye, "cute" really isn't the word that comes to mind. But for her mom, cute was fine, probably even a compliment. For her, it always felt like an insult, like some kind of mocking accusation that she should be twirling a baton or batting her eyelashes and ringing a bell to bring in some more donations for the Salvation Army.

Her mom cleared her throat, her hands absentmindedly twisting the gold filigree chain of her Steelers logo pendant.

"Just ignore your dad this week. He's being a real ass because of Sunday's game. You couldn't help that they were playing it at the theater. That wasn't your fault. Just ignore him."

She pushed up the sleeves of her red flannel pajama top and stepped deeper into the room. To Angela, it looked like she was searching and the first thing she thought of were all those brochures about Seattle colleges. Shoved haphazardly into her desk and dresser drawers, they were easily identifiable and an immediate way to start a fight. Angela stepped in front of her mom, acting like she was interested in her shirt and angling to cut off her searching gaze.

"Is that a new shirt?"

Her mom nodded, biting her lip and looking amused.

"You're interested in my shirt?"

"Sure. It looks comfortable."

"Okay. What is it? Are you hiding something? Is there a boy up here? Drugs? Illegal wildlife?"

"Ha, ha. Of course not, and about Dad, I usually ignore him as like part of standard operating procedure, so I'm not sure why you're telling me this. I have a lot of homework, Mom, so can I get back to that or are you going to be in here for a while?"

"Wow. So you really are hiding something, aren't you?"

"Mom, no! Seriously, I'm just tired and I have a lot of work to do."

"Work?" Her mom walked right past her, heading toward her bookshelves and the dresser. She needed a distraction. And fast.

"So do you have these kind of talks with Dad about me?"

"Excuse me?" That stopped her mom in her tracks, pivoting to face her.

"I mean, you're telling me to ignore Dad and just be a sport. Do you ever tell Dad to get over his superstitions and just realize that he has no control over the game? It's magical thinking, Mom,

I've read about it, there are scientific studies that show these kind of people—"

"Magical thinking? Now THAT sounds made up. You can't believe everything you read on the internet. Oh Angela, don't take it so seriously. It's just a joke with your dad. You know how he likes to take things to an extreme."

They'd been down this road before. Why did she even bother? Even though her mother would never come out and say it, deep down Angela knew that her mom also thought she was a bad luck charm. Everybody did. Even Robbie's mom had gotten wind of the superstition years ago and refused to let Angela come around on game days. It was ludicrous. A bunch of grown-ass people who took a game so seriously that they didn't care how it affected her at all. There she was, living and breathing right beside them, and they all chose to spend their life in service to some team that they didn't even really know. The Pittsburgh Steelers didn't know or care about them like she did but all these people would cast her aside in favor of their beloved team.

Her mom lifted herself on her tiptoes, reaching into the bookshelf and pulling out an old, frayed teddy bear wearing a Steelers sweater.

"Wow," she said, looking between Angela and the teddy bear. "I'm surprised you still have this. Really surprised." She looked at the bear, nostalgia gray and cloudy across her hazel eyes.

Angela watched how her mom looked past her and around her but never directly at her. It had been like this ever since she'd gotten her eyebrow pierced.

"Why would you want to do that to yourself?" her mom had said when she came home bearing her new piece of hardware.

She hadn't even tried to explain, but it was something about wanting to be different than who she was and where she was. It was something intangible that she couldn't even really describe but definitely something that her parents, a former football player and captain of the colorguard squad, would never understand.

Angela stood up, grabbing the bear from her mom's accusing grasp. So what if she kept a Steelers teddy bear in her cupboard? It had been a childhood gift from her grandpa that she'd had as long as she could remember. And now her mom was looking at her with a smile, like this one little hidden toy actually meant something. Angela shoved it back into the shelf, back toward the shadowy cobwebs alongside her yellowed copies of *Little House on the Prairie.*

Without a single glance toward her mom, she sat down with her laptop. "Get out of my room."

Jen

Friday at noon, Jen and her mom pushed through the web of pedestrians and traffic on Sixth Street toward the Renaissance Hotel. She rarely went Downtown save for parking in the garages for Pirates or Steelers games and on days like those, the city streets were a black–and-gold patchwork of people headed across the bridges toward the North Shore. This afternoon, she watched the dark-suited business men and women talking on cell phones and stepping into cafes and cabs and thought of how she had felt as a little girl, riding on the network of highways and bridges that bordered the triangular tip where Downtown existed. It had always seemed then like she lived in a real city, and she remembered thinking that the angular glass turrets of the PPG buildings looked like a magical castle where a princess might live.

Stepping through the gilded doors of the Renaissance and into the main lobby with its the tall marble pillars, Jen felt suddenly very princess-like herself.

At that exact moment, they saw Desiree waving at them from beside a mahogany chair. She felt her mom's breath on her neck as she whispered through clenched teeth: "Don't get your hopes up too much, honey. I don't think their prices will be very reasonable."

Reasonable? There was nothing reasonable about planning a wedding. And for god's sake, she was their only daughter—reason had no part in any of this.

"So glad you're here," said Desiree. "They gave me a new girl to deal with today. Never even heard of her, but we'll see what we can do."

Jen nodded, grateful but feeling slightly worried as she saw her mom appraising the room with judging eyes.

Desiree tapped on her watch. "If this new girl isn't down here in one minute, I'm going to complain. Do you have any idea how busy I am?"

Just as she said that, a tall, busty blonde with dark brown eyes approached with a hesitant smile.

"Ms. Salvatore?" She held a black leather binder against her chest and wore a slim black pantsuit that accentuated her curvy figure. Although professionally dressed, there was something about her vampy red lipstick and exaggerated up-do that reminded Jen of an old-fashioned pin-up girl. Something about her seemed especially colorful, like a black-and-white movie painted in color, a touch too vivid to be taken seriously.

"I'm Megan," the girl said, extending a long, slender hand. Jen shook it and relaxed. Megan had a firm grip. The kind of handshake you could trust.

"If you want to follow me upstairs, I can show you a couple of room options and we can talk availability."

Jen nodded, following. At the foot of the sweeping red carpet staircase, she looked at her mom and smiled. "This is it. I don't care about reason."

Her mom's face turned a shade of gray. "We need to be practical. Would you rather us spend the money on the wedding or help out when the baby comes?"

Jen gripped the cold ivory banister and sighed. First, her mom insisted on a wedding. Then, she refused to pay for a nice one. If this was some passive aggressive way of dealing with things then it was working remarkably well. She was definitely pissed.

The first room they looked at was small, maximum capacity about 50 and only one small window overlooking the traffic on Sixth Street. Jen watched her mom nodding and pursing her lips as Megan explained that this was the cheaper of the two ballrooms.

"I don't really think 50 is realistic. We both have big families. What's the biggest room you have?"

Up until this very moment, she had absolutely no intention of inviting nearly any of Dave's family, but she wanted to see how far she could push things.

"Okay, follow me." Megan guided them toward the end of the balcony and swung open a door into the most beautiful room Jen had ever seen. Immediately, Jen knew that this was where she was going to get married. She held her breath, looking around the room. It was simply decorated, buttercup walls, ornate crown molding, and shiny green trees in each corner. The centerpiece of the room was the long wall of floor-to-ceiling windows framing the Allegheny River, the yellow arches of the Roberto Clemente Bridge, and the blue curve of PNC Park.

"I love it," she gushed. "How much is it?"

Desiree looked at her, one eyebrow raised.

The sales girl, Megan, pushed a loose strand of hair from her face and opened her binder. "I'm sorry. I should have looked at this before I brought you in here. It's booked every Saturday until May."

"What about Sunday?" asked Desiree.

Megan browsed a calendar, her face pinched. She sounded unsure of herself. "The first one is in November. November 20."

"Nobody gets married on a Sunday," said Jen's mom.

"They do if it saves them a couple thousand dollars," said Desiree.

Jen's mind raced. November 20. November 20. Who were the Steelers playing that day?

"I don't know if we could save you a couple of thousand dollars, but if you have a budget I could work with you to stay within that."

Yes, yes. Budget. Jen looked to see if her mom was paying attention, but she was looking at something on her phone.

"Is there a game that day?" she said, looking up from what Jen now realized to be a calendar.

Megan nodded. "Yeah, it's an away game, versus the Ravens."

"I don't know. I mean we'd have to have it after the game of course. But Mom, don't you think that would work?"

Her mom looked as tired as though she'd spent the entire day in the kitchen cooking pierogies. "I don't know, Jen, that seems so fast, it's barely a month away, how do we plan a wedding in a month?"

Desiree cleared her throat. "I like to think that I have some experience in this department and I will tell you, Beth, that it's going to be a whole lot easier on you planning a wedding in a month at a hotel than it would be doing it yourself at the Polish Club."

"Yeah," said Megan. "Once we get something set up, our staff can do most of the leg work for you."

Jen looked at her mom, hopeful. "Yeah, see, you'd be saving time. And it's sooooo pretty, Mom, please? Can we just look at the prices?"

Her mom sighed, uncrossing her arms. "Okay. I guess it doesn't hurt to look."

Jen dug her heels into the plush carpet, perfectly pleased.

Week 7: Steelers vs. Cincinnati Bengals
(W 27-13)

Angela

It came to her on the way home from school, an innocent conversation about which teachers they could dress up as for Halloween ending with the decision to go as Patty.

And about ten minutes later, in Patty's bedroom, Angela waited for Robbie to get out one of those godawful holiday sweaters that Patty sometimes wore. It was an easy outfit, all she had to do was wear the sweater that day at work and school. Sure, about 99% of people wouldn't even know who the hell she was supposed to be, but she and Robbie would and that was funny enough.

Robbie approached Patty's dresser with a sigh. "I don't know. Maybe this isn't such a good idea."

"Not such a good idea? I feel like this is the best idea we've ever had," she said pushing him off Patty's bed and toward the dresser. In the mirror, Angela saw Robbie's red lips part as he shrugged.

"I just, well, what if she notices a sweater is missing? Or who is going to even get who you're dressing up as?"

Angela pushed him, the metal studs of his belt buckle pinching against her palms. "Come on, Robbie, she's not going to notice at Halloween if her Easter sweater is missing, and even if people don't get that I'm your mom, just that I'm a person who wears holiday sweaters is totally funny enough."

Robbie squatted down, pulling the drawer open. "I don't really see where it's that funny, but whatever. Here they are, take your pick."

She knelt down. The sweaters were stuffed so tight into the drawer that they nearly popped out as she poked and prodded.

"Mm, not the black one, or the Thanksgiving, but oh, oh, I think that's the one…" She stopped, pointing at a pink one near the bottom of the drawer. She had a feeling it was for either Easter or Valentine's Day and laughed to herself, thinking about how shocked the kids at school would be to see her in pink instead of her usual black.

"Can you imagine the look on Nancy's face when I head off to school wearing pink? Her and Dom will be falling all over themselves." Grinning at the thought of her parents' surprise, she tugged at the sweater. It didn't budge. She dug her hand deeper into the drawer.

"The dumb thing is stuck on something." Digging to get underneath it, her hand hit a glossy surface that definitely wasn't part of the dresser.

"What the hell is this?"

"What the hell is what?"

"I don't know, it's like some sort of a box." Angela dipped both hands into the drawer and tugged. When it finally gave, she fell backwards, a small chest falling onto her lap and a bunch of sweaters falling into seizures on the rug.

They looked at each other. Robbie held his hand out to block the box. "Come on, let's just put it back. If it's like love letters or sex toys that belong to my mom, I will vomit. Seriously, I will kill myself."

"Quit being such a drama queen," said Angela as she popped the latch open.

The box was filled with sexy lace panties and thongs. Robbie shielded his eyes, looking like he was about to throw up. "Put it away."

Put it away? She had known Patty for her entire life, and never once had she imagined that Patty wore or was even aware of anything outside of white granny panties. The idea that she might have some secret double life of passion was totally awesome: accountant by trade, sex slave by choice; mom by day, swinger by night. The possibilities were endless, each one of them a welcome alternative to seeing Patty as just another sad-sack, suburban robot mom. If Patty had a secret sex life, then anything was truly possible. Angela rummaged through the box. She yanked out some papers. Envelopes. Red ones. Each one imprinted with a return address for one "Ginger Mae" at a post office box number and made out to the same mailing address. Angela flipped through the envelopes, imagining that Ginger Mae was Patty's prostitute name and that these were thank you notes to her biggest clients. Or perhaps how she sent her pimp his share of the money. Suppressing a laugh, Angela unfolded a white piece of lined paper underneath the envelopes.

"Wait," she said, looking over what appeared to be some sort of a log sheet reading: Player Name, Date, Panties Sent, and Score. She threw it at Robbie, disgusted.

"This isn't, it can't be, she isn't..." Angela was tripping over her own words, her tongue ring suddenly heavy in her mouth. Patty was sending her underwear to the Steelers. God. So even in her double life, Patty was doing something that still had to do with the status quo around town. Even her alter ego was just another depressing sports fan who believed that some stupid superstition somehow put them in control of a game. Just like her parents.

Robbie groaned, throwing the paper back. "Oh gross. She's sending football players underwear? Really. I mean, who does that? Seriously. Who does that?"

Angela snickered, her tongue finding its way again. "Your mom."

Robbie twisted his mouth, his black eyes darting back and forth as he grabbed the box and shoved it back into its place. He slammed the box shut and crammed it into the drawer. Angela folded the sweaters, putting them back into place.

"I don't think I want to be your mom for Halloween anymore."

Robbie slammed the drawer shut. "Good. I honestly don't even want to look at my mom anymore." Underneath his gray t-shirt, Angela noticed that his thin arms were shaking. He turned around and she bit her tongue, silent as she followed him out of the room.

Jen

Jen looked around the small crowd at Morgan's, wondering how many other couples did their wedding invitations at a bar. There were probably a few out there, but she had never exactly aimed to be one of them. Dave had insisted on being involved in the process and thanks to his weekly game of pool with the guys from a competing auto garage, Wednesdays were spent at Morgan's.

"It's too smoky in here. Do you really want your unborn baby exposed to so much secondhand smoke?" she said, pulling a list of names and addresses from her purse.

Dave shrugged. "My mom smoked when she was pregnant with all of us, and we turned out fine." He dug into his pocket and dropped a few crumpled sheets of paper onto the table.

Jen grabbed them, looking at his scratchy writing in smeared blue ink. The list looked like it had been through the washer or something, but most of the names were legible.

"This is kinda long, Dave. I thought I told you 75 each."

"Yeah. About that. My mom gave me like the dream list of who she wants to invite and then said we can narrow it down from there."

"So then she'll be mad at me when I cut one of her friends."

"Nah, she'll be fine with it. She just wanted to give me the max, you know. Start reading me names and we'll decide." Dave took a drag on his cigarette and waved to some guys coming in the front door.

Jen looked at the list, aggravated. The Renaissance Hotel wasn't cheap. If some second cousins had to be left out because she was having a fancy wedding, then so be it. That view of the North Shore was a much better gift than anything some second cousins would probably give.

She ticked through Dave's list, marking the first few with stars—his mother, her boyfriend, Dave's three brothers, his half-sisters, and his uncle Ronnie. With significant others and kids, the list was already at 20. The next person on the list was Dave's cousin Theresa, followed by the number 5.

"Five for Theresa? She wants to bring her latest fling and all three of the kids?"

Dave nodded. "Why wouldn't she? You're pregnant. Don't tell me you're going to make it one of those no-kids-allowed affairs."

Jen groaned, marking a star beside Theresa's name. Dave was right, but the issue wasn't about kids. It was about the kind of kids. Theresa's kids were bad, the kind with messy hair and food on their faces who ran and screamed like a pack of wild hyenas. The

Cincinnati Bengals had more class than these little punks. She grimaced, imagining them climbing underneath tables, tripping old people on the dance floor, and possibly setting a small fire while Theresa half-heartedly screamed at them from across the room. But she was trying to be open to his family, and imagining the drama that would come from not inviting those kids wasn't pretty. They would be invited, but that didn't mean she wouldn't be praying for some nasty flu bug to take the whole lot of them out of commission for the day.

She counted up the stars. 40. The next few names better be good.

"John Pinkerton? Who's that?"

"Stevie's parole officer."

"Stevie's parole officer? You want to invite your brother's parole officer to our wedding?"

"Yeah. He's a helluva cool dude."

"No. Not gonna happen." She crossed off his name.

"Larry Imhoff?"

"My mom's chiropractor. She's at his office once a week. She feels close to him."

Jen rubbed her head. "No, we are not going to invite chiropractors and parole officers when there are plenty of close friends on my side who had to be cut. Tell me who the rest of these people are."

Dave grabbed the list. Trying not to lose control of herself, she felt her heart pounding as he explained the last couple of people, mostly neighbors who he barely knew, and even a couple of names he didn't know. He shrugged. "I don't know, I guess cut'em, but I think we should put back John and Larry. I swear they are cool dudes."

"We are not having a parole officer at my wedding."

"It's just how we met him all those years ago. Now, we're all cool. Just give me that one, okay? And then you can invite all your little friends at the salon or whatever."

"All my friends at the salon? No, I can't even do that. Do you know how big my family is? Do you know how many people we had to cut? I can only invite Sarah and Amy and maybe Allison if some of my cousins can't make it."

"That's lame. It's your wedding."

"It's OUR wedding." Dave kept referring to everything as hers: her wedding, her baby, like it was something completely outside of him. It was like he didn't even care. "This is your wedding too, ya know. And the invites need to be sent this week, so you better start caring."

He rubbed his forehead and looked toward the back of the room. She knew he was more interested in playing pool than the invitation list. "Do you even care? Do you even care one bit about all this?"

"Of course I care. God, Jen, I'm asking you to include one person on the guest list you don't approve. Just add John and then you can have the rest of my guests. That's the deal."

"Fine. He's on. But the chiropractor is out."

Dave snorted. "What if somebody needs an adjustment at the wedding? Shouldn't we have a doctor on hand?"

"Chiropractors aren't doctors. And I'm not finding any of this funny right now." She knew she was being a bitch but these days, once she got started, she couldn't stop. On top of the stress of Bobby being away, now she had the anxiety of planning a wedding and preparing for the baby. She always imagined pregnancy was supposed to be the happiest time of your life—you and the man you love eagerly awaiting the birth of your child. It always seemed so magical and miraculous. But this felt like hell. Her legs and back hurt, she had so much gas she could barely make it through a haircut without excusing herself to the ladies' room and she felt so fat and gross and disgusting that she didn't even want Dave touching her. He'd slept on the couch every night since she moved in.

And watching him now, as he nodded at Shannon for another draft, her mind raced. Was he doing this because he loved her? Or because he felt obligated? She needed to get out of there, and soon, before her anxieties came to a rolling boil and she blew her stack. She stuffed the papers in her purse. Dave obviously didn't want to help, and she didn't want to nag him anymore. She was tired of nagging. Tired of being her.

"You going back to my place?"

His place? She'd been living there nearly a month. And he was still calling it his?

She stood up, keys in her hand. "OUR place. I'm going to back to our place."

Dave shrugged. "Oh yeah, that's what I meant." She saw him leaning in to kiss her cheek and turned the other way.

"Have a good night," he said, heading to the pool table and leaving her waiting at an empty table.

Shannon

Shannon poured another beer and smiled as Larry walked into the bar with his signature toothy grin. It was the wide-mouthed kind of grin that might have looked crazy on another person but suited Larry just fine. He was a friendly guy and treated every room he entered like it was the most important place he'd ever been. While he paused at a table to greet a pair of regulars wearing black biker jackets, Shannon pulled out a Miller Lite bottle and sat it in front of his regular stool, second from the pool table. It was Wednesday night and, just like every Wednesday night, the boys from Larry's Garage and Mike's Auto Body were enjoying 25-cent wings, $2 pitchers and an evening's worth of pool.

Larry sat down with an exaggerated sigh. "How was your day, Miss Shannon? Better than mine, I hope."

"It sucked. I felt like I was stuck in traffic all day." Earlier that afternoon, she had collected samples from McKees Rocks and got stuck in a backup on the West End Bridge that stranded her for an hour and a half during rush hour. It was typical, but lately the traffic seemed worse. Or maybe it was just her ability to cope.

"With that job of yours, you probably were. Where's about?"

"West End Bridge."

"Accident or something? You should get another job. Like I always say, if you wanna do some bookkeeping and scheduling, I'd hire you in a heartbeat. Beth's mom does a lot more talking than she does working these days."

Larry's mother-in-law kept the books down at his garage. But he was always bugging Shannon about taking over even though she didn't know the first thing about keeping books. There were days when her job was annoying, but getting paid to sit in traffic wasn't the worst fate. It seemed far worse to be stuck in an office all day. At least her job offered some sense of motion.

"Don't be startin' that. You know I'm not comin' to work for you. But thanks for the offer. It's just all the construction right now, when they get it all done, it's all gonna be just fine."

Larry groaned, wiping his bald forehead with a thick hand. "I thought ya grew up here, kid. Don't you know the construction is never done?"

"I'm an optimist. Speaking of growing up, you just missed Jen."

"Nah, I seen her out on the sidewalk. That girl. Coming to a bar to do her wedding invitations and now she's all in a twist because she said Dave wasn't takin' it seriously."

Shannon nodded. She'd noticed that Dave and Jen were poring over lists and envelopes and had assumed as much. Jen was the only member of Larry's family who made her feel uncomfortable. There was something about her that was slightly abrupt, a tone in her voice that always sounded bitter.

"A wedding and a baby. Big couple of months for your family, huh? Audrey told me Des hooked you up with a real fancy wedding package too."

"Ha. I wish Des would have hooked us up with a damn way to pay for it. But I guess that's what the old man is good for, right? We wanted to throw her something nice, you know a big party for everybody, but she's insisting that it's gotta be fancy. She should be damn near glad we're willing to put any money out for her at all. God love her, she's my little girl, but she's so stubborn. Stubborn and damn near rotten sometimes. Dave's in for a helluva ride with that one."

Smiling, Shannon glanced back at the pool table where Dave stood in his backward white cap and Penguins t-shirt. His mouth was open in a half-smile and his blue eyes sparkled like city lights on the rivers. Talking to Dave, you knew he'd grown up rough, but there was an essential kindness about him that softened Shannon's heart. She'd thought many times since they'd announced the engagement of how unfair it seemed that mean girls like Jen always landed nice boys like Dave.

Larry continued talking. "God, it's funny how different kids can be. Now, you take Bobby for instance. He'd go out of his way to do for somebody else. That kid's been nothing but easy since the day he was born. Only took Beth an hour to have him. An hour! Beth waited 16 hours with Jen and she came out screaming and hasn't shut up since. Now I'm telling you again, I love that little girl with all my heart, but she's stubborn as the day is long and always has been. You'll see when you have kids of your own, Shannon, just how different they can be."

She swallowed. "I think I know a little bit about that. Me and Darla have nothing in common except our parents."

"That's probably not true. You gals seem like you get along real good."

Shannon shrugged. Seemed. The only reason it seemed like that was because Darla was the only person besides Audrey who she ever hung around with.

"So, tell me about the wedding."

"What's there to tell?"

"When is it?"

"You're not gonna believe this, but it's on a Sunday night. Can you imagine the nerve of somebody getting married on game day? And it's my kid. But that's the only night they could get. I know, I know. What the hell, right? But consider yourself invited. You and your sister and that boyfriend of hers, the construction guy, he's good people."

"Jack?" Shannon liked just saying his name, the feel of it on her mouth. It was a manly name, sturdy and strong just like him. "No, I don't think that would be right. I'm sure you guys are trying to trim costs, I don't need an invitation."

"It's not an invitation, Shannon. It's an order. Bring 'em. Bring 'em all. I'm paying for the damn thing; better be some people I like there! And bring a date." He winked at her and she felt herself sinking into the soles of her cherry Doc Marten boots.

"Oh, no." She blushed, feeling the heat rising along her chest like the stagnant air on the West End Bridge earlier today. She'd been too low on gas to run the air-conditioner so by the time she started moving her clothes were sticky with sweat. Why did things always have to turn to dates? Except for moments like this, she felt perfectly content being single.

"Yeah, I'm sure you got somebody up your sleeve, don't you now? I see how all the boys come in here looking at you. You're a real heartbreaker. Pick one of 'em and take 'em for a spin at the wedding."

Take 'em for a spin. People acted like dating was no more serious than test-driving a car, just something to do on a Saturday afternoon. But she didn't like doing that, either. She'd had the same silver Honda Civic since 1997.

She looked up at the TV screen. Fox Sports Network was running a highlight show of the Steelers' previous game against the Bengals. After a disappointing loss to the Jaguars while Roethlisberger was injured, he'd started this week and led them to an easy win against their AFC conference rivals. Monday night, they'd meet Baltimore in yet another conference game. She clicked her tongue. "What you thinkin' about the score for Monday's game?"

Larry snorted. "That's between me and my bookie. But I'd be happy to hear your predictions if ya got one."

Shannon smiled, then felt the cool flush of relief as Dave approached the bar with three empty pitchers.

"Fill us up, Shannon," he said, smacking Larry on the back.

Shannon grabbed the pitchers and started pouring.

Megan

Perfect. The bus would be at her stop in about five minutes, and her wallet was nowhere to be found. Frantic, she dumped the entire contents of her brown bag on the oriental rug and rifled through receipts, ticket stubs, empty gum wrappers, lipsticks missing their caps, a broken compact, three candy necklaces, and a green plastic spider ring. Between her dull headache and vague recollection of last evening, she couldn't even remember where she'd seen it last. Aside from a lot of shouting and pressing against bodies in the black-lit interior of Bar 11, she couldn't come up with anything that made sense during the night except letting a college freshman with a fake ID bite off her candy necklace and dancing, quite excitedly, along to "Crazy Bitch" with an old college acquaintance who happened to be back in town for a job interview. Somebody named Ray paid for most of her drinks, and when her friend Bret had dropped her off last night, she'd had no reason to look for her wallet. In fact, she remembered feeling grateful last night that she'd even remembered her keys at all. Losing keys was quite the bitch.

She scooped the garbage back into her bag and ran into the kitchen, interrupting Emily's breakfast. "Can you spare some bus money? I lost my pass. And my wallet."

Emily didn't look up from her bowl.

Megan sighed and held out her hand. "Excuse me? Bus money? I need some. I'm gonna be late if I don't leave in like 2 minutes. I'll pay you back tonight."

"Sorry, I don't have it."

"You don't have two dollars? C'mon, I'm good for it. I must have left my wallet in somebody's car last night. I'll get it at work or something."

Emily crossed the room, dumping leftover milk into the sink. The milk looked yellow and reminded Megan of all the blowjob shots she'd done the night before. Her stomach writhed a little, then a lot when Emily turned around and crossed her arms over her chest, coolly detached.

"Look, Megan, I'll give you bus money when you give me the back rent you owe."

Back rent? Megan tried to think. Okay, there had been July. And August. But she'd made a full payment the end of September and Emily had pronounced them even.

"I thought we were cool. And this is only $2. If you don't give it to me so that I can get to work, then you're gonna have a helluva lot worse problems than two months back rent."

Emily sighed, a heavy exaggerated one that Megan swore she heard landing on the kitchen floor with a sickening thud. "I can't. I'm sorry. I've been thinking about it and talking about it, and I just feel like you are taking advantage of me. I mean, look at all those new clothes you bought for work and you go out every night of the week, so I just feel like you have your priorities. And rent obviously isn't one of them. And if you don't start paying me every month, you're going to have to find somewhere else to live."

Megan felt like she'd been struck across the face with a brick dipped in acid. "First of all, I told you things would get better once I start getting a regular paycheck, not tips. Second, it's none of your business what I spend my money on, thank you. And third, is this really something you believe or some nonsense that Mike is filling your head with? Don't lie to me. I know he doesn't like me."

Emily threw up her hands and walked out of the kitchen. "It IS my business what you spend your money on when you're my roommate and you're supposed to be sharing the rent. And no, this is nothing that Mike is filling my head with. He's, they've, just helped me realize things that I was too blind to notice."

"He? They? Who is they?"

"Mike and Kevin."

They were in the foyer now, Megan with her bag falling off her shoulder and Emily with her french-manicured nails on the mahogany banister. Megan wanted to grab that hand and bite it until it bled. It was an ugly thought and maybe a little abnormal for a twenty-eight-year-old girl to wish that she really could settle all of her disputes with a little bit of violence. But she'd always envied that among her male friends. Guys just kicked the shit out of each other and moved on. Girls had a way of letting things stew inside the old emotional pressure cooker until they exploded into all-out psychological warfare. To her, backstabbing always seemed just as dangerous as an actual stabbing. This was why she usually didn't like other girls. And yet, she'd once been stupid enough to think that Emily wasn't like the other girls she knew, that Emily was above backstabbing.

"I'll have your fuckin' money faster than you can blink, Emily." Megan regretted the words as she spoke them, but there was something about being pushed into a corner that made her unleash her claws. Where was she going to get nearly $1000? Unless she started charging for it down on Liberty Avenue or stripping down at Bare Elegance, that kind of moolah was a next-to-impossible feat.

On the steps, Emily smiled an arrogant little grin. "Great. I need it by November 1." She spun on her heels, disappearing upstairs.

Megan wanted to strangle her. Instead, she grabbed her keys and ran out the door, hoping that if she drove to work, she could charm the doormen into valet parking her car without charging. She unbuttoned the top two buttons of her blue blouse and pushed up her bra. November 1. That bought her a few days at least. And maybe with luck, Emily and Mike would break up by then and they could just forget about this little incident.

Week 8: Steelers vs. Baltimore Ravens
(W 20-19)

Desiree

There was nothing more exciting than a Monday night game against the Ravens, especially when that Monday night game fell on Halloween. An hour before kickoff, Desiree and her mom ate gyros in a window booth at Salonika's on Sixth Street and watched the parade of crazies. It was a cool night, crisp like an apple straight off the tree.

"Oh my god, did you see that one?" Desiree pointed, then covered her mouth and laughed. Across the street, a woman dressed as an angel held hands with a giant banana.

Audrey looked and shook her head. "Where the hell are all these people going? I hope it's not to the game. If some moron sits in front of me dressed as a damn banana, they are gonna be one helluva bruised banana after I'm done with them."

Desiree poked at her salad. "There must be some party down here somewhere. There's way too many people dressed up. We should have gone as Ravens fans!"

"And get our asses kicked? No thanks!"

Desiree looked away as her mom bit into a gyro. She tried to concentrate on the scene outside, the steady stream of Steelers fans and people out celebrating Halloween. Across the street, she noticed a young family exiting the Arthur Murray Dance Studio. The husband and wife, both in regular clothes, held the hand of a dainty Cinderella. Neither the mom nor the dad wore anything black and gold, a sight so unusual on game day that Desiree immediately assumed they were foreign—Russian ballroom dancers, most likely. They were certainly lithe enough to be athletes of some sort. Their daughter looked no older than four or maybe five. She had long black hair and bangs that framed her delicate pale face. She wore a puffy blue dress, clear shoes, and a silver tiara. Even from across the street, she glittered and glowed.

"Look how cute," said Audrey with a full mouth. Desiree glanced over, seeing that her mom was pointing to the same little girl.

"Yeah, I noticed her, too. She is cute." Just then, an older couple approaching the dance studio stopped to chat with the couple. As if on cue, the little girl spun in a perfect circle, then tucked herself against her mother's legs as all of the adults laughed.

"You noticed her? Well, that's a surprise. I didn't think you ever noticed kids, except maybe to notice how much they were annoying you."

"God, Mom, you act like I'm some kind of monster. Just because I'm not afraid to call it when a kid is being an asshole doesn't mean I hate all of them."

"Just most of 'em, right?"

Desiree looked at her salad. "No, I mean some of them are okay. I like Robbie and Kristen alright."

"Now you do. But you didn't care much for them when you first met Tom, did you now?"

Desiree stiffened. Everybody—Tom, Patty and her mom—thought she didn't like Kristen and Robbie back then. But it wasn't true. It was just that she didn't know how to act around them. When she first met them five years ago, they were just old enough to understand that their parents were splitting up and smart enough to be looking for somebody to blame. She knew that drill well enough because she had watched her mom go through it three times and she remembered how bad it sucked. How bad she hated anybody her mom dated because she knew they were just temporary. They were just as cool and aloof as she'd once been with her mother's beaus and she knew that falling over backwards or kissing their asses wouldn't win them over. In fact, that would probably make it worse. But the fact that she didn't gush over them or go out of her way to win their affection made everybody think that she didn't like them at all. That was the farthest thing from the truth. She sympathized with them, with the silent anger behind Robbie's black eyes and the tender hurt in Kristen's little voice. She could still remember the first day she met them, the awkward silent lunch they'd had at Eat'n Park followed by an excruciatingly long afternoon at the zoo. They'd looked at her like she was as strange to them as the elephants or the laughing hyenas, somebody they couldn't even begin to imagine. And she'd looked at them like they were as dangerous as the wild tigers and lions, ready to attack.

"Everybody says that, but it's not true. I always liked them, it just took a while to adjust. Maybe it's really true about the biological clock, but I just really feel like, I don't know, like maybe I would actually consider having a baby."

Audrey dropped her gyro onto her plate. "Oh no. Don't be scarin' me like that, Des."

"Mom, I'm not joking." This was exactly the reaction she'd been afraid of.

"Really? You're not kiddin'? When did this come over you?"

"I don't know. I've been helping Jen with the wedding and talking to her about the pregnancy and everything and I don't know, I just feel like maybe it's time."

"Time? At thirty-eight? I'd say you're damn well out of time."

"That's not true. Look at all the celebrities who are having babies now—Madonna had her first around my age, and now she has another. I'm not past my prime."

Audrey held up her hand. "Des, those are celebrities. They've got access to the best healthcare in the world and probably have a team of nannies to raise their kids. You think Madonna's changing dirty diapers? Please. You don't wanna be near 50 when your kid is in elementary school. And Tom would be way past 50! Did you talk to him about this?"

"Not yet. It's just something I've been thinking about." She didn't want to say that she was afraid he'd have the same bad reaction.

"Let me say something, as your mother. Your biological clock probably is tickin'. Hell, the alarm's probably blarin', but it'll pass. Don't have a baby just because you're feeling all hormonal. You've seen with Robbie and Kristen how challenging it is to be a parent. I just, now don't take this the wrong way, but I just don't know if you were cut out to be a mom. I'm telling you, once it happens, you just give up a part of yourself. You lose your right to be selfish. I've known you your whole life, Des, and I'm sure you could do that, but I don't think you'd be as happy as you think you'd be."

Don't take this the wrong way? Her mother was going to sit there and tell her she wasn't going to make a good mother and then say don't take this the wrong way? What other way was there to take it?

"That's just plain mean. You're gonna tell me about being selfish? Me? What about you? You think you're so self-sacrificing, moving us around and getting a divorce every time you meet a looker down at the corner bar?" She curled her hands into fists, waiting for a reaction.

"See, this is what I'm sayin', Des. You have a kid and no matter what you do, no matter how good you think you are, you wind up thirty-eight years later listening to them list your faults. Is that really what you want?"

No, that wasn't what she wanted. If anything, that was her worst fear. And right now, she just wanted to leave, to head out and watch the Steelers game and get away from her mom.

"C'mon," said Audrey with a shrug. "I didn't think we were going to be so serious tonight. Can't we get outta here and start getting some drinks, get the party started?"

Even at 55, all her mom wanted to do was get the party started. Some things never changed. She looked outside. It was closer to game time and the sidewalk crowds were thinning. The sun had just about set, casting the city in a ghoulish gray. From her left, she watched a lone man approaching the window. He wore a purple Ravens jersey and a brown hood like the Grim Reaper. His face was painted black, and Desiree couldn't help but stare, accidentally making eye contact. She looked away, but he stopped in front of the window, staring in at her and her mom, pointing to his jersey with a huge smile that revealed a plastic set of fangs.

"Jagoff," said Audrey as he walked away. "I really hope we mop the floor with some Ravens blood tonight."

Desiree nodded, slipping on her fleece jacket. She suddenly felt very cold.

Jen

Jen stepped into her parents' living room. It was dark, like nobody was home. Strange. The plan was to meet here and watch the game together. She'd come straight from work, not even stopping for gas even though she was nearly on empty.

"Mom! Mom? Where are you? The game's about to start."

She turned on the big screen TV and walked toward the kitchen. There was something about the silence that was unusual, and she felt overtaken by her fears. Something had happened to Bobby and they were afraid to tell her. That was the only plausible explanation for why there wasn't anybody around. She swallowed, entering the dining room. No lights were on in there or in the kitchen, and she imagined walking in on her parents, their heads bowed and crying.

Just then her mom appeared in the hallway. "Oh," she said, stopping in her tracks, hand on her heart. "Goodness, Jen, you scared me. I didn't hear you come in."

"Is everything okay?"

"Yeah. It's fine. I just worked late. C'mon, do you want something to drink? Milk? Orange juice? I think I'm going to take a beer."

"I'm fine, but where's Dad? And Dave?" She followed her mom into the kitchen.

"They just called. They worked late too, so they're just gonna watch the first half down at Morgan's. Said we're welcome to come down, but I'm too tired to head out. You?"

Watch the first half at Morgan's? They'd made specific plans to watch the game together.

Her mom pulled a frosty mug out of the freezer and started pouring in a bottle of Yuengling.

"Are you sure? Dave didn't call."

"They knew you'd be here."

"But we were going to watch the game together."

"Well, you still can. Head on down to Morgan's. I won't be offended."

"I don't want to go to Morgan's. In case you haven't noticed, I'm pregnant, and I really don't want to spend all my time in a bar."

"Suit yourself."

Jen bristled. Just what she needed right now—as if it wasn't bad enough having Dave trying to grope her all weekend in spite of the fact that she said she wasn't interested in sex right now, now her mom was going to make her feel like she was uptight?

"I'm not going to Morgan's."

Her mom opened a bag of tortilla chips. "Fine. Then looks like you're watching it with me."

"No, I'm watching it with Dave. I'm calling him, and he's coming here." She followed her mom into the kitchen and pulled up her phone. No answer. She dialed again. No answer.

"He's not answering his phone."

They were in the living room now, and her mom grabbed for the remote, turning up the TV. The roar of screaming fans down at Heinz Field saturated the room as the Ravens took possession of the ball. Usually that sound was exciting, but tonight, it just felt irritating. Dave was supposed to be here.

"Let him be, Jen. They are coming here at halftime. That's good enough. Don't be a pest."

"I'm not being a pest! I just want to watch the game with my fiance."

Her mom glared at her, her mouth fixed into a hard, thin line. "You're having a baby, Jen. It's about time to stop acting like one."

"What's that supposed to mean?"

"That as miserable as you are right now, can't you just shut up for a minute and let me watch the goddamn game in peace? I had to work overtime today to help pay for that fancy wedding of yours and I really don't want to listen to you complaining all night, okay?"

Jen turned her head, looking away out the front window. All along the street, houses were dark save for a couple of windows. She imagined the whole neighborhood huddled around their TVs: parents and kids, husbands and wives, everybody watching the game like a solid family unit. And here she sat with her mom, unmarried and pregnant, while Dave sat at some bar less than 2 miles away. She rested her hand on her stomach, trying to forget about this moment and imagine the baby. Trying to imagine it as a real honest–to-god little person. She couldn't see it, though, just like when she was a little girl and she used to have dreams about marrying a faceless groom. She couldn't see its face. And that was okay, she didn't need to see who it was going to look like or if she should be stocking up on pink or blue baby items. She wanted it to be a surprise, the anticipation of the unknown as tantalizing as a football game, not quite knowing how things would turn out. Pressing her hand on her lower abdomen, she wished that she could feel something more than a layer of fat. But so far she hadn't felt a bit of stir. Still. She knew it was there. And just knowing made everything feel a little better.

Megan

Of course she was the only who dressed up. Not that it mattered. Not like dressing up like a zombie cheerleader was even too far off from the actual outfit she'd probably have worn. And sure, Mike and Emily had given her a couple of looks like they just couldn't believe her, but who the hell really cared? It was Halloween. The Ravens were in town and they were at a Monday Night Football party.

Her friend Ryan didn't seem to mind that she'd mistaken his invitation as an excuse to dress up.

"Why don't you sit on my lap?" he said when she first walked in. And now, near the end of the game, he still sat beside her, tickling the exposed flesh on her thighs and poking his fingers in the slits on her black shirt.

"Behave," she said, winking at him and casting a disapproving glance at Emily, who sat tucked in Mike's arms. They'd been avoiding each other since their fight on Friday morning about bus fare. Turns out she'd left her wallet in her friend's car and she'd gotten it back on Saturday with money to spare. Not that Emily needed to know that.

Looking back at Ryan, she tickled his ear. He swatted her arm away, but she could tell by the look on his face that he liked it. He was an old friend from high school who lived a couple blocks down from her on South Graham. She hadn't seen him in ages until they ran into each other shopping in the Strip District back in June. Since then, they'd hung around quite often. And in the small world that is Pittsburgh, it turned out that Ryan's roommate worked with Mike. But even Emily couldn't spoil her good time. She'd been flirting with Ryan for years now, and last month he'd finally dumped his flat-headed anorexic girlfriend.

Everything was going well except for the game. The Ravens had answered each Steelers score with one of their own and even after a Heath Miller touchdown opening up the 3rd quarter, she felt tense. Baltimore was 2-and-4; a game with them wasn't supposed to be so close. So she was especially pissed when her mom interrupted it with a call. Her mom always called at the worst possible times. Usually she'd just ignore it, but tonight she actually needed to take it.

"Hey," she said, walking onto the front porch of Ryan's building, a space as huge as the old Victorian-style house where he lived. This wasn't a conversation anybody needed to hear. She went to the farthest corner, sidestepping a large pile of faded Yellow Pages stuck with dried leaves and sticks.

"What's going on?" Her mom sounded exhausted and annoyed. Nothing new about that.

"What's going on? How about Steelers versus Ravens? Is Dad really not there watching the game?"

"Oh, that. Right. No, I'm in DC today. I've been working all day and I've been thinking about your little request."

Megan caught her breath. *Your little request.* As if she was an annoying five-year old asking to ride her bike after dinner. Admittedly, asking for two months rent at this point in her life was annoying, but she didn't have any other choice. If she didn't pay Emily by the end of the week, Emily might throw her out. And if that happened, it was either back to Mom and Dad's, on the floor at some rando's house or asking for yet another loan to pay for a security deposit and rent somewhere else.

"So, what were you thinking?"

"I'm thinking, no. Absolutely not. We can't keep bailing you out, Megan. You're twenty-eight. If you aren't paying your rent, you're going to have to deal with the consequences."

"So is this what you think, or what dad thinks?"

"Your father and I are on the same page with this, Megan. I'm very serious. We are not going to bail you out."

"But Mom, I'm going to pay you back. I'm getting a paycheck now, not just tips, and once I get the check, it's all yours, but I don't get paid until next week and she wants her money this week."

"Megan, it's the same old song and dance every time, and you never pay us back."

"That's because you don't need the money like I do. I am your only child; it's your job to take care of me. What, you need to save some money so you can remodel the bathroom for the seventeenth time?"

"Maybe I do. Do you really think that my parents or your dad's parents were bailing us out every time we got into financial trouble when we were your age?"

"That's totally different and you know it. You were married and had me at my age. I'm all alone."

"You're right. I was married and had a child at your age. I was an adult."

Megan clicked off the phone and threw it across the porch. It ricocheted off the arm of a green plastic chair and into a corner on the opposite side. She stomped toward it, stewing. What did her mom know about acting like an adult? Her mom grew up wanting to be a nurse and a mother, and she'd achieved both those goals by 23. She had no comprehension of living in a world where dreams didn't work out quite the way you'd planned or where there were no dreams at all. For a long time after she'd dropped out of Pitt, she'd imagined herself becoming an artist. She loved to paint, but except for doing the first-draft sketches of her tattoos, she'd hadn't done too much drawing in the past few years. Still, in the back of her mind, she always felt like it was an option, that someday she'd get around to it and maybe, just maybe, support herself doing gallery shows or painting beads. But right now, she had other things on her mind. Like making sure she had money for the weekend.

"Now that didn't look very smart, did it?"

Megan spun around. Kevin. Of course. Perfect. She knew he lived here, too, but was hoping there wouldn't be a run-in since Emily had mentioned he always worked late. If it weren't for him, she might not even be in this mess. "I don't need your comments right now."

She popped her phone back together. It wouldn't quite snap into place, but the screen was lit up like it still worked. Kevin pushed his hands toward her phone. "Need help with that?"

She snatched it away. "I don't need your help. It's your big mouth that got me here in the first place."

Kevin backed up, his mouth open with complete surprise. He wore gray suit pants and his blue shirt was unbuttoned enough to reveal a tuft of brown hair sticking out of his undershirt. "Wow. You really lost me on that one."

"I was just fighting with my mom. And the reason I'm fighting with her is because Emily is making me pay two months rent and she wants it by Friday. Apparently some dudes named Mike and Kevin got into her head and made her think I'm some pathetic mooch who's taking advantage of her."

"Oh."

"So you're not going to deny it?"

"There's nothing to deny. I was present when a conversation occurred about the rent situation at your apartment. But I don't recall anybody being called a pathetic mooch."

Megan stood up straight, pulling down her skirt. She noticed Kevin looking at her long legs and then looking away really fast. That glance, almost imperceptible, made her feel more confident about the direction of this conversation.

"Look, I know you don't care, but I had some issues the past couple of months and just didn't have it. Emily said she was okay with it." Emily had never exactly said that she was okay with it, but that was none of Kevin's business.

Shrugging, he reached in his pocket and pulled out his keys.

She cleared her throat. "So aren't you going to ask for the score?"

"Excuse me?"

"The score? You know, of the football game?"

"I think I can wait until I get into my apartment. Besides, I'm more of a baseball man."

"Baseball!" She almost laughed. The Pittsburgh Pirates hadn't had a winning season since she was in junior high, and while going to those games was still fun she didn't know too many people who put baseball ahead of football. The Penguins maybe, but the Pirates? She wanted them to win, too, but diehard Pirates fans were either just assholes with a victim complex who liked to bitch and moan about how all of the others sports fans in town didn't give respect them or naïve fools still stuck in some other world back when the Pirates were contenders.

"So what, you're still stuck on those glory days back in ninety-two?"

"Something like that." Kevin turned away from her now, concentrating on opening his mailbox. She turned toward the leaf-covered street; the trick-or-treaters were long gone but the air had just turned the sinister kind of cold where it seemed truly possible that goblins and demons might be afoot. She moved toward him, angling for a shield from the wind. He darted sideways, dropping a piece of mail. They reached for it at the same time and when their hands touched, he dropped the envelope. She almost wanted to laugh. The last time she'd seen him, he'd seemed all too comfortable lording it over her, but without his tie and jacket and business associate, he seemed like frightened prey.

"Can you call my phone?"

"Huh?"

"My phone," she said, waving it in front of his face. "I want to make sure it's not broken."

He nodded. She called out her number. He dialed. It rang. She hung up.

"Oh, well, looks like it works. Guess we better get in there to watch that game, now. You coming over to Ryan's?"

Opening the door, he stopped at the first door. "I had a long day. I think I'll be reading about this one in the paper tomorrow."

"So what, you're, like, not from here or something?"

"I'm from Latrobe."

"Oh. Yeah. Rolling Rock Beer, huh?"

"You would know a town by its brewery."

"And you would be the only person in Western Pennsylvania not watching the Steelers game."

"I think that might be an exaggeration."

She nodded toward the number on his apartment door. "Number 1, huh?"

"Do you know how bad it sucks moving furniture up stairs? I did that in undergrad. I'm too smart for that now."

"And if you're really smart, you won't be talking about me behind my back anymore."

"Don't give me anything to talk about."

"Touche." She winked at him, starting up the stairs.

On the third step, she turned around. "Oh, and Kevin, just because you have my digits, don't be calling me all the time."

"I already deleted it," he said, closing the door.

Megan frowned. What a condescending douche.

Patty

Eating lunch at her desk, Patty couldn't decide what was more acute—her exhaustion or her gnawing sense of paranoia. The exhaustion was easily accounted for: last night's game was decided by a field goal with about a minute and a half left in the fourth quarter, at which point it was close to midnight. By the time she'd felt comfortable enough that the Ravens weren't going to answer with a score and headed upstairs to package a pair of black lace boy shorts for tight end Heath Miller, it was nearly one in the morning. From her vantage point in the middle of Accounts Payable, it was apparent that nearly everybody in her office was suffering from the same fatigue.

The paranoia was harder to dismiss. She turned her eyes from her co-worker Mark's empty desk and back to the *Post-Gazette's* sports page. She didn't like to use the internet much at work. Sports was a neutral topic. Other sites, like ones that offered parenting advice or even the dating sites where she sometimes lurked just to see who was out there, felt too incriminating.

She looked over her monitor as Mark came back to his desk from lunch. He ate in their company cafeteria every day and although he'd given up on Patty joining him there, he always came up talking about the lunchroom buzz as if she was actually interested. The office politics and cliques down there made her uneasy, and she didn't want any of her co-workers' silent judgments on how much food she picked from the buffet.

"So," said Mark, removing his jacket and hanging it by his desk. "The lunchroom was abuzz about the game. That one was a real squeaker. You stay up for the whole thing?"

Patty nodded. Of course she stayed up for the whole thing.

"You watch it at home or out somewhere?"

"Home." Patty snapped her Tupperware soup bowl shut and clicked her mouse a couple of times as if she was returning to work. Mark usually didn't pry into her personal life. Nobody did except the receptionist, Joni, who still insisted that Patty join her for singles night at the Green Tree Holiday Inn. It was called

"Second Time Around" and held every first Friday of the month. Politely, she always declined. It wasn't like Mark to dig into details like this. But perhaps this was just another example of her paranoia.

She watched as Mark adjusted his pink paisley tie and pulled out a stack of expense reports and receipts. Although she half-expected some sort of disapproving look or questioning glare, his face looked consumed with the dull tedium of work. She turned back to her computer screen and blinked. Her desk was stacked with similar piles of expense reports, receipts, balance sheets, and empty coffee mugs. *#1 Mom* said a black one with red lettering. When the kids were little they'd given her one just like it, but that was long ago broken, and she'd bought this one for herself at a clearance sale after Mother's Day. She blinked, hoping she could rid herself of this nagging feeling as easily as Kristen could brush off any request to do chores. Still, it lingered, like something bad was about to happen. It was probably just PMS. But this morning, she hadn't had time to drop off her package to Heath Miller and knowing that it was inside her bag with her laptop, only separated from her co-workers' eyes by a thin piece of black leather, made her even more nervous. And then there was home. Robbie had been acting really strange. For the past week, he was acting way too compliant. He sat through family dinner night without starting a fight. When she asked him to do chores, he did them without a word, and he actually called his dad a few times without prompting. Although she'd once wanted him to behave this way, now it just felt suspicious. It reminded her of how Tom acted shortly before she'd found out that he was flirting with Desiree. He'd suddenly become engaged in their family—helping out with the kid's homework, tending to the lawn, and even asking her about her day. She'd thought that the nagging feelings of doubt he'd been voicing about their relationship were subsiding. It had blindsided her when she found out about Desiree.

Looking over at Mark, she bit her lip. He cocked his head, concentrating on his computer. He had bright blue eyes and a helpful smile. He was openly gay, but in a conservative office like theirs, even open was halfway shut. That's why she liked Mark so much. They had a mutual understanding that what happened after work didn't enter the office.

She thought of what had Kristen said a few weeks ago about the kids at school calling Robbie a fag. Suddenly, even though she knew he was at school, she wanted to talk to him. She wanted to hear his voice. If she could just talk to Robbie for a minute, she knew she'd feel better.

Shaking, she dialed his number, expecting his voicemail. He answered on the second ring.

"Mom?"

"Robbie? What are you doing?"

"You called me."

"I know. I just wanted to, um, see if you kids could stop at the store to get some milk on the way home."

"Milk? We have milk."

"We need more. I want to make a casserole tonight." Crap. That was a dumb lie. Now she'd have to make a casserole tonight. But hearing his voice alleviated some of her tension, although the background noise sounded strange for high school. She swore she heard cars.

"Robbie, where are you? It sounds like you're in traffic."

"What? No, I don't know what you mean. It's just in-between classes, a lot of background noise."

"Oh. Well, have a good afternoon. And get that milk."

"Sure, Mom, will do." He hung up without saying goodbye. Before Patty could put the phone down, she saw Joni coming toward her. She held the phone tight to her ear, the dial tone droning as Joni passed.

They made eye contact and Patty winked as if she was still on the phone. "I love you too, Robbie."

Angela

"Dude, what the hell was that all about?" Angela felt ready to puke. Robbie's mom had just called and asked where he was. They were on East Carson Street, where they always were now on the days when they had gym class.

Robbie shook his head, then stuck his hands into his tight jean pockets. "Do you think she knows we're skipping?"

"God, I hope not. But if she busts us on skipping, then we can call her out on her panty-sending." She didn't even have to look at him to know he was rolling his eyes. "Oh come on, you never thought of using that little knowledge for blackmail? Seriously?"

"I still don't want to talk about that."

Even though it was still some stupid sports superstition, the idea of Patty sending panties to football players was too epic not to talk about. And ever since she'd mailed her applications to three schools out west and completely ignored the deadlines for Pitt, she definitely wanted to keep the conversation off anything to do with her. Nobody needed to know anything about her plans until they were definite.

"I'm sorry, Robbie, I just can't help it. It's just so juicy. I mean, your mom has this secret life. Aren't you interested in that?"

Angela darted, trying to avoid a circle of khaki-clad girls standing outside a restaurant, but the coeds stopped them anyway.

"Free coupons for The Locker Room," a blonde girl chirped, thrusting a handful of coupons into their hands.

They kept walking. "What's The Locker Room?"

"I don't know, some restaurant Hines Ward is opening."

"Oh dear, that's just what we need. Mediocre food backed by a sports celebrity. Didn't anybody learn their lesson from Britney Spears' restaurant?"

Robbie shook his head. "For somebody who wears so much black, you sure know a lot about celebrity gossip."

Angela laughed. "And for somebody who wears eyeliner, you know way too much about football."

"It's a Pittsburgh thing," he said. "You wouldn't understand."

"Hardy har har," she said, sticking out her tongue.

"Anyways, I think my mom wants to go to this place. She mentioned it one time."

"Oh god, that's, like, too perfect. She'd like totally leave some underwear there or something. Let's give her the coupons."

Robbie shook his head. "First of all, ew. And second, no, because she never leaves the house unless it's to get groceries or go to work."

There was something hard in Robbie's voice. Time to change the subject.

"Speaking of weird things that parents do, how about Dom totally called into the 'DVE radio show on the way home from the game last night?"

Around Pittsburgh, sports fans began debating the highs and lows of the game before the final buzzer sounded, and many of them did it on public forums like radio or TV talk shows. It was equal parts appalling and amusing. Her dad listened to and watched these kinds of programs with the same devotion that she reserved for The Smiths or The Cure. Once when she was stuck watching one of those shows with her dad, they heard a toilet flush in the background of the call as somebody spoke to a stone-faced newscaster about the merits of a playoff system for college football. Her and her dad still talked about how funny that was.

Robbie laughed. "That's awesome. Did you hear it?"

"No, my mom told me. Even she was embarrassed. She said he was bitchin' about special teams or something and he dropped the f-bomb and they dropped his call. Typical, huh?"

"You seriously waited this long to tell me that? Dom Wyckoff gets kicked off a radio show. I feel like that's front page news."

Angela shrugged. It was funny that her dad got censored on local radio, but the fact that he was calling into a radio show at all was totally annoying. He was interested enough in football to play armchair quarterback all week, but since she'd started her senior year, he hadn't once asked her how school was going or what she was planning for college. It wasn't like she wanted to sit down with him and have a heart to heart like some ABC Family movie, but it would be nice if he'd at least pretend to be interested in something other than football.

Robbie's laugh pulled her back into the moment. "Why haven't we ever pranked one of those shows? We should so call from the bathroom and flush the toilet while we're talking."

"That's been done. It would be funnier if we called and said we were from the Locker Room and said some crap about the first hundred people to show up would get a free jersey or something."

Robbie held the door open for her at The Exchange. "That's kind of evil. But if we did that, I'd definitely want to be camped out here so we could do some mullet-counting."

"Ha! That might beat the Ribs Fest." There were so many mullets in Pittsburgh that, once at the Ribs Festival that Dom and Nancy always dragged them to, they had counted 67 mullets. Granted, femullets counted twice, but it was still a pretty astronomical number for one evening.

Inside the store, they parted ways, Robbie heading toward the used video games and Angela toward the vinyl. They were having the perfect afternoon, but Patty's call was totally weird. She didn't know what, but something was definitely up.

Week 9: Steelers vs. Green Bay Packers
(W 20-10)

Shannon

Stuck. Again. Shannon tapped on the steering wheel and flipped through the radio stations: Static, static, nineties song, classic rock, country, country, and country. She popped in a CD and sighed, looking out the window of her car. Outside, it was cold but sunny, a clear bright day. From where she sat now on the North Side, the shining concave roof of the Convention Center and a dense network of yellow bridges arching over the muddy Allegheny dominated the view.

There were moments, driving, when she saw the city glittering in the midday sun like this and its sheer beauty caught her breath. *This is where I live. This is where I belong.* But sometimes, she imagined picking up and leaving, just getting in her car with a suitcase and driving until she was far enough away that she could start over. She imagined living silently among people, maybe in a small desert town. She'd dye her hair blonde and get a waitressing job at a greasy spoon diner. If people asked her, she'd spin stories about what she'd left behind—a dead lover, maybe, or a family in crisis that she could no longer help.

But even if she ever left, it wouldn't be because she didn't like Pittsburgh. It would be because she was tired of being lonely, and lately, tired of thinking so much about Jack.

The phone rang, startling her. It was Darla. Of course. Answering it, she felt a twinge of guilt. It was almost like Darla had a sixth sense about when she was thinking about Jack.

"Hey, girlie girl, what ya doin'?"

"Sitting in traffic. What am I always doing?"

"I just wanted to say that I did get the invite to Jen's wedding. So Larry was really serious that Jack and I can come."

"Yeah, I guess he was." Shannon swallowed, disappointed. The only reason she'd given Darla's address to Larry was because she thought he was bluffing about inviting her.

"You know it's on a Sunday, right? The day of the Ravens game. That's kind of weird—don't you think?"

"Mm, it's at night. I guess this late in the game, you have to take what you can get."

"Ha, well you can bet that Jack will never let me have my wedding on a Steelers' game day. He takes that stuff about as seriously as you do."

Shannon braced herself. *My wedding.* The very words gave her a headache. She knew that Darla wanted to get married, but had never heard Jack's opinion on the matter. This sounded like some kind of a confirmation that marriage was something in the works.

Darla cleared her throat. "You know I'm bad at RSVP stuff, so if you could just tell Larry that would be great."

"Tell Larry what?"

"That we're going to the wedding, dummy."

"Oh yeah. The wedding. Okay, I'll tell him."

"Okey-dokey. Well, I gotta go now, sis, I'm pulling into some wicked traffic on Centre Avenue." As always, Darla hung up before Shannon had a chance to reply.

Dropping her phone onto the seat, she sighed: another long day, another traffic jam, and another wedding without a date. The car in front of her moved and she followed it closely, merging onto Route 28. At this point, traffic was always backed up. On one side of the road, the old Heinz plant loomed. Its abandoned smokestacks and huge buildings were a reminder of Pittsburgh's industrial days but had recently been converted to expensive loft apartments for trust-fund hipsters and yuppies. On the other side of the road, Penn Brewery rose like a mighty brick fortress, and on the hillside beyond it, the modest homes of Troy Hill dotted the landscape, most of them still stained and ashen from those very same years of industrial prime.

Darla and Jack were discussing marriage? There was exactly no reason right now why she shouldn't just pick up and leave. She had no intention of ending up like those forgotten homes on the hill.

Megan

It was Friday night, and the crowd at Jack's was at maximum capacity, just the way she liked it. Squeezed in between a chunky sorority girl with sleek brown hair and a grizzled man with a faded Harley-Davidson shirt and long gray beard, Megan felt right at home. She wiggled a little closer to the bar, pulling her white tank top dangerously low and winking at the bartender. He came to her, smiling, and she grinned, ignoring the disgusted stare of the sorority girl who had been standing there first. After he gave her a Jack and Coke, she held it above her head, slipping through the sweaty crowd and into the side of the bar where a group of her co-workers sat by the window, commenting on pedestrians' clothes and celebrating Katie Maloney's 23rd birthday. Katie and her crew rarely went out and didn't know how to have a good time when they did, but when they had invited her after work, she decided to come along for the ride. She knew enough people in the city that even if she started the night with nerds, she'd eventually find another group she liked better.

"What kind of a shot do you want to do, Birthday Girl?"

Katie looked at her watch. "Oh, no. I have to drive back to Plum tonight. I can't be drinking like that."

Megan rolled her eyes. "It's only nine-thirty. You can stand a shot. You look like a Kamikaze girl. I'm buying. No arguments!" She lifted her Jack and Coke, drank it in three gulps, and slammed it onto the table. "Refill! Pitcher of kamikazes, coming right up."

For the second time in ten minutes, she stood at the bar. The bartender caught her eye and smiled. He was pretty cute, although he looked a little too young. She didn't mind young, but there was something babyish about his face that irritated her.

"Another Jack and Coke and can I get a shaker of Kamikazes? Enough for five?"

He nodded and she smiled, imagining those boring girls' faces when she came back with the shots.

She felt a warm hand on her waist.

"Hey, stranger," said a familiar voice. Interested, she turned around. Seeing who it was, she groaned. Kevin.

"Dude. Are you stalking me or are we stuck in the plot of some badly written romantic comedy?"

"Badly written rom-com," he said. "But geez, Megan, do you always have to act so excited to see me?"

Wearing a blue and white plaid button down shirt and jeans, he looked like the total prep that he was. If she was destined to keep running into somebody again and again, why couldn't it be a muscular tattooed bodyguard or somebody of equally strong stature? She'd heard that Ben Roethlisberger hung out at Jack's during the week, but she always missed him when she was out. But Kevin? This guy was always around.

"I'm good with Emily now."

"None of my business, but that's good. Paid up your dues, I guess?"

She wrinkled her nose. "You could say that. We're good though, that's all you need to know."

Over the chorus of Christina Aguilera's "Dirrty," she could barely hear herself talk and she wasn't about to go into detail about the payment plan she'd brokered with Emily: $500 this check and the rest at the end of the month. Still, she felt better telling him that things were okay. Grinding her hips in rhythm with the music, she accidentally grazed him, noting his uncomfortable expression as he moved away. Prude.

"That's good," he said. "I'm glad things are okay." He scanned the bartenders, surveying the taps with an expression of irritation. "So is this your hangout?"

"The world is my hangout. What, you never been here before?"

"Not since I was 21. Hasn't changed a bit. You think they could get some better beer on tap. Evolve or die, right?"

Better beer. So Kevin was one of those people hell bent on showing how sophisticated and classy he and his city were in any given situation. Craft beer and heirloom tomatoes have their place, but why was it that people who liked that sort of thing had to look down their nose on everything else? Not every grocery store could be Whole Foods, and not every bar had to be super trendy or brew their own beer. There was nothing wrong with art galleries or trendy pastry studios, but there was something wrong with people who wanted the new and hip to totally erase the past.

"You can't change Jack's. That's not right."

"You can change anything."

"That doesn't mean you have to," she said, feeling pissed. When the bartender delivered her drinks, she threw her money on the bar and practically ran away, barely mumbling a good-bye to Kevin. The place was getting more packed by the second and the whiskey was really starting to hit her. The neon lights above the bar felt piercing, and her body temperature was rising. She wanted to take her shirt off. Not that her tank top was much to begin with, but any form of clothes felt suffocating once she started drinking.

Balancing the glasses and cups in her hands, she pushed through the narrow hall between the bars when another hand landed on her waist, this one cold against her skin. She turned around to swat somebody off, then laughed when she saw it was Ryan.

"Hey, just the person I wanted to see. You up for the game on Sunday night? Got an extra ticket. It's $80. You good for it?"

Megan leaned into his chest, thinking. Good for it? She barely had enough for food after she paid Emily the $500. But tickets to the game? With Ryan? She had to do it. This was the Steelers versus the Browns. Not a game you wanted to watch on TV. The kind where you needed to be there, needed to stand there and scream as loud as you could.

"Of course I'm good for it!" Ryan slapped her five, pointing to his phone. "I'll call you with details later. It's gonna rock."

"I gotta get back to my friends."

"What?"

The music turned from Christina Aguilera to Molly Hatchet without anyone in the bar batting an eye, an event that Megan was pretty sure only happened in Pittsburgh.

"My friends!" she screamed. "Gotta get back! You gonna be here?" She gestured toward her drinks.

"Yeah, I'll be out front. Come over when you're done."

"I will." Pushing through the crowd, she faked a smile while she calculated where the money from this check was going. Surely Emily would understand if she could only give her $420 this time. It was only $80 less. She could work a wedding and make that in one night. Sure, it would extend her payment plan a little, but going to the game would be worth it.

Patty pulled a steaming pan of eggplant parmesan out of the oven and screamed for Robbie.

"Robbie! Dinner's ready. You don't have to eat it down here, but get it while it's hot."

Carefully, she transferred it to the counter and pulled out plates. Kristen was staying at her friend Vanessa's house for the night—they were supposed to see a movie, then spend Sunday morning working on an upcoming group project for their English class. Even though she'd checked Kristen's overnight bag to make sure her schoolbooks were there, she had a feeling that their night out had less to do with movies and more to do with Jeff. She thought about calling Vanessa's mom, Anna, just to check up on things, but Anna was a few years younger than her and had three other kids besides Vanessa to worry about—Anna would surely think she was just being overprotective.

"Robbie! Get down here."

Again, no reply. After spending the entire afternoon with Angela, he'd been in his room for the past three or so hours. She screamed a third time. No reply. Patty looked at the meal and sighed. She didn't want to eat alone. Even if Robbie only came down long enough to eat at least it would be human contact. Climbing the stairs, she raised her voice.

"Robbie, I'm coming to your room. I asked you to come down for dinner. Don't make me break down the door."

She knocked on his door.

"Robbie!"

"I'm not hungry. I'll come down later."

"You've been hiding in there all night. Come down and humor me for about twenty minutes."

"I'm not feeling real good. I want to be in bed."

"What's wrong? Are you coming down with something? Let me come in and check on you."

Anytime one of the kids said something about being sick, her mind always went directly to the darkest place—something was seriously wrong: what if he had a some kind of terminal disease? She needed to see him. She pounded her fists on his door.

"Robbie. Open this door. Right. Now."

From inside, she heard him moving, and this time when he spoke, his voice sounded closer, like he was standing right beside the door.

"Mom, I'll open the door. But you have to promise me that you won't freak out."

"I won't freak out, I've seen your messy room before."

"No, Mom. You have to promise. "

"Okay, okay, I promise. I won't freak out." She held her breath as the door slowly opened. Robbie stood there looking down, his hair a flaming shade of magenta.

Patty gasped, telling herself not to freak out. It was only hair dye. It could be changed. But why was he dying his hair pink at all? Why had he, for one second, thought that was a good idea? If he was already such a target, wouldn't this make it worse? And then for a fleeting moment, she actually thought that maybe he brought some of the teasing on himself. Immediately, she felt guilty. How could she think something like that about her own son?

"Come on, Mom. Say something. I know you're mad. It was Angela's idea. We can dye over it. I was just afraid to do it for a few days so it doesn't fall out or something."

Of course it was Angela's idea. Patty took a deep breath.

"Robbie, I think you need to see your dad tomorrow."

Robbie shook his head, eyes wide. "Oh no. I'm not going to see dad like this. I mean, he's probably traveling anyways. Or going to the game with Des. I'll call him and go over next week, but not tomorrow."

"No, Robbie. I think you need to see him now. I'm going to call him."

She turned around, walking down the stairs and feeling somewhat unsure about what she was doing. She had promised not to freak out, but she hadn't expected pink hair. And she didn't even know how to deal with it or if there was even anything that needed to be dealt with. He was a teenager. Teenagers did stupid things all the time. If Kristen did the same thing, she wouldn't bat an eyelash, but with Robbie it seemed like doing this had to be some kind of cry for attention. Maybe even help. And to be honest, it just made her tired. She was worn out from dealing with this kind of stuff day in and day out. Living alone with two teenagers was enough to drive anybody crazy. So let Tom deal with this one. He deserved it. She was pretty sure the only sleepless nights he spent were ones worrying about some stupid work project and how he was going to keep Desiree firmly ensconced in her materialistic lifestyle. No, she was sure he'd never laid awake at night worrying about how a bunch of dim-witted high school kids were emotionally abusing their sensitive son. Behind her, Robbie protested all the way into the kitchen, but shut up as soon as she picked up the phone.

Tom answered on the first ring.

"Hi, it's me," Patty said, turning away from Robbie. "Can you take Robbie to the game tomorrow night?"

On the other end, she heard Tom sigh. "Is something wrong? You sound upset."

"No, everything's fine. I just really think that Robbie needs to spend some time with you. I mean, how long has it been, Tom? August?"

"That's only because I'm away all the time for work and every time I do ask the kids to come over, they always have plans. Why don't I come over during the day and see him? The game is at 8:15. That's late on a school night."

"He's seventeen; I think he can handle it. And he's free all day tomorrow so if you want to spend the day with him, you can do that too. Here he is, you can make your plans."

She handed the phone to Robbie, smiling. He glared at her with narrowed eyes, shaking his head but accepting the phone.

"Hi. Yeah. You don't have to take me to the game."

He paused while Tom talked.

"You do? No, Dad. I know you're busy. You probably want to take Des. It's fine."

Patty half-listened, pleased with herself. Tom got to see the kids on all the happy occasions—let him deal with this one and see what it was really like.

"They seemed happy today," he always said, bringing them back from a day at the mall with him and Desiree—Robbie with a bag full of video games and Kristen with enough clothes and jewelry to last her a school year.

Right, she always thought, of course they acted happy as long as Tom's credit card was smoking. Let him deal with how happy they were going to school every morning or how joyful they were doing homework every night. Those were the moments that defined parenthood, not afternoon shopping trips and dinners at trendy restaurants in Shadyside.

Robbie hung up the phone. "So Dad's coming to pick me up at three tomorrow."

"He better."

"What's that supposed to mean?"

"That I just asked him to take you to the game, so he better be taking you to the game."

"Why are you acting like such a jerk?"

"I'm not acting like a jerk. I just got you tickets to a Steelers game, so don't be crying on my shoulder at the moment."

"You sound jealous, Mom."

"Jealous of what?"

"That I get to the game and you don't. That Dad invited me."

"Robbie, your dad didn't just call you up and invite you to the game. I had to tell him to do it, and now you're acting like he's some kind of a saint?"

"I'm not acting like he's anything. But he's certainly better than you right now."

Patty winced, handing him a full plate. "Better than me? Why, did Dad make you dinner tonight? Or drive you to Angela's this afternoon? Or help you with your Social Studies assignment? All he does is buy you stuff, but I guess that's all it takes. I guess next time I want you and Kristen to act like you like me, I need to drop a few hundred on video games and clothes, right?"

Robbie crossed his arms, pushing the plate away. "Oh yeah, that's right Mom. I forgot, you ARE some kind of a saint. Oh, everybody bow down to St. Patty, she cooked dinner tonight!"

"Don't you DARE talk to me like that! I'm your mother!"

Robbie's mouth twisted into a defiant sneer, the kind of look she expected from Kristen when she told her to get off the phone.

"You're such a freak!" he screamed.

Without even thinking, as instinctively as she might blink, Patty slapped him across the face. After she hit him, she left her hand in the air, stunned.

"I'm sorry, Robbie. I'm sorry. I shouldn't have done that. I'm so sorry." Biting her lip, she tried not to cry. She had never slapped either one of the kids. But what he had said: *You're such a freak!* It was like he truly hated her.

"Robbie, I'm sorry." She stepped forward to hug him, but he jerked away from her, running up the stairs.

The air hung heavy and stale in the kitchen. For a moment, she stood there, staring at the pan of cold pasta. Then, trance-like, she scraped the full plates back into the pan and covered it with foil, shoving it in the fridge.

Desiree

She had every intention of telling him about her recent thoughts on kids when they were interrupted by Patty. She didn't call very often, at least not as often as some nightmare ex-wives who Desiree had heard about, but she had a knack for calling at exactly the wrong time—in the middle of sex, the tail end of a fight, or just when a movie they were watching was starting to get good. Sometimes, it took all her self-control not to explode. Sure, she knew up front that he had this other family, but nothing, not even her experience with her mom's ex-husbands, had prepared her for exactly how much his other family would affect every single second of theirs.

One phone call from Patty could entirely derail the tone of an evening. And tonight was no exception. When Tom hung up the phone, he was clearly irritated. She'd been watching a *What Not to Wear* marathon on TLC and he abruptly changed the channel to college football.

"Hey! What's that all about?"

"You've been hogging the TV for half the day and I'm sick of watching this!"

"You just came in here 15 minutes ago!"

"And that was 15 minutes too long."

"Well, I'm still watching!" She grabbed for the remote, but he dodged her, moving to another chair. About five minutes ago, she was imagining that once this episode ended and she saw the transformation of Leah from Fargo, she'd turn off the TV, cuddle up to Tom, and raise the possibility of having a baby. Now, he seemed so annoyed, she barely wanted to be in the same room with him.

"Robbie's gonna go to the game with me tomorrow."

"What?!"

"Yeah, that was Patty and she pretty much just insisted that I take Robbie to the game. I really couldn't say no."

He could have very easily said no: *No, I have plans with my wife.* It was that simple.

"You can always say no. There's always a choice."

"Des, I can't say no to Robbie."

"Did Robbie ask you or did Patty? I mean, Robbie turns us down every time we try to hang out with him, and now, all of a sudden, he wants to go to a Steelers game? Sounds fishy."

"Fishy?"

"Yeah, like Patty wants Robbie to go the game for some reason. She's just mad because we never give her the tickets." In the early proceedings of their divorce, Patty had tried to fight for the rights to the Steelers tickets, but Desiree had fought right back, telling Tom that if Patty got full custody of the kids, the house, and a huge chunk of change in child support, it was only fair that he get something.

Tom shook his head. "Patty asked and then put Robbie on the phone. He was clearly standing there the whole time, so what could I do? She said I hadn't seen the kids since August. That has to be a lie."

"We try to see them all the time! I don't know why you let her speak to you like that! Give me that phone. I'll call her and give her an earful."

"Des, just drop it. It's done. I'm taking Robbie to the game. It's not the worst thing that's ever happened and besides it's going to be cold tomorrow night, and I know you hate going when it's cold."

"Let it drop? I don't want to let it drop." Her patience was wearing thin. She'd planned this night to go so differently and Patty had ruined everything.

"Then what do you want to do?"

"I want you to call Patty and stand up to her. Tell her that you'll take Robbie to a game on your terms, not hers."

Tom shook his head, turning up the TV volume. "C'mon, Des, you'll survive. It's just a game. Robbie is my son."

Desiree stood up. It took all her might not to scream until her throat bled. My son. He said it so condescending, like she could never possibly understand.

"You know what, Tom? I wanted to talk to you tonight about something. I've been thinking lately that I want to have a baby. But I can see now that it's a bad idea. A really bad idea. You're too stuck on your other ones to care at all about what I want."

She huffed away, grabbing her laptop. It was time to do some online shopping.

"A baby?" Tom sounded completely blindsided. "What? You can't just say something like that and walk away. Come back here so we can talk—"

But she was already upstairs. As much as Tom said he wanted to talk about it, she couldn't do it. The moment, maybe even her desire, had vanished. Who was she kidding, anyways? She'd missed her chance to have a family. Instead of getting to build one, like everybody else did, she'd married into one. She slammed the door to their office shut and turned on the computer. The top stories on the Post-Gazette were about Charlie Batch, the backup quarterback who had taken over for Big Ben after he was injured a few weeks ago. Batch hadn't seen a lot of playing time over the past few years, and they'd really only won last week's game against Green Bay on the strength of their running game. She felt the same anxiety about Batch starting that most Steeler fans did, but she also wondered what it must feel like to be the backup, only getting to play if Roethlisberger couldn't. The NFL paycheck surely wouldn't hurt, but she couldn't help thinking of how often she felt like the second best to Patty. She logged onto Neiman Marcus and browsed through gold jewelry. After a minute, she heard Tom's heavy breath on the other side of the door. He knocked lightly.

"Desiree, open up. Don't be like this. I love you. Can't we talk?"

I love you. He loves me, she told herself. He really does love me. If he didn't, he wouldn't be here, he'd be two bridges and a tunnel away in the house with Patty and his kids. He loved her. He really did. But right now, the way she felt, it wasn't nearly enough.

141

Week 10: Steelers vs. Cleveland Browns
(W 34-21)

Jen

On the ratty couch at their apartment, Jen cuddled against Dave's leg. Their apartment. She was still getting used to the sound of it: their apartment, their wedding, their baby. As much as she accused Dave of being the one who couldn't use the word *we*, it didn't roll off her tongue as easily as she'd hoped, either.

Earlier that day, she'd checked her e-mail, and there was a message from Bobby. As hard as she tried, she couldn't get it out of her mind:

Jen, I know that your wedding is next week and you have no idea how much I wish I could come home for it. I know you will be a beautiful bride. But I just have to say this, I love you and I like Dave, but you need to know that you aren't obligated to marry him just because you are pregnant. Mom said you don't seem very happy right now. And I hope that you aren't doing something just to be stubborn, just because you want to show how grown up you are or something stupid like that. If you are getting married, I only hope that you are really in love. Life is too short, you don't want to spend any time being miserable just to make a point. I understand if you are mad that I'm writing this. I just hope that you are taking things seriously. Be good to Mom and Dad and tell Dave I said hi. Love, Bobby

Usually when Bobby wrote, she replied right away. But today, she didn't. She couldn't. Even now, hours later, she tried to come up with some sort of a reply. Some way to explain it all away. Everybody in her family was so overprotective, they just couldn't deal with the fact that she was finally making a decision without them.

She felt Dave pushing on her head. "Get up, I need a smoke." Sitting up, she watched him put on a black hoodie and duck outside. Alone in the living room, she closed her eyes, imagining what she would say to Bobby: *Do you know how well he treats me? He always goes outside to smoke now because I asked him too. And last week, he washed my car and cleaned the bathroom because my back hurt.*

And it was true, Dave was a thoughtful guy. He'd make a good dad and a good husband. And she loved him. Didn't she? She was attracted to him, and she liked to hang out with him. Sometimes he really annoyed her with his stupid sense of humor, and sometimes she felt like there were things she couldn't tell him, like he always thought her and the girls at the salon were so crazy with their gossip and theories on all their customers. But, overall, she could tell him stuff. Couldn't she?

Dave came back inside, tossing his work boots on the floor. "Put those on the shoe rack," she said. He rolled his eyes, but moved them to the shelf.

Jen tried to concentrate on the game. It was more than a little nerve-wracking that Ben Roethlisberger was injured and not playing at this point in the season. But they were still playoff contenders, and their game plan was always dependent on the run, not the pass. If they could keep it going, they might make it all the way this year.

"Do you think we'll go to the Super Bowl this year?"

Dave shook his head. "I doubt it."

"You doubt it? What kind of fan are you?"

"An honest one. I just don't see it. Too many injuries But, I mean, you never know."

"Well, I have faith in them. I think they'll go all the way this year. They'll do it for us."

"For us?"

"Yeah, like they're gonna get one for the thumb, you know, to give us the ultimate wedding present."

"You're crazy sometimes," he said. She felt crazy, that was for sure, but how could she not when so many things were up in the air—watching the Steelers play so well was the only thing that made her feel like everything would be all right. And right now, she really needed that.

Megan

The sound was deafening, even with a 27-to-14 lead in the fourth quarter. As Cleveland prepared to punt, the entire stadium stood on their feet, waving Terrible Towels and screaming into the black November night. Backup quarterback Charlie Batch had been injured in the first half, and his replacement Tommy Maddox sucked.

Standing on her tiptoes in platform boots, Megan was almost as tall as Ryan and about three times as loud.

"Gooooooooooooooooooooooooo Steelers!" she screamed as the Cleveland kicker punted the ball. On the field, Cedrick Wilson caught it and everybody cheered, then sat down. Once Maddox ran onto the field, the whole place got so quiet it felt like you could hear somebody sneeze on Mt. Washington. The ebb and flow of the home crowd gave Megan shivers. She gripped Ryan's arm.

"I'm so glad you got tickets for this game."

"Yeah, it's awesome." He looked down at his phone. "Hey, Porter's calling. He's out in the South Side. Wanna head there after?"

Megan bit her tongue. "I don't know. I have to be to work at eight tomorrow."

"Aw, come on, don't be lame. We'll get you home before then." Ryan winked at her. Ryan was looking damn good. And she hated the thought of going home, alone, without him.

"We'll see." She leaned into him and he moved his arm, wrapping it around her shoulders. It felt safe. And cozy. So safe and cozy that she almost missed it when Verron Haynes ran for a 10-yard touchdown on fourth down. She stood up, screaming, shouting and high-fiving all the people around them.

"Come on," said Ryan, holding her waist. "You can't say no now. We gotta celebrate."

Megan looked around. The stadium was bleeding fans fast, black-and-gold jackets clogging the upper-level stairways.

"Okay. But we're not leaving now. I don't leave a game till it's over."

Ryan saluted her. "Yes, ma'am. We're here to the bitter end."

She poked him in the side. "Don't call me ma'am! And tell Porter we're coming."

Ryan pulled out his phone and started texting. Megan sighed. From their seats, she could see the Renaissance Hotel looming on the corner of Sixth Street. She imagined herself there in the morning, hung-over or maybe still a little tipsy, barely able to think.

Even so, on her feet smiling and watching the parade of fans hitting the exits, going out seemed like a very good idea.

Desiree

It was well after one in the morning when Desiree heard the garage door open. Even though she'd been up in bed watching Lifetime, she clicked off the TV and bedside lamp and buried her head in the pillow. Since their fight last night, she'd avoided Tom entirely. She wasn't still mad, exactly. She just didn't want to communicate, so she'd gotten up at eight to do yoga and stayed out shopping and tending to various errands until well after the time when she knew he'd leave to pick up Robbie.

Downstairs, she tracked Tom's motion by sound: first, the keys in the basket on the counter; then the fridge door opening and closing; next, footsteps on the stairs. She pulled the white duvet closer to her face, nestling into her satin pillow. If Tom thought she was asleep, there was no way he'd bother her. Or maybe not, she realized as the lights turned on and she surprised herself with a loud gasp.

Tom laughed. "Ha! You're up!"

Trying to sound sleepy, she pressed her face into the pillow. "I wasn't until you banged in here like a bull in a china shop."

"I'm not like a bull. Come on, aren't you going to ask how it was?"

She'd expected him to still be a little bit cool from the night before, but his voice sounded unusually excited, like it did when he had good news to share.

"How was it?" she asked, trying to sound as disinterested as possible.

"He had pink hair."

"Huh? Who?"

"Robbie! Robbie dyed his hair pink. Bright flaming fluorescent pink."

"No way. And Patty let him? Why would she let him do that?"

Desiree couldn't believe it. Not that she'd ever tell Tom or Patty, but she had plenty of homosexual friends and could see the signs and Robbie had them all—unusually quiet about girls, a little bit too neat, a fascination with style, and a female best friend who monopolized all his time and attention.

"No, no. I don't think so. I mean, you should have seen her face when he came downstairs to see me. She wanted a reaction for sure."

"What did you do?"

"Nothing." He shrugged, peeling off his fleece. "I mean, what could I do? I wanted to pound some sense into him, but I wasn't going to do it in front of Patty and then, after I was around him a while, I kind of got used to it."

"Used to it? Pink hair on your son? Used to it?"

"Yeah, I mean it's dark enough. I don't know. It just seemed like if I said anything, I was giving into him and Patty."

"Did you talk to Patty about it?"

Tom went into the bathroom, the sound of water obscuring his voice for a moment.

"Huh? I didn't hear you."

"I said, no, I didn't go in when I dropped him off."

"Do you think you'll call her? To talk about it?"

"What's there to talk about? He'll dye it back. He's a kid. It's what they do."

Desiree stiffened as Tom flipped on his electric toothbrush, the noisy vibration filling up the room. *It's what they do.* Tom could really be oblivious. He and Patty just couldn't seem to see that Robbie was acting out in this passive aggressive manner because he was afraid to tell them that he was gay. This was a kid who broke down crying when Mandy Moore died at the end of "A Walk to Remember," for god's sake. And now he was dying his hair pink? What else could it be? But saying something like that would make her sound like a bitch, like she was picking on Tom's kids. And that never went well. What Tom and Patty needed to do was sit down with Robbie and tell him that they loved him no matter what, but that dying his hair back to a normal color would make his whole life a lot easier. Besides, wasn't fluorescent hair color a little dated? In the nineties, that thing may have been cool, but nowadays it just made you look like a loser mallrat. Robbie was a bright, interesting kid. He could do better.

She moved toward the edge of the bed, waiting for Tom to climb in. As he did, one hand reached for her back.

"I'm tired," she said, looking the other way.

"I am too, but I could still…"

"I can't."

Behind her, she felt him rolling toward her, the heat radiating off his body. "Are we going to talk about what you said last night?"

"No."

"Oh. So that's it? You say that you want to have a baby and I'm just supposed to ignore it?"

"I've said that I wanted a Jaguar for about three years, and you've ignored that. I think you know the principle."

"Yes, but a baby? Don't be offended, but it was a little bit shocking."

"Don't worry about it. I must be PMS-ing or getting too much estrogen at the office or something."

She'd spent the entire day talking herself out of it, listing all the reasons she shouldn't have a kid—love handles, ugly maternity clothes, too much time off work, morning sickness, no alcohol for nine months, and the difficulty of finding a reliable babysitter during the Steelers home games. She'd thought of all those things, but there was only one real reason why she knew she could never go through with it: Fear. The fear that she was too old to be pregnant. Or that something would go wrong with the pregnancy or the baby. Or, worse than any of that, that she wouldn't be a good mother. She imagined herself in a nursery, pulling her hair out as a baby screamed and all the while Tom would stand behind her, hovering: *Patty never had this problem.*

"So that's it?" he said. "You really didn't mean it?"

"I said I don't want to talk about it." Feeling bad, she rolled over, rubbing Tom's arm. He responded by pulling her so close, she could barely breathe. She ran her fingers along his neck and her fingernails up and down his arm. He leaned forward, kissing her so hard she fought for breath. Her hand made its way down his stomach and he let out a loud, contented sigh. That was the good thing about men—no matter what you said to them, they were easily distracted.

Patty

Thursday night, Patty rallied the troops for yet another family dinner with one thing on her mind—grades. Two days ago, Kristen and Robbie had begrudgingly showed her their report cards. Kristen's was typical—As in English, Spanish, and Gym, Bs in History and Life Science, and Cs in Algebra II and Wood Shop. A C in Wood Shop? Had she shown up for class at all? But a C in Wood Shop was much less worrisome than that awful report card Robbie had brought home. Granted, if Kristen had brought home the same grades, she would have received a standing ovation, but this was Robbie. He got straight As. At least he used to. This term, he got an A in German and World Cultures, a B in English and AP Biology, and a C in Gym and Calculus. For a high honor roll student, this was bad.

As Robbie and Kristen took their seats with their usual sullen expressions, Patty dished up the chicken and broccoli casserole.

"So Robbie, are you going to change your hair this weekend?"

It was still pink. And Patty was still sore that Tom hadn't even commented on it.

"You should change it," said Kristen. "It's just stupid. Like, people are seriously talking about it, and it's embarrassing to me."

Patty clenched her teeth, afraid of what Kristen was going to say next.

Robbie stuck his tongue out. "Like I care what a bunch of dumb freshmen are saying."

"Well, I do. They're saying you look hot. It's gross."

Patty almost choked. They were saying he looked hot? Not that he didn't. Robbie was a good-looking kid, a little skinny and gangly right now but in a couple of years when he filled out, he was going to be quite handsome. But had it really taken pink hair for girls at school to notice him? What was wrong with kids these days?

Looking at Robbie, he didn't seem very interested that anybody would be saying he was hot.

"Who's saying that?" Patty asked, her own curiosity getting the best of her.

Kristen smirked. "Kelsey Scanlon. She's, like, all about Robbie now."

"Kelsey Scanlon? That little skank?"

"Robbie, that's no way to talk about a girl."

"She IS a skank, though. Don't think I haven't heard about what she does underneath the bleachers—"

"Robbie! That's enough!"

"I think she loves you," said Kristen. "Maybe you guys can get matching shirts at Hot Topic and have some goth wedding."

"Kelsey isn't goth, she's some lame-ass Fall Out Boy groupie, and I don't shop at Hot Topic."

Hot Topic? Fall Out Boy? They sounded vaguely familiar, and Patty was pretty sure she didn't like either one of them.

Patty tried to stay on topic. "Whenever you're ready to quit fighting with your sister and dye it back, the dye is in the bathroom closet."

Kristen stuck her lower lip out, pouting. With her light brown hair in a ponytail and without the thick black eye make-up she'd recently taken to wearing, she looked like a little girl about to throw a fit.

"Why don't you ever buy me hair dye?" demanded Kristen. "I want to dye my hair black"

"Kristen, your hair is fine. I only did this because we need to fix Robbie's hair."

He smiled. "Now that Kelsey says she likes it, I have to. She's gross. I can't even believe you're friends with her."

"I can't even believe you're my brother."

They paused long enough for Patty to change the subject. "So how are your classes, Robbie?"

"Fine."

"What about Calculus?"

"Are you seriously going to ride me about my grades right now? In front of her?" He nodded toward Kristen.

"Oh, c'mon Robbie. I know you got a C, what's the big hairy deal? I get Cs all the time."

"I'm not trying to ride you, Robbie, I'm just wondering why somebody who has always done so well in math is suddenly struggling."

"Did you ever take Calculus?"

"Yes. Freshman year of college, and if I'd had the opportunity to do it in high school, I would have been much better prepared."

"I want to major in English or German, so it doesn't really matter what I do in calculus. Why bother?"

"You bother because if you're going to be in a class, you should take it seriously and work your hardest."

"I've worked my hardest for like twelve years now, getting good grades. I figure it's time for a break."

Patty understood where he was coming from. He had worked really hard through school, even though he knew that he wanted to go to Pitt, where his scores and grades were far above average. She'd tried to convince him to apply to Carnegie Mellon University, but he was firm on Pitt since that was where she and Tom had graduated from and Angela was going to go there too.

She wanted to say more, but that moment in the kitchen last week was still so fresh in her mind. The slap. She didn't want to push it.

"I just hope that's not your attitude next year in college."

"It won't be." Robbie stood up, carrying his empty plate into the kitchen, where she heard him rinsing. When he walked back in, he stopped for a second in the doorway, glaring at her. "Besides, if you're so worried about my grades, why don't you call Dad and try to get him to lecture me? He didn't care about my hair, so maybe he won't even care about my grades."

Patty started to say something, but he disappeared fast.

Kristen looked at her, one eyebrow raised. "What's that supposed to mean?"

All week long, she'd assumed that Kristen knew what happened on Saturday, but her confusion was unmistakable.

"I don't know," she said, feeling relieved.

Across the table, Kristen leaned in for more casserole.

"You should really make him dye his hair back tonight. It's really gross to hear people saying that my brother is hot. I thought it was annoying when they were saying he's gay, I mean not even annoying because, seriously, like, who cares, but honestly, Mom, I'd much rather have a gay brother than somebody who all my friends are drooling over because, seriously, Mom, if you have a hot older brother, then how do even know if your friends are really your friends, or if they're just, like, trying to get to your brother?"

"Kristen, I don't care if your brother is hot or gay or hot and gay. He's your brother and you need to quit complaining about him all the time."

Kristen shrugged, twirling one finger in the air. "Yeah, yeah, yeah."

Shannon

Saturday afternoon, Shannon stood in her panties in the Kaufmann's fitting room. There were so many other places she'd rather be. Hanging out at Morgan's and getting pumped for the Pens game later that night or, better yet, at home in bed. But Audrey had insisted that they go shopping together. And what had started as a way to chip in on a wedding gift for Jen and Dave had turned into an excuse for Audrey to pick out frilly dresses and beg until Shannon finally agreed to try them.

The first, a sleeveless red number with a crinoline skirt was dismissed as "too juvenile" and the second, a navy blue shift dress that Shannon liked was vetoed by Audrey as being "too matronly." The final, a sheer black halter dress, looked like it barely had enough material to cover up one leg, but Audrey had insisted that she try it on.

"Try it, you might like," she insisted, practically shoving her into the fitting room.

Or she might try it and be embarrassed that she was trying to fit her thirty-something ass into something from the junior department. Rolling her eyes, Shannon slipped it off the hanger and stepped inside. Tugging it into place, she leaned forward, throwing her hair down and tying the black ribbon around her neck. Standing, she was pleasantly surprised by her reflection. The dress wasn't nearly as sheer as it had looked on the rack, and there was a metallic sheen to it that made both the dress and her olive skin look nearly luminescent. Shannon smiled. At least this time, she wouldn't be embarrassed to step out of her dressing room and into the sea of weary looking middle-aged mothers and whiny teenagers shopping for winter formal dresses.

"C'mon, Shannon. Ya gonna be in there all day or what?"

Before she even fully opened the door, Audrey clapped her hand over her mouth. "Goodness, Shannon. You look amazing."

Shannon shrugged, taking center stage at the three-way mirror. Spinning a little, she smiled again. She did look pretty good. The dress fit like it had been made especially for her, hugging her curves in all the right places and hanging just far enough above her knees to show off her lean legs.

One of the waiting mothers, a round woman with a snowflake sweater, nodded with approval. "You look great, honey. I hope you're going to buy that."

Audrey nodded. "She sure as hell is."

"Thanks," said Shannon, nodding to the mother. She turned to Audrey, laughing. "I don't have anywhere to wear a dress like this."

"What about Jen's wedding?"

"No, I already have a dress for that."

"But it ain't *that* dress. I think ya gotta get it."

"It's seventy dollars, Audrey. I don't have that kind of money to spend on a dress I'm going to wear once."

"C'mon Shannon, live a little."

Behind Audrey's shoulder, the waiting mother made eye contact with Shannon and nodded. Shannon blushed, heading into her dressing room. Audrey held out her hand, holding the door open. "Seriously, Shannon. I'm going to hold this door open until you promise to buy it."

"But I have that black-and-white dress for the wedding. You know, the one I wear to the Christmas parties."

"Stop it. That thing must be damn near ten years old."

Audrey didn't have too much room to talk about wearing old clothes. She'd been wearing the same leather Steelers jacket since they'd met ten years ago. And it was already ancient then.

"So if I buy this dress, will you buy a new Steelers jacket?"

"No way. That thing's good luck, but this dress, Shannon, I'm telling you, you have to buy it."

"It's just a dress."

"Kid, it is not JUST a dress." Audrey elbowed her way into the room.

Shannon flinched, kicking her jeans and boots into the corner. "What are you doing?"

"I'm trying to show you this dress. Now, stand right there."

She followed Audrey's orders, positioning herself on her tiptoes in front of the mirror.

"Now pull your hair back like you would for a party."

Sighing, Shannon twisted her hair into a loose bun. This was the kind of thing she expected from Darla or her mom, not Audrey.

"Now, you just look there and tell me if that's just a dress."

Shannon looked. It was true. This was no ordinary dress. With her hair pulled back, she could see the slim lines of her collarbone and shoulders and how even they looked sexy against this dress.

Audrey grabbed her elbow, shaking her head. "Shannon, I've known you for ten years and I think you're a very beautiful girl. But I've never seen you look this beautiful."

Shannon swallowed. She couldn't remember the last time somebody had sincerely called her beautiful. Sure, the guys down at Morgan's were quick to tell her how hot or sexy she looked on any given day, but they were also drunk and most of them quite horny. Audrey spoke with the solid conviction of a nun.

She twisted the tag. $70. It seemed like a lot of money for a dress, even a dress this nice. She pushed Audrey out of the door. "Fine. I'll get it, but if I'm broke till my next payday, you're gonna have to feed me."

"Honey, after you show up in a dress like that, you're gonna be too busy fighting off the men to worry about eating."

Week 11: Steelers vs. Baltimore Ravens
(L 16-13 OT)

Jen

Jen buried her head in her hands and tried to hold back the tears. No. No. This was not supposed to happen. All season long they'd been playing so well and now, on the day of her wedding, the Steelers lose to the Baltimore Ravens? In overtime? All afternoon as hands flurried about doing make-up and hair, zipping and unzipping dresses, the game had played on the hotel TV and about every woman who looked at the score or watched Tommy Maddox being sacked for the third, and then the fourth, time, had made a remark about it being just a game.

Right. Maybe for some people. But not to her and Dave's families and friends. The Steelers were way more than just a game—a religion, perhaps; a genetic trait that one couldn't deny, like having red hair or webbed feet, maybe. But a game? Who were they trying to kid?

Everybody waiting in the banquet room right now was feeling a twinge of disappointment about that very "game" that had just been played, and the thought of going out there to face them all made her sick. Instead of happy faces, they'd be disappointed, and what about Dave? He was never in a good mood after a loss. Would him and his friends spend the rest of the night debating every last third down or would they man up and enjoy the night for what it was?

The whole season, she'd felt like there was something magical about this team, like they were destined for something great and that her association with them had, by extension, destined her for something great too. But what if it was all in her head?

"Football teams lose, Jen," her pragmatic cousin and maid of honor, Sandi, had said with a roll of her eyes about an hour ago when Jen told her that she thought the game was a sign. And now, sitting on a toilet in an ivory dress stretched tight over her budding baby belly, she was still listening to Sandi trying to cheer her up.

"Come on, Jen. It's just a game. It doesn't mean anything. If it rains on your wedding day, do you think it's a curse?"

Jen closed her eyes. Sandi didn't understand. That morning, she'd prayed for a sign. Some kind of special signal to let her know that she was doing the right thing. But they'd lost. To Baltimore.

"I think it's a sign, Sandi. I don't think I'm supposed to do it."

Sandi moaned. "Am I gonna have to get your parents?"

"Yes, yes. Get my parents. I think I need to leave."

Jen imagined that her parents might be a little upset, but surely they would understand. If she didn't want to get married, they couldn't make her. It just wasn't right.

After what felt like forever, her mom and dad poked their heads into the bathroom.

Her mom crouched down, wrinkling her silk dress. Her expression was pained. "We've got guests waiting. What in god's name is going on?"

Jen whimpered.

Her mom's look changed to one of alarm. "Is it the baby? Are you feeling okay?"

"The baby is fine. I just don't think I can do this."

There, she'd said it. Wasn't that what they'd been waiting for her to say ever since she'd announced the engagement? She waited for a hug or an "I told you so". Instead, they exchanged careful glances.

Her dad stepped forward, putting his hand on her beaded shoulder. "Everybody gets cold feet on their wedding day."

"No, no. This isn't just cold feet. I can't do it."

"Why not?"

"Because I asked God for a sign today and the Steelers lost, and I think that's my sign and it's telling me that this is the wrong thing to do."

"You called us in here to cancel the wedding because the Steelers lost?" said her mom, her eyes on the verge of fury.

"It's a sign!"

"It is NOT a sign, Jen," she continued. "It's a coincidence. People are out there waiting for a wedding, and we are going to give them one." Her mom reached for the makeup bag, pulling out a tissue and a mascara wand. "Let's just get your eyes fixed."

"No!" Jen jerked away. "I'm serious."

"Can you give me any other reason why you shouldn't get married than the Steelers? Is David treating you right?"

No, there was nothing else. But wasn't a gut instinct enough?

"Okay, then let's get your eyes." Her mom reached for her face, and Jen batted her hands away.

"Get your hands off me." She heard the mascara tube rolling across the tile floor. Her dad, previously quiet, stepped forward, his face puckered and red. He grabbed her left arm around the bicep.

"Young lady, if you can give me ONE goddamn good reason for not doing it that does NOT involve a football game, then I'll listen."

Jen shook her head, frightened. He pulled her up, a little rough, but covering his tension with a strained laugh. "Then get the hell out there and get married." When he dropped her arms, she rubbed them, wounded.

They were really doing this. They were going to make her get married. No, they couldn't. She would run. She would run away. But looking at their stern eyes, she knew there was no backing out now. It was too late. For twenty-plus years they'd indulged her, and now, when she really needed them to, they wouldn't budge.

She turned to the mirror, wiping the runny mascara off her cheeks and mourning that Bobby was a million miles too far away to come and save her.

Desiree

Watching Jen and Dave stand in the corner reciting their vows underneath a canopy of tulle, Desiree felt proud. Sure, Jen had looked snow white with horror as she walked down the aisle and Dave kept shifting on his feet like he might pick up and run screaming out of the room. But wasn't that what weddings were all about—staring down your worst fears and anxieties and deciding that you were going to share them with somebody else for the rest of your life? Or, more likely, until you both got mutually bored enough that it was time to move on.

But even then, you'd always have the memories of your wedding day. And wouldn't Jen be lucky to look back on hers and know that she had spared herself the humiliation of a fried chicken buffet at the VFW? The room looked absolutely magic, like a wedding cake come to life— thick ivory tulle over every surface and a spray of baby's breath and ivory and pink roses on every table. After Jen met Dave at the altar, the lights were dimmed, allowing the hundreds of tea light candles to illuminate the room in an amber glow. Behind them, the lights of the bridges and the North Shore framed the young couple in the wide picture window. It was absolutely stunning.

Much better than the County Courthouse where she and Tom had traded their vows. As an event planner, everybody had expected her to have a huge wedding. Something straight out of the fairy tales. But Tom had already had a wedding a million years ago with Patty and look how well that had worked out. Plus, in her twenties she'd stood as bridesmaid in seven weddings, only two of which still existed by the time she tied the knot. And then there'd been all those weddings with her mom. Weddings were a fun thing to attend and an even more exciting thing to plan, but when it came time to participate in one, she felt oddly serious—like the less they did, the luckier they'd be.

Besides, as much she tried to deny it, so many bad things had occurred to her at least a hundred times before she finally decided on the courthouse: How could she have a fairy tale wedding with Tom, when he'd done it before? And what if when she walked down the aisle it reminded him of that other time he got married? Yes, he wanted to marry her and likely any thoughts he'd have would be nothing about that other wedding or Patty at all. But just the idea bothered her. And it didn't help that his mom still kept up the pictures from that first wedding even after all these years. She'd seen how young, innocent, and blissful Tom had looked in the pictures. And she didn't want anything on their day to possibly remind him of that moment. Because if he thought of that, then he might remember how far he'd come from that day—the sexless, loveless marriage he'd felt trapped in by the time she met him. If he started thinking like that, he might not want to go through with it again.

So the courthouse it was. Not that it really mattered. She'd lived vicariously through enough brides and thrown enough fancy parties at work to satisfy her wedding needs for a hundred years.

Still, at times like this she couldn't help but wonder: what if she'd given herself a chance?

As if on cue, a baby started whimpering, softly at first then louder, until a trashy looking girl in a backless red dress stood up near the altar, picked up the crying baby and strutted out of the room. Desiree leaned in closer to Tom, resting her hand on his leg. He hadn't brought up the baby conversation again, and for that, she was grateful. She really didn't want to talk about it, was just about ready to close the door on that one. But what if? What if this time she gave herself a chance?

Megan

As the bride and groom took center stage for the first dance, Megan stood in the corner, writing on a clipboard and trying to look busy. She wanted to go home, curl up in bed, and watch the highlights of the day's game. The Steelers had lost and from listening to the garbled WDVE reception in the hotel kitchen she knew that both their running game and their passing game had struggled today. She wanted to go home and see the highlights for herself. And more than any of that, she desperately wanted a drink. She NEEDED a drink. But being in charge made sneaking off and hitting the bar nearly impossible. Ever since she'd shown up for work at noon to get things started it had been one disaster after another. First, there wasn't enough tulle, so she'd had to send somebody to Michael's. Then the normal night chef had called in sick. Thank god she'd been able to sweet talk Marlon into coming in on his day off. He'd done such a good job that nobody seemed to notice the difference.

Between the wait staff and the wedding guests, somebody had been at her almost all day with a command or question: Is there a coatroom? Where will the deejay set up? Are we supposed to put the bread at the table before or after the wedding starts? Champagne at every table or just the bridal party's? Where are the bathrooms? When do they cut the cake? Should the cake already be cut so we can serve it immediately or can it be delayed? Do you know who made the almond cookies at the cookie table?

She'd always envied the managers. All they did was give orders, they didn't have to break their backs working. How wrong she had been. Trading in her pencil skirt and silk blouse for black pants and an apron sounded like heaven. Responsibility was overrated. Both her mother and father were managers at their jobs—was it this bad for them? She hadn't had time to eat anything since this morning and her last cigarette had been during the ceremony a good two hours ago. About the only interesting thing that had come out of the wedding was that she'd found out that Desiree, the balls-to-the-wall event planner who'd set this whole thing up, was married to her cousin Angela's best friend's dad. She'd known Tom Salvatore for years and had only heard of his new wife. What a strange little world to meet her this way. Not that she cared, really, but it would be a nice little tidbit of gossip for her parents next time she needed to keep the conversation shallow.

She looked at her watch. A little before nine. A couple more dances and hopefully this party would be ready to break. Maybe she would tell Larissa that she was going to be late for tomorrow's staff meeting. Probably not a good idea considering she'd had to call off last Monday after the post-Steelers game partying on the South Side got carried away.

A mousy girl in a hotel uniform approached her. She was new enough that Megan barely knew her, but her nametag said Jamie. "Megan, what are they doing with the centerpieces?"

They were supposed to do something with the centerpieces?

"Ask the mother."

"Which one?"

"Which one what?"

"The mother of the groom or the bride?"

Megan rubbed her head. She had never realized what morons most of her coworkers were. "The mother of the bride, of course."

"I did and she said to ask you."

Of course she did. Because that was the answer to every question today: Ask Megan. Like she actually had any answers.

"Well, I don't know. Keep'em out until people leave, we can break'em down then."

"But aren't they going to give them to people?"

"I don't know."

"Well, can you find out? Because we might need to do it now."

"Look, I don't care what the hell they do with the centerpieces."

Jamie's face fell and Megan immediately felt bad. It was bad enough that everybody at work thought she was a lush, now they'd call her a bitch.

"I'm sorry, Jamie, I didn't mean to snap. I'll find out."

Jamie crossed her arms over her chest, her mouth twisting into a disgusted sneer as if Megan was the most incompetent person she'd ever seen. "I'm waiting."

God. Nothing like going from crumpled to bitchy in about ten seconds flat. Megan scanned the room for Desiree, positive that she'd know what to do. As the bride and groom danced, Megan watched the line to the bar swell and wished she was part of it. She needed whiskey. But she couldn't, at least not for a couple of hours until this party was totally shutting down. An open bar had never looked so tragic.

Shannon

Of course Jen and Dave were going to play Journey slow songs at their wedding. That was the kind of couple they were—two parts cheesy and three parts classic rock. Shannon could think of about a million slow songs better than "Faithfully" but still, watching the crowded dance floor fill with couples made her a little sad. Especially when Darla pushed at Jack enough that he finally stood up, taking her hand and working their way deep into the crowd.

What a dumb song. A cheesy dumb song. There was absolutely no reason to feel bad about sitting out a Journey slow song. In fact, it was much worse to dance to it, to stand up and act like you took that kind of sugar-coated thing seriously.

"Mm, these almond cookies are heaven. I wonder who made them? I asked that slutty-looking girl from the hotel staff, but she didn't know," said Audrey, pushing over a heaping plate of cookies.

Shannon picked up a ladyfinger, then groaned as the pastry flakes settled on her dress. What a waste of money. This afternoon, modeling the dress in her bedroom, she'd had a good feeling about this night. Like there was going to be a single, normal, handsome man at her table. Or Jack would confess his love. But there didn't seem to be a single man over the age of 22 or under the age of 50 in the whole place. And even though both a teenager with a bad moustache and a creepy octogenarian had complemented her dress, nothing about either of those moments felt very good.

On the dance floor an older couple shifted, bringing Jack and Darla into view. Even in four-inch heels, Darla just barely grazed the top of his shoulder, her head resting on his chest, comfortable and easy. Jack looked serious. As they came full circle, Shannon saw Darla's mouth moving. Of course she was talking. She never quit. As the music swelled into an overstated chorus, Shannon looked away. She'd sat out millions of slow dances. Why was this one ripping out her heart?

Audrey cleared her throat. "Mm, even with all the man problems I've had in my day, moments like this, ya sure wish ya had one, don't ya?"

She'd felt Audrey noticing her watching Jack all night and knew that if she spoke one word of agreement it would all come spilling out. Shannon touched her eye like her contact was bothering her and stood. "I have to go to the bathroom." She put her head down, refusing to look at anybody.

In the hallway, alone now, it felt easier to breathe, but she still couldn't relax. Then, pushing open the bathroom door, she almost screamed as Desiree ran into her.

"I'm sorry," said Shannon, hoping Desiree wouldn't try to talk to her. The last thing she needed was small talk.

"Shannon? Are you okay?"

Shannon nodded. "Fine."

Desiree grabbed her arm. "My ass you're fine. You look like you're going to cry."

"Des, I really don't want to talk about it…" Her voice broke, caught in a sob. Desiree grabbed her, pulling her tight. She choked out a few more sobs then pulled away. "I'm sorry, it must be PMS or something. Can't get a hold of the emotions tonight."

"Oh geez, Shannon. Cut the crap. I know what's going on. I've been watching it all night."

"Watching what all night?"

"You. And Jack. You got it bad for him, and the way he watches you, I'd say he's about the same."

"Desiree, that's just ridiculous."

"It's not ridiculous. It's the truth. And I've been in your situation before, so I should know. When I met Tom, he was still married."

"Yeah, I know, but I always thought —"

"Always thought I was a homewrecker? I'll tell you what happened." Desiree set her purse on the counter, sighing. "Well, I won't tell you everything that happened, but let's just say that I didn't plan to fall in love with a married man. We were working together on events all the time and the more we were together, the more I liked him."

"Really?"

"Yes. I could talk to him, you see. Maybe because he was married, he didn't see me sexually at first. So we could just talk and joke and be ourselves and suddenly, it was something more."

"Yeah, but this is different. This is my sister's boyfriend."

"Have you told either of them?"

"Oh no, I couldn't. I can't."

"How does he make you feel?"

Shannon bit her lip, wiping off eye makeup and sighing. She didn't know if she could describe it. Or if it would make any sense. She'd been thinking it for all this time, but putting it into actual words felt as cheesy as that Journey song.

"He makes me feel like I'm at home." Just saying it, she felt lighter, like she'd lost a hundred pounds.

Desiree shook her head. "Tell him."

"I can't. It's selfish."

Desiree shrugged, handing Shannon a tissue. "Some people call it selfish. I call it self-preservation."

Shannon rolled the words around her head—*Some people call it selfish. I call it self-preservation*—they sounded full of hope, like a glimmer of good things to come.

Week 12: Steelers vs. Indianapolis Colts
(L 26-7)

Shannon

All she wanted to do was watch the Steelers and Colts game with friends, throw back a few Yuenglings, maybe a whiskey shot or two, and forget all about that horrible mess that Darla had cooked on Thanksgiving, not to the mention the disapproving way she'd grilled her all day about prospective boyfriends and career choices while her parents didn't even try to defend her.

"You look like a puppy got shot," said Audrey, tying an apron around the waist of her skinny jeans. "Chin up, dear. What can possibly be that bad?"

Shaking her head, her hair covering her face, Shannon wished she could hide behind it forever. "I hate her." Audrey pushed a draft across the counter.

"You don't hate her. She's your sister. You don't like her. There's a big difference. You can dislike somebody and still love them."

Shannon curled her hand into a fist and set it on the bar. As usual, Audrey was right.

Around the bar, all of the tables were full, and over in the back a game of pool was starting up. She watched Dave breaking balls. He winked and she nodded, turning back toward Audrey.

"Why's Dave here? He just got married last week. You think he'd be at home." Audrey shrugged. "He's here because he's a man."

The last thing she wanted to think about was men and what they did. Fortunately, Jack had spent Thanksgiving with his family in Indiana County rather than sticking around for Darla's turkey disaster. She'd missed him, sure, especially since he was probably the only one who would have been able to see, like she had, that the bad food and poor planning were nobody's fault but Darla's.

But when Darla pulled the burnt remains of the turkey out of the stove, she'd somehow turned it all around on Shannon: "Maybe if SHE would have gotten over here and helped in the morning instead of sleeping in all day, this wouldn't have happened."

Meanwhile, when Shannon had offered to come early to help, Darla had refused, saying that she could do it on her own. And just like always, her parents went right along with Darla's martyr routine, assuring her that frozen pizza would be just fine.

Frozen pizza for Thanksgiving? Who did that?

"I guess Dave didn't take too much of a honeymoon, did he?" she said, trying to change the subject.

Audrey laughed. "Guess not. Jen talks so damn much, he probably needs a break already. I still can't believe they're married. Seems like yesterday, I was bouncing Jen on my knee." Shannon nodded.

Somebody tapped her on the shoulder. Shannon spun around. Larry grabbed her by the shoulders and pulled her into a hug.

"There's my favorite girl! What do we think about the score tonight?" Larry laughed, loud and from the belly, then rubbed his head. Shannon shrugged.

"24-21 Steelers," she said.

Larry flagged over Audrey. "The lady here says 24-21, Audrey. Get her a drink on my tab for the prediction." Audrey smiled, tongue firmly in cheek.

Larry took his usual seat, leaving an open seat between him and Shannon. An open seat which she didn't think too much about until three beers later, when the Colts scored an 80-yard touchdown on their first possession and Jack sat down next to her.

"I thought I might find you here."

She was really feeling her alcohol by then. Her arms felt loose, like if she just let them hang limp, they might float up above her head. But even in her haze, she knew it was completely strange for Jack to just show up like this.

"What are you doing here?" She didn't want to look at him. Looking at him made it real that he was there.

"I didn't want to watch the game alone and when I talked to Larry at the wedding, he told me I should come down here to watch the games." Jack's arm muscles rippled beneath his black shirt. Shannon nodded. She knew that Darla was at work.

"Plenty of other places to watch the game," she said, taking the very last ounce of her beer and wiping her mouth with her hand. She caught Audrey's eye.

"Hey Audrey, Jack here wants a drink."

Shannon watched Audrey's smile grow as Jack asked for a whiskey and coke, then turned her head, glued to the TV. "You really shouldn't be here."

Jack looked around. "Now, is that how you treat all the customers?"

"Hell yeah, it is," said Larry. "That's what keeps us comin' back!"

Indy had one touchdown and a field goal under their belts by the time the Steelers finally scored their first touchdown, but Morgan's still exploded in hugs and high-fives as Hines Ward caught the ball. Larry ordered a round of shots for the bar and everybody cheered, hopeful. But by half time, trailing by 9 points, the momentum on the field and the mood in the bar had fallen fast and furious. So far this season, the Colts were undefeated. Everybody hoped the Steelers would end that tonight, but when Roethlisberger threw an interception toward the end of the 2nd quarter, it was starting to look like it wasn't going to happen.

But while the other regulars had taken to shaking their heads and swearing, Shannon and Jack had inched closer and closer with each passing whiskey shot until their barstools were touching, their legs grazing. She wanted to put his hand on her thigh, to feel the weight of it against her flesh. They were so close it frightened her. No matter how much she wanted this, it was wrong. Excusing herself for a moment, she went to the bathroom, splashed cold water on her face and hoped she would snap out of it. When she stepped out of the bathroom, Jack was there, waiting, like an answer to a question she hadn't yet asked. Their bodies crashed into one another, and for a moment, both of them lingered, the heat of his breath on her neck and in her hair.

"You smell good," he finally said. When she looked at him, he was leaning into her, his eyes closed. She wanted to reach up and kiss him, to pull his mouth to hers and never let go. But instead, she panicked, brushing him away and mumbling apologies. It was time to go home.

Megan

The game totally sucked and the night wasn't going much better. No matter how much fun she'd had sharing drinks, rants, and laughs with all of the old dudes at Nico's, there was no amount of free drinks and compliments that could cure a game like this. So when Indianapolis scored a field goal and brought the score to 26 to 7, she pushed her drink away and grabbed her coat.

"No, don't leave, babe. The fun's just begun," said a portly Italian man in a black Steelers turtleneck. He was in his late sixties, if not seventies.

Slipping on her puffy white coat, Megan shook her head. "I can't watch this anymore. I gotta work tomorrow. I need some sleep."

What she really needed was to be at work on time. Every day following a Steelers game she rolled in late, and even though Larissa hadn't said anything, it was only a matter of time until she did.

"You can sleep when you're dead," he replied with a wink. Earlier in the night, he'd told her she made him all wet when she spouted off some statistics about the Steelers' defense this season. She smiled at him, patting his arm affectionately.

"You're killin' me, girl," he said, amidst the laughter of the other patrons. Standing, she made her way to the door in spite of his protests.

Outside, she hugged her coat closer to her body. All around, houses turned dark as residents both old and young gave up on the game and turned off their televisions. Alone, she thought of her family scattered across the South Hills: her grandma, alone in her three-story house and watching the TV in her bedroom, no doubt muttering curse words and shaking her head at this point; her cousin Angela, sleeping probably while Aunt Nancy and Uncle Dom stayed glued to the game; her dad in the basement family room and her mom most likely in bed. On Thanksgiving her mom had said something about being away, but Megan couldn't remember when or where. She tuned out her mom like she tuned out the broadcast announcer's commentary on the Steelers.

It was late, but she wasn't ready to go home. She headed down Pearl Street toward Liberty. With luck, maybe somebody she knew would be out and she'd find a companion for a walk or get some good gossip. Surprisingly, the sidewalks and streets of Bloomfield were nearly deserted. With its abundance of Italian restaurants, grocery stores, and bakeries, it was known as the city's Little Italy. It wasn't exactly New York City but it was a far-enough cry from the suburban cul-de-sac where she'd grown up that it sometimes felt like she was living in an entirely different city. Tonight, every streetlight was wrapped in white, green, and red garland and twinkling Christmas lights.

At the corner of Pearl and Liberty, she glanced to the right toward Lot 17. Another night, she might have wanted to stop and say hi to Todd, but she wasn't quite that lonely. Instead, she headed the opposite way, pausing a block away in front of the Pleasure Bar, entirely surprised to see Todd in the front window there. They made accidental eye contact. She offered a brief wave and continued walking.

Not three seconds later, she heard footsteps behind her and a girl's whiny voice.

"Come back here, whore."

Before she even had time to think, Megan felt a yank on her hood and spun around, fists curled.

"Who the hell are you?" she said, looking down on a petite brunette with an eyebrow ring and a corduroy pea coat.

"Todd's wife."

Megan stepped back. On the list of last things she needed to happen right now, this was right up there with alone time with her mom or sitting next to a smelly dude on the bus. Feigning ignorance, she extended her hand. "Nice to meet you."

Todd's wife wasn't much for pleasantries.

"Stay the hell away from my husband, bitch." Obviously drunk, she tottered on her black platform boots, falling sideways then standing up straight, swinging a wild punch into the air.

Megan grabbed her forearm, holding it tight. "I don't care whose wife you are, don't EVER call me a bitch or a whore." Todd's wife twisted, unable to break free. Outside the Pleasure Bar, Todd and a handful of curious gawkers spilled onto the sidewalk.

"Missy, get the hell back here," screamed Todd, running toward them.

"Tell this bitch to let me go."

"I said, don't call me a bitch." Megan pushed her forearm backwards. Missy winced.

"I'll quit calling you a bitch. Now lemme go."

Megan glared at Todd. He looked pathetic and scared, and she regretted ever doing anything with him at all. He was about as tough as a box of tissues. Staring him straight in the eyes, she dropped Missy's hand and started to turn around. Halfway through her pivot, Missy flailed at her again, this time connecting a fist to her shoulder. Megan swallowed. Sometimes playing dirty was the only way. As Missy's tiny fists pummeled her torso, she leaned forward, yanking Missy's thin coat over her head and beating on her hockey-style amidst the hoots and hollers of a suddenly crowded sidewalk. Missy was tiny but tenacious, kicking and scratching at her face as Megan clawed at her back and sides. She felt Todd stepping in and tried to move away, but he was too quick, pulling them apart and holding each one of them by the bicep.

He looked at Megan then shoved her away. "Get the hell home."

She touched her face. It felt tender and she imagined bruises forming on her ribs and neck. Her skin was tender like that; the tiniest imprint left behind a mark. Missy was bent over, dancing around Todd's arm, trying to get free.

"I said to get the hell outta here," repeated Todd, pointing down the street.

Missy screamed. "Yeah, I'll call the cops on you, bitch. Assault and battery."

Touching the side of her face, Megan realized for the first time that she was bleeding. She'd barely felt it, but Missy must have scratched her. That was going to look just great at work tomorrow.

For a second, she hesitated, scanning the group of onlookers further down the street and wishing that somebody she knew, really knew, was there to help her, but the faces in the small crowd were only vaguely familiar and far too pleased with what they had just seen to offer any support. She tugged on the hem of her miniskirt, pulling it down just a little, then turned around, disappearing down the first side street she came to and hoping that Emily or Mike wouldn't still be up when she got home. Some things just weren't worth explaining.

Desiree

All she wanted was to get some Christmas shopping done. Ever since she'd told Tom that she didn't want to have kids, she'd been slowly trying to convince herself of the opposite. Or that at least she'd consider it. Or that there was no way she could be a worse mother than most of the heinous mothers she knew. Seriously, as much as people acted like pushing a kid out of your vagina qualified you for sainthood, she was convinced that some of the most truly awful people in the world chose to breed, while the others, the truly good, didn't. For instance, there was a girl at work, Janie, one of the few people in the office who wasn't a sniveling idiot or asshole and she'd been trying for years to get pregnant without any luck. But airhead Amanda in Secretarial Services? She had gotten pregnant after a booze-fueled one-night stand with one of the very married sales reps.

Desiree browsed through some lackluster jewelry at Saks, then turned her attention to the Old Navy web site. As the screen loaded with its obligatory pictures of shiny, happy, acne-free teenagers wearing jeans that looked like they'd been purposely dragged through the mud, Desiree noticed the sidebar advertising kids' clothes and clicked. Funny how the same carpenter jeans that look ridiculous on a fifteen-year old looked downright adorable on a toddler.

Desiree moved her mouse over the sizes then logged out. What was she doing?

On her home page, the cursor blinked in the Google search box, just waiting for a question. Desiree clicked on it and typed: Getting Pregnant. She closed her eyes, and when she opened them, a million sites displayed—Baby Center, Baby Hopes, Web MD, and American Pregnancy Association among others. She clicked on the first link. She knew how to get pregnant, but it didn't hurt to look. Right? She wasn't getting any younger, and this stuff was supposed to get harder as time goes by.

Scanning the first page, she felt the muscles tightening in her neck. Desiree scanned the sidebar and clicked on the Infertility link. Maybe this could give her some info about the odds for somebody her age: *Your chances of conceiving decrease drastically after you turn 30.* Like she really needed a web site telling her she was old.

She read on. As if it wasn't bad enough that there was only about a 36-hour window in any given month that you could actually get knocked up, it seemed like pretty must everything she could imagine affected fertility: alcohol, drugs, body fat, seafood, vitamin B6 and a bunch of other stuff she had never once given a second thought to. Her stomach tightened as she imagined going through years of pain and dismay as a series of negative pregnancy tests flashed before her eyes. What the hell was wrong with her? Three months ago, she'd never thought twice about chasing around a rug rat of her own. Now the idea of being infertile seized her heart with such despair she wanted to fall on the floor and sob.

Patty

On Friday afternoon, Patty entered her building fresh from Monte Cello's Pizza, floating on three huge slices of pepperoni and mushroom and an extra large Coke. Pushing through the revolving doors, a restricted number rang her cell phone. That was strange. Typically, she knew every number that called—work, Kristen, Robbie, Tom, and her cousin Sally. On the third ring, she answered.

"Hello?"

"Hello? Patty Salvatore?"

"This is her."

"This is Mrs. Marshall, Robbie's guidance counselor. Do you have a few minutes to talk?"

Patty took a breath, immediately assuming the worst: Robbie had been in a fight.

"Sure. Is everything okay?" Patty ducked into a stairwell.

"Yes, well, not exactly, but I'll explain. I'm a little concerned about Robbie. Academically."

"Believe me, ever since Robbie brought home that last report card, I have been on him about bringing up those grades."

Mrs. Marshall cleared her throat. "I'm glad to hear that you're so involved. Robbie has always been a good student. And I think that's what got the teachers talking."

"Talking. About what?"

"About his attendance. His Calc teacher, Mr. Simpson, says he misses at least one class per week and his gym teachers say he rarely shows up."

"That can't be right. Robbie hasn't stayed home sick one day this year. I'm up when the kids leave, so I know."

"You're exactly right. I did some research, and he doesn't show up with any sick days. The only conclusion I can draw is that he's showing up for homeroom and then leaving."

Leaving after homeroom? How in the world could he leave after homeroom? Angela! Her and that car of hers. She was probably talking Robbie into skipping.

"How is he leaving? Doesn't the school have some kind of system in place to prevent this?"

"Mrs. Salvatore, we have over 400 students in each grade. There is no way to monitor every single one of them at every moment of the day. We leave that up to our parents."

Patty burned. First, to be called Mrs., then, to be accused of being a neglectful parent. Who did this woman think she was?

"Mrs. Marshall, I have to go. I'm going to talk to Robbie and handle this, and I assure you there won't be a problem going forward."

"Yes, that's good. But maybe you should come in one day to meet with us, you, Robbie, your husband. We can all sit down and troubleshoot to get at the real problem."

"Oh, I think I already know what the real problem is." Yes, she was about five feet four with black hair and a pierced lip. "My ex-husband and I will handle this on our own, thank you." She clicked her phone shut, Mrs. Marshall still talking.

Angela

Eighth period study hall and there was nothing, absolutely nothing, to do. She tried to read the worn copy of *On the Road* she carried in her backpack for occasions just like this but couldn't concentrate. She should have skipped out on classes earlier. Even though she'd already applied to the University of Washington, she had requested so many other pamphlets and brochures from various schools that she liked to intercept the mail to avoid any questions from her parents. They were still under the impression she was going to Pitt in the fall.

Three years ago, her mom had left her job as a secretary at a local transportation company and became an office manager for the Office of Parking at Pitt, a definite step up, but one that her mom insisted she had taken solely to help pay for Angela's tuition. Angela had never asked her to do that and hated how every time her mom had any complaint about her job, it came back on her.

"I don't like the way they run things either," she would tell whatever friend or relative who happened to be listening to her rant. "But I can't think about leaving until Angela's out of school."

If that's how she really felt, then she should be thrilled at the prospect of Angela going somewhere else. If her parents really cared about her future, they would know that she needed to create a whole new life away from this city and away from Robbie. And how could they even blame her? They should be happy. Her dad had spent the last two weeks teasing her that she was the reason for the Steelers' recent losing streak. It would be just as well for everybody when she left.

A chorus of laughter at the front of the cafeteria distracted her. Looking up, she watched a group of cheerleaders in matching purple-and-white track suits laughing. She glanced around, hoping the teacher, Mr. Smathers, would tell them to be quiet. Unfortunately, he was nowhere to be found. The same couldn't be said of Brad Wellesley, who happened to look up from his notebook the exact moment she did. He smiled and waved, then stood up, walking over to her seat.

"What's going on here?" he said with a smirk. "Lookin' for me? Can't go one period without me, huh?"

"No, I was looking for Mr. Smathers. I thought this was a no-talking study hall."

"And who are you? The study hall police?"

"Something like that."

Brad sat down across from her, pulling the book out of her hands. "Hey," she said. "I was reading that."

"No, you weren't. I saw you looking around the room. Face it, Bad Luck, you're just as bored as the rest of us." She grabbed for the book. In their scuffle, a white slip of paper floated out and onto the floor. Brad swooped down, picking it up before she had a chance to react.

"Buy one, get one free at The Locker Room? Geez, Angee, are you a closet Hines Ward fan? I knew it! You can't live in this city without liking at least one Steeler. Your secret is out!"

She grabbed the coupon out of his hand and shoved it into her bag. "I don't have a secret. And don't call me Angee, it sounds like some mafia wife in New Jersey."

"Okay, Bad Luck. I won't call you *Angee*." The way he emphasized Angee made her want to slap him. How could the same guy who helped her protect Robbie also be such a world-class dick? "But seriously, why do you have it?"

"No reason."

"There's gotta be some reason."

"Nope."

Of course there was a reason, but she wasn't about to tell Brad. Ever since she and Robbie had found that box of panties in Patty's room, she couldn't stop thinking about Patty. In some weird way, she wanted Patty to know that she knew about what was going on and even that she thought it was kind of cool, even if it was related to the stupid Steelers. At least it was something vaguely interesting. The day they found the box, she had noticed Patty used a PO Box to send the panties, and she imagined sending Patty a letter with the coupon, instructing her to go to the Locker Room on a certain night and time. Then, she would be there waiting.

Sure, at first Patty would be mad, but after Angela explained her fascination with the whole enterprise, she'd surely let Angela in on her secret. And maybe then Angela could let her in on her secret about applying to schools in Washington state, and maybe Patty could offer her some advice about how to tell her parents, and they'd see for a second that they weren't that much different. Maybe they could even be friends. As much as she hated to admit it, Patty was the kind of parent she'd always wanted. There was something so deeply maternal and kind about the way Patty treated Kristen and Robbie, she wanted Patty to see her in the same kind of light. But she knew that Patty only saw her as a problem, the red-headed step-child who kept Robbie constantly in trouble. But if Patty could get past that, they'd see how alike they were: two people who don't quite fit in, who thrived on secrets just to get them through this place they called home.

Week 13: Steelers vs. Cincinnati Bengals
(L 38-31)

Desiree

She hated going to the bathroom during halftime, but today she just couldn't hold it. Standing in a line with about a hundred or so women dressed in head-to-toe Steelers gear and sporting various shades of red faces from the cold temperatures, Desiree was surprised when she heard somebody screaming her name.

"Desiree? Desiree DeNunzio?"

If somebody didn't know her married name, that only meant one thing—she hadn't spoken to her in about fifteen years. After she moved back from DC in 1997, she'd cut the majority of her old crew out of her life. Some because all they ever did was go to the South Side every weekend to get shit-faced like they were still 21 and others because right after high school, they went totally white trash—trailer park, multiple husbands, clothes from Wal-Mart, the whole redneck deal. It wasn't that she believed she was better than them, it was just that while she was gone, she'd become accustomed to a certain style of life and even though she had desperately missed Pittsburgh, she wanted to maintain her new ways. Her mom had mocked her when she'd gone for the apartment in Shadyside rather than a duplex in Millvale, but it had all been part of the plan. And now she and Tom had a very comfortable life in a part of the city known for its wealth. The plan had worked.

Gritting her teeth, she turned around, scanning the crowd for a familiar face but only seeing a visibly pregnant woman standing by the sink waving her gloves.

The lady looked damn near menopausal and still had big hair straight out of 1988. Desiree tried to place her but couldn't.

"Desiree!! It's me, Becky Sulkosky!"

Becky Sulkosky? Quickly, she scanned that part of her brain that kept track of things she didn't want to think about. Sulkosky. Sulkosky. Nothing came to mind.

"From cheerleading? I was a sophomore, you were a senior. C'mon, the basketball playoff game in Erie? I was the one who everybody said gave Tommy Elliott a blowjob on the bus?"

There was a slight titter among the drunk women in line and one of them repeated the word "blow job" and made a fist pump, her Steelers charm bracelet jingling as it moved. Becky Sulkosky. She'd been known at school for her big hair and her open legs. Desiree glanced at her swollen belly and naked ring finger. Apparently some things never changed.

"Becky. It's nice to see you," she said, praying that the bathroom line would start moving.

"It's good to see you, too. So, how have you been?"

"Great, thanks."

"I thought you moved away from here."

"Yeah, I went to D.C. for a few years after college, but I moved back."

Becky shook her head. "Nobody can leave the Burgh, can they?"

At this exact moment, Desiree wanted to leave the Burgh quite badly. She shrugged. "I guess not."

"So, you married? Divorced? Single?"

"Married."

"That's just great. Kids?"

Feeling her body becoming stiff, Desiree tried to force a smile and run her usual "Are you kidding?" schtick she'd done so seriously for the past 17 years. Averting Becky's eyes, she caught sight of yet another pregnant woman at the sink, and suddenly it felt like the whole place was knocked up.

"No," she said, hoping that Becky wouldn't pick up on the slight hint of disappointment in her voice.

Becky immediately picked it up. "Oh. I see. Can't make the babies, can ya? Sorry to hear that. You know, Ginny Pagewell, from my grade? I heard she just adopted some babies from China. I mean, everything else is made in China these days, may as well get your kids from there too!"

Desiree couldn't remember the last time she had wanted to punch somebody in the face so badly.

Desperate for a change of subject, she turned it back on Becky. "I see you're still able to make the babies, huh?"

Becky rubbed her belly, proud as a weatherman who'd been the only one in town to predict a blizzard. "This is number 5. My oldest, Mariah, is pregnant too. Just turned 18. The apple doesn't fall too far from the tree."

"Are you married?"

"I was, but we're gettin' divorced. He didn't want no more kids and didn't like that Mariah and her boyfriend were livin' with us. Whatever. They're all lazy bastards, right?"

Desiree shrugged. "I guess it depends on where you find 'em."

The women in front of her took a giant step forward and Desiree followed, desperate to get away from Becky. Unfortunately, Becky followed her like they were in line together.

"So, I guess you're still a snobby bitch, aren't you?"

Desiree turned and saw Becky's nostrils were flared and her thin lips set in a determined line. "So did you get yourself a real yuppie husband who will put up with your goddamn attitude? Heaven knows, everybody in Shaler thought you were too big for your britches."

"Right. So that's why you were so anxious to talk to me a couple of minutes ago. Everybody wants to hang with the snooty bitch."

Becky turned to the women in line behind them, trying to rally support. "Do you hear how this lady's talkin' to me?"

With the Steelers losing by four points to the Bengals in a game with serious playoff implications, the mood in the line was already tense. Desiree imagined that a similar incident in the men's room would most likely turn into a brawl and was relieved when the other women ignored Becky. Becky wasn't quite so pleased. She raised her voice: "It's just as well you never had kids—we don't need more of your kind in this world."

It was all Desiree could do not to grab her by the neck.

"Isn't the game starting soon, Becky? You should probably get back to your seat. I imagine it takes you a while to move up the stairs, waddling like that and balancing a beer and a cigarette." Desiree peeled back her black leather glove, pointing at her silver

TAG Heuer watch. Becky's face crumpled, and then she huffed off.

Finally, it was her turn in line. She went into the stall, hung up her purse and sat on the toilet seat, not caring how cold or dirty it was. She literally didn't have the strength to stand. And when the person in the next stall flushed and somebody else turned on the hand dryer, she leaned forward, finally letting herself cry.

Megan

She awoke with a start. Somebody's cell phone rang incessantly, the strangled chords of "Barracuda" filling up the room. She was on an unfamiliar bed, in an unfamiliar room. The ring sounded insistent. Aggressive. Like it was daring her to pick it up. But she didn't know where it was coming from or just exactly where she was. Talk about déjà vu. In the dim light, she made out the shape of her purse on the floor. She reached for it, fumbling to find the time. It was 8:00. She'd started drinking at Ryan's house around ten this morning, the game had started at one, and beyond that, things were, well, fuzzy. She knew that the Steelers had lost and vaguely remembered moving to a second destination sometime after that. An after party at somebody's house, perhaps?

She stood up, a little unsure of herself. Looking in the mirror, she smoothed down her jean skirt and Flashdance-style Steelers sweatshirt and looked around. Wherever she was, this was totally a dude's house. The place was a mess. The beige walls and orange-and-brown shag carpet were totally bleak. Creeping out the door, she walked down a narrow hallway, stopping short at the sight of a handsome black-haired man on the couch in a pair of boxers.

"Who the hell are you?"

"Bill," he replied with a smile. "I know Ryan's roommate." He said it as if that was supposed to help things. As if that would just clear everything right up.

"Well, Bill, can you put on a pair of pants and take me home?"

He smiled again, and the more she looked at him, the more she thought he was a total creeper. And good-looking creepers were the worst. They thought the world owed them everything. Her head pounded as Bill stood up. That morning, she had promised herself that she wouldn't get drunk. But once she got started, everybody loved to egg her on.

"Take you home? So soon? But you only woke up." Bill winked at her, and she winced.

"And I'm leaving. Now." Grabbing her coat off the floor, she put it on and started to open the door. Bill stood up, pushing it shut with the palm of his hand.

"C'mon, I'll take you. I was just joking. Can I get you a glass of water at least?"

"I guess." A glass of water really did sound like heaven. She followed him into the kitchen and he handed her a glass. Thanking him, she drank it fast and turned around. Bill grabbed her, pulling her waist toward him and nuzzling her neck.

"And what are you going to do for me?" His voice in her ear sounded like pure poison.

"Nothing, jackass." She elbowed him, trying to get away. He grabbed her arm, pulling it behind her back.

"So is that how you are, Megan Sullivan? A cock tease? Ryan said if I took you home, it was guaranteed pussy."

"Ryan wouldn't say that. He's my friend. Get away from me, you asshole." She twisted her arm, breaking free and diving toward the door. He grabbed her by the ponytail and spun her around. He smelled like whiskey and Axe body spray.

"Ryan did say that. Guess you need to get to know your friend a little better."

She kicked him in the shin. "Leave me the hell alone and I won't call the police."

"Ha! The police? And what would you tell them? Dressed like that, you really think they're going to take YOUR side?"

He had her by the wrist, trying to drag her down the hallway. She resisted, shouting, and then he pushed her into the wall, shoving his hand up her skirt.

"C'mon, baby. I heard you like it rough. Now, just lemme in."

As he fumbled to push her panties aside, Megan brought her elbow down hard on his shoulder. When he faltered backward, holding his arm, she bolted, running out the door and stumbling into a back alley. She broke into a run, heading for the nearest street corner to catch her bearings. The nearest sign said 36th.

Lawrenceville. She could walk home if she must, although her breath was so ragged, she felt like she might pass out. Beginning to walk, she headed toward Butler Street, flipping through her cell phone to see whom she could call for a ride. Ryan was obviously out. And Emily. She'd run back and tell Mike and they'd have endless conversations about what a mess she was. Surprisingly, she couldn't even place half of the names in her phone. Hot Guy from Dee's Café? Undergrad from 80's night? What kind of contacts were those? Well, there was one name but, no, she couldn't call Kevin. This would just be too rich for him. But it was freezing cold and even with the adrenaline pumping, she was half-afraid she might pass out. She dialed.

"Hello?" She heard noise in the background. Shit. What if he was with Emily and Mike?

"Hi, Kevin. It's Megan. I'm sorry to bother you. I had a little incident, and I was wondering if you could give me a ride."

He paused and the music dissipated.

"Well, I'm in my car coming back from Sports Rock right now, where are you?"

"Are you alone?"

"Actually yes. Are you planning to seduce me?"

The word seduce made her want to puke.

"I'm walking toward Butler Street. Near Arsenal school."

"I'm almost there. Can you wait in the Rite-Aid parking lot?"

"Yeah."

She was a few blocks away but made it there fine. She waited by the mouth of the 40th Street Bridge for a few moments before Kevin arrived. He swung open his car door and she jumped in, not even wanting to look at him.

"Thanks," she mumbled.

He turned toward Bloomfield.

"Is everything okay?"

"Fine."

On the radio, the Mighty Mighty Bosstones started to play. Kevin groaned, switching the station. "Can you believe they still play this stuff?"

She laughed. "I know! There is so much good music out there and they play the same song all the time. The Mighty Mighty

Bosstones were relevant for what, like five minutes in the 90s when the movie *Clueless* came out?"

Kevin laughed. "Exactly! I sure wish the X would fire their programming director and get with the times."

"Fire him? Yeah, like from a cannon."

Kevin laughed again. "I didn't know you were so passionate about music."

There were a lot of things that Kevin didn't know about her.

Leaning her head against the window, she watched the dirty row houses flying past as they climbed the hill toward her house. Earlier in the weekend it had snowed and its dirty remnants were piled on the sidewalks and curbs. Everything, even the Christmas lights, looked dingy and dull, like the whole place had been dipped in an ashtray.

"Megan, I don't mean to pry, but are you sure you're okay?"

Okay? Was she okay? Some guy had just tried to push himself on her and Kevin wanted to know if she was okay. And what could she say? That maybe she had deserved it because she was partying too much? Or that maybe she didn't even have any friends because people like Ryan, who she trusted, called her guaranteed pussy? But the important point was that nothing had happened. Sure, maybe some creepy guy had tried to push himself on her and implied that everybody thought she was a slut. But she'd gotten away. And it didn't matter what people thought.

She cleared her throat. "As okay as I'll ever be."

She felt relieved when he didn't try to pry anymore. They approached her house in silence, and he dropped her off with a thanks and good-bye. The lights in her house were on and inside she saw Mike and Emily poised at the dining room table, looking at each other and laughing; an exchange so pleasant and easy that she couldn't help but envy them. Growing up, all she'd ever wanted was a relationship, that one person who idolized her and worshipped the ground she walked on. But somewhere along the lines, everything had gotten so distorted. She'd become so set on trying not to get hurt that she had pushed away everybody and anybody who tried to love her—her parents, boys, and even Emily. And now, the very thought of this intimate exchange between Emily and Mike made her feel sick. She paused on the porch, trying not to cry. She needed to go inside, fake a smile, smoke a joint, and go to bed. In the morning, things would make sense. Feel better. Taking a deep breath, she turned toward the street. A lone car circled its way around Friendship Park then disappeared.

Patty

Monday morning, Patty sat at the dining room table amidst a pile of bills, cookbooks, and catalogs. Only 20 days away, Christmas weighed on her mind like a box of dynamite. There was too much to do for just one person. This weekend, she'd pulled the decorations out of storage, but the two Rubbermaid bins hadn't emptied themselves and two days later still sat full by the fireplace. Maybe today she'd get around to tackling that. After she was done with paying bills, cleaning, groceries, and her Monday morning ritual. But looking up from her shopping list, she eyed the brown package addressed to Brett Keisel and wondered why she even bothered with the panty routine.

For almost five seasons, she'd been doing this and she hadn't once received anything back in the mail. Not that she expected one of the players to actually write her, but it might be nice to get some kind of an acknowledgement that her packages were received. Perhaps the head office might recognize what a dedicated fan she was and send her a discount card at the Steelers Team Store.

All she wanted was for the Steelers to make it back to the Super Bowl, but at the rate they were going, with three losses in a row this late in the season, they were so far off from a playoff bid that the nightly sports cast had turned into a regular math class, offering up countless scenarios for how they could possibly get one. The only scenario that would work now was if they won every single game for the rest of the season. And while most years she would have thought it was possible, she didn't have the same hope for this year. During Sunday's game, one of the Bengals had wiped his feet on the Terrible Towel after scoring a touchdown. If seeing that wasn't enough to push this team to victory, she didn't know what was.

Pushing the package aside, she reached for a low-fat cookbook and sighed. Why bother? With low-fat cooking or the panties. Nothing she ever did mattered. If she cooked a nice meal for the kids, they just complained that she didn't make dessert. If she finished an extra-hard project at work, her boss rewarded her with even harder projects. And even if she got Kristen and Robbie everything they wanted for Christmas, she knew it wouldn't compare to whatever Tom and Desiree would give them on Christmas Eve.

And besides, after the fight she'd had with Robbie this weekend, she barely wanted to buy him anything at all. Yes, she had been wrong when she slapped him a few weeks ago. But he'd been out of line too. And this weekend when she'd confronted him about skipping school, he'd turned it all around on her. Like she was some deadbeat parent who didn't pay attention to anything he did.

"Maybe if you paid more attention to us than the freakin' Steelers, you'd notice the things going on in our lives," he'd accused. But when she asked him what was going on, he'd fled to his room and stayed there pretty much the whole weekend.

Closing the cookbook, she started writing a list of things she needed to do this month. But all she could think about was how angry Robbie had been: *the freakin' Steelers.* He'd spit the words at her like he was talking about some abusive boyfriend. He liked football! And what did he mean about her not paying attention to him? The kids were always welcome to watch the games with her. Robbie and Kristen had video games, homework, and friends to round out their lives. She had football and a panty ritual. And she deserved every minute of it. At least the Steelers couldn't betray her like people could. Tom had left, and someday soon, the kids would, too, but she'd always have the Steelers. Individual players might come and go, but the spirit of the team always remained the same: one reassuring thing in an inconsistent world.

So why all the fuss from Robbie? Then it dawned on her. Angela. Maybe some of her anti-football rhetoric was rubbing off on him. She stood up, looking for the phone book. She would call Angela's parents to tell them about Robbie skipping school and that he was no longer going to be allowed to hang out with her. Just looking for their number she felt elated. Sure, Robbie would be mad at her for a while, but he'd come around. And maybe not being associated with her would help him out at school. Maybe he'd finally find other friends, boys from nice families who would invite him over for dinner and to play video games. He'd finally start doing normal boy things instead of dying his hair pink on a Saturday afternoon. Yes, she thought, phone in hand. Get rid of Angela. This will solve everything.

Angela

When she got home from work, her parents sat on the couch, their faces unusually somber and their gazes singularly focused. Peeling off her coat and hoping to ignore their latest joke or rant about her role in the recent Steelers losing streak, Angela nodded at them and headed upstairs.

"Angela. We need to talk. Sit down." Her mom pointed at the recliner. Reluctantly, she sat. This better be good.

"Is everything okay?"

Her mom crossed her legs and leaned forward. "Angela, I got a phone call this afternoon from Patty Salvatore."

Patty? Why was she calling?

Her mom continued. "She said that Robbie has been having some problems with his grades and that last week the guidance counselor called and said that he's been skipping school. Patty seemed to think that you were responsible."

Angela started to protest, ready to deny anything at all costs.

"I called the school and talked to Mrs. Marshall and she said that your teachers also confirmed that you've been missing school."

As if on cue, her dad leaned forward. "So what do you have to say for yourself, young lady?"

"What do I have to say for myself? Mm, maybe that I hate school and was trying to save Robbie from getting his ass kicked every day? You don't understand, I had to get him out of there or he was going to get beat up. It was the nicest thing I could do."

Her parents exchanged glances. They had this way of looking at each other that cancelled out the presence of anybody else in the room.

"It's nice that you were trying to help Robbie," her mom began. "But Angela, this is really unacceptable."

"It's my senior year. So I skipped a couple of classes? I mean, my grades are the same as always, so what's the big deal?"

"The big deal is that we can't trust you. We've given you more than your fair share of freedom, but all we ever get in return is your bad attitude and stuff like this."

"My bad attitude? Oh yeah, I have such a terrible attitude that I get straight A's and I've been working since I was 16 to pay for my own car insurance. Yeah, terrible, terrible attitude."

"Stifle it, Angela, and let your mother finish!"

Her mom continued. "Patty said that Robbie isn't allowed to hang out with you outside of school right now. And your punishment will be no car privileges until the new year."

"What?!"

No car? They had to be kidding. And no hanging out with Robbie? What the hell was wrong with Patty? Who'd gotten her panties up in such a bunch that she would actually do something like that and keep her son from his only friend in the whole world, the only person who really looked out for him?

"You heard it. No car. Hand over the keys. Now." Her dad stood up, holding out his hand.

Angela pulled her arm back, hiding the keys. They were not taking her keys. Her car was like a home on wheels, the only place where she could really get away.

"No! You can't. I am not giving you my keys. I can't hang out with Robbie and you're going to take away my car? Why don't you just kill me?"

"Stop with the drama and give your dad your keys," her mom said. Angela jumped up, skirting past him and toward the stairs.

"Over my dead body."

"Angela. The keys!"

Her mom grabbed her hand. Angela swung it away. She knew she was pushing things. Her mom's face was red and agitated. "Oh yeah, so the Steelers lose a few games and this is your way of sweet revenge?"

Her mom grabbed her arm, holding it tight. "This has nothing to do with the Steelers. Now give me the keys."

A few years ago, an act like that might have prompted her to accuse them of child abuse. But tonight, as bad as things were, she could feel freedom lapping at her feet like the gentle tide of the river. It was only a matter of time until one of the schools where she'd applied accepted her and she had her ticket out of this hellhole.

She dropped the keys into her mom's open hand. "Here. Take'em. I can't wait till I get away from this stupid town next year."

Her mom tilted her head, raising an eyebrow. "What's that supposed to mean?"

Angela sighed. It was as good a time as any.

"I only applied to schools in Seattle, and that's where I'm going even if I don't get in."

She watched her mom's face switch from stern accusation to complete bewilderment. "Where? But Angela, you can go to Pitt for free. I got a job there! You said you applied."

"I never said I applied. You just assumed I did because that's what you wanted me to do. I don't want to go there. I don't want to be here."

"Quit talkin' to your mum like that." Her dad rose now, standing near the front door like she was a flight risk. They looked sincerely worried, more worried than she'd ever seen them look. Her mom walked away, sitting down and folding her face into her hands. When her shoulders began to shake and she let out a big sob, her dad approached, resting his giant hand on her shoulder. Angela paused, still on the first step. Her dad glared at her, a look so mean and disdainful she almost felt bad. He shook his head and pointed upstairs.

"Go to your room, Angela. We'll deal with this tomorrow."

She nodded, stomping up the stairs. She hadn't expected her mother to cry. Or her dad to look at her so awfully cold. She'd done a lot of rebellious things in her day and through it all, they'd maybe shook their heads or wagged their tongues, but never any real discipline and never any tears. They always just turned things into jokes, like her life was a page out of some crummy sitcom and didn't matter at all. But now her mom was crying? Now?

As she climbed the stairs to the attic, all she could see was the one person who was responsible for all of it: the one person with a mouth so big that she'd just had to be a tattletale.

She thought of the coupons in her book bag and the fake letter she'd imagined penning. She'd thought, even hoped, that her and

Patty could be friends. How wrong she'd been. When she got to her room, she pulled out a pen and started writing a letter. Ginger Mae was going down.

Shannon

On Tuesday night, after a week of fantasizing about that moment outside the bathroom with Jack, Shannon decided to call him. It wasn't like she'd never called him before. He was Jack. If things got weird, she'd turn it into some question about what Darla wanted for Christmas. It would be fine.

During a break in the usual flow of people, she disappeared into the kitchenette, shutting the door tight.

Fingers trembling, she dialed. He answered gruffly, like he'd just gotten out of bed.

"Hey."

"Hey. Are you busy?"

"No. What's up?"

What's up? It sounded so casual. She didn't know what to say. *I think I love you? I wish you'd have kissed me last week?* None of that seemed very casual.

"Um, I —"

He interrupted, his voice coarse. "Shannon, before you start, I just want to say that I'm sorry about what happened last time I saw you. How I acted." He stopped. She imagined him closing his eyes, his mouth in a thin line.

Shannon caught her breath. "Oh, I don't really know what you mean."

In the background, she heard cheers erupting from the TV—a hockey game, probably.

"Shannon, I think you know what I mean, and I just want to say that I acted out of line. I had too much to drink. I'm not that sort of guy."

Shannon's heart raced. What sort of guy? The kind who hit on his girlfriend's sister? Or the kind who cared about her?

"Don't worry about it, I was just going to call and see what you were getting Darla for Christmas but you know, the bar just got slammed so I, uh, I gotta go."

She hung up fast, the dial tone ringing in her ear. She braced herself against the counter, pushing aside a jar of Chex Mix. It was hard to imagine the last time she'd been so embarrassed. Her whole body felt like a third degree burn.

Back at the bar, Glenn and Larry were parked at their usual stools, their attention divided between the Pens game on one TV and clips of the Steelers' upcoming opponents, the Chicago Bears, on the other.

Larry winked at her. "Think we can win this weekend, Shannon?"

"No. I think we're gonna lose."

Larry and Glenn gasped. Larry pushed at his chest, faking a heart attack and laughing.

"You don't EVER predict that our boys are gonna lose, do ya ,Glenn?"

Glenn laughed. "Not unless you bet a lot of money on the opposing team! But we're winning this game. You gotta have some faith, Shannon. And whiskey. Two of the most important things in my life."

Shannon nodded, grabbing a bottle and pouring double shots into plastic cups. She felt sick in the pit of her stomach. She wished she could turn off Glenn, Larry, and the TV and go home, pull the covers up over her head, and just be still.

She didn't want to think about anything. Not Jack. Not Darla. And especially not football. But as she leveled off the shots, all she could think about was the Steelers' last trip to the Super Bowl, all those interceptions that Neil O'Donnell threw in the Arizona desert. More than 10 years later, she could still taste the stench of that defeat.

Larry caught her eye, smiling.

"Shannon," he said. "It's still early. We've had some bad luck, but don't call it a day just yet." He looked at her intently, a spark in his eye carefully trained on her. She knew that he wasn't just talking football tonight, that he had seen her faraway looks and was reassuring her in some small way that whatever it was, she would get through just fine. She didn't believe it, but she stared back at him for a moment, grateful.

Glenn cracked the awkward tension of the moment, slapping his fist on the bar with a loud yelp. "And four losses in a row, Shannon? What do you think this is? Cleveland?"

Larry looked away from Shannon then, patting his friend on the back and laughing. She slid the amber shots toward them, leaning against the edge of the bar, so close that she could see every hard line on their faces and smell every cigarette they'd smoked that day. Picking up their shots, she noticed them twisting a little under her gaze.

"Sorry, guys. I'm just tellin' the truth," she said. "Sometimes you lose."

As they drank, she grabbed their crumpled dollar bills and counted, slow and methodical, ignoring coarse hands on plastic cups and the rise and fall of their Adam's apples. As they finished, they returned to their usual pose at the bar, waiting for her, just like everybody else, and wanting something more.

Week 14: Steelers vs. Chicago Bears
(W 21-9)

Jen

As she surveyed the room looking for a good place to put the crib, Dave sat on the couch watching the game, beer in hand. Sure, the bedroom was the logical location, but they could barely open their dresser drawers now that she'd brought in her queen bed. How would they possibly fit a crib? Looking in the corner of the living room, she realized the bookshelf full of video games and DVDs was the only place that might work.

"What do you think about the crib over there?" she said, pointing.

She waited for his reaction, and then felt irritated when he barely shrugged. "Whatever you say."

"C'mon, Dave, don't you have an opinion on where we put the crib?"

He flipped the remote, turning up the volume. "Not right now. I thought you said you wanted to watch the game."

She sighed. She had promised to watch the game today. But ever since the wedding, she hadn't made it through one entire game. Every time she saw the Steelers, she felt angry, as if they were betraying her with these recent losses. She'd relied on them to win on her wedding day and they hadn't. They couldn't be trusted. And who really could be? Once she might have said Dave or even her parents, but now everybody felt like a stranger out to get her. Was she losing her mind? Or were these the pregnancy hormones acting up?

Looking sideways at Dave, she felt guilty. He was attractive and attentive, and for the longest time, she'd believed him to be everything she wanted, but lately, it just wasn't enough.

As the game flipped to commercial, she shook Dave's arm. "So what do you think about Jared for a boy or Jayden for a girl?"

Dave chewed on a potato chip and frowned. "I veto both. But seriously, I thought we already decided Dave Junior. Jayden sounds like a stripper name."

"I guess Dave Junior is okay, but I really like Jared too."

The commercials ended and the game resumed. Dave was barely looking at her, so she stood up, walking into the kitchen. The sink was full of dirty dishes, but she didn't feel like standing on her feet long enough to wash them. Her ankles were swollen and standing too long hurt her back. Sitting at the kitchen table, she sighed, flipping open her laptop and thinking of her next letter to Bobby. She knew that her parents had told him about her little breakdown before the wedding. But he had been kind enough not to bring it up in their latest correspondence. Instead, he'd congratulated her and even admitted that he was a little jealous. He had broken up with his last girlfriend months before he was deployed, and he suggested that it would be nice knowing he had a girl to come back to. A wife, he said.

It made her sad to think of Bobby longing for something he didn't have. He was a nice guy who always picked the wrong girls. Her parents said it was because he wasn't ready to settle down. She wondered if that would change when he came back. Maybe then he'd be ready for the right girl. She wanted to write to him and tell him that marriage wasn't at all what she'd thought. That it could be lonely and sad. That Dave slept on the couch most every night now and that he didn't even care that they barely made enough money to afford daycare or all the baby equipment they needed. She wanted to tell him that she was worried she had made the wrong decision and that she hadn't even been able to watch the Steelers since the wedding. But she also didn't want him to worry.

She stared at the screen for a long time. The cursor blinked in the blank e-mail screen, like the ultimate triple dog dare. She minimized the screen and looked out the window. Outside, it was beginning to snow. With a layer of fresh snow, even their dingy street looked beautiful, its crammed row houses transformed into a magical Christmas village.

"Hey, Dave. It's snowing. Come look at it, it's so pretty."

"I can see it on the TV. It's really a blizzard out."

"That's not the same. Come look out the window."

"It's Steelers ball. I'll look during the commercials."

She pressed her forehead against the cold window, knowing that he wouldn't bother to come during commercial break. He was merely trying to appease her, with no intention of actually doing so.

Shannon

As the Steelers drove toward the end zone, the snow swirled in great white waves like the ocean just before a storm. She could barely see the field. Or feel her feet. And she definitely couldn't believe that she was standing next to Jack.

All week she'd dreaded today's game, knowing that Darla and Jack would be there. Together. But this morning Darla called her, sick as a dog, begging her to take her ticket. She protested at first but, as usual, Darla was insistent: Jack had promised to do some work around the house on Monday and she wasn't going to let him take one of his buddies and get shit-faced and too hung-over to do anything the next day. Shannon gave in and a few hours later, Jack was picking her up for the game. They'd parked Downtown, walked over the Roberto Clemente bridge in a snow squall, drank a few beers at Firewaters, then waited in line at the gate, all the time immersed in conversation. She wanted to know about his house and he wanted to know about her job, about how she liked it, or what she wanted to do next. What she wanted to do next. She'd almost stumbled on the question.

"What do I want to do next?" she'd repeated while they sat at the bar in Firewaters.

"Yeah, like where do see yourself in five or ten years? Come on, everybody has some kind of a dream."

But she couldn't say anything because lately, all her dreams included him and she knew that was a dead-end dream, so she just ignored them and tried to focus on other stuff. She'd become a master at Sudoku and crossword puzzles recently, anything to avoid thinking about him.

"I don't know. Nothing specific. Just to be happy, you know. Whatever that means."

He smiled, winking at her and buying her another drink. "I know what you mean. I think Darla has my life planned out for me for about the next 20 years. But I like to take things as they come."

The glint in his eyes made her twist, uncomfortable in his gaze. He looked at her like he knew that she had it bad for him. She hated being played for a fool. She pointed to a man at the bar with slicked back brown hair and a soul patch.

"He's cute," she said, pointing at the stranger even though she didn't think he was attractive at all. She would do anything to change the subject. But nobody in the room held a candle to Jack.

Three hours later, they stood on their feet with the rest of the stadium, straining to see the play through the wall of snow. As frozen as she was, she couldn't imagine anywhere else she'd want to be.

As the team lined up at the end zone, Shannon patted her hands together, hoping they'd score. After about his seventh beer, Jack had started hugging her every time they scored. She wanted to feel his arms around her again.

On the field, Jerome Bettis ran 5 yards for his second touchdown of the game and the crowd went crazy, the whole stadium jumping and screaming, Terrible Towels waving. Jack grabbed Shannon, pulling her close. As their eyes met, he smiled, the kind of relaxed, carefree smile that she always wanted to see but that he barely made around Darla. He leaned forward and she felt like her heart might explode as he pulled her tight against his chest, his lips so close to hers, she could smell his last beer. Timidly, he pushed closer, his breath warm on her cold mouth. A shiver went through her like she might pass out as he kissed her hard. She'd been waiting for nearly a year to do this, and in all of her fantasies, it had never been this perfect. This moment. This kiss. As his tongue rolled gently across her tongue, she felt herself melting into the concrete floor. From behind them, an obnoxious voice yelled, "Get a room!" and there was a patter of laughter from others in their section.

Pulled from their moment, they slipped out of their embrace, Shannon blushing as the entire section behind them began clapping and hooting and hollering. They sat down, ending the cheers. Jack slipped his arm around her and pulled her close. Shannon leaned into him, relaxing. The snow fell so thick now that she couldn't even see the seats a few rows down from them, the visibility nearly non-existent, like there was nobody here but them.

Megan

Monday morning, Megan struggled to stay awake during the weekly sales meeting. She'd been having difficulty concentrating the past week or so, and the monotone voices of management didn't help. Today's topic had been the changes to the menu beginning in January. She couldn't imagine anything less interesting. Somewhere between learning that the au gratin potatoes now featured rosemary and that the veal piccata was being eliminated, she'd mentally checked out. When the meeting adjourned, other staffers made small talk, lingering at the table as she darted out of the room and toward the kitchen.

She had a couple of questions for the Executive Chef about a substitution for an upcoming kosher wedding. But more than that, she needed the time away from her desk. Now that she was used to her new position, she found it to be dull and tedious. On a day like this, she longed for the action-packed scene of the kitchen. Serving was dull and tedious too, but at least there was always something to do. Being busy made the time go faster. She'd show up for work and barely realize that it was time to go home. In her new position, she watched the hands of the clock crawling by like slugs and could barely wait to run out of there at exactly 4:56.

This weekend, she'd spent enough time by herself that she didn't want to spend her workday isolated as well. Thanks to a bad head cold, she'd barely left her bedroom the entire weekend, sleeping most of the day and waking up only to watch *The It's Alive Show*, filling the void of the night with tinny shrieks and screams of damsels in serious B-movie distress. Usually, these movies were her favorite, a good way to make her laugh. But this weekend she'd actually found herself crying after a particularly brutal massacre scene, as cheesy as it had been. There was something about it that reminded her about what had happened last Sunday, the innocent girl waking up with the wrong stranger. All week long, she'd tried not to think about it and had done a pretty good job until seeing that. And why should it upset her, really? Nothing had happened to her at all. She'd gotten away from that stupid loser and could easily chalk the whole thing up to bad luck. But what if she hadn't gotten away? And what if what he had said about Ryan was true? That she really was known for being nothing more than guaranteed pussy?

In the kitchen, the familiar voices of her old crew were boisterous amidst the ovens and fridges. The whirring beaters, whisking spoons, and chopping knifes drowned out her thoughts. She popped her head into the main office and saw that Chef Picard wasn't in yet. Usually he came around ten, but this morning's snowfall was delaying a lot of people who drove. Stepping back into the kitchen, Marlon hooted as he saw her.

"There she is! Why you been a stranger?"

She smiled, shrugging. "Absence makes the heart grow fonder."

"So how 'bout that game?"

"One for the ages," she said, not really wanting to talk about it. She noticed a bowl of chocolate icing on the table and reached for a spoon.

Marlon batted her hands away, laughing. "Keep your hands outta there."

"Geez, I was just looking at it!"

"I saw the intent in your eyes." He wiped his hands on a towel and stepped closer. Uncomfortably close. Moving away, she felt his hand grabbing her ass.

"And speaking of intent, when you gonna come over to my place for Round 2?"

She jerked away. "Not suitable for work," she said, hoping he'd get the drift that there was not going to be a Round 2 and that he needed to let her go. She didn't exactly regret that there had been a Round 1, but it certainly hadn't been good enough to warrant a second go at it or a hand on her ass during work. She looked around the kitchen and suddenly it felt like everybody was looking at her and laughing, like they'd heard everything he'd said and seen his hand on her ass and were thinking of how typical this was. That of course she'd slept with Marlon.

Marlon leaned closer, winking. "Oh right, my bad. It's our little secret. That's even hotter." He grabbed her ass again.

She pushed his hand away, furious. "I'm serious. Don't touch me."

Marlon laughed, stepping back. "I was only joking."

She pushed him. "Joking? You call that joking? That's sexual harassment."

"Megan, are you okay? You know you're my girl. I don't mean no disrespect."

She knew. She knew. Marlon wasn't the enemy. As much as he teased her, she always felt like deep down, he really did respect her. But she couldn't stop herself, something inside giving way like a rockslide on Route 28. "You don't mean no disrespect? You grabbed my ass like I'm some whore, and you don't mean no disrespect?"

Suddenly, she realized that the kitchen was eerily silent, everybody staring at her and Marlon. She pointed at them. "Oh, and don't you all just love this, right? The dumb slut gets what she deserves, huh?"

Everybody looked down, staring at their feet and fidgeting at their respective work stations.

"Megan! What is going on here?"

Shit. Larissa. How long had she been there? How much had she seen and heard? Megan spun around, blanching. It was quite clear by the pinched look on Larissa's face that she'd heard about the whole damn thing.

"Show's over! Get back to work!" Larissa barked at the kitchen staff as she pushed Megan into the main office. Closing the door behind her, Larissa folded her arms over her chest.

"Larissa, I'm sorry, I can explain."

"I don't want explanations. Megan, you have to learn to leave your personal life at home. You've been noticeably late at least three times, missed several staff meetings, and how about all those bruises on your face a couple of weeks ago? That didn't look very professional at client meetings."

"I'm sorry, it's just been a bad couple of weeks but I can —"

Larissa held her hand up. "I'm sorry that you're having a bad time but I put myself on the line trying to help you and if there's one more incident, I'm done defending you."

Megan tried to think of some way to defend herself, but there was nothing left to say except I'm sorry.

Patty

In the parking lot of the Brentwood post office, Patty stepped out of her minivan with a triumphant smile. On the morning after a victory against the Chicago Bears, it finally felt like there was reason for hope. Yes, the Steelers needed to win every last regular season game to even win a chance at the playoffs, but after yesterday's game, that didn't look like such a long shot. After battling injuries earlier in the season, Jerome Bettis had run 101 yards in bad weather conditions. Just watching him rush like that, she had a feeling she was going to be seeing him running next month in the Super Bowl, in his hometown of Detroit.

With a silent prayer for another victory, Patty dropped this week's panties, addressed to Bettis of course, into the mail slot and turned the key to her box.

Inside, a white envelope was stuffed tight into the hole. Figuring that it had been stuck in the wrong bin, she looked at the address, shocked to find that it was addressed to Ginger Mae. There was no return address, but it was stamped with a Pittsburgh seal.

Taking a sharp breath, she looked around the vestibule. Save for an elderly woman cussing under her breath as she fumbled with her keys, the place was deserted.

Heart pounding, Patty stuffed the envelope into her purse and marched to her car where she ripped it open, exposing a letter typed on Steelers letterhead. She could barely catch her breath as she read.

Dear Ginger Mae,

On behalf of the 2005 Steelers team, I'd like to say hello and thank you for your letters. Although we have many fans that send us letters, particularly items of clothing, none of them have been as persistent and intriguing as the ones sent to us by you. There is always locker room discussion after a victory about who will be getting Ginger Mae's panties this week. While we understand and respect your right to privacy, we would very much like the chance to meet the mystery woman behind the underwear. Along with some business partners, I recently opened a restaurant/bar called The Locker Room on East Carson Street. Enclosed is a voucher for a free meal. Please know that I have given your name to the hostess with instructions to seat you at the best table in the house and to call me immediately if you are ever to come dine at my establishment. Go Steelers!

Sincerely,
Hines Ward, #86

When Patty finished reading the letter, she tucked the voucher into the plastic fold of her checkbook with her other coupons. Then, she crumpled the letter into a ball and peeled out of her parking space so fast, she smelled the rubber burning for miles.

Angela

Glancing up from her macaroni and cheese, Angela surveyed the cafeteria. It was pretty grim. Closest to the salad bar, the jocks and cheerleaders laughed and flirted. Over by the windows, the band geeks loudly discussed last night's chorus concert. At the table nearest her and Robbie, some science fiction geeks discussed the nuanced meanings in the latest episode of *Battlestar Galactica*. And across all these different tables, Angela noted the same theme. The same theme that united everybody in this damn city but her: Steelers gear. Sweatshirts. T-shirts. Polo Shirts. You name the type of clothing and chances were good that one of her schoolmates owned it in black and gold.

She looked at Robbie's Oasis shirt, another 90s throwback they'd salvaged from the Red, White and Blue. She frowned.

"Won't you even like consider talking to your mom?"

"About what?"

"About how unfair this is. About how she is ruining our senior year."

Getting rides from her mom to and from school and work was torture. For the first week, her mom had been so miffed about the college news that they'd barely talked. But this week, she'd acted all friendly and tried to make small talk, as if Angela had actually chosen to spend time with her and wanted to chat it up like the Gilmore Girls.

Robbie shook his head. "I'm trying not to talk to her at all if I can help it."

"At least try. Doesn't she know that we were skipping school for a reason?"

He tilted, his head, confused. "We were?"

She paused, swallowing her words. Hints had been made, but she'd never officially told him about why she'd decided to bail that first day. Sometimes, Robbie could be very oblivious to social cues. Like, it was very obvious at school that the boys thought he was gay and most of the girls too. But he seemed totally oblivious and usually irritated when people said anything about it. Even her. Not that it bothered her, really; people called her a lesbian all the time. She wasn't and didn't really care if people thought otherwise. It was pretty apparent to her that Robbie was gay, but if he didn't want to talk about it, then she minded her own business. That's what being a real friend was all about.

She shrugged. "Of course there was a reason. We don't like gym."

"I don't think that will be a very compelling argument."

"So you're not even going to try?"

"It's only for a month."

"Only a month? That's forever!"

"You're a drama queen."

"You don't seem very upset."

"There's nothing we can do about it. This time next year, we'll be at Pitt and none of this will matter." He pointed his finger around the cafeteria. She was still waiting for the right time to tell him that she hadn't applied. It was time for a change of subject. There was something else she'd been waiting to tell him, and this did seem like the right time for that.

"Yeah. Anyways, how is your mom?"

"My mom?"

"Yeah."

"Why are you asking?"

"Oh, I'm just curious."

There was an edge to Robbie's voice. "Why?"

"No reason."

"Angela."

"Okay, okay. I might have sent her a letter."

"A letter?"

"Mm-hm. And not to her. To her alter ego."

Robbie dropped his fork mid-bite. "You did what?"

He looked really irritated, but she was sure that once she told him the whole story, he'd laugh. But he didn't. She told him the whole thing, how she'd snuck back into Patty's room months ago to get the P.O. Box number. How she'd saved the coupon from the Locker Room. And she told him about the letter she'd written and mailed—a letter from one Hines Ward to one Ginger Mae. Robbie looked stunned.

"You did that?"

"Yeah." He made it sound like a bad thing. But she was proud of herself. Patty had done her wrong and she deserved some kind of payback. And what was the big deal? It was just a stupid letter that would either make Patty totally paranoid or give her some jollies.

Robbie finally spoke. "There's something wrong with you."

"What?"

"That's just mean."

"Oh, and banning us from hanging out together isn't? She knows we only have each other."

"But my mom is really sensitive. This sort of thing could really mess her up."

"Robbie, your mom's sending panties to the Steelers. I think she's already messed up."

"Stop it," he said, shoving his books into his bag. "I don't want to talk to you right now."

"Oh, please. Now who's the drama queen?"

"No, Angela. It's like my mom always says, you have no regard for anybody but yourself. None."

With those parting words, he left her alone at the table. She watched him walk out toward the library and considered following, but didn't. Why did everybody think she was so selfish? Trying to save Robbie's skin had gotten her into this mess. Scanning the room, she looked for Brad. He knew the truth and could straighten this whole thing out. But he wasn't there. All that was there was a bunch of people who she didn't like, cracking lame jokes and sporting Steelers shirts. It was the same sad story of her entire pathetic life.

Week 15: Steelers vs. Minnesota Vikings
(W 18-3)

Megan

Alone in her bedroom on Sunday afternoon, Megan squeezed her legs into her chest and tried to muster emotion, any kind, for the game at hand. The Steelers were leading the Vikings, 6 to 0. Any other Sunday this would have been cause for cheers, smiles, high-fives, and a round of shots. Watching games was comforting, a tradition as familiar as her grandma's sweet potato casserole at Thanksgiving or the first warm day of the spring when you could finally wear open-toed shoes and mini-skirts for a night out on the town. Today though, she felt nothing. Not one single thing. And it had been like this ever since her run-in with Larissa on Monday. All week at work, she'd done her job with a distinct lack of feeling. She was phoning it in, like her and her dad always said about a seasoned player missing a tackle or fumbling the ball. She'd been holed up in her room the whole weekend; the people in her print movie poster, *Attack of the 50 Foot Woman,* were about the closest she'd come to human contact for three days. And the worst part? Nobody seemed to care. Hell, nobody even seemed to notice.

Emily had barely been home the whole weekend, coming in and out for short periods both mornings, presumably to grab her stuff and head back to Mike's. And the phone hadn't rung at all. As much as she wanted to believe that it was because everybody assumed she was busy with something or somebody else, she couldn't help but wonder if maybe what it really meant was that nobody cared. At all. Even her dad, who she could usually count on for one phone call before or during a Steelers game, was totally MIA. Even after she had left a message on their machine last night.

"Hey, it's me," she had said, trying not to cry. "Just calling to say hi. Give me a call when you get a chance."

In her mind, she'd assumed that "when you get a chance" would translate into "as soon as you hear how broken your daughter sounds on the answering machine." But now, she imagined them listening to it and ignoring it. There she goes again, they probably said.

Looking at her silent phone, she picked it up. Maybe they were really busy. That had to be it. There was no way they would just ignore her call. Maybe if she called now, she'd see it was all just a big misunderstanding and feel a little bit better. It rang once. Then twice. Come on, the game was on a commercial break. There was no reason not to answer the phone.

"Hello?"

"Dad? What's going on?"

"What's going on? I'm watching the game." He sounded abrupt, a lot ruder than he should have been given the score.

"Yeah. I called last night. Just wanted to see what was—"

"Hey, it's coming back on. I'm gonna hand this over to your mom right now."

She began to protest but stopped, hearing the phone exchanging hands.

"Megan. What are you doing?"

"Didn't you get my message last night?"

"Huh? Oh yeah, we got that."

"Why didn't you call me?"

"Why? Is something wrong?"

"No, but, I mean, I said to call me back."

"You said when we got a chance. My office holiday party was last night and today's been hectic. You wouldn't believe who I ran into at Giant Eagle this morning—Gracie Wilkinson."

Gracie Wilkinson. Her high school best friend turned enemy turned stay-at-home mom to three kids in the suburban development where they'd both grown up. Seeing her at the grocery store was hardly surprising. Nor was her mom actually thinking she cared. When she and her high-school boyfriend, Chad, had broken up after senior year, she'd thought she could count on Gracie, but Gracie had gone behind her back and befriended Chad's new girlfriend. And here was her mom acting like it was 1995 and they were still the best of friends.

"Stop it, Mom. I didn't call to talk about Gracie. And none of those sound like really good reasons for not calling me back."

There was a long pause on the other end of the line. "I was trying to talk to you, Megan. I thought that's why you called."

That was partially true. But she'd never really been good at talking to her mom. "I mean, I just think that if your daughter calls, you should call her back."

"Megan! You are infuriating!"

"Infuriating? Me? Because I want you to call me?"

"Stop it. You know exactly what I'm talking about. If I call you too much, then you're on me about riding your back, and now I wait a day to return your call, and you treat me like a criminal."

"I'm not treating you like a criminal. I just asked a question."

"And I answered it. Now, what do you want? Do you want to talk to me or not? I don't have time to sit on the phone all day hoping that my daughter wants to listen to me."

Megan cringed. No matter how hard she tried, talking to her mom was impossible. There was something unspoken between them that she could never get past, a wall as formidable as the hills surrounding Pittsburgh, except even more impenetrable. She'd never found a tunnel or a bridge that could bring them eye-to-eye.

"Right now I don't want to talk to you. So fine." Except she did. She wanted, nothing more, than to talk to her mom. To talk to anybody at all. But the notion made her as helpless as she would be if somebody forced her to stand on the overlook at Mt. Washington and pinpoint the window in her Bloomfield bedroom. It was impossible to even know where to start.

"Fine. I'll have your dad call you back when the game is over." As the phone went dead, Megan hurled it across the room. It hit the door, exploding into two parts. She watched it fall without moving, not even bothering to pick it up.

Shannon

Wednesday evening, when Shannon finally showed up at Darla's place, the door was open and loud laughter and talking emanated from the kitchen. All day, she'd been expecting the call from Darla. The break-up call. What she hadn't expected was the invitation to come over to offer moral support. Usually Darla had an army of friends from the hospital waiting in the wings for just these types of crisis situations.

But when the call came in, Darla said she wanted to be alone. Granted, she also had a food order to put in. And now, carrying the requested two gallons of Edy's Peanut Butter Fudge ice cream, Klondike bars, Cool Ranch Doritos and what felt like the entire baked goods section at Giant Eagle, Shannon wondered if Darla had wanted her support as much she wanted free groceries.

"Darla? Darla?" Stepping into the kitchen, she stopped, surprised to find a tableful of vaguely familiar women who she recognized as Darla's co-workers at Presbyterian Hospital.

"SHANNON!" Darla squealed, jumping up and nearly suffocating her with a bear hug. She grabbed the grocery bag away and immediately began pulling out goodies, pointing at the three women at table. "You know my friends, right?"

She remembered meeting them all at various points and had heard Darla talking about them so much she felt like she did know them. Unfortunately, she couldn't even remember their names.

She nodded anyways. "Yeah, good to see you." They nodded at her then went back to talking. Since they were still wearing scrubs, she figured Darla must have called them to come over after their shifts ended hours ago. Judging by the two empty bottles of wine on the table, they'd been having quite the time.

She stepped backwards, whispering to Darla. "I thought it was just going to be me and you."

Darla nodded. "I know, but when I called off, I told Dani and she told Terry and Karen and, well, they just stopped on by. Wasn't that sweet of them? They know how to cheer a girl up."

"Right." Shannon nodded, faking a smile. As relieved as she was not to be alone with Darla, spending the rest of the evening with three women she barely knew was just as intimidating, if not more.

"So, Shannon, you still working down at that bar in the evenings?" said one with purple scrubs and long, curly hair pulled into a severe ponytail.

"Huh? Oh yeah. Still there."

"Do you meet a lot of guys that way? Maybe we should get Darla a job on the side, what do you think?"

At that, all four of them exploded into laughter, heckling and catcalling Darla and shouting about meeting men and talking so fast and loud that Shannon stood still, waiting for a break in their revelry to give an answer. Finding none, she sat down, close to Darla and the back door in case she needed to make a quick exit. After what seemed like forever and the opening of one new bottle of wine and five full glasses later, they finally shut up when one with pink scrubs and graying hair and a mole at the tip of her nose held up her glass for a toast.

"And this one to Jack. May his penis fall off."

Darla squealed, adding, "His very SMALL penis!"

All the women laughed, uproariously, clinking their glasses with a fervor that left quite a few drops of burgundy wine on Darla's white tablecloth. Shannon faked a smile, drinking her glass in three gulps. The ladies laughed. "That's the spirit," they said.

Shannon tried to smile again but what little spirit she had left had been extinguished with that toast. She felt like she might die if she didn't get out of that kitchen in about five seconds flat.

The conversation somehow shifted to the topic of their new physician assistant's manly parts—Dani maintaining that he was packing a big one and Terry insisting that his lack of confidence meant it was uncomfortably small. Shannon made a point of looking at her watch and yawning.

"I think I should be going. I have to get up early."

Her fears that an early departure would provoke resistance were entirely wrong. In fact, nobody, not even Darla, seemed to notice that she was going extra early. Darla gave her kiss on the cheek. "Thanks for coming, chicka."

Chicka? This was a woman whose heart had been broken less than seven hours ago and now she was smiling and saying cutesy words like "chicka"? Darla had no idea what it was like to be in pain. No idea.

Angela

Study hall, Thursday morning, Angela sat in the library doodling on her latest Calculus test. When she noticed Robbie coming in with the rest of his English class, she tried not to look too obvious, watching intently as they sat at the round tables closest to the computers. Straining her ear, she made out a few words from Mrs. Gianni, something about the literary canon and finding a good book to read over the break. Then Mrs. Gianni sat down and started writing in a notebook, and the class dispersed into different parts of the library. Robbie disappeared into a tall aisle of non-fiction, and Angela seized the opportunity to talk to him. The week since their fight he hadn't returned her calls, e-mails, texts, or approved a single one of her MySpace comments. She'd had enough. Marching down the aisle, she spotted him staring off into space, arms folded, looking entirely uninterested in anything the library had to offer. They made eye contact and he started to move.

"Stop," she said, quickening the pace to grab his arm. He wore a black hooded sweatshirt zipped up to his chin.

"What are you doing?"

"I need to talk to you."

"There's nothing to say." Robbie bent his knees, leaning sideways into his red Chuck Taylors.

"C'mon. I left you like a million apology e-mails and texts. Why are you still mad?"

Robbie backed away from her. "It's not that I'm mad, it's just —"

"Just what? C'mon dude, spit it out."

She could tell by the way he glared at her that rushing him wasn't her best move.

"It's like if you'd done it to me, you know, it would be fine and I'd be over it. But you, you went for my mom. That's just—low."

Low. He was right. It was low. Going for Patty was a pretty classless move. But she'd been so angry. And hurt. What right did Patty have to try to keep her away from her best friend and get her into even more trouble with her parents? Ever since the grounding, even though the Steelers season was on an upswing, things at home had been excruciating. Every day her mom left Pitt paraphernalia and applications on her bed. And each night at dinner her dad made a point to talk about how little money they had to do just about anything, including paying for college tuition. They seemed to think that there was something they could do or say to change her mind. They just didn't get it—she didn't belong in Pittsburgh. She needed a new start. Here, she'd run into people from high school on campus or she'd spend every day with Robbie and her life would be more of the same. She'd always be that angry girl who couldn't watch Steelers games and emasculated all the boys with her sarcasm. In Seattle, things would be different. She'd dye her hair lighter and get crushes on cute boys who knew more about Kant and Nietzsche than they did Bradshaw, Swann, or Lemieux. Looking at Robbie, she frowned. A million times she'd said I'm sorry, and a million times he'd said it wasn't enough.

"Right. I hit below the belt. I know. We covered it. But just let it go."

Crossing his arms over his chest, Robbie shrugged. "I don't know if I can. I mean, you don't understand my mom. The last thing she needs is somebody attacking her."

"I sent an anonymous letter to her alter ego. I'd hardly call that an attack."

"She doesn't need people pointing out her flaws."

"I didn't point out any flaws, Robbie. I'll show you the letter. It was perfectly innocent."

Robbie shook his head. "Look she's been acting totally weird lately, so don't say it was perfectly innocent."

"Well, how do you know she's not acting weird about something else?"

"Because there's nothing else. It's this. She got your letter and you freaked her out, and now she's all wide-eyed and nervous, exactly like she was after my dad left. Like all these years of her getting over it and now she's right back where she —"

"Dude, you are blaming way too much on me. It wasn't that big of a deal."

"I bet it was to her."

"Well, what do you want me to do? Write a letter to Dr. Phil and we can go to his show for a heartfelt confession?"

"This is done. I'm not talking about it anymore. Have a good Christmas." He started to walk away, and Angela pulled him back.

"Have a good Christmas? So you're going to keep this up over the whole break?"

He shrugged like he wasn't sure he cared. It was too much.

"That's cold, Robbie. But I really think I've made the right decision about colleges."

"What decision?"

"I'm not going to Pitt next year."

"What?"

"I only applied to schools out west. I want to move to Seattle."

Robbie took a step back, his face white like she'd threatened to punch him in the mouth. For an anxious moment, she thought he was going to cry, but instead his face went blank then gave way to a fake, mechanical smile. She knew that he was processing it, slowly realizing that all this time she'd been lying. And she wanted him to be mad, to get angry, to have some kind of dramatic reaction to let her know that he cared. But he didn't.

"Merry Christmas," he said, turning around and walking away. For a moment, she stood alone in the aisle, waiting for him to come back. And then, finally, it became clear that he wasn't—not now or maybe ever.

Week 16: Steelers vs. Cleveland Browns
(W 41-0)

Desiree

9:00 PM on Christmas Eve, Desiree sat quietly on the couch,trying to concentrate on the game. With the Steelers leading the Browns 34 to 0 in the third quarter, it was clear that they were going to win. Even Tom, who always watched until the bitter end, had started working on a crossword puzzle.

As the game broke for commercial, Desiree tried to ignore both Tom and his kids, a nearly impossible task.

As Kristen returned from what seemed like her hundredth trip to the kitchen for more sweets, Tom looked up and said, "Here's one, Kristen: a five-letter word for 'like some mouthwashes.'"

Shaking her head, Kristen settled into the other side of the couch and stuffed a cookie into her mouth. "No clue. Ask Robbie."

As she spoke, crumbs dropped onto her red cashmere sweater. Desiree braced herself, trying not to say anything. That sweater wasn't cheap. It deserved a lot better than cookie crumbs. Kristen kicked Robbie in the arm.

He looked up from his new iPod. "Any other clues?"

Tom frowned. "Not yet."

"Call Mom if you're that stuck," said Kristen, holding yet another cookie. "She's a whiz at those."

Desiree's eyes darted toward Tom to see his reaction. If he even thought about calling Patty, she was more than ready to wrestle that phone right out of his hand.

To say the day had been trying was an understatement. Not only had the kids barely said thanks for their mountain of gifts, Kristen had spent most of the day whining that she wasn't with Jeff, and Robbie had spent most of the day talking about Patty in terms so glowing that it was all Desiree could do not to knock that smirk right off his face. Not exactly the nicest thought, but a person has their limits. And those limits did not involve listening for over an hour to Robbie, Kristen, and Tom talking about memories of Christmas past. If they wanted to reminisce, fine. But they needed to do it on their own time and not when she was trying to cook them a healthy, holiday-appropriate dinner. And speaking of cooking, those limits certainly did not include periodic phone calls to Patty to update her on the progress of the sweet potato casserole: "Mom," Robbie had reported. "Desiree's sweet potatoes taste bland, what do you put into yours to make it taste so good?"

As helpful as Patty's butter-laden reply had been, it was information Desiree already knew. And when dinner was finally served, the kids picked at the spread, barely eating anything and swearing that they just couldn't wait until tomorrow's Christmas ham.

"Mom is the most amazing cook ever," Robbie had declared as he dumped his leftovers into the garbage disposal. "Tomorrow is gonna be kick ass."

About a hundred times, Desiree had given Tom that wilting "I'm dying here" look to indicate her fraying nerves. And about a hundred times in return, Tom responded with a strong nod and pursed lips, a clear warning that he knew she was upset but was going to do absolutely nothing to remedy the situation.

At Kristen's suggestion to call Patty, Desiree caught his eye and delivered withering look number 101. Hurriedly, Tom looked back down at the paper. Robbie whipped out his cell phone, already dialing.

"Here," he said, handing it to Tom. "Just ask. It will only take a minute."

Desiree jumped up, intercepting the call and hanging up. The living room became very quiet, all eyes on her as the phone in her hand began ringing. It was obvious that Patty had seen the number and was calling back.

"Answer it," said Robbie.

She clicked the ignore button and stuffed the phone into her pocket.

"What'd you do that for?" Robbie stood up. Nearly six foot, he was a good six inches taller than her, but she didn't flinch. He weighed about 150 pounds, barely enough to remain grounded in a heavy wind.

She looked between him and Kristen. "Because you two may not realize it, but you're supposed to be spending Christmas Eve with me and your father and that does not mean calling home every 5 minutes."

Kristen immediately pointed at Robbie. "Hey, that was all him, not me."

"I don't care who it was. It's rude to me and your dad. Right, Tom?"

Even from the corner of her eye she could tell that Tom was hedging, that he was going to carefully negotiate his next few words, afraid to upset her or the kids. Before he could speak, Robbie moved closer to her face.

"It's rude to call our mom? What do you even care?"

The words hung like the humidity on a stormy summer evening, threatening to suffocate them all. She thought about her turmoil of thoughts over the past few months, the sudden desire to have kids and the decision that it was probably too late. And there they all stood watching her, none of them, not even Tom, privy to her struggle. And yet, they stood there and judged her, like she didn't care about anything in the world, especially not them. If only they knew. If only they had the slightest fucking clue.

She swallowed. "I care, Robbie. Because like it or not, you and Kristen are probably the only goddamn kids I'm ever going to have. And for once, I'd like a goddamn memory that's about the four of us and doesn't include your goddamn mother. And the answer to your stupid crossword is Scope! It's SCOPE, you goddamn fucking morons!"

Her piece spoken, she spun on her heels, hoping to get away fast and hide the impending waterworks. Behind her, the living room remained quiet, and she imagined them frozen in position, wondering what had gone so miserably wrong.

Patty

Ever since she'd gotten the letter, Patty had been working furiously to forget about it. There was no way that one of the Steelers could really be writing to her. No way. Chances were good that somebody had discovered her secret, perhaps even somebody from work, and was trying to make a fool of her. But then again, what if a Steeler really did want to meet her? Surely they'd noticed her dedication over the years, and maybe they were just trying to reward a good fan. And it was those kind of crazy thoughts that made her determined to focus on any other thing but that crumpled letter.

Fortunately, Christmas was the perfect time for distractions, so she'd spent the past few weeks obsessively shopping and transforming their house into a Christmas wonderland, complete with an entire Steelers-themed Christmas village on the mantle. There were so many things to do to keep busy, and she'd done a yeoman's job of it, perfectly portioning out every minute of every day into some pursuit that did not involve thinking about that letter. She'd done so well for so many weeks.

And now Christmas Eve was here—her least favorite night of the year. The night she spent alone while Robbie and Kristen had a sweet little family holiday with Tom and Desiree. Usually, she tried to save a few last-minute things to do for the evening to avoid spending it entirely devoid of activity. But this year, she'd been too efficient. Every last thing was done. Every bow tied, every ribbon curled, every holly hung. Except for watching the evening Steelers game, she had nothing to do. It had been nice for a while, though, because Robbie had called her several times throughout the night to update her on various going-ons and ask random questions. But around nine, the phone rang one last time and by the time she got to it, he'd hung up. Despite a few frantic calls back to him, there'd been no answer and now she sat in her recliner in the wake of a Steelers victory, thinking about what to do next. It was Saturday night and even thought she didn't usually pack up her panties until Monday, there was nothing else to do. Besides, tomorrow would be too busy.

That's it, she decided, looking at the silent cell phone and closing her eyes. First, she'd wrap up some panties for Ike Taylor, then she'd take a long hot bath. A glass of wine and a sleeping pill later, she'd be in heavenly slumber by ten thirty. Heavenly slumber that would not include worrying about what kind of amazing gifts Desiree and Tom had just given Kristen and Robbie.

She headed upstairs, carefully packaging a red lace G-string. And as she did, she finally let herself think about that letter and, thinking of that letter and of her impending bath and a good night's sleep, she felt hopeful for a change. It was a long shot, but she decided to add an extra note to her package. *Dear Hines, I received your letter last week and am interested in meeting you. Love Always, Ginger Mae*

She wrapped the pink note around the envelope and pushed it into her drawer. She wasn't entirely sure that she'd actually send it. But something about it felt right. And for once on Christmas Eve, she didn't feel so damn lonely.

Megan

The announcement came early Christmas morning via text, before Megan had barely opened one gift: a picture of a diamond ring. Emily and Mike were engaged.

"You just get a message you got fired or something?" said her dad. Megan looked up, startled. She hadn't even noticed him watching her.

"Huh?"

"That face you just made. The angry face. Shelley, did you see that face she just made? Just like when she was little and —"

"I saw the face, Nick. It just seems like she's a little old to be making it on Christmas morning," her mom said, folding her arms over her chest. In a pink cashmere twin set and black slacks, she looked the picture of confidence and poise at nine in the morning.

Reaching for another box, Megan slid her cell toward the couch. " And I'm also a little too old for my parents to talk about me like I'm not even in the room."

"Well, what was it? A hot date cancel on you?" her dad said with a wink.

A hot date? Usually her dad left the prying to her mom. He seemed about as interested in her personal life as she was in his. That was the thing with parents and children, at a certain point they just needed to acknowledge the other's existence and stay uninvolved in the particulars.

She shrugged. "No hot date. And I didn't make an angry face. One of my friends got engaged. That's all."

"That's all," her mom repeated, obviously excited. "That's fantastic news. Who was it? I thought most of your friends were already married."

Most of her friends were not already married. Most of her friends from high school were already married, yes. But she had so many more friends than that, so many more networks and clusters of people than her mother could ever conceive. But she knew exactly what her mother was getting at: *I thought most of your friends were already married. Unlike you, Megan, the last unmarried twenty-eight-year-old in all of Pittsburgh.*

"Most of my friends aren't already married, actually. But this was Emily."

"Your roommate? I didn't even know she was dating anybody."

"Yeah, but she only met him in September. This seems a little too fast."

Her dad groaned. "That's a lot too fast! I thought she was a smart girl."

"She is a smart girl," said her mom. "Sometimes a few months is all it takes. Maybe if you were a little more open to the possibility, you'd see that. Of course, you need to finish your degree before you go rushing into a relationship."

Megan stood up, the unopened box on her lap hitting the floor with a solid thud. "So which is it, Mom? School or a man? Because when I was in high school and wanted to marry Chad, all you did was try to break us up so I could go to school."

"You were too young. You needed to finish school first."

"Yeah, and maybe if you'd have let me go to school with him, he wouldn't have cheated on me."

He wouldn't have cheated on me. Megan couldn't even believe she said it. But it was true. Her mother had pushed her into college at Pitt to keep her far away from Chad at Penn State; far enough away that they'd broken up by the end of first semester. And it hadn't been her fault at all. Back then she was just another love-struck teenager who thought her entire life was all mapped out. And then Chad had cheated with a sorority girl from Philly who later dumped him for a third-stringer on the football team. Still, seven years later, she got a bitter taste in her mouth remembering that final conversation with Chad.

"I don't know what to say, Megan," he'd said without trace of regret in his voice. "We just weren't right for each other."

"Weren't right for each other? We were talking about getting married!"

"We're young, Megan. You only get to play the field once. I'm not going to marry the first girl I date."

It sounded like the sort of thing her mother had been telling her the whole four years she'd dated Chad: *You're so young, Megan. Don't tie yourself down to one boy.*

If playing the field was what everybody wanted her to do, she'd spent the last few years exceeding their wildest expectations.

"Megan," her dad said. "It wasn't your mother's fault that Chad cheated on you. He was a doofus. You were too young to see that."

"Yeah, but then when I got confused about what to major in, what help was Mom then? Not much, because all she could push down my throat was her life. What she wanted to do. I didn't want to go into freakin' health care administration. I don't even know what the hell that is. She could never just let me make up things for myself. Always pick, pick, pick."

"I'm sorry you feel that way, Megan. I've never meant to pick on you. It's just that I think that you have a lot more potential than you give yourself credit for. You're a very smart girl, but you don't seem to see it."

A very smart girl? As much as she hated to admit it, hearing her mom say that felt pretty good. But it didn't really change anything.

"Thanks, Mom," she said, trying to be nice, but still frowning.

She looked at her dad, hoping he'd say something comical to alleviate the tension. But his face was pinched, full of concern. "Hey, kid, you're not really that unhappy with your life, are you?"

She concentrated on opening a set of Steelers beer mugs from her aunt and uncle. She turned them over in her hands, tracing the emblem with her finger.

"No," she said, unable to put into words how she really felt. It wasn't that she didn't like her life, it was just that everything and everybody was always changing, always pairing up or settling down or having kids or moving away, and she just wanted everything to stop, for everything to stay the same. Once upon a time, she'd been the one who everybody followed, now she was the one forever being left behind. But how do you tell that to your parents? On Christmas morning?

She tried to laugh it off, shaking her head: "No, no. I love my life. It's really friggin' great."

She hoped it sounded sincere enough for them to actually buy it.

Angela

Waiting in her room on the tail end of Christmas, Angela felt something bittersweet bubbling up as she contemplated her gifts and thought of how different things would be next year. If she stuck with her plan, she'd be flying in from Seattle for the holiday, armed with exciting stories about a life outside of the Burgh. Circumstances like that might even make her feel nice toward her parents. And while she'd once worried about Robbie and even fretted over her decision, his recent silent treatment made her realize for once and all that going away was really the best decision.

She sat down on her bed, looking at the pile of clothes her mom had bought her, most of them ones that she'd never be caught dead in, but her mom of course wished she would embrace—a black sweater with pink accents, an oversized Pitt sweatshirt (good for around the house at least) and a knee-length, gray pencil skirt. The sweater and the skirt looked like an ensemble fit for a job interview, and she couldn't for the life of her comprehend what her mother might have been thinking when she picked that one. But then again, she couldn't really comprehend much of anything her mother thought. Or anybody else for that matter.

Her brief feelings of melancholy vanished with a knock at the door. "Angela, phone for you," her dad said.

She opened the door, hesitantly taking the phone, wondering who it could be.

"Hello?"

"Ang."

It was Robbie. In spite of herself, she felt thrilled. Practically elated.

"Hey, what's up?" she said, her voice barely concealing her excitement.

"My mom got your letter."

"Huh? Oh, why? Did she say something to you? I mean, if she did that's crazy…"

"She didn't say anything. I snooped in her room this morning. She was all caught up in some drama about a mini-skirt that Desiree bought Kristen and didn't notice me slipping away."

"So what, you found it in her drawer? It's not a big deal. I thought we were done with this, honestly. I told you I was sorry. I just needed to vent my frustration and that was a perfect way—"

"I didn't find the letter. I found her reply."

Angela stood up on her knees, surprised. "Her reply?"

"Yeah, she wrote back, like saying she wanted to meet them."

"No way! So she took it seriously?"

"Apparently. And don't sound like you're about to start laughing. This isn't funny."

Angela sighed. Robbie could be such a square sometimes. If there was nothing else amusing in her life right now, this was a little bit funny. Her attempt at official Steelers stationery had been amateur at best, and if Patty had swallowed that she was pretty gullible. Or she just wanted to believe so badly that she'd overlook even the largest flaws. Angela was pretty sure she'd even gotten their mailing address wrong.

"I'm not laughing. I mean, okay, I am laughing. Robbie, that letter I wrote was so obviously a fake…."

"She didn't think so."

"I'm sorry, but what do you want me to do about it?"

"Apologize."

"I've apologized to you about one hundred times."

"To my mom."

The thought of confessing what she did to Patty made her face burn. She hadn't meant to cause any problems. She just wanted Patty to squirm for a while, just like she had chafed without her car keys and the whole world's knowledge of her Seattle escape plan.

"Don't you think that would be, like, pouring salt in the wounds or whatever?"

"How?"

"Well, right now she thinks they did it and she's writing back asking to meet them, but when they don't reply, it will just fade away. She'll realize it was a mistake or a joke or whatever."

On the other end, she could almost hear Robbie contemplating. She crossed her fingers, hoping he'd see it her way.

"I guess."

"You don't guess, you know. Just let it go and I promise if anything else of this ever comes up, I'll give myself up."

"You promise?"

"Promise?"

"Just like you promised we'd get an apartment together in Oakland next year?"

Angela bit her tongue. "Robbie, just because I want to go somewhere else to college doesn't mean I don't want to be your friend."

"But you didn't even apply to Pitt."

"But I can apply anytime. They have rolling admissions." She paused, unable to believe that she'd actually said that so easily. Her mom's constant comments were starting to affect her.

"I don't know, Angela. I just don't feel like I can trust you anymore."

She winced. His tone sounded more like her doubting parents than her best friend since kindergarten. Was this really what growing up was about? Disappointing everybody you loved unless you always did exactly what they wanted?

"You don't have to trust me for now, Robbie. But don't ignore me, these past few weeks have been—"

"The freakin' worst ever?"

"Yes!"

Robbie laughed. Angela smiled. "I mean, this whole day was so terrible, thinking that I couldn't call you to tell you all the embarrassing things my dad said once he got drunk at dinner—he told my cousin Megan she was skanky hot."

"Well, your cousin Megan is skanky hot."

"I know. I think of it more like she's Pittsburgh hot, than skanky hot, but you don't freakin' say that at Christmas dinner!!!"

"Yeah, well speaking of Pittsburgh hot, Desiree completely yinzed out last night over a crossword puzzle."

"Yinzed out? Details, details!"

Listening to Robbie's story, she felt comfortable for the first time in weeks, just like old times.

Jen

There were so many things about Bobby that were different—he seemed more serious, somber at times, and he seemed a lot more interested in drinking for drinking's sake. But one could easily excuse these kinds of things. He was, after all, returning home from war. It was hard to imagine that just seventy-two hours earlier he'd been in the Middle Eastern desert. He sat now, beer can in hand, cracking jokes with various aunts and uncles who'd spent the day at their parents' house. Everybody, it seemed, had come back home to see Bobby. Everybody but Dave.

After a long week of fighting and silent treatments, Dave had decided to spend Christmas with his mother, just like they'd planned about a month ago. But those plans were made before they knew Bobby was coming home and Jen just didn't get why Dave couldn't see that. Seeing Bobby was important. Way more important than heading up to Butler County. But Dave didn't think so. So early this morning, after a very curt gift exchange (video games for him, a new Steelers jersey for her), Dave had dropped her off at her parents' place and headed on down the road. He hadn't even kissed her goodbye, a bad sign by any standards but especially so for a new bride who was expecting a baby in less than four months. If she and Dave were already so rocky, what would a screaming baby add to the situation? If something didn't change with them soon, things were going to erupt.

Thinking about all of it, Jen felt a heavy flutter in her gut. Lately, she felt the baby moving, and sometimes it startled her. They were just the slightest taps, like goldfish in a tiny bowl always hitting the sides. It was supposed to be reassuring, she knew. These little taps were signs that the baby was alive and healthy. Still, its sudden presence scared her. It was here. And it was making itself known. She rested her hand near her belly button. Then, scanning the room, she noticed Bobby watching her with a smile. He broke away from the amateur game of poker beginning at the dining room table and sat down on the floor beside her. As he leaned his shaved head into the armrest, he let out a comfortable sigh.

"It's kicking," she said. He regarded her swollen belly with a raised eyebrow.

"So why didn't you go with Dave?"

Why didn't she go with Dave? What kind of question was that?

"Because you're here."

"Yeah, but I think you'd want to spend Christmas with your husband."

Jen felt her chest tighten. Dave had said the same thing, in a similarly accusing tone.

"Bobby, I can't even believe you're asking me to explain myself. I came to see you. You should be happy."

"Yeah. And so should you."

"What's that supposed to mean?"

Bobby rolled his eyes and finished off his beer. His eyes looked droopy, like a cartoon character's eyes pulled forward by a heavy weight. "I mean, all those damn e-mails about how unhappy you are. About how horrible things are with Dave."

She snapped to attention, sliding forward. "I never said I was unhappy or that Dave was horrible!" Abruptly, he pushed her back into the chair.

"Really? All this woe is me, Mom and Dad forced me to get married, Dave never understands what I'm saying, blah blah blah." Why was he being so mean to her? Jen glanced around the room, hoping somebody had noticed what was happening and would step in. While the women worked on the remnants of the day's cookies and pies in the kitchen, the men leaned seriously over their poker game, shot glasses close to each hand. No, she and Bobby were alone in the living room, and nobody seemed interested in intervening.

She pushed his arm away from her. "You're drunk."

"And you're spoiled."

Spoiled? If she didn't know any better, she might think that Dave had put him up to this. Or her parents. All three of them were always singing the same tune. But Bobby, he was different. He understood. When everybody else dismissed her as though her emotions were no more significant than a buzzing housefly, Bobby listened to and comforted her. Why was he doing this?

"Bobby, that's mean."

"It's true. You get married and then you can't even spend Christmas with his family because you have to do things your way. You saw me last night, and you can see me tomorrow. You could have gone with Dave."

"But I didn't want to go with Dave."

"Exactly. And Jen doesn't do what Jen doesn't want to do. And everybody else just has to get with the program."

The force in his voice startled her. As defensive as she felt, she knew better than to keep throwing gas on the fire.

"I look at you, Jen, and I think how lucky—you live close to home, you're married to your high school sweetheart, you're having a baby. Must be nice. I'm here for a month and then I have to go back for a year. If I ever come home for good from this, if I make it back outta that place outside a body bag, what's next? I'm never gonna be normal after this, ya know, I'm never gonna be right. And what girl deserves to be married to a guy like that?"

The gravity of his voice and the sheer force of his words nearly knocked the wind out of her. *Go back to trashing me,* she wanted to say. *It's much better than listening to this.* Deep down, she feared that everything he said was true. What if things really were never right for him?

He turned around, his eyes weightless for a moment, searching her face for some kind of answer. She wished it were that simple, that something could really be said to make him feel better. If such a thing existed, she had no idea what it was. She put her hand on his shoulder and held on, as if that alone was enough to save them both.

Week 17: Steelers vs. Detroit Lions
(W 35-21)

Shannon

She should have known better than to stop by her parents' house on a Saturday afternoon, especially on New Year's Eve. Of course Darla would be there trying to grub some free food for the week or sharing her latest sob story of loneliness and neglect. Ever since Jack and her broke up, barely a conversation went by when Darla didn't start to cry about some injustice that had happened to her—a rude elderly man who had cut her off in traffic, an electrician who wouldn't budge on price, or a coworker who told her she needed to stop bringing her personal life into the job. According to Darla, the whole world oppressed and she was its number one victim.

Shannon opened the kitchen door and shoved a bag of food containers toward her mom. "I was out this way and I thought I'd drop these off," she said, one hand on the doorknob like she was in a giant hurry.

Her mom looked in the bag, smiling. "You didn't need to make a special trip, but while you're here, you may as well sit down. Darla and I were just having a cup of tea."

Shannon glanced at the counter, trying not to make eye contact with Darla but surveying the delicately arranged china cups and sugar dishes.

"Sorry, I'm running errands. I should probably go."

"Who runs errands on New Year's Eve? C'mon, Shannon, just sit down and have a cup."

She looked at her mom, whose eyes now seemed beseeching. Even her mom needed a buffer from Darla these days. Shannon sighed, feeling guilty, like she owed it to her mom to stay.

"Um, I guess," she said, checking her watch as if she really had someplace to be. "But just one."

Darla clapped her hands together, grabbing a yellow teapot and filling a white filigree cup. Shannon picked up a tea bag and

"

dropped it inside her cup, watching the brown tea seep into the hot water and wishing it would go faster.

"So what are you doing tonight, Shannon?" Her mom's stool was close to hers, their knees almost touching. Darla sat across the counter. At the very question, Darla laughed.

"Like you even need to ask that, Mom. Shannon spends every major event at Morgan's. She's probably working."

"Actually, this year, I'm not. I have other plans." As soon as she said it, regret flooded her brain. Why didn't she just let Darla think she was going to Morgan's?

Darla picked it up like a fish on a worm. "Other plans? What kind of other plans? Tell, tell, tell."

"Yes, Shannon," her mother said. "Do tell."

"I just meant, you know, I'm going to do something with Audrey but not at the bar. That's all."

As lies go, it was very unconvincing.

"Liar," said Darla. "Your face is red. You have plans, but not with Audrey. Who is he? What's his name?"

"He?"

"Yeah, I mean I didn't say anything at Christmas, but you've been acting so moony lately, I just know you must have a man."

"I haven't been acting like that."

Her mom interrupted. "I wouldn't call it moony, but you definitely have been acting a little distracted. Is everything okay?"

Darla snorted. "Of course everything's okay. Shannon's just finally getting some, that's all."

Shannon blushed. "Darla!"

Laughing, her mom playfully poked her shoulder. "Oh Shannon, Darla says that kind of stuff in front of me all the time. I may be your mother, but I'm not dead. So, are you?"

"Am I what?"

"Getting some?"

Shannon felt like her face might melt right off her skull. First Darla, and now her mom, trying to pin her down to admitting something like some motley tag team in amateur wrestling. Yes, all right, so getting some had distracted her lately. But there was no way she was going to confess that to these two nebby-nosed

Nellies and put them on the scent trail that might lead them right to Jack.

She stood up, indignant. Her tea had barely turned a light shade of tan, but she was ready to go.

"I'm sorry, guys. I don't like being ganged up on like this, so I'm leaving."

Against the protests of her mom and Darla, she dumped her tea down the drain. As she opened the door, Darla made one last plea. "Oh, come on, Shannon, be a sport. If you leave now, we'll just have to talk about you all evening."

Shannon stepped outside. "Right. As if I'm supposed to believe that's different than any other time." The door slammed shut behind her with the harsh sound of finality.

Megan

At five minutes until midnight, for the first time in about nine years, Megan wasn't drunk, nor did she care if there was anybody around to kiss when 2006 hit. It was actually a pretty liberating feeling, no doubt helped by the fact that this party had lame written all over it and the only reason she was there at all was because it was at her house. Emily and Mike were so pleased with their engagement that they'd decided to have friends over on New Year's Eve to celebrate the news.

An engagement party? Please. Just one more excuse for people in relationships to get gifts and accolades. As if finding a partner was truly an accomplishment. Any asshole could fall in love and get married to another asshole.

Staying in her room all night seemed like a preferable option to this party. Hell, pretty much anything was better than this. But Megan had given all her Christmas money to Emily to pay off her outstanding debts. Emily hadn't said so much as a thank you or recognized the sacrifice she was making at this time of the year, but she had asked that Megan stick around for the party, to hang with her pretentious grad student friends and Mike's obnoxious co-workers. She'd even asked Megan to prepare the vegetable tray, no small task considering these nerds could eat their weight in organic produce. Any party she'd ever thrown revolved around a keg, beer pong table, and pizza. But this was a wine-and-cheese crowd. In fact, one of the skinny girls next to her was talking wine like it was a PhD dissertation.

Megan studied the girl as she swirled her red wine around in the goblet, took a sip, and sighed. "It's a little too warm for my tastes. I keep telling Emily that if she really takes wine seriously, she needs to invest in a wine chiller."

A few other guests agreed with this statement, which somehow devolved into a rating of the best places to get wine in Pittsburgh. Megan sunk into the couch, trying with all of her might not to stand up and punch this jagoff in the jugular. It would certainly spice up the party. And just as she was thinking that the moment couldn't get any worse, Kevin crept up beside her on the couch, completely drunk.

"How's my lady?" he said, casually draping an arm over her shoulder. She leaned away, taking another long gulp of beer. Although she'd been drinking a few hours now, she barely had a buzz. She looked at her bottle, wondering if Emily had slipped her non-alcoholic. No, it was definitely regular.

"I'd be better if I was somewhere else, but at least I don't have to worry about getting home."

Kevin laughed, but it sounded more like a gurgle. He was extremely drunk and the closer he got to her, the more she smelled Old Spice. Old Spice? A drug store scent like that surprised her, given his penchant for new and better things. Didn't they sell men's fragrance at Banana Republic or J. Crew? Hurriedly, a preppy-looking chick Megan didn't know pushed champagne flutes their way.

"For the toast," she explained, darting through the crowd. Megan sniffed her drink. It smelled slightly less pungent than Kevin. Sitting next to him felt awkward but safe. As drunk as he was, he still seemed too nice for unwanted passes. Although, as the seconds approached toward the New Year the better a midnight kiss sounded. No, she told herself. A midnight without a kiss won't kill you. Besides, it wasn't like all the midnights she'd had with kisses had ever worked out. Maybe all of this was happening for a reason—a sober New Year's Eve might be a start fresh.

On the TV, the golden ball began its descent over Times Square. For a moment, even all these stupid party guests seemed slightly tolerable, even collegial, as they all counted down: "Ten, nine, eight, seven, six, five, four, three, two, ONE!"

On the TV and throughout the neighborhood, noise erupted—the celebration in New York City, the clanging and banging of pots and pans as drunken neighbors took it to the streets, and the distant roar of fireworks from Downtown. Megan stood, clinking her cup with the guests nearby, then chugged her champagne. Finishing, she walked upstairs, hoping there wasn't a line for the bathroom. There were enough guests and chaos that she didn't notice Kevin following her until she realized she wasn't alone in the upstairs hallway.

She spun around. "Are you looking for the bathroom? You can go first." She gestured toward the closed door on the right.

Kevin stepped toward her, then grabbed her waist, pulling her close and drunkenly kissing her. Surprisingly, his mouth wasn't altogether uncoordinated. In fact, if it had been any other guy on any other night, she might have said he was an awfully good kisser. Instead, she pushed him away, wiping her mouth.

"What the hell are you doing?"

"Don't you want your New Year's kiss?" He fell back against the wall, knocking a picture frame crooked. Then he moved toward her again. She knew it was Kevin and that he was drunk, but all she could think about was that asshole last month. Stopping him at about three inches away, she slapped him across the face. Hard. He clutched the side of his face and she immediately saw a red mark forming. His eyes opened wide, clear now, like he'd totally sobered up.

"What the hell was that?"

"What the hell was you trying to grab me just now?"

She needed to go into her room and lay down. It wasn't that what he did upset her. It was that, for the first time in a long time, she actually believed something a guy said—that he didn't mean to do anything wrong. Maybe, just maybe, he was kissing her because he really liked her and not because he thought it was a guaranteed fuck.

"I wanted to kiss you, Megan. God, you're a real piece of work, aren't you?" He paused, studying her carefully, something in his eyes softened and she felt immediately exposed. He put his hand on her forearm. "I'm sorry. I didn't mean anything about it."

"I'm sorry, too," she said, removing her arm from his grip before she could get too comfortable. "I'm going to go into my room for a few minutes and you're going to go back downstairs. When I come back out, we're going to pretend like this never happened."

"Okay, if that's what you want. I'll do it."

It wasn't what she wanted at all, but for now it would have to do.

Jen

Standing in her parents' kitchen washing dishes, Jen knew exactly what she was doing. She didn't want to do dishes any more than the next female at the New Year's party, but time in the kitchen, even with the smelly sauerkraut, was still time away from Dave. He was parked on the same chair where just last week Bobby had told her off and admitted that he was afraid for his future. Bobby had gone up to Seven Springs with some of his friends. She hadn't seen him in two days now, but the words still rang in her head, clear as the crystalline icicles hanging outside. All week they'd haunted her, and all week she'd avoided Dave more and more. It was a surprise he'd even decided to come today at all, but that probably had more to do with the fact that the whole gang from Morgan's was hanging out.

In spite of Bobby's advice, she couldn't stop thinking that maybe the best thing for everybody was if she just moved back home. Her parents would be willing, of course. And Dave might be mad for a while, but he'd get over it. And who knows? Maybe he wouldn't even care. The thought of coming home and raising the baby in her childhood room felt so much more comforting and manageable than staying with Dave in that awful, cramped apartment. Maybe it would be better for the baby if she cut things off now, before they could get attached.

"What's new, pussycat?" chortled Uncle Mark. He had a laugh that could wake up a corpse. Jen threw him a weak smile.

"Not much."

"Getting ready for that baby?"

"Something like that. I don't even know where to start."

"Well, I'm sure the parents will help you out."

At that point, Dave walked in, rummaged through the fridge, and cracked open a beer. "Help out with what?"

"Baby stuff."

"Damn right they will. And Uncle Mark too, right?"

In spite of herself, Jen laughed. "Uncle Mark didn't even buy us a wedding present."

"Hey now," Uncle Mark said, laughing. "You know it's the woman's job to do them sort of things. Now that I'm divorced, I can't be relied upon for nothin', Jen."

"The woman's job," Jen repeated. "No wonder you're divorced."

"And now you owe us," said Dave, leaning against the counter. "And the way I see it, you owe us twice, for the wedding and the baby."

Uncle Mark laughed and staggered a little. He was pretty drunk. "Let's see. Well, how about I just paid to go in the Super Bowl ticket lottery and if we get'em, I'll give'em to you two young bucks."

Dave lunged forward, almost knocking him down. "I'd like to shake on that."

"Dave, don't be silly, we can't go to the Super Bowl. I'm six months pregnant."

As Dave turned to face her, his face completely crestfallen, she immediately felt guilty. All she could hear was Bobby, over and over: *You're lucky.*

Wiping her hands dry, she turned to Uncle Mark, poking him in the belly. "Are you serious?"

"Deadly."

"Uncle Mark, you're so drunk you won't even remember this tomorrow."

"I will too remember this, and I'm not drunk." Jen tried not to laugh as he put one finger on his nose and tried, unsuccessfully, to walk in a straight line.

Dave patted his back. "You are drunk. But you WILL remember this in the morning, now, won't you?"

"Yes. I will definitely remember that I promised you tickets that we have about a one in a thousand chance of getting to a game that we have about a one in a hundred chance of making it to. Best damn deal I ever made!"

Dave shook his head. "Now, now. Why you so pessimistic, big fella?"

Uncle Mark looked at Dave. "Cuz I'm sorry, but it ain't gonna happen. Not this year. We're sixth seed for the playoffs. All our games will be away. Do you know how hard it is to win three playoff games in a row on the road? It's about as hard it was keeping my marriage together for fifteen years. And I'm telling you, Dave, that was DAMN hard."

He laughed then, but it quickly faded as Dave crept closer toward him, grinning. Jen winced. Dave looked like a downright crazy person, and she wasn't sure what he was about to do. Uncle Mark was right. The whole idea was crazy. Dave needed to leave things alone.

"But Mark, what you don't seem to understand is that anything is possible. Anything."

Uncle Mark snorted then walked out of the kitchen. Jen kept watching Dave. It had been a long time since she'd seen him that happy, so transparent with optimism. She wished he'd looked that excited during any of their numerous events this year—the proposal or the wedding. But seeing him like that now made her desperate to believe in anything. Maybe he was right. Maybe this year the Steelers really would make it to the Super Bowl. And maybe, just maybe, they would be there too.

Angela

Standing on the curb outside the theater, Angela wished her mom would hurry the hell up. Her shift had ended at five-thirty, and now it was nearly six. On a snowy New Year's Day, the parking lot looked deserted, just like it had the whole day. It was stupid her boss had scheduled her for an afternoon shift at all; it wasn't like anybody ever showed up for matinees on the day of a Steelers game. The entire day had been one giant waste of time, save for the paltry thirty-five bucks or so she'd get in her next paycheck. And, of course, the Steelers had won, securing them another week of play. Another week of agony. Playoffs just heightened the spirit, made everything seem a little worse. Friday at school everybody would be decked out in their black and gold. Radio stations would start playing all those miserably catchy fight songs. And her parents would become even more determined to keep her out of the way on game day. January football was pure hell.

"Bad Luck! What you doin' here?" Oh great. Brad. Of course he would show up at a time like this.

"I work here, asshole." She turned around, annoyed and ready to give him a tongue-lashing. But the buxom blonde standing beside him stopped her dead in her tracks. Marci Updyke. The bitchiest of the bitches. The girl who had been giving hand jobs underneath the cafeteria table since freshman year but who acted so sweet and nice and innocent that half of the high school faculty would probably hail her as an example of chastity and kindness. Girls like her made Angela sick. Being able to sniff out fake bitches was one of her strongest character traits. And Marci was one fake bitch. One fake bitch who was holding Brad's hand.

"So, can you get us a discount?" He playfully tugged at Marci's arm. Marci gave a quick smile, barely acknowledging Angela's presence.

Thinking of a witty reply with Marci standing so close was harder than she'd expected. Not that it mattered, considering most anything she did say would be way too intense for Marci's pea brain to process.

"I can't," she finally said. Wow. *I can't.* She'd really outdone herself on that one.

And it figured that just as she looked away to ignore them, her mom's minivan came into view. Why her mom drove a minivan, she had no clue, but she did, and there she was, pulling up to the curb in all her purple Chrysler glory.

"Bad Luck, is that your mom? Are you going to introduce us?"

"Shut up, Brad." She threw her bag over her shoulder and ran toward the car.

"Thanks for showing up so freakin' late," she said, slamming the door shut.

"Nice to see you too, my darling daughter. And who was that couple you were talking to?"

As the van pulled out of the parking lot, Angela watched them heading into the theater together, Marci's long blonde hair whipping against the wind.

"I'd hardly call them a couple."

"They looked cozy to me."

"Cozy. Like that means anything. Brad would get cozy with a mummy if it could tell him he played a good game."

"Brad? I've never heard about him. What's his dealio?"

"Leave the slang to the teenagers, Mom. Brad's just the moron with a locker next to mine. That's all."

"That's all. Sounds like there's a lot more to it than that."

"There's not."

"C'mon, Ang. I saw you looking in the mirror like you were watching them. You wouldn't be doing that if this Brad boy didn't mean something to you. And what about this good game? What sport does he play?"

Now she'd done it. Her big mouth always got her into trouble.

"Mom, I said I didn't want to talk about it."

"No, you didn't. Come on. What sport? Last question, I swear."

She lowered her voice, watching the twinkling Christmas lights of residential homes. "Football."

"Football! Oh my goodness, you have a thing for a football player. Wait till I tell your dad!"

"Okay, it's not a thing and you're making me really mad now. Do NOT tell Dad anything. There's nothing to tell."

A few blocks from their house, they stopped at a four-way stop sign. Last night's coating of snow looked gray and gross. And while the neighborhood still blazed with twinkle lights and Christmas trees, even they seemed dull, filling the streets with a tarnished glow.

"I'm just teasing, Ang. I won't say anything to your dad about your football player boyfriend."

"He's not my boyfriend!"

"I'm kidding! What's that you and Robbie used to say? Take a cold pill?"

"A chill pill. Seriously, Mom. The slang is killing me."

"I'm so sorry that I get things wrong. I'll try to be the perfect mom or whatever. Like Robbie's mom."

"I've never said Robbie's mom was the perfect mom."

"You've said enough things to compare us to let me know you think she does a helluva better job than me."

Angela looked at her mom sideways now. In profile, her mom's face was so slender, like a fragile doll that could easily break. Was she being serious?

"I don't compare. I just said once that she was a good cook."

"And that Robbie's house is ALWAYS clean. And that him and Kristen have TVs in their rooms. And that Patty goes to three different grocery stores if she can't get the exact thing that they asked for at one."

Perhaps those things had been said, once or twice or maybe five times. But Patty was better than her parents in some ways. It was just plain fact. If her mom didn't like it, then she didn't like it. Angela had never thought of her mom as somebody who even cared if somebody said those sorts of things. Both of her parents seemed so impervious to life. As they pulled into the driveway, Angela tried to think of something nice to say.

"I don't know. I didn't mean like you have to be like Patty. It's just that she does things different, ya know. And sometimes it would be nice—"

"What? If I suddenly got all Leave it to Beaver and started wearing housedresses?"

"No! If you listened to me sometimes."

There was a long dramatic pause, the tension palpable.

"Oh. So now you're saying I don't listen to you?" Her mom hit the steering wheel with her hands, like she was really mad, but just as Angela was about to apologize she started laughing. "I'm kidding, I'm kidding. I really got you on that one! You looked like you were going to cry!"

Angela jumped out of the car. Of course her mom would make light of her honesty. That, it seemed, was the only way that anybody, her mom, her dad, or even Brad knew how to interact with her. And Robbie wondered why she thought playing a prank on Patty was okay. It was what people did. At least all the screwed up ones she knew.

Patty

It was happening. Regular season was done and the play-offs were here and suddenly everything seemed a little more palatable, even the hundreds of potholes messing up Route 51 on her way to and from work. Except for the fact that Robbie had started talking to Angela again, winter break had gone so much better than she'd expected. Usually, the kids acted completely tortured that they had to spend even five minutes with her. But this year, probably because he realized he'd soon be out of the nest, Robbie was exceptionally nice. And sure, Kristin had spent her fair time pouting that Patty was not letting her keep the slutty miniskirt that Desiree had given her for Christmas, but even she'd been pleasant on Christmas Day. Even when Patty had refused to let Jeff come over for dinner. Patty didn't know what had gotten into the kids since their night with Tom and Desiree, but whatever it was, it seemed like it had really made them appreciate her and she wasn't about to question it.

And there was something even better than that. Yesterday, while mailing her note to Hines Ward, she'd gone inside to pay her PO box dues and purchase some stamps. Usually, the Brentwood post office staff was a bunch of craggy old ladies with cigarette breath and dried hair. But the new worker was on duty, the gentleman she'd seen a few months ago and thought was very handsome. She often gave in to the occasional crush (one of the security guards in her building and a pizza delivery guy from Italian Village Pizza), but something about this gentleman really stopped her in her tracks. Maybe because he was catching her at one of her happier moments, but she couldn't help but think that this gentleman was pretty darn friendly to her. And there was something about the awkward way he handed over her items that made her think there was something else there.

And their exchange had only heightened her sense of interest:

"So, you new here?" she'd asked, trying to stretch out her time at the window.

"No," he said. "About six months."

"Really? That long?"

"Yeah. And you're in here every Monday morning. You just never come inside."

"Every Monday?"

"Yes. Sorry for speaking out of turn, I'm not stalking you or anything, ma'am. It's just that the post office routine is pretty constant, so you begin to know people's little, er, quirks."

"Quirks?"

And then suddenly she realized. He knew. He knew all about her letters to the Steelers and was still talking to her as if she was a totally normal person. And she didn't even care. Maybe he'd even seen that letters were now coming in from the Steelers. Maybe he thought she was pretty damn important.

"Yes. Quirks. That's how I'd put it. And just between you and me, it's those occasional quirks that make this job somewhat bearable." He winked at her.

She couldn't think of anything to say. Here was this handsome man practically telling her that he knew her secret, and she felt so comfortable that she almost blabbed the whole thing to him: The Steelers want to meet me!

Fortunately, self-control kicked in, so she just smiled and offered, "I do what I can."

But nibbling on last night's leftovers at her desk, she realized that this chance meeting with Mr. Post Office was a sign. She was ready to tell somebody about her secret. She was ready to get it off her chest and seek advice. And maybe, just maybe, consider actually showing up at The Locker Room. On New Year's Eve she'd promised herself that this year would be different. After years of her ritual, she'd finally been contacted by a Steeler! Life was full of surprises. What if she actually met one of the Steelers? And what if the man at the Post Office continued talking to her? And what if the Steelers won the Super Bowl? All of it combined was enough to make her burst. And she needed to tell somebody. The bad part was that after about 24 hours of deliberating over who she could tell, she'd realized that there was only one person in her entire life slightly insane enough to appreciate and maybe even encourage all of this: Desiree.

Waiting at the entrance of The Original Fish Market, Desiree checked her watch once, then twice. It was unbelievable how nervous she was. This was lunch with Patty. Patty, of all people! But something about Patty's tone on the phone, the upbeat, almost chipper way that she extended the invitation had struck fear into her heart. Since she'd wanted to discuss whatever it was in person and not on the phone, it had to be pretty bad. And while Patty was not what she would consider a confrontational person, she'd seen Patty handle the kids before and knew that she could reign over things with a smug sense of authority. Any other time, that sort of thing would roll right off her back. But coming down from these past few weeks of indecision and anxiety, the thought of the slightest criticism made her whole body feel limp. And it had to be criticism.

She'd even narrowed it down to two possible complaints. One, that Patty was going to tell her stop buying clothes for Kristen. Or two, Patty was going to have some commentary on the Christmas Eve melee. Surely, Robbie and Kristen had reported back to her like good little spies. And who knew what they had said? That Desiree was a crazy woman, screaming and yelling at them and their father? Patty would certainly have a field day with that one. In the aftermath of the divorce, she'd been very clear that the last thing the kids needed to see was any kind of strife between any of the adults. Everybody was supposed to put on their fakest smiles and grin and bear it no matter what conflict they were having. That, Patty said, would be best for the kids. Desiree didn't disagree that this was a good approach for the kids, but considering they'd spent the first ten or so years of their young lives watching the strained and tense relationship between their parents, it was safe to say that Patty's sweeping rule was a classic example of too little, too late.

And speaking of too late, Desiree was just about to call the whole thing off when she saw Patty ambling her way.

"Sorry I'm late," said Patty.

"That's fine, but chop chop. I have a meeting at one."

Desiree waved down the hostess and they were quickly seated. After a moment of strained small talk and table arranging, the two women faced each other quietly. After waiting about five seconds for Patty to say something, Desiree started talking. And there was nothing really to talk about at all; she barely had a clue what noises her mouth was making, but all of a sudden she was chattering non-stop about the last time she took her cat Mitzi to the vet. Desiree knew that Patty was only feigning interest, but she just couldn't stop talking until Patty took a crumpled letter out of her purse and placed it on the table.

"What the hell is that?"

"Desiree, I have to tell you something that I've never—that I never thought I'd tell anybody."

Oh, dear god. Holding her breath, Desiree skimmed the letter. Something about somebody named Ginger Mae, the Steelers, and a possible meeting at The Locker Room. Desiree looked at Patty, feeling even more confused.

"You found a note written to a stripper?"

Patty reached for the note. "No, no, no. This is stupid. Just give me that back and forget I ever showed it to you."

Desiree held onto the note. "I don't get it."

"Don't get what?"

"Why you're showing me that note."

Patty took a deep breath so exaggerated that for a moment Desiree wondered if she was ever going exhale. When she finally did, it was with a long sigh. "Because it's not a note to a stripper."

"Then what the hell is it? I think I just went into menopause waiting for you to tell me what's going on."

"Ginger Mae is…"

"Yes?"

"Me!"

Shaking her head, Desiree looked back at the letter, still attempting to figure out what Patty was saying.

Patty continued, "You remember how I found out about you, right?"

Did she remember? What kind of a question was that? Of course she remembered how stupid she'd felt when Patty had intercepted the interoffice envelope of perfume-soaked panties meant as a flirtatious joke for Tom.

"Patty, really, I thought we were past that."

"We are past that. I just asked if you remembered."

"Yes, and it's very embarrassing—I honestly didn't know he was still…"

She trailed off, unable to say that last word. He'd told her he was separated from his wife, he seriously had. But it turned out that he'd been referring more to his own mental check-out on the marriage than an actual physical state. If Patty was going to try to bring that up again and make her feel bad, she was busting out of this place, right here and now.

As though Patty sensed her fear, she held up her hand. "This isn't about you. This is about me."

"You?"

"Yes. I don't condone what you did, but, all in all, I thought it was a very good idea."

"A good idea?"

"Yes. So the football season after the divorce, I started—doing it."

"Doing what?"

"Sending panties. To the Steelers. Every week for the past five seasons."

Patty? Sending panties to the Steelers? Desiree bristled. Patty laughed.

"Not MY panties. Sexy panties. Very sexy panties."

What? Desiree could barely process what she had just heard. Not so much the panties, but the fact that Patty had a secret life. Patty? And here she was telling her little story, explaining how vindicated and sexy she'd felt as she mailed the panties each week, her eyes aglow and her hands and face more animated than Desiree had ever seen before. Of all the people she knew, Patty was the most stoic. She was like a blank slate, a quiet reserve of dignity and pride who never let anybody in. Desiree remembered Tom saying once that it was this coolness that he'd found so troubling in their marriage. "She never showed any emotion," he said. "Sometimes I just wanted her to react, goddammit. But she never did." But here she was now, as excited as an eighteen-year-old girl on prom night, all this time holding in her secret ritual.

Desiree interrupted Patty's monologue. "Well, what are you going to do about it?"

"Do about it? Oh, nothing. I think, I think I just needed to tell somebody. And I thought, well, I don't know. I just thought that since I kind of stole your idea you might, you might understand."

The strange thing was that she did understand. Maybe not the vindication or the panties part, but certainly the secret life. Wasn't that exactly what she'd been doing all season long with her fantasies of babies and motherhood?

"Patty, this letter says you can meet Hines Ward. I think you should do it."

Maybe nothing would ever come of her own secret life, but bringing Patty's to life sounded fun

"Oh, no, I think that might be a bit too much."

Desiree reached across the table, firmly placing her hand on Patty's. "I'm only going to say this once. If you want to do this, I'll be right at your side."

"You will?"

"Definitely."

"You'd really do that?"

"Of course."

"Really?"

"Patty, I told you I was only going to say it once."

Desiree pulled her hand back onto her lap, scanning the restaurant. Suddenly, everybody looked more interesting, all of them hiding their own secret lives, the whole place somehow connected in an intricate web of secrecy. For a moment, Desiree considered telling Patty about wanting a baby, but it was just a passing thought. As much as she liked this new feeling, she wasn't quite ready to share.

AFC Wildcard Playoff
Steelers vs. Cincinnati Bengals
(W 31-17)

Megan

She loved the intensity of the play-offs and had felt buoyed by the prospects of the AFC Wild Card all week. The Steelers were playing their conference rivals the Cincinnati Bengals and all cards were on the table. If they lost, it was all over. And if they won, it was just the beginning—they'd have to play two more playoff games until they were even in the Super Bowl. And then they'd have to win the Super Bowl! It was a lot to expect for them to win three road games in a row after having just won four games straight to end the regular season. But the anticipation had given some shape and normalcy to her otherwise uneventful week.

Still, in spite of three voicemails for game day parties and an even stranger invitation from her parents, watching the game alone felt like the best option. Considering that two of the invites were from acquaintances who also knew Todd and his crazy wife or Psycho Bill who'd try to attack her, neither of those sounded appealing. The third invite was from Marlon at work. She knew he was just trying to get back in her good graces and she wasn't having it. Not quite yet. He was having about the whole kitchen staff over for the game and there was no way in hell she was going to give them all the satisfaction of talking and laughing behind her back. The only times she went into the kitchen now were when it was absolutely unavoidable or she was touring with an especially nosy client who just had to see every last part of the hotel.

Her parents were having a playoff party with her aunts and uncles, and as much as she enjoyed analyzing the game with her dad, showing up alone to a family party felt like holding up a white surrender flag: *Yes, guys, you're right! I have absolutely no social life on Sunday afternoons.*

Going downstairs around four, she noticed Emily in the dining room. Oh, great. That's just what she needed right now—Mike stopping by to pick up Emily. But as she sneaked a peek from the kitchen it looked like Emily was studying. Dressed in sweats and a ponytail, she definitely didn't look ready for a night out on the town. Megan opened a bottle of beer and stepped toward the table.

"Is it gonna bother you if I'm watching the game?"

Looking up from a pile of books, Emily looked tired. "No, I'm finishing up here actually."

"Oh. Plans with Mike?"

"No, he went to the game."

The thought of that little geek going to a playoff game was pretty sickening, but Megan held back the gagging.

"Really? And you didn't go?"

"Too much schoolwork."

"Oh." Megan crossed past the table, curiously looking at the books, something about Educational Psychology and Management.

The tension between them felt thick, like the kind of soupy summer air you could actually see. She just wanted to get away as fast as possible. In the living room, she flipped the channel to the game, arranged her beer, chips, and dip on the coffee table and leaned into the couch, ready for a victorious evening.

Meanwhile, Emily remained in the dining room, pounding away on her keyboard. School had just started a few days ago; did she really have so much homework it had to be done right then? Wasn't that what weekdays and libraries were for?

Megan turned up the volume, not too loud, but just enough that maybe Emily would get the point and head upstairs. She heard the click of a laptop, making her even more confident that Emily would go away soon. After all, she deserved some alone time in the living room. She'd spent the last month or so barricaded in her room while Emily and Mike made out and mooned over each other all over the first floor. Before she'd paid all her rent money she'd felt the slightest hint of guilt being down there at all, but now there was absolutely nothing that Emily had to hold over her head. If she wanted to go into her room and pout that Megan was using the TV, then let her go. And as if she'd said that aloud, Emily walked into the living room. She paused, looking at the TV.

"What time does it start?"

"4:30."

"Yeah, I bet Mike's having fun. He went with Kevin."

"Kevin went?" The way she'd said that almost sounded eager. Hopefully, Emily didn't pick up on that.

"Is that so surprising?"

Of course she picked up on it. "No. I mean, he always seems like he has better things to do than watch the games."

"Oh, you noticed that too? I felt like maybe he was an asshole at first, but Mike said it's like a nervous thing. When he doesn't know people he's nervous and kind of easily distracted."

Wow. That definitely summed up Kevin.

"But he's really nice after you get to know him. Like a really good, solid guy."

Megan smiled. "You filming a pro-Kevin service announcement?"

"No. I'm just saying, that's all. He's nice. And he thinks you're really smart."

Kevin had said she was smart? That wasn't the usual type of thing she heard guys saying about her. It was actually much better.

"And why would he say that?"

"I don't know, he just always says nice things about you – like that you're funny and stuff."

"Really?"

"I think he might have a little crush."

She didn't want Emily to know how much that excited her. She looked away.

"Well, ya know, who doesn't?"

Emily stood with one foot on the stairs and it almost looked like she was looking longingly into the living room. Things had been so awkward with them lately and deep down she just wanted Emily to say she was sorry. That she hadn't meant to totally ditch her and that they'd still be friends even after her and Mike got married. But Megan had been through this song and dance routine enough to know that it probably wasn't the case. But maybe it was her fault, too. It wasn't like she really tried to be friends with anybody who got married. In fact, she usually felt compelled to stay away. Maybe, just maybe, it didn't have to be that way.

She cleared her throat. "So, are you gonna to watch the game with me or not?"

Surprisingly, with that one single question, the mood in the room went from frosty to warm. Emily smiled and nodded, her ponytail bobbing. "Yeah, that would be great. Just let me go upstairs, and I'll be right back down." She disappeared upstairs.

Megan sighed. On TV, the Steelers were running onto the field and a stadium full of Cincinnati fans decked out in orange and black were booing. The Steelers didn't look phased by the crowd's animosity, laughing and slapping five with one another as they ran toward the bench. Some days, it didn't matter how unfamiliar the territory, you just had to hold your head up high and do what you had to do. If the Steelers could do that in Cincy, then she could certainly enjoy an afternoon game with Emily. Right?

Jen

The Steelers were still trailing, but when they scored at the end of the first half Jen just knew that the momentum was about to shift. What was that Dave had said? *Anything is possible.* She wasn't sure he believed that when it came to anything other than football, but that level of optimism was slightly encouraging. God only knows she had a negative streak that affected both of their lives for the worse. She had to of been the only person in the world who didn't want to know the sex of her baby just because she didn't believe that the ultrasound could get it right. What were the odds? 90% accurate? That was about as accurate as that broken condom that had landed her right here, carrying around a gut the size of a bowling ball. Not that she minded her bowling ball gut anymore, she thought, rubbing it affectionately. If there was anybody who was going to change her life, it was going to be this baby boy or girl. And boy or girl, it would be a Steelers fan. And by now, they already had enough Steelers, Penguins, and Pirates baby clothes to last an entire year. They were set then, no matter what sex this baby was.

As the game broke for commercial, she motioned to Dave. "What do you think?"

For the first time since they'd been married, she felt comfortable asking him something without getting a snippy response.

"I think we're goin' to the Super Bowl," he said, confidently putting his arm around her shoulder. For a moment, the sensation made her wince, but the longer he kept it there, the more comfortable it became.

"Me, too."

"Really?"

"Yeah!"

"So we finally agree on something?" His voice sounded hesitant and she pulled away from him, realizing at once that he'd also noticed the problems between them. She'd thought he couldn't see it at all, that she was the only one suffering while he was oblivious to anything wrong.

"Finally? That's kind of a strong word."

He stood up, disappearing into the kitchen. "God, Jen, I meant we agreed, that's all. Now, can you just drop it before we start to fight?"

Through the kitchen door, she watched him standing in front of the fridge, belaboring a decision on which beer or leftovers to choose. His body was tense, his face tight, and his shoulders clenched like he was holding everything back. Even when she didn't mean to she always said the wrong thing. She started to retort, to say that maybe he should drop it or that she wasn't the one trying to start a fight. Instead, she took a deep breath. Think of Bobby, she told herself. It had become like a mantra. Not like she had to remind herself to think of Bobby—his words forever weighed on her thoughts—but what she wanted to remember was his message on Christmas day: you're lucky. Lucky. Start acting like you're lucky. Did lucky people get pissed off about every little thing that anybody said or did they let things roll off their back?

She waited until Dave came back in with a bowl of cold spaghetti and an Iron City beer. "I'm sorry. I didn't mean it that way just now. I just meant that I'm surprised you'd say that because I didn't think you'd noticed."

"Noticed what?"

"That we fight so much."

Dave shook his head, spaghetti sauce dripping from the corners of his mouth. "No shit, Sherlock."

"Oh. Yeah. So, you do?"

"A deaf and blind man would notice that. It's all we do. I mean, I don't know what got you started, but for the past 3 months I can't do nothing without a comment."

"Hey, hey, hey. Let's not start pointing the finger here. I agree that we fight, but I don't want to start fighting over who causes the fights."

"Yeah," he said, taking a swig of beer. "Guess that's as pointless as trying to convince Cincinnati that Kimo didn't take Carson out on purpose."

Shortly into the game, linebacker Kimo Von Oelhoffen got through the Bengals' offensive line and landed on quarterback Carson Palmer's knee. The injury was severe enough to sideline him for the rest of the game. Unfortunately for Bengals fans, Carson Palmer was their strongest chance for a playoff victory. And even though it was obvious to Jen that it was truly an accident, there was no way that any Bengals fan worth their salt would believe it.

"Yeah, I guess it is that bad. Well…" She wanted to say I'm sorry, but she wasn't quite there yet.

"Well?"

"Well, at least we can both agree that we're going to win this game. And that this is what the Bengals get for disrespecting the Terrible Towel last time we played."

Dave looked at her, then tipped his beer can to her and winked. "Right. At least we can agree on that."

Shannon

As the game ended, Jack crossed the room, looking out the large bay window that was the centerpiece of his second floor bedroom.

"It's snowing," he reported, pulling on the downy beige drapes. "Looks like you'll have to stay here tonight."

With the curtains parted, she could see the snow swirling through the thick, black night. From that vantage point, all she could see were the tips of trees, branches twisting high into the air, the snow gliding easily past them. Shannon yawned, stretching her arms up over her head and arching her back. Staying over was fine with her. Staying here in this room forever was fine with her.

They'd watched the entire game in bed, the heat of their bodies keeping each other warm. It was as romantic and lustful as Shannon had ever imagined, and the sheer idea of it still overwhelmed her. They'd been seeing each other for almost a month now, but her desire for Jack was insatiable. Just seeing him, she wanted to sink her teeth into his skin. She wondered sometimes if he could possibly feel the same. And when he crawled back into bed and began softly kissing her neck, she realized yes, that he definitely could.

He was nibbling her ear when the phone rang. Immediately, Shannon felt her stomach sinking into her knees. Darla was the only person with timing like this. She gave Jack a gentle push, but he didn't budge. "Mm, they'll leave a message."

The phone quit ringing, then started again. There was no denying it was Darla now. She was the only person rude enough to think that her calls were so important she'd just call until somebody answered. Jack groaned. He must have figured out the same thing. Shannon answered.

"What do you want?"

"I want to talk to my sister after the game, that's what!!!! Ya-hooooooo! Goooooooooooo Stillers!"

There was so much screaming and shouting in the background, Shannon could barely make out a word she was saying, but this was obviously a drunk dial.

"Yeah, good game. I'm kind of busy now. I'll talk to you later."

"Don't hang up, sis! We're making plans, thinking about road-tripping it to the next game or something or maybe just having a big party at my place and I want you in on it. So I had to call you, like, right now."

Darla's words were slurred and exaggerated. Shannon looked at Jack and rolled her eyes.

"So, are you in on it?"

"In on what?"

"In on partying with me for the next game?"

"I'll have to see."

"Come on, don't check your schedule, just say yes!"

"I said I'll have to see."

Darla began laughing, that tinny giggle of hers that people always said was so cute but always sounded to Shannon like cackle of an evil witch. "Oh," she said. "So you're like with your secret boyfriend, right now, right?"

Shannon felt herself blush. It was about time to hang up the phone. "I told you I'm busy right now."

"Okay, okay, okay, you can bring him too." Darla paused for a moment and Shannon could hear a lot of high-fiving and shouting. When Darla returned to the phone, she kept screaming. "Bring him too. Okay, love you. Bye!"

Shannon hung up the phone, annoyed. As she laid back into the bed, Jack put his hand on her belly. Shannon didn't move it, but she wanted to.

"She wants me to watch the next game with her," said Shannon.

Jack didn't say anything, his eyes closed. "Well, she's your sister. It wouldn't hurt."

"But what about you?"

"I'll be okay. You can come over after. It might be good. It will keep her off your back."

What did he care about keeping Darla off her back? Or did some small part of him still want to please her?

"No, I'm not watching it with her."

"Why not?" Jack reached his arm over his head, covering his eyes with his forearms.

"Because I don't want to, dammit." There. She'd said it. Jack moved his arms, his green eyes penetrating her gaze. He winked at her.

"Then there you have it. Don't go. We can watch it here again." He tickled her belly and she squirmed. "Maybe it's good luck."

She nuzzled closer to him, and he pulled her in tight, his breath hot on her face. "Yeah," she said, closing her eyes. "Maybe it's good luck. Maybe we're good luck."

She found his lips. He responded, turning her on her back and swallowing her mouth into a deep kiss.

Patty

Monday morning in the post office, Patty couldn't help but smile. The Steelers had won yesterday and that nice-looking gentleman was working the front counter again. Paused at a table, she pulled her envelope from her purse, sneaking glances toward the counter. There had to be a reason to go in there and ask a question or buy something, but she couldn't think of one off the top of her head. She could go inside to mail this letter, but that seemed a little desperate, didn't it? And what if he asked questions? It was one thing suspecting that his curiosity was piqued by her weekly packages, but it was a whole other thing busting inside and handing it over to him hook, line, and sinker. No, she wouldn't do that. Besides, with her luck, she'd get one of the grizzled old ladies who looked like they lived for cigarette breaks and video poker. That wouldn't do at all. In fact, the one with a hooknose was looking at her suspiciously right now.

She turned back to her envelope. There was nothing more to look at. It was stamped, addressed, and ready to go. All she had to do was drop it in the box. But he was busy with another customer and wasn't looking out toward the vestibule at all. She could just go in there and buy a pack of stamps, but that seemed too obvious. She dug through her purse, made an exasperated face, and headed outside. Maybe she could just stand there a few minutes until he was done and then go back in as if she'd forgot something. It was freezing, a typical winter day in Pittsburgh, entirely too cold and grayer than anybody should have to endure. All the cars in the parking lot were caked with rock salt and they were barely through the halfway mark of the long winter. The worst was yet to come. If January was gross here, February was like a black pit of despair. Unless you counted clearance sales on Valentine's Day candy, nothing good ever happened in February.

Patty pretended like she was walking to her minivan, trying to count out the seconds. Desiree would definitely not approve of this type of behavior—it was too timid and socially awkward for her taste. It would be nice, just every once in a while, to capture Desiree's raw confidence and just rush headfirst into things rather than sitting on the sidelines, forever counting the costs. But she was in accounting—counting costs was what she did best.

She turned around and went back inside the door. This time, his customer was gone and he leaned against the counter, talking to the other two ladies. He pointed at something in the back and Hook Nose shrugged then disappeared from view. Was he a manager? It certainly looked like the women had some kind of reverence and simultaneous distaste for him. He had salt-and-pepper hair clipped short, grayish blue eyes, and an extremely stocky build. And he's probably married, she thought, getting out her key and opening the box again. The way he talked to the other women, he was definitely barking orders, and when he finished, he leaned against the counter, seemingly relaxed. The easy way he carried himself was what she liked most about him. And that same demeanor also probably meant he definitely wasn't married. Men that age still married had a beaten-down look to them. He looked easy and free. Definitely not attached. So maybe he was gay? No, no, he wasn't gay. Just then, closing her box, he looked up. They made eye contact then she turned back to her box, hoping he wouldn't think she was looking. She busied herself with her keys and purse, cringing as she heard a door opening. What if he tried to talk to her?

"Good morning," he said. His booming yet comforting voice filled the entryway.

"Good morning," said Patty, glancing back. He carried a ring of keys and stopped at the supply table.

"Looks like we're low on things out here," he said.

Patty put her hand on the door.

"How about that game yesterday?"

She turned around, startled. "Excuse me?"

"The game. Yesterday?"

"Oh." She must have looked like a real moron, but honestly, thinking about him just now had totally made her forget about the Steelers. Unbelievable. "Yeah, the game."

"Sure thing. I wouldn't want to be a Cincinnati fan today, that's for sure."

"I wouldn't want to be a Cincinnati fan on any day," she said. He laughed from deep inside, like he really meant it. She smiled.

"Spoken like a true Steelers fan," he said, shaking his head. "I moved here from Philadelphia about ten years back, and that's my favorite thing about this city."

"What's that?"

"The women know their football. Ain't like that in Philly."

Patty paused, not sure what else to say. So he wasn't from Pittsburgh? For some reason, that made him even more interesting.

"Well, ma'am, I see you're on your way. You have a real good day."

On my way? She had forgotten she was standing with a hand on the door.

"Oh yes, on my way. Busy day. Well, you have a good one." She smiled then almost ran to her car, lightheaded and dizzy like a fourteen-year-old girl.

Angela

Leaving work on Wednesday night, driving home felt like a life sentence. They'd let her go early, so her parents wouldn't be expecting her for another half hour. With no destination in mind, she drove right past the turn off for her house near Baldwin High School and continued down Route 51 as it changed from the strip malls and doctors' offices of the suburbs into the abandoned buildings and shady used car lots of Carrick and Overbrook. Some nights, driving felt like the only option. And since she'd only had her car back for two days, this ride felt especially victorious. As long as she kept driving, she didn't have to think about anything from her daily life. Not the fact that it actually really annoyed her that Brad really was dating that stupid 'ho Marci or that her parents were in a Steelers-playoff-induced euphoria.

Things still weren't perfect between her and Robbie. Just today at lunch he had walked away when she complained about all the Steelers banter on the morning announcements, but he was over it by 7th period. Just like he'd get over her not going to Pitt next year. If Robbie, or anybody else, had been listening to her for the past few years, he would know that her heart wasn't attached to going to Pitt. And if Robbie really wanted to, he could go to any college. Yet he seemed perfectly content with just staying here. What was his problem? At the light by the Liberty Tunnels, or as her dad would say, "The Tubes," she waited in the turning lane, headed toward Downtown. Waiting at this light, with the way Mt. Washington rose above the road like a curtain separating the city from the suburbs, it would be nearly unbelievable for somebody new in town to think that just through the tunnel was an actual city.

As a kid, driving through the tunnels had always felt so exciting. Coming from home, it was hard to imagine that anything could exist on the other side of the hills, and sometimes as a kid, she had half-expected that the city wouldn't be there at all, that it was all some kind of a dream. Downtown Pittsburgh felt hundreds of miles from the cloistered suburban streets and side roads of Whitehall. It was easy to think their close proximity was just a sleight of hand, a trick of the eye. She remembered holding her breath as they drove through the tunnel back then, imagining that the city didn't really exist at all, that it was forming as they drove, skyscrapers being built and roads being carved out of the hills. Tonight, she didn't hold her breath but tapped her brakes, following the lead of every motorist ahead. Why people slowed down in tunnels, she would never understand, but around here, it seemed to be one of those universal things that made you a person, like taking a crap or enjoying sex. The dirty walls looked like a gray blur as she floated past them, the concrete tube nothing more than a holding cell for bad fluorescent lighting and the red glow of taillights. And without much traffic, it felt like mere seconds until she was at its mouth, exiting onto the bridge and fast assimilating to the city lights, the Downtown skyline and the black waters of the Monongahela River flowing beneath her.

Entering the city now, she felt her chest swelling up with an odd sense of pride. She didn't want to be here, yes, but she couldn't deny that the city looked spectacular at night, especially the spiky turrets of PPG Place, a building she'd once childishly thought of as a castle. It was hard to remember being that innocent. But now that she knew she was going away, something inside seemed to let her look at the place without being cynical. In her rearview mirror, the hundreds of homes nestled along the South Side Slopes and Mt. Washington were nothing but orange, yellow, and white lights, twinkling like Christmas. She took a right onto the Boulevard of the Allies, riding in the shadows of

Duquesne University and high above the industrial Parkway, where commuter traffic squeezed in and out of the city every single morning and evening.

She had seen enough pictures to know that Seattle had a different look than Pittsburgh, newer and greener—probably way more beautiful with its blanket of evergreen trees and the looming shadow of Mt. Rainier. She'd seen in one of the University's brochures that there was a fountain on campus where you could see the peaks of Mt. Rainier from about 50 miles away. You can't do that at Pitt, she thought as she merged onto Forbes Ave, a cramped and dirty street with its rows of coffee shops and chain Mexican restaurants leading to the college's crown jewel, the Cathedral of Learning. More than 36 stories high, it was a stunning gothic building that soared high above anything in this part of town.

She'd only been in it once, with Robbie's family. They'd taken the kids on a tour of the Nationality Rooms—a series of classrooms based on other countries and cultures. There had been Japanese, Norwegian, and Persian rooms and at this point she remembered none of them except that they mostly seemed cold and uncomfortable. What she did remember about that day was how genuinely excited Mr. Salvatore had been, showing off his college stomping grounds. He'd taken them all over the Cathedral and up and down Forbes Avenue, capping it off with a dinner of fries and hotdogs at The Original Hot Dog Shoppe, a nondescript greasy spoon serving up extra large and super cheap portions of every heart-attack-inducing food one could imagine. It was the first time Angela had seen him appear to be excited. Whenever she visited Robbie as a little kid, his dad usually wasn't there, and when he was, he always seemed focused on something else, he'd been working full-time and going to school at night back then. She remembered that about their house—that Patty always tried to keep the kids out of Tom's way, as if he couldn't be bothered. Meanwhile, both her parents acted like such embarrassing fools anytime somebody came around that by the fourth grade she wanted no parts of bringing any other friend over than Robbie, lest Dom and Nancy try to engage the whole crew in some cheesy sixties throwback dance party with her dad pretending to Elvis.

Robbie's house is so quiet, she always told her parents. His parents are so normal. And then Patty and Tom had gotten divorced and the house had become even quieter and she'd liked it even more. But thinking back on it now, that quiet didn't seem as comforting as she'd always thought. It seemed like fear, like something sad. As Angela drove past the Cathedral, she felt a stab of guilt for what she'd done. She'd turned Patty into a joke, just like her parents occasionally did to her. It wasn't very nice. Maybe Robbie was right. Maybe she did need apologize to Patty. No, she thought, making a left onto Fifth Avenue and slowly circling back to where she'd started. It would be worse at this point to admit what she'd done. The best thing was to forget about it. To focus on the great escape.

AFC Divisional Playoff
Steelers vs. Indianapolis Colts
(W 21-18)

Jen

Now that she was nearly six months pregnant standing up from a seated position was becoming increasingly difficult. The soft, comfy couch cushions at her parents' house didn't help. But when Troy Polamalu dived for a Peyton Manning interception, fumbled, and then recovered the ball, Jen was on her feet faster than she imagined possible.

"YES!" she screamed, slapping Dave and her dad high-fives. With a little over five minutes left, the Steelers had a 21 to 10 lead over the Indianapolis Colts in the AFC North Championship game and with this interception it could only get wider. As her heart pounded, she felt the baby kicking at her ribs. Uncomfortable, yes, but a little Steelers fan needed to get his or her cheers in too. During a game like this, it was easy to forget the rest of the world. It was probably how you were supposed to feel about church, but to her, this kind of happiness and freedom only came from football.

Unfortunately, football also had the power to fill her with rage. So when the play ended and the referees began congregating on the field, Jen felt her blood beginning to boil.

"What the hell are they doing?" she screamed, stomping her feet. The baby responded with another swift kick in the ribs.

Dave looked at her. "They're reviewing the play."

"I know they're reviewing the play, but why? He had possession the whole time!"

She pointed at the TV where it played over in slow motion: Troy dived for the ball, the ball became loose but he maintained possession, and then he was tackled. It looked pretty cut and dry.

When the referee came back on and said that it was still the Colts' ball, her dad threw the remote across the room, Dave and her mom started cussing at the refs, and Jen felt her heart sinking, a feeling that continued over the next minute or so as the Colts scored a touchdown and then a two-point conversion. With a score of 21 to 18, suddenly nothing seemed quite so cut and dry.

The game broke for commercial, and as other people headed into the kitchen for refills, Jen sunk deep into the couch, kneading a cushion on her lap and praying to somebody, anybody, that the Steelers would win and hoping that nobody was watching her.

"You really got your panties in a twist about this one, don't ya, Jen?" said Uncle Mark, returning from the kitchen with a piece of kielbasa on his plate. She didn't know how people who called themselves fans could eat at a time like this.

"Why shouldn't she?" asked Dave, a fresh beer in hand. "We gotta win this week and next if we want your Super Bowl tickets."

"Yeah, kids, only 3 points and next week's game are keeping you from the prize."

Jen tried not to grimace as her mom came into the room at that exact moment.

Her mom raised an eyebrow, looking at Mark. "What's this about Super Bowl tickets?"

"I told Jen and Dave they can have the tickets if we get them in the lottery."

"Why in the world would you do a thing like that?"

"Wedding and baby gifts," replied Uncle Mark.

"If you want to give them a nice gift, you can give them the money that all of that would cost so they can start saving for a house." She moved her disapproving glare from Mark to Jen. "And you, young lady. You shouldn't even be entertaining thoughts of going to a Super Bowl. You're going to be almost 7 months pregnant."

"I'm pregnant, not handicapped. Seriously, Mom, if we get tickets to the Super Bowl, I'll go if I have to deliver it in the aisles."

Dave laughed. "That's my girl!"

Jen looked down, avoiding the weight of her mother's stare.

"It's a football game," her mom said, disapprovingly. "There will be others."

No, if the Steelers made it to the Super Bowl and finally got their fifth Super Bowl ring, the legendary one for the thumb, then it was a lot more than just a football game. In fact, all of this—the Sunday afternoons and the playoffs—had become so much more than a game. They felt like a life preserver, the only things holding her afloat. This week had been about the best of their marriage so far, Dave coming home every night on time, countless hours spent together watching ESPN and examining the local coverage and speculating about this game. If the Steelers lost today, things might go right back to the way they were. No, the Steelers were going to win—today and next Sunday. They were going to make it to the Super Bowl. And they were going to be her saving grace.

Shannon

The mounting tension was palpable. Jack sat on the edge of the bed, wearing nothing but a pair of black track pants and a worried expression. Shannon stared at the TV, where the Colts and the Steelers were lining up for a field goal. Since Indy's last touchdown had brought the score to 18 to 21, Jerome Bettis had fumbled a Steelers ball at the goal line, leading to a recovery by Indy's Nick Harper. Fortunately, Ben Roethlisberger had tackled him, but in those split seconds while Harper ran, Shannon felt her heart beating furiously, her whole body filled with adrenaline as the horror of Bettis' fumble switched to hope when Roethlisberger tackled Harper.

But now there was this: a 46-yard field goal attempt by the Colts. If Indy tied the score, their shift in momentum and a home field advantage might just propel them to a win in overtime.

Shannon crept to the edge of the bed with Jack, holding her breath. Please, please, please. Miss it. Miss it. Miss it. As the announcers bragged up the kicker's accuracy and he poised into position, she shut her eyes, pressing her face into Jack's arm. How awful it was to think that entire seasons, perhaps even entire careers, could come down to just one kick. One foot, one ball, one kick that could spell the difference between moving onto the next round of the playoffs or packing up and going home.

It didn't seem fair that anything in life could be determined by something so small. But then she began to think about her and Jack. If Darla hadn't gotten the flu last month and sent her to the game with Jack, would they have been here together at all? Was there really such a thing as fate, or was it all just random acts of cause and effect? In her hard of hearts, she wanted to believe, to truly believe, that something larger was at work, that it wasn't all such chaos, that some guiding force was leading them along. But waiting for this one single kick, the whole future felt up for grabs.

Megan

HELL YEAH! HELL YEAH! HELL YEAH! HELL. YEAH. In the final seconds of the game, Indy's kicker Mike Vanderjagt, kicked wide right to miss a field goal and the crowd at Sports Rock Café was on their feet, screaming and hugging like Oprah had just given them all cars. Megan was so happy that it didn't matter one bit that she'd just spent every last dime she had on Jack and Diet Cokes and chicken wings or that she had no idea how in the hell she was going to get home. Sure, she was looking to turn over a new leaf and give that kind of thing up, but this was the playoff season, and the Steelers had just marched into hostile territory and pulled off a nail-biting victory.

As the boys she'd been sharing a table with for the last quarter ordered a round of shots, her entire body ached with the stress of the afternoon's game. She felt so exhausted from watching it that it was almost as if she'd played herself.

"Yo, Eddie," said a lanky kid wearing a Terry Bradshaw jersey. "Make sure you get one for this one." Megan saw him looking at her with a mischievous gleam in his eye.

"Oh, no," she said. "This one's done. Enjoyed the game, guys. I gotta find my ride." Scanning the crowded bar, finding anybody seemed nearly impossible. As far as the eye could see, it was a crush of black-and-gold bodies, high-fives, and sloshing beers.

"A ride?" he said. "I'd give you a ride anywhere, honey."

"That's very nice of you," she said, putting her hand on his chest.

She knew it was the kind of gesture that led to another, and for a second, she surveyed his angular face, the way his brown hair just skimmed his cheekbones. He was cute in a puppy dog kind of way. About three months ago, she'd definitely have made out with him, maybe even more. But tonight, she didn't feel like it. The emotions she'd experienced during today's game felt like she'd been riding the Thunderbolt at Kennywood all day long. All she wanted to do was go home and go to bed. And perhaps strike up a text message conversation with Kevin. Last week, she had gotten bored at work one day and texted him to see if he'd respond. Since then, they'd spent about the whole week trading witty quips and flirtations. To be entirely honest, she'd kind of wanted to watch the game with him, but he was watching back home in Latrobe with his high school buddies. Whatever. These geeks at Sports Rock had been a fun afternoon diversion. Removing her hand from his chest, she flashed him a smile. "Enjoy your shots."

"Come on, where you rushin' off to? You got a boyfriend?"

"Try ten."

"I'd believe it."

"You better. No, it's been a long day. Time to hang it up, head home, and get ready for work tomorrow."

"Work?" He spoke the word like he didn't understand the concept.

"Yes, it's called a job. You know—menial labor in exchange for a paycheck?"

"Haha. I mean why are working on Monday morning? I don't even schedule classes until 1:00."

"I'm not in college."

"You're not?"

"No. Past that."

"So how old are you?" He cocked his head, eyeing her up and down.

"28. Geez, dude. I gotta go."

"28?"

"Yes, you wanna write a headline about it? It's time for me to go. I gotta find my friend." She'd ridden here with Katie from work, but now in the sea of straight blonde hair that seemed to stretch the length of the bar, Katie was entirely indistinguishable.

The kid named Eddie was returning to the table with a tray of shots. Her lanky sidekick gave Eddie a hearty push as the shots hit the table. "Dude, this girl's 28."

She rolled her eyes. "Okay, and you guys are how old?"

"Twenty one," they answered, looking at her as if she'd just taken her shirt off to reveal a Peyton Manning tattoo. 21? She'd expected 22 or 23, not that it mattered. Katie had just turned 21 back in November, but this was different. Spending an entire day flirting with 21-year-olds felt a little desperate.

"That's why she needs to go home," said Eddie with a laugh. He looked her up and down like a total creeper. "Grandmas get up early in the morning."

Everybody at the table exploded into laughter. Grandma? At 28, she was still way hotter than any young skanks these douchebags had a chance with. She wasn't sure if she wanted to flash them or punch them in the face and felt relieved when the crowd parted by the bar and Katie became visible. Best-case scenario here, she walked away and forgot the whole thing happened. A bunch of geeks calling her grandma? Damn. This day had gone from totally awesome to downright irritating in about ten minutes. Without looking at them, she walked toward Katie, waving frantically and ignoring the "Yo, hot Grandma" catcalls from the little boys.

Patty

Thursday evening, Patty stood at the corner of Carson and Seventeenth waiting for the light to change.

The night felt charged, prickling with possibility. Patty stood on the sidewalk waiting to cross the street. Overhead, Steelers banners waved in black-and-gold arches. Signs taped to business and apartment windows chanted "Go Steelers" and every car that passed sported a Steelers flag, bumper sticker, or license plate. As people walked in and out of the storefronts and bars, they smiled at one another, some of them shouting "Here we go, Steelers!" to the cars stopped at traffic lights.

As she stepped into the crosswalk, the grizzled driver of a red Chevy Cavalier gave her the thumbs-up sign. Two months ago, this kind of thing might have startled her, but tonight she flashed him a smile and threw out her own thumbs up. This was a good week— the Steelers had won again on Sunday and on Monday morning at the post office she'd talked even more with Ron. He lived in Castle Shannon and had two daughters: one at Pitt and another married with a kid back in Philly. At the end of their brief conversation, he'd told Patty that he looked forward to seeing her again. Just thinking of it made it her smile as she crossed the street.

In front of The Locker Room, Desiree waved. "What are you smiling about?"

"I'm not allowed to smile?"

"No, you are. It just looked kind of like a delirious smile. Like the kind somebody makes right before they kill a crowd of innocent bystanders."

Patty laughed. "I never took you for such a cynic."

"You'd be surprised," said Desiree, pushing open the door.

Inside, a bored-looking hostess in a white polo shirt and black pants leaned against a podium. She straightened up a little as they walked in.

"Two?" she asked.

Patty nodded. "I was told my name was in your book."

"Huh?"

"My name—Ginger Mae."

The girl wrinkled her nose, skimmed the book, and shook her head.

"I don't see anything, but there's not really, like, a system for reservations or anything."

Desiree stepped forward. "Look, honey, these weren't reservations. These were instructions. This one here is a VIP. Hines Ward told her that she'd get the best seat in the house if she were ever to come in here and that you should call him immediately to tell him that she's here."

The hostess looked Desiree straight in the eye. "Right. And if I had a dime for every time somebody gave me that line, I'd be rich." She shrugged. "Do you want a table or not?"

They nodded and she led them to a corner booth right across from the bar.

"Des, maybe we shouldn't bring up the whole Hines Ward thing anymore. Let's just enjoy our dinner. That girl didn't sound very promising."

"Nonsense. That twit didn't know the difference between a reservation and her asshole."

As they settled into their seats, Patty watched the swinging doors to the kitchen, thinking how nice it would be if Hines Ward walked through with his thousand-flashbulb smile lighting up the entire room. Instead, she watched as a parade of college-age servers, bartenders, and cooks filed in and out of the kitchen, engaged in raucous conversation and carrying various trays, utensils, and condiments. This was silly. And it had all been Desiree's big idea. She seemed more interested in meeting Hines Ward than Patty did now. The truth was that the person she wished to see right now wasn't even a Steeler. It was Ron.

"Hi, Patty," he'd say. "I wrote you that letter to get you here alone."

She tried to get the thought out of her head.

"Desiree, I think I have a crush on somebody."

"Really? Who?"

"This guy who works at Brentwood Post Office."

"What are you going to do about it?"

"What do you mean?"

"Are you going to ask him out?"

"I couldn't do that."

"You could!"

"No, I haven't dated since college. I don't even remember what it was like."

"Women ask out first these days. It's a whole new ballgame."

Of course Desiree would think it was that easy to just ask somebody out, but Patty needed to be sure before she could make any move. She scanned the restaurant, noticing a flash of black clothing and milk-white skin that reminded her of somebody.

"Did you see that?" She pointed at the stairs. "I think that was Angela."

Desiree turned around. "Robbie's friend? Why would she be here?"

Patty nodded. "I don't know. Robbie and her were supposed to be doing something tonight. What if they came here?"

"They wouldn't, okay? And I don't want to spend dinner talking about Robbie. Let's talk about your crush or what we're going to say when we meet Hines."

"I think we should forget about meeting Hines tonight. He's probably already in Denver for this week's game."

"I know. You know every time an event at work has been planned where I could meet him, something crazy comes up and I don't get to go. Like one year I got the flu and another time it was Kristen's chorus concert."

"You missed out on meeting Hines Ward to come to Kristen's chorus concert?"

Desiree shrugged. "Yeah, last year. It's not a big deal."

"Why didn't you tell us? Kristen would have definitely understood."

"I guess. I had already promised her, backing out didn't seem right."

Patty started to say thank you but Desiree interrupted: "So tell me about this guy. Your crush."

"Tell you what?"

"I don't know, name, age, social security number. What do you mean, *tell me what?* It's called girl talk, Patty. Get with the program. What does he look like?"

What does he look like? Girl talk? Patty started explaining how she'd met Ron. Something about being around Desiree made her feel like a teenager sharing her naughty thoughts with the other girls at a sleepover. She was beginning to understand why Kristen liked her so much.

Dinner went by so quickly that Patty almost forgot why they were here until the check came and Desiree announced that she wasn't going to pay her portion of the bill until they called Hines Ward to tell him that Ginger Mae was here. When the waitress said that they weren't allowed to call Mr. Ward, Desiree promised her fifty dollars if she could get around that rule.

"You shouldn't have done that," said Patty, already putting on her coat. "We should just go now."

"We're not going anywhere," said Desiree through clenched teeth.

A tall gentleman wearing Dockers and a black shirt approached their table.

"Hi, ladies. I'm the manager here, Tim. I heard that you were looking for Hines. Is there something I can help you with?"

"Nope." Patty slid out of the booth. "We'll just be leaving."

Desiree motioned for Patty to stop. "Come on, Patty. Show him the letter. I'm not leaving until you show him the—"

"Desiree, let's just leave." Patty stood up.

"A letter. What letter?" He held his hand out for it.

Patty fumbled through her bag, then handed off the letter like a little kid giving a forbidden toy to the teacher. First Desiree and now some strange restaurant manager— she may as well have agreed to an all-access interview with Sally Wiggin.

Tim raised his eyebrow as he scanned the letter. "This seems like some kind of a hoax. I mean, I could be wrong, but I'm pretty sure that somebody in the front office goes through all the fan mail and that the players never see it."

Patty took a step back, leaning against the corner of the nearest booth. *Somebody in the front office goes through all the mail.* Her heart felt like it was going straight through her body, down her stomach and bowels into her legs, dropping past her feet and through the wooden floor, somewhere far beneath this moment, this excruciating moment with Desiree looking at her wide-eyed and Tim the manager offering to take her phone number.

She saw it all very clearly: five seasons' worth of panties, cards, and envelopes in a pile somewhere in the company mailroom, the kind of damp, concrete room with cracks in the walls and boxes everywhere, a staff of three, or maybe even two, who read her letters each week and got a good laugh.

Right then, Patty looked up and saw Angela. Beside her, Robbie stood still without expression or emotion, just a blank absence from which Patty could not turn away, a deep empty space.

Patty turned, abruptly, her eyes filling with tears as she left before she could listen to the string of expletives Desiree was spewing toward Robbie and Angela.

Outside, she doubled over, gripping her stomach and dodging past a horde of expectant fans smiling as they staggered down the sidewalk. She leaned against the building, standing still and trying to block out what had just happened—that terrible blankness on Robbie's face. How could she have been so stupid? How could she for a minute have thought that this wasn't some sort of a joke? Of course it was a joke. Just like it was just a joke that Ron was nice to her. It was his job for god's sake. He was a manager. He didn't look forward to seeing her any more than anybody else in her life did.

Before she knew it, Robbie tugged at her arm. "I didn't do it. It was Angela. It was just meant to be a silly joke. Mom. Mom? Mom?" He said her name like a question and she saw a raw vulnerability about him that she hadn't seen since he was a toddler. It was that same look he used to get when he thought he had lost her in a crowd, panic creeping through his features in slow motion—his whole world about to crumble. Standing beside him with her sideways haircut and dark eye shadow, Angela looked about just as terrified as him.

"Mrs. Salvatore, I'm really sorry. It was just a prank. We didn't think you'd actually come here. We were coming downstairs to tell you the truth, but Desiree did it too fast."

"Don't blame this on me, you little brat," snapped Desiree.

The kids kept talking, but she'd stopped listening, leaning against Desiree for support, holding onto her arm and this moment, Robbie and Angela's apologies swirling in the air like thin threads of smoke.

Angela

This was not how it was supposed to happen. Nobody was supposed to cry. Her and Robbie were supposed to casually walk by Patty's table to interrupt the dinner and make sure nothing weird happened. But Patty and Desiree must have eaten really fast because by the time they came by for the sneak attack interruption, Tim was already reading that stupid letter. And now here she was on Carson Street, frantically apologizing to both Robbie and Patty.

"I'm sorry. I didn't think you'd actually care this much," she explained. "Mrs. Salvatore, I didn't actually think you'd come here and try to meet Hines. It was just a stupid prank. I was just so mad after you busted on us for skipping school."

But neither Patty nor Robbie would even look at her. Unfortunately, Desiree stared her down like she was the last designer purse on sale at Saks.

"You little scheming brat! I've always known you were a bad kid, but this just takes the cake. You are downright cruel. Cruel. I feel sorry for your parents."

She imagined her parents witnessing this scene and wondered if they would see her side or if they would be just as mean as everybody else. Chances were good they'd be just as mean. Nobody ever took her side. But she wasn't going to let Robbie's stepmom make her feel guilty.

"Oh yeah? Well, I already told Patty I'm sorry, so you can just butt out. And you know who I really feel sorry for? Anybody who has to see you without your makeup on."

A glimmer of rage flashed through Desiree's eyes, and for a moment, Angela thought she was going to get decked, but Robbie intervened.

"Shut up, Angela. Maybe you should just leave."

His dark eyes were full of sadness and regret, like he'd done this all himself. Angela swallowed. The cold air made her chest feel tight, like it was ready to collapse. She felt awful, she truly did, but she knew that none of them would believe her. Yet, if she really didn't care, why was she here at all? She could have just let Patty make a fool of herself on her own. But when Robbie came to her upset that his mom was going to The Locker Room, they'd decided to come just to make sure that she didn't make a fool of herself. Sure, she could have saved them a lot of grief if she would have just told Patty straight-out like Robbie wanted. But she just couldn't believe that Patty was actually clueless enough to fall for this.

"Mrs. Salvatore, you really need to know that this wasn't Robbie. It was me, and I didn't mean to make you so upset." Patty let go of Desiree's arm and leaned in toward her. Her breath smelled like onion rings.

"And just what did you mean to do?"

"I didn't mean to do anything, just like scare you or something, I guess. I was just so mad after you got me in trouble with my parents for skipping school."

"So that's what this was? Revenge?"

"Something like that."

"So you never thought for a moment how this might make me feel?"

"Yeah, I mean, I thought that maybe you'd feel scared or worried that somebody knew your secret but—"

"But you never thought for a minute that maybe I wouldn't be scared? That maybe this was something I'd been waiting for? That maybe for a few minutes, this would make me feel like a woman, like the kind of woman who could meet Hines Ward or ask a man out? Like the kind of woman with confidence?"

Patty's voice cut like a needle through skin. Angela felt herself shrinking. "I never thought of it that way."

"Of course you didn't, because all you were seeing was your funny little joke. Let's make fun of Patty. Because, hell, isn't that what the whole fucking world is always doing? Making fun of poor, stupid, fat Patty?"

She'd never heard Patty swear before. And obviously neither had Robbie or Desiree because they both let out surprised gasps. Angela reached out to grab Patty's arm. "I don't think you're stupid at all. It wasn't like that. Actually, I thought it was kind of cool what you were doing, I just—I'm really sorry, okay? Isn't that enough?"

Patty jerked her arm away from Angela's grasp. "No, it's not okay. Do you know what it's like to be treated like a punching bag your entire life? My parents, my ex-husband, and now my kids and their friends? Why don't I just get on the local news and let the whole damn city make fun of me? Why not?"

She turned toward the street corner, flailing her arms and screaming, "Hey, South Side, my name is Patty Salvatore and everybody I know thinks I'm a goddamn loser."

Oh shit, this was certainly not how this was supposed to go down. Angela stood back, frozen to the sidewalk, as Robbie and Desiree wrestled Patty away from the corner.

"Show's over," said Desiree, as Patty continued to scream. "Robbie, ride home with your mom. I'll help you to the car." All of them began acting as though Angela didn't even exist, helping Patty across the street like they were trying to restrain a homicidal maniac.

She watched them disappear down the side street, her feet and whole body still anchored to the ground. She imagined her parents, their jokes flying this past weekend as they went out of their way to prevent her from watching the game with them. When the theater had cancelled her shift last Sunday, they'd pretended to disconnect the cable so she couldn't watch TV at all while they went out to watch the game with her Uncle Nick and Aunt Shelley. Yes, she knew exactly what it was like to be nothing more than a punch line.

Desiree

The walk to the car was the worst. The dinner she could forget, even that awful scene on the street with Angela and Robbie, but walking Patty to her car while Patty made low murmurs in between a cry and a moan was sheer torture. Since Patty wasn't one for open displays of emotion, the fact that she was so overcome by it now could only mean two things: she was seriously this upset about being played for a fool, or, even more frightening, she was finally coming to terms with a lot of things that may have been building up inside for a long time. And what those things were, Desiree didn't want to imagine.

Sitting in her parked car, watching Patty's taillights fading into the distance, she slumped onto the steering wheel. She shouldn't have pushed so hard at the restaurant just now. She shouldn't have taken Patty up on any of this in the first place. Two intelligent, grown women should have known better than to be entirely waylaid by some bogus letter written by a 17-year old. Looking back, the letterhead wasn't even all that convincing, and just the very idea of Hines Ward writing it was totally absurd. It was almost like they were both in such desperate need of something, anything, to believe in that they'd latched onto this stupid letter like it offered the answers to their prayers.

Desiree sat up straight up now, buckling her seatbelt then pulling onto Carson Street. She felt sorry for Patty, for her being so lonely that the letter had meant so much. Just the sheer idea of it had been enough to make Patty actually reach out to other people—first her and then this Ron guy at the post office. Dining with Patty tonight was like being with an entirely different person—somebody who wasn't just going to roll over and let the whole world piss on her. No, tonight at dinner, for a brief moment, Patty had been somebody with a glimmer in her eye. Somebody with hope.

But just as quickly, that glimmer vanished; those final moments entirely extinguishing any sense of mirth or joy that had existed just moments before. In some ways, Desiree felt like she wasn't any better than Angela or Robbie. Sure, Angela wrote the letter. But she hadn't forced Patty into doing anything. That was all on her. She'd forced Patty into dinner and then forced her into talking to the manager. Why couldn't she have just left well enough alone? The sheer idea of something other than her own internal baby drama was so compelling that she hadn't given a second thought to what could happen. And now, for the second time in her life, she was to blame for Patty's unhappiness.

Cruising past Downtown and the gray dome of the Mellon Arena, Desiree pulled onto the Veterans Bridge heading into the North Hills. Years ago, when they'd decided on living arrangements, she'd insisted on going north. In a city where neighborhoods were divided by tunnels and bridges, choosing the North Hills when Tom's family lived in the South Hills had seemed as definitive as moving from New York to LA. To her, it was a statement, putting just enough distance between the old and new family that she didn't have to be constantly reminded of them. In the North Hills, they'd started fresh. Made a life for themselves at restaurants, stores, and parks where memories belonged exclusively to them. Now, watching the city fade to black, the distance seemed bittersweet. Maybe in a different life, she could drop by Patty's house, offer some support. Maybe in a different life, they could be friends. God only knows they could both use one—Patty with those ungrateful kids and her with an empty bed night after night. Some nights, she liked the empty bed, the open schedule, and the independence. But tonight, guilty as she felt, she wanted nothing more than to hold onto Tom, to press her face into his neck, their arms intertwined so tightly it was hard to move, much less unravel.

AFC Championship
Steelers vs. Denver Broncos
(W 21-10)

Megan

It wasn't a fairy tale exactly, but later in life she'd think back on it like that: the entire day like a long dream she recalled in striking detail—the plaid couch where they watched the game, that Hines Ward touchdown just before the first half that brought the Steelers to a 24-3 lead, and the tears of joy as the Steelers celebrated on a snowy field in Denver. Even Emily, who seldom seemed moved by sports, squeezed Megan's hand at the end of the game, a gesture so surprising that Megan couldn't tell which made her cry more, the game or Emily's hand—that little squeeze of friendship like they'd come full circle, that bygones would be bygones, that no matter how engaged Emily was, they would still be friends.

And then there was Kevin, buttoning up his navy coat and asking if she needed a walk home. She nodded, standing up so fast she nearly knocked over a bowl of chips. Of course she didn't need a walk home; it was freezing cold outside and she could easily go home with Emily and Mike. But this was a day for soaking up the atmosphere. All over Friendship, horns honked, firecrackers popped, and people cheered on the streets. As they stepped out onto the porch at Mike's house, a car waving Steelers flags passed, all of its young riders tipsy and screaming.

In solidarity, Kevin pumped his fist at them, prompting one of the kids to stick his head out of the window and scream, "Here we go, Steelers! Here we go!" The car slowed to their pace, serenading them with Steelers fight songs all along South Graham until another vehicle behind them prompted them to move.

"Moments like this really make you love Pittsburgh," said Megan, wishing she could wrap the entire city in her embrace.

Kevin smiled. "Or hate it."

She looked down at the sidewalk. Hate it? After two weeks of flirty texts, she still couldn't read him. When he glanced toward her, their eyes locking, he laughed.

"I didn't mean me. I meant, you know, I'm sure there's somebody out there annoyed by all the noise: 'those damn kids and their fireworks!'"

She laughed. "True."

As they turned onto Friendship Avenue, there were even more honking cars and black-and-gold flags and banners waving. It felt like everybody in the city was on a porch or sidewalk, toasting to the game. One group invited them to join, but they declined, continuing their walk in a comfortable silence. Talking seemed like a good way to ruin the moment. As the rounded curve of Friendship Park came into view, her and Emily's place on the left, she thought maybe something to say was in order. Some kind of thank you or confession of mutual adoration or gratitude for the game. But when Kevin wrapped his leather-gloved hand around her knit mittens, she felt good enough to die. There weren't any words that needed to be said. She looked at him and smiled, then looked away, bashful. She hadn't felt that way since she'd first kissed Chad in the 9th grade. It had been a long time since holding hands had sent shivers down her spine. It felt nice, innocent even, like finding herself, unexpectedly, exactly where she wanted to be.

Desiree

After the game, after all of the hullabaloo on TV and Tom's nearly immediate invitation to the Super Bowl from corporate, Desiree snuck into her room and dialed Patty. She hadn't talked to her since Thursday, but she wanted her to know, to really know, that she hadn't meant to hurt her.

"Hello?" Patty answered like she always did, with a question. Her voice sounded less enthusiastic than one might expect considering the Steelers were going to the Super Bowl.

"It's me, Desiree."

"Oh, hi."

"You don't sound very excited."

"I am. I think I might still be in shock, I had kind of given up hope."

"I just wanted to see how you were doing."

"I'm fine. And I'd like to just forget about all that, so if you're going to be like Robbie and try to convince me to send one last pair of panties to the team, don't bother."

"Robbie's trying to convince you to send something?"

"Yeah. He says after all this time, if I don't do it this week, something bad might happen."

It made some sense. The week before the Super Bowl was a pretty bad time to abandon a game-week ritual.

"What if he's right?"

"So, you were calling with an agenda. No, I'm just fine not doing it, thank you, so if everybody could just mind their own business —"

"I did call with an agenda, but listen Patty, it wasn't about panties. Or football."

"Great. What's that?" Patty's voice was borderline snide, but any hint of emotion was better than none.

"I was going to tell you that I didn't mean to push you about the whole Hines Ward thing, but I do kind of still hope you take my other advice from that night."

"Other advice?"

"Yeah, about that guy from the post office. I think you should ask him out."

"Are you crazy? I'm not even going to talk to him after this."

"But Patty, you should! I mean, this was just one stupid thing. Someday we might all look back and laugh at it. You can't just roll over and take it up the ass. Just shake it off like nothing and move on, and if this guy doesn't say yes, somebody else will. I don't want you to give up without a fight."

She heard Patty sniffing. "Thanks for the input."

"I'll let you go."

"Bye."

Desiree hung up the phone, then realized that Tom was standing in the doorway.

"Who were you talking to?"

"Nobody."

"Nobody? Then why's your face so white, like you just got bad news?"

Desiree touched her face. "Don't be silly, it's not white. I'm fine. Everything's fine."

Tom sat down beside her, taking her hand. "I'm sorry."

"About what?"

"That I'll be leaving you on your own for the game. It's kind of a boys-only thing in the box."

"It's fine."

"I'm sure you can go down to the club or Morgan's and watch the game with your mom."

She hadn't even considered that. "Yeah, I'll figure something out."

10 years ago, she'd watched a Steelers Super Bowl in a suburban restaurant in Bethesda, Maryland, missing her mom and her hometown like mad. Maybe watching it with family this time would be nice. Or maybe—no, that was silly. Why would she watch it with Patty and the kids? They surely had their own plans.

"Des, I've been meaning to talk to you—"

"Huh?"

"That conversation we had—about you wanting a baby…" His voice trailed off, like he wasn't sure what to say.

Closing her eyes, she sighed. She'd been so consumed with work and this drama with Patty, she'd barely thought about it. She thought of how lonely Patty had looked that night after The Locker Room.

She opened her eyes. "I don't know, Tom. Sometimes I think maybe I don't want a kid half as much as much as I want a friend."

"A friend? You've got plenty of those…the Martins, the Stewarts, all the girls at the office."

"I know. It's just that I don't feel like I can talk to any of them, like really talk to them, like about my feelings."

"Is that what you need? To talk about your feelings?" Nervously, he laughed. "I thought I was your best friend."

She squeezed his hand. "That's nice. It's just that you're hardly ever here these days."

Tom wrapped his arm around her and she rested her head on his shoulder.

"Well, I don't know what to tell you about that. Except that once this quarter's over, I'll hopefully be home some more."

He'd been saying that for the past few years now, but every quarter was more of the same.

"What if I invited my mom over here to watch the game? And Patty and the kids?"

"Patty?"

"Yeah. Patty and the kids. I think I'd like that. Is that weird? I could invite them over here. I really want to watch the game with the kids."

"You do?" Tom looked a little confused, but just shrugged. "If that's what you want."

"It is, Tom. It's definitely what I want."

And for the first time in a long time, she meant it.

Patty

Monday morning and back at the post office. And no, this had nothing to do with Desiree or Robbie or even Kristen's constant pleas over the past week to mail the panties. She was doing this because she had to. It was the only way.

"Excuse me," she said, marching right up to the empty counter. "I'd like to cancel my post office box." A haggard woman started to call her over but was cut off by Ron.

"I'll help you," he said. "Cancel it? Are you sure?"

"I've never been more sure of anything in my life."

It was the honest truth. And to be even more honest, she found it really difficult to breathe with Ron standing there in front of her. He smelled like sausage and eggs. She appreciated a man who ate a big breakfast. It was the most important meal of the day, and everyday, she had to yell at the kids to remember to eat it. But this was no time to get caught up in the breakfast habits of a stranger.

"Do I need to fill out something?"

Ron moved abruptly as if an alarm had gone off. Digging through a file cabinet, he finally came back with a form for Patty to complete.

"You need to complete this circled section, then we need a signature at all the Xs"

Patty leaned down, scribbling her name and address and signature. On one hand, she felt triumphant. Like this one single act was a kick in the face of everybody who knew about her little secret. She answered her critics with every line of her pen: *I'm done with this. I don't need it anymore.* On the other hand, it felt bittersweet. Without the post office box, she'd have no reason to come here and see Ron.

Sliding back the form, she noticed him frowning.

"Did I do something wrong?"

"No." He shook his head. "It's fine. I guess this means you won't be stopping by to see me anymore."

Pen still in hand, she halted, embarrassed. Great, was she really that transparent? Maybe it was a good thing she was canceling. She couldn't take too much more of everybody in her entire world using her for their own entertainment.

"I'm sorry," said Ron, clearing his throat. He looked at her with concern. "That sounded wrong. Maybe what I should have said is, I guess this means I won't get to see you anymore."

She took a sharp breath, stunned. Yes, if that's what he'd truly meant, then he had definitely said it the wrong way the first time. And now, knowing that he actually wanted to see her, she couldn't help but blush. She didn't know what to say. The paper was signed and there was really no reason for her to be lingering at the counter except for Ron. She thought of how Desiree had said that she just needed to ask him out. But she just couldn't open her mouth to say the words.

"Oh, brother," said the craggy old lady who'd been sorting piles in the background. "Won't one of yinz just ask the other one out? I'm goin out for a smoke, Ron. And when I come back, this better be straightened out." She put on a tattered coat and disappeared into the back of the office.

"Well," he said. "That was awkward. But would you?"

He looked at her as if he wanted her to finish saying it. But she couldn't. He had to say it. The truth was that she'd been the one who'd asked out Tom a million years ago in college. And she'd always wondered, if things had been the other way, if he had really liked her enough to gather the courage and ask her out on his own, would they still be together?

Finally, he smiled. "Would you like to go out sometime?"

Patty nodded. "Yes. Yes, I would like that."

"I guess I should get your phone number?" Patty liked that he sounded just as unfamiliar with this as her.

"It's on the form," she said, pointing to the piece of paper still in his hand.

"Oh, yes," he said, embarrassed. "I have it, then. Maybe next Saturday?"

"Yes, Saturday is good."

"Okay, then I'll call this week and we'll plan the details."

She smiled so big it practically hurt her face. "Okay, we will. I'm sorry I have to go now, I have to get to work, but I'll…I'll look forward to hearing from you."

Ron smiled, waving good-bye. There was something about him so sincere that she just knew he would call. Outside, climbing into her minivan, she felt a tremendous sense of relief. Just two months ago, she would have never believed that the Steelers would be in their 6th Super Bowl the same weekend that she'd have a date. She closed her eyes for a moment, leaning into the headrest and imagining how proud Robbie and Kristen and even Desiree would be. It was a feeling she had never thought she could get on her own without the help of Ginger Mae, and now that it was here, she hoped it would never go away.

Angela

It wasn't like she ever liked family dinner, but three days before the Super Bowl, the mere thought of spending uninterrupted time with both of her parents filled her with such dread that enduring an entire conversation with stupid Marci Updyke seemed preferable. It was bad enough that the Steelers were in the Super Bowl, but of all the teams for them to play, why in god's name did it have to be the Seattle Seahawks? Ever since the match had been announced—Pittsburgh vs. Seattle—her parents had been cracking all kinds of jokes, sending all kinds of e-mail forwards about how much stronger and better the Steelers were compared to the coffee-soaked, tree-hugging residents of Seattle. And her dad, who had before either very deliberately not tried to nag her to stay or really just wanted her to get the hell out of town, was now trying to place a friendly wager on the game: "They win, you go. We win, you stay."

Angela just rolled her eyes and left the room almost every time he started—as if she was going to let her entire life course be decided on the fate of one game.

When her mom placed a steaming bowl of pierogies and caramelized onions in the center of the table, Angela braced herself, expecting the jabs to be thrown quick and easy. As her dad helped himself to a full plate, her mom made eye contact and began talking.

As soon as Angela heard the words, "We got a phone call from Patty Salvatore," she pretty much blanked out. Not Patty. Not again. Hadn't ratting her out for skipping school been enough? Did she really have to rat her out for the stupid panties prank? Especially after Angela went over there last weekend and apologized so honestly and profusely that she'd actually cried as she tried to explain to Patty exactly how well she understood the pain of constantly being the butt of jokes and exactly how much she regretted making somebody else feel the same way. Wasn't that more than enough of an apology?

"Look," Angela said, interrupting. "I'm sorry for what I did to Patty but I apologized and I really want to move past it."

Her mom put her fork down. "What are you talking about?"

Her dad perked up. "You did something to Patty?"

"Angela. Patty didn't mention you doing anything to her."

Wait. They didn't know? So Patty hadn't told them? Interesting. But why the hell else would she have called? Angela took a deep breath. "Oh. It was nothing. I just meant that the other night I, um, ate the last bowl of chocolate ice cream when I was visiting Robbie and I thought she would, um, be kind of pissed about that."

Her dad laughed. "The lady does like to eat."

Her mom poked his beer gut. "Kind of like somebody else I know." She turned to Angela. "I don't think it was an issue."

"Then why did she call?"

"I don't know," said her mom. "I guess because she's you know, parent of the year, like you're always saying."

Oh, great. Not that again.

Her mom laughed. "No, I'm only kidding. She is a good mom. Probably better than me, I'll admit that. But anyways, after talking to her, I just feel really bad about some things that your dad and I have done and said, and I want you to know that we would really like it if you came with us on Sunday and watched the game at Grandma's house with the family."

Angela looked at her dad, studying his face for any sign of anguish or disgust, but he actually looked as sincere as her mom. She waited for a moment, not sure how to respond. It wasn't that she wanted to watch the game at all—football was still a barbaric, asinine game—but the idea of being asked to watch it with the family, something that hadn't been offered to her for almost ten years, felt pretty good. It was surprisingly nice to be included. And all because of Patty. She almost wanted to run away from the table and call her on the telephone. Somebody had finally stepped up to the plate for her. Watching her parents' expectant faces begin to become slightly irritated, she realized that she had yet to reply to their invitation.

"I'll have to think about it. I mean, I guess in a way I just kind of knew I'd be alone that night, and I was already kind of looking forward to that."

She wanted to make them wait for it, but she was going to say yes. It wasn't about going to watch the game or supporting the stupid Steelers, it was about accepting her parents' request, about admitting that deep down, she really did want to spend time with them, even if they were super crazy and annoying. They were her parents, for god's sake, and goddammit, she loved them.

Shannon

At this time of night on a Friday, the bar was unusually slow. Sure, it was snowing, but that sort of thing never kept away the regulars like Dave or Larry or Glenn. But tonight, the occasional straggler who did walk through the doors was either a regular she didn't like (the kind who she'd had to cut off one too many times) or strangers picking up six-packs. Still, the air felt festive and everybody was friendly enough, so she couldn't really complain. It was just quiet, that's all. Some nights she wanted to drown in the noise of the bar, the frenetic sounds of clinking glasses and shouted orders. But on a night like this, the only constant sound in the bar was Audrey calling out greetings to customers and firing a line of twenty questions at Shannon.

"C'mon, Shannon. You really haven't decided what you're doing for the Super Bowl?"

The expression on her face made Shannon's skin crawl. Hadn't decided was the diplomatic way of putting it. Had been trying not to think about it was slightly more accurate.

"I don't see why yinz don't just go to Larry's. Or maybe come watch with me out in Desiree's hi-falutin place. Darla won't be at either of those places."

"But they'll all know."

"Know what?"

"That he was Darla's boyfriend. Everybody will act all nice but they'll be thinking I'm a floozy."

Audrey cackled. "Do you know proud I'd be if somebody thought of me as a floozy these days?"

"I just don't want people talking about me behind my back. I think it's better if Jack and I stay in like we've been doing. We're just fine that way."

"You can't hide out forever."

"Who says?"

"Me. And I've been around a lot. You should listen to me."

Shannon turned away, concentrating on the slight layer of condensation in the front of the six-pack cooler. Did it always do that or did they need to call somebody? It was going to be a long weekend. It would be a damn shame to have a broken cooler. Just then, the door opened, a gust of arctic air swirling inside like a slap across the face. Shannon looked up, chilled, and there was Jack. Stomping his feet on the mat a few times, he brushed the snow off his shoulders and smiled.

"What are you doing here?"

"Nice to see you too, honey," he said. "I didn't feel like sitting home all night; thought I'd come hang around." He leaned over the counter, smiling. She leaned forward, allowing him a quick peck on her cheek.

"Geez, Shannon," said Audrey. "I've seen people go in for appendectomies with more enthusiasm than that. Give that man a kiss."

Jack winked at her. "Yeah, Shannon, give your man a kiss."

He puffed out his lips in an exaggerated pucker. Shannon was just about ready to swat at them both when her phone started ringing. She caught her breath, looking between Jack and her cell. He knew the ringtone and offered up a mild shrug as she answered it.

"Hello?"

"Hey, girl. You got six packs of Yuengling, right?"

"Yeah, why?"

"I invited the girls over after their shift tonight for a little drinky-drink and thought I'd head over to Morgan's to pick it up."

"Where are you now?"

"Home. Why you so interested?"

"It's just snowing, that's all. Maybe you could go some place closer to home."

"Shannon, I think my car can make it over the Highland Park Bridge. Besides, I gotta run to Giant Eagle for some snacks too. See you in fifteen."

Darla hung up the phone before Shannon could say another word. Frowning, she put the phone back on the counter and looked at Jack.

"You gotta leave."

"What?"

"Leave. You're gonna have to. Darla's headed over here. I don't want a scene."

"It doesn't have to be a scene, Shannon. We're all grown-ups here."

"See, that's how little you know Darla. It most certainly will be a scene. Now, you go on home, and I'll see you in a couple of hours."

Parked on his chair like a statue on a bench, Jack didn't budge. "And what if I don't go?"

"Jack, I'm serious here. You need to leave. You shouldn't have even come here. It's just asking to get caught. You start showing up here, people start talking, Darla starts listening, and we have one big mess on our hands."

For a moment, Jack watched her intently. She looked away, uncomfortable. Underneath the flickering fluorescent lights, Jack's anger was tangible, his angled features sharper and piercing like he was about to open his mouth wide and let out some god-awful feral scream. Then he stood up, putting on his jacket. She exhaled, once again able to breathe.

"Thanks," she said, leaning her face forward, hoping for a less chaste kiss than what she'd given him just minutes earlier. This time, he was the one who pulled back.

"Maybe we shouldn't," he said. "Wouldn't wanna get caught."

"C'mon, Jack, don't be like that. I'm just trying to keep the peace. I'll see you in a few hours."

Jack shrugged. He opened the door, allowing in a thin stream of swirling snow. As the door slammed shut, the snow melted quickly onto the floor, little tiny dots of water the only proof he'd just stood there.

When she turned around, she saw Audrey shaking her head. "Sometimes I don't get you at all."

"I don't wanna hear it, Audrey."

"Well, you're gonna. You know how much time I spent feelin' sorry for you when you were pining for him? And now you got him and you're gonna treat him like that?"

Shannon felt her temperature and her voice rising. "Treat him like what? Like a person with common sense who doesn't want to hurt her sister's feelings?"

"No, like a person who can't let herself be happy no matter what the costs."

From behind, Shannon could hear the seal of the door popping, more snow and wind blowing inside the bar. This time, it was Larry and Glenn and a group of heavy-set guys she barely recognized, all decked out in Steelers garb and obviously intoxicated from a happy hour or long liquid dinner. They bellied up to the bar, shouting orders, and she let herself sink into the moment.

Someday soon, she'd have to choose—Jack or Darla. Someday, probably much sooner than she'd expect, the choice would have to be made. She honestly didn't know who she was going to pick yet, but she knew that this time, it would be a decision she made for herself, not for Audrey or Darla or even Jack. But for now, on a snowy Friday night two days before the Super Bowl, it was nice to let herself be distracted by the thirsty crowd at the bar: the motions of work, the rhythmic pace of taking orders, filling glasses, and taking cash. There was something about it that felt like love.

Jen

Saturday morning, Jen held perfectly still, her round belly exposed and cold in their harsh white kitchen. Dave leaned over with a paintbrush, adding the finishing touches to a Steelers logo painted around her now-protruding belly button. It had taken a little longer than expected, thanks to the baby's kicks and punches, and their estimated time of departure had changed from 11 to 1. Her mom, of course, had called one million times, urging them to leave earlier because of storms, but Jen didn't see any reason to get there any earlier. The only rooms they could find were nearly an hour away from Detroit itself, so all they had to do when they arrived was grab some food and fall into bed.

She still couldn't believe they were going at all. And she really wished that Dave was in a somewhat better mood than he'd been all morning. The painting was laborious, she knew, but he'd gone for her stupid idea. He didn't have to say yes, but he had, so now he needed to grin and bear it. It wasn't exactly comfortable for her to sit still for over an hour, but she hadn't complained. At least not in the past twenty minutes.

"Move a little to the right," Dave directed, like a master painter.

Jen shifted and then shuddered a little as the wet brush touched the side of her swollen belly.

Dave pulled the brush away. "Come on, you have to stop moving or I'm never gonna get this done."

Obviously, he was stressed, but she wasn't sure what about. It could be about the game or some conflict he'd had at work that week, or maybe her mom had gotten into his head with all the talk of the storm. Or maybe this little arts-and-crafts time was making him face the fact of the baby and he felt overwhelmed and frustrated.

"Maybe if you'd gotten home at a decent hour last night, we could have gotten done with this then."

Dave leaned forward, his face pressed so close to her belly that she could barely read his expression. When he finished and looked up at her, he rolled his eyes. "And maybe you didn't have to go to bed at nine on a Friday night."

Jen cupped the sides of her belly with her hands. "And maybe I did."

Just hearing him completing a full sentence made her feel somewhat better. He'd been so silent this morning that she could barely stand it, especially after all the excitement of last week and the impending trip. How could he be in a bad mood on Super Bowl weekend? And how much longer would she have to sit with her belly exposed for this thing to dry?

"I'm tired, okay, and we have a lot of stuff to do, so whatever you're getting at, I don't want to go there."

"Whatever I'm getting at?"

"Yeah," he said. "You're going somewhere with this and I'm saying I don't want to hear it."

"Of course not. You never want to hear it. It's perfectly fine for you to stay out every night at Morgan's and then come home and say two words to me the whole night. But if I want to spend the night at my parents' or I don't wait up for you, you get all pissy."

At the kitchen sink, Dave ran the water, rinsing off the paintbrushes and cups, his black t-shirt puckered just above his ass. Jen noticed that his hips looked thicker than usual, like he'd been putting on weight. Last night, she had sat at home half the evening, wondering where he was, why he was taking long, and assuming he was at Morgan's.

She waited for a beat. "Well, are you going to say something?"

He turned around.

"You really want to know what I was doing last night, then why didn't you just ask?"

She'd called his cell a million times with no answer and finally collapsed into bed before he'd come in. This morning, she'd been too annoyed to ask. She'd just wanted to get this done so they could get on the road.

"Believe it or not, these painting kits were pretty hard to find. I had to go to four different places last night just to get the right colors."

"You went to four different art stores? I don't even know where four different art stores are."

"Yeah, I didn't either, but everywhere I went was out, so one Michael's was directing me to the next one, and then JoAnn Fabrics was sold out and then I had to go a Pat Catan's clear in Murrysville to find the damn thing."

She imagined him out in the snow last night, head tucked into a black hood, ducking in and out of craft stores all around the city. It was so tender a thought, such a nice thing that he had done, and here she was finding fault like always.

"I'm sorry," she said, unsure of how to proceed.

"Right. The hormones." He could barely look her in the eye.

"No!" she said, surprising herself with the amount of passion in her voice. "Not the hormones."

"What?"

"No. It's not hormones, Dave. I mean, it is and it isn't. I'm scared, Dave. I'm scared like I've never been scared in my life. We're going to have a baby and sometimes I don't even think we have anything in common except sports and I don't know how to be a mom or a wife and Bobby's not here and I'm just really freakin' terrified all the time now, and I don't know how to stop."

She put her head down, ready for him to call her a baby—the typical response that everybody gave her when she complained about anything. What all those people hadn't realized was that she wasn't looking for somebody to agree with her or fix her problems. She just wanted somebody to listen. She felt Dave's hand on her shoulder.

"You're scared? I mean, why didn't you just say that? I'm scared, too. I mean, what do I know about being a dad? I'm the one who's scared. You're going to be a great mom!"

"I am?"

"Yeah. You are. Like, the really good kind."

"Really?"

"Yeah. Geez, Jen, why didn't you just say that before, instead of actin' all crazy all the time?"

She started to speak but stopped. It was only now that she'd realized how she was feeling. Looking down at her stomach, she heard Dave stepping away and washing brushes in the sink. "Give it another 15 or 20 minutes to dry, then we should start loadin' up the truck, see if we can't get outta here any earlier."

It was a relief that he just jumped to the next topic. That he didn't make her explain herself any more than she had. Right now, she just wanted to see her belly.

"Can you bring me a mirror?"

Dave nodded, leaving the room, then reappearing in a few minutes with a round vanity mirror. It was small, but it would do. He held it far enough away that she could see the whole thing. It looked even better than she had expected—a thick black ring circled her bulbous belly. The middle was filled in with white, and the three diamonds of the logo arched out in lines of thick blue, yellow, and red from the tip of her swollen navel. It was beautiful. She wanted to hug it and take a picture. She admired it with a sincerity that bordered on religious zeal, as though this one logo could solve all the world's problems. Stroking the sides of her belly, she was careful not to touch it, turning to the side and looking at it every which way. When they'd first decided to do it, she had thought mostly of what other people would say when they saw it— her coworkers or friends, her mom and dad and Bobby. But now, it felt like something uniquely theirs, for private consumption only.

Dave shifted on his feet. "Is it okay? We can wash it off and start again if you don't—"

"No. I love it. It's perfect." She reached out, taking his hand and pressing it carefully against the convex rim of her bare belly, just beneath the wet paint. His hands flooded her flesh with warmth and she felt the baby stirring from deep inside, her own little family, fragile perhaps, but at this very moment, filled with hope.

Acknowledgments

I'd like to thank Chuck Kinder, Marah Gubar, Cathy Day, Missy Raterman, Susan Gottfried and my former MFA classmates at Pitt for providing invaluable editorial input along the way; Steve Barton for cover design and Michelle Hammons for photography.

In addition, so many people helped and encouraged this project along the way but especially Lauren Hughes, Heath Maksin, Heather Bell, Steven Welch, Kara Pryke, Bob Scott, Melissa Cooper, Erin Metnick Taylor, Christina DuBrock, Nicole Lesovitch, Kim Revay, Natty Soltesz and Leah Herman.

Pittsburgh has a great and welcoming network of local bloggers who continually inspire and impress me. Thank you all for doing what you do and I'm so happy to be a part of your community.

Thanks also to my family members – my mom and dad and my big brother Bill who kept telling me to get it done.

And last but certainly not least a big thanks to Jason for his steadfast support and faith in me and to our beautiful girls Jordan and Eden.

www.ingramcontent.com/pod-product-compliance
Lightning Source LLC
Chambersburg PA
CBHW032055050726
47590CB00001B/284